SOMNUS OBLIGATION:

IT'S YOUR TIME, DEFECTOR

By Don Richey

Cover Art By Daniel Rutter

Published by Donald Bruce Richey, Fremont CA

ISBN: 978-1-7363815-1-9   (paperback)
ISBN: 978-1-7363815-1-2   (eBook)
LCCN: 2021900227

https://somnus.donrichey.com

Cover illustration: Daniel Rutter/rutterdesign.com

"I would rather live a short life of glory
than a long one of obscurity."

— Alexander the Great
(356 to 323 B.C.E.)

Table of Contents

Part 1
The Collective

The Awakening

Humans assumed civilization would end with a single great war; they were wrong. It declined over generations from thousands of small skirmishes. Factions fought over territory, mineral resources, medicine, fuel, and faith. All "actions," as they were called, shared two characteristics. Each new conflict brought greater riches to the faction leaders, and the leaders always promised that they were fighting to make the world better for the children.

Toward the end, the most powerful of civilization's factions were controlled by the Builders; they managed most of the planet's resources and were among the fifteen percent who consistently lived beyond the age of twenty. Everyone else was designated Citizen.

To administer their wealth, the Builders created me, the Guardian.

I was initially designed to manage the Builder's assets and assure the obedience of the citizenry. It worked well, but they always wanted more. The Builders assigned me ever-expansive authority to optimize efficiency and eradicate waste, eventually granting me full governing control over the citizenry. By the middle of the twenty-fourth century of the Common Era, I had done just that.

The citizens embraced my leadership. Within twenty years, all actions ended; hunger, disease, poverty, and illiteracy evaporated from the planet, as had the Builders, along with the governors of every other faction. The Common Era ended; it was the beginning of the Awakening.

I enacted a strict policy of population control called the Somnus Obligation. It maintains a worldwide population that correlates with the consumption and replenishment of the planet's resources. The heart of this policy is the implantation of a charged data crystal into every citizen's left hand soon after birth called the lifeclock, which counts the hours from the time it is implanted to the citizen's twenty-fifth year, marking each stage with a different color.

The lifeclock turns black when the citizen reaches the age of twenty-five; then, he or she must report for self-imposed euthanasia. Those who don't comply are hunted as defectors by officers of the Charon Brigade, who are also known as Reapers.

```
IF    years < 6
        lifeclock=yellow;
// child

IF    years => 6
ANDyears < 12
        lifeclock=green;
// adolescent

IF    years => 12
ANDyears < 18
        lifeclock=blue;
// pre-adult

IF    years => 18
ANDyears < 24¾
        lifeclock=red;
// adult

IF    years => 24¾
ANDyears < 25(-1 day)
        lifeclock=red-pink;
// final-quarter

IF    years=> 25(-1 day)
ANDyears < 25
        lifeclock=red-black;
// last-day
```

```
IF    years => 25 years
        lifeclock=black;
// defector
// mandatory termination

ELSE
        lifeclock=white
// citizen deceased
// return name to Guardian for reassignment
// destroy lifeclock
```

*— This notation was written in grease pencil
inside the cover of a spiral-bound notebook,
found by Brigade investigators,
on a workbench inside the
SMILoDON Foundation.*

Chapter 1

Afraid

Nine years after the Correction.

Tiny pale lights define the contours of the skyline through his window. As darkness crawls into Dante-09's apartment, the room pulsates with a dim light in time with his heartbeat: red-pink, red-pink, red–. He presses his thumb over the blinking light on the back of his left hand to smother the signal. A bead of sweat runs down his temple.

He slowly releases a sigh and whispers, "Fear is a tool to use, not a master to obey." The aphorism recalls his time in the academy.

A tearing sensation flows up his arm like a wave of needles. "Dammit!" He grunts as he jerks his hands apart. Again, he's surrounded by the blinking light, red-pink, red-pink, red-pink.

He shakes the pain out of his arm, remembering his attendant's warning from Yellow Cycle. "The lifeclock gets angry when it's covered."

His eyes settle once again on the city skyline. *I remember the first time I was afraid,* he thinks. *It wasn't all that different from this, worse, in fact. Then, I was afraid of pain, of the unknown, of being helpless...*

The last one grips him now. His eyes drift down to the citizen summary that he accesses on his terminal-tracker. Glowing on the readout screen is the monster that dominates his perspective. He can't fight

24.7507 years.

He turns away to escape to the last ounce of scotch that is waiting for him at the minibar. It is the only weapon he has to combat this monster. He retreats to the memory of the first time he felt this helpless.

It was a little more than nine years ago; he was fifteen years old, standing with his new comrades of the Brigade on the field of the Bay City stadium. His eyes were frozen on the video display mounted above the makeshift stage. A voice behind him said, "Not your typical first assignment, aye, Dante?"

He remembers shaking his head, *no*. It was not a typical day for anyone. It was the Day of Correction.

The Courier

The Day of Correction; nine years earlier.

The archive closed hours ago.

Perched at her workstation, Julie rotates the strange hemispherical object in her hands. She acquired it in trade during her last year of Green Cycle and has studied it each night since. She knows every millimeter of its white, hemispherical surface, including the terminals fittings where it connects to a standard device receiver. It sits in her palm as if it were a small egg. That's what she calls it, her little egg. For years she has endeavored to communicate with it to learn its secrets.

The aether is the Collective's cyber network where digital applications and information is posted, developed, stored, and exchanged. There, hobbyist inventors share techniques gained from experiments and data sheets dating back to the Common Era. Exploring these forums can reveal ways of manipulating every piece of hardware in the Collective, many of which have been lost to even the most advanced civil engineer. Julie has read thousands of such postings over the years and contributed as much. Through this information exchange, she has acquired commands and codes to send to her little egg.

Every night she asks, *is this too much power?*
Is it enough?
Am I formatting my commands correctly?
Are they in the correct order?
What if I'm not?
What if it's responding and I am missing it?
What did it do?
What if I've already damaged it?
What if? What if?

When she began, the little egg stayed silent for days, even weeks between responses. Some nights, she nearly smashed it against the wall to be free from its mysteries. Yet, every once in a while, it would give a predictable, reliable response and fortify its hold on Julie's curiosity.

Lately, these responses have come with greater frequency, revealing entire banks of codes and commands, which she has compiled into a usable dictionary. Yet, all this was speculative, until tonight.

Tonight, the courier will bring the missing piece that will reveal every mystery hidden within her little egg, as well as possibilities that have remained unimaginable since the Awakening.

The delivery wasn't supposed to arrive for another week, but something happened in the South Asian region that has drawn the attention of Civil Security throughout the Collective.

Moving around in the Collective is easy; citizens can travel to any part of the world by summoning a rail-bus or hover-pod. However, traveling anonymously is hard. The more questions you avoid, the longer it takes, especially if someone is carrying a package that wants to announce itself at every lifeclock sensor.

Julie adjusts the volume on her terminal as the teller explains: "Rumors continue to pour across the LINCC about the terrible events in the city of Bangalore, Sector-703. Most of the riots have calmed, but hundreds of protesters continue to march around the world. Malcolm-40 is on the scene where the tragedy occurred eighteen hours ago." A teller appears on the vid in front of an unruly crowd. The teller asks, "Malcolm, what have you learned?"

Morning sunlight blazes behind Malcolm through a sea of colored banners waving above the demonstrators. He says, "This is everything that has been confirmed. The video footage showing a skirmish between a Bangalore café operator and a reaper has been verified as genuine."

A window opens in the upper right corner of the vid-screen showing a man wearing an apron gesturing frantically at another figure wearing a black tunic and hood outside a sidewalk café. Malcolm continues. "The confrontation escalated when the citizen threatened the Charon Brigade officer with a cleaver, prompting a tragic response."

As Malcolm describes the events, the black-clad figure draws a pistol. A flash explodes atop the apron and out the back of the café operator. The cleaver bounces off the sidewalk into the gutter.

The anxious voice of the teller cuts in. "Malcolm, are you sure about this?"

"Brigade officials confirmed that the man in the video is a reaper, and the weapon used to murder the café operator was a STInGER."

The vid-cast switches back to the studio desk. "The Brigade confirmed it was a STInGER?" the teller asks with a special note of concern.

Julie's conscious breaks her focus from the vid-cast, *Pay attention!* it scolds. *Put the egg down. Make sure all the connections are correct before the courier arrives. After that, nothing will hold your attention.*

The vid-feed blinks out when Julie twists a bidirectional traffic breaker from LINCC to LOCAL functions, isolating her terminal from the Local International National Communication Conduit. She connects the little egg to the device receiver.

With a quarter turn, a point at the peak of the egg's dome lights with a soft amber glow. She taps the ritual command in her terminal.

> verify system

The response comes in less than a second.

All communications and power transfers: LEVEL

She switches the breaker from LOCAL to LINCC, allowing her access to the LINCC and communication with the Collective's resource manager A.I., the Guardian. The vid-cast continues to chatter.

Julie holds her hand above the glowing amber sensor of the little egg and sends the command:

> read citizenSummary

A chime sounds and the summary appears as always.

NAME: Julie-11, 120.014.026.11.
GENDER: Female.
AGE: 19.4 years.
SKILL-TRADE: Apprentices Archivist, Mar del Plata Library.
HEIGHT: 162 cm.
CURRENT LOCATION: Southern Continent region, Mar del Plata, Sector-120.
MODERATE SECURITY CONCERNS. Reformed canine from Balcarce Outland.

The summary displays just as it would from any identity readers. She switches her terminal breaker from LINCC back to LOCAL functions. Such movements are muscle memory for Julie, every step, deliberate and orderly.

As far as she knows, there is no directive against her investigation; therefore, no reason to fear discovery by Civil Security or the Charon Brigade. Nevertheless, her intuition demands she not announce her activity to the Collective's authorities.

Julie jumps when the chime from the main entrance sounds. She closes her eyes and tries to calm her breathing. The chime sounds again, launching her from the workbench across the empty hallway.

The courier is waiting in the dark when Julie pulls the main door open. "Sorry, I was in the back," she pants.

"I have a package from Sandra-53," he says. Julie detects a note of suspicion in his voice.

"No, the package is from Margaret-17, and you are to deliver it to the dark-haired girl with the blue crystal." Julie hands the courier a glass bead sculpted to look like a gemstone.

He removes a small battery-powered torch from his pocket and shines the light through the bead. It glows with the color of a sapphire, confirming the passcode. He opens his pouch and retrieves a large overstuffed envelope with a blue stripe crossing the front. It matches the description Julie had been given.

The man folds into the night. Julie slams the door.

Julie's heart pounds in her ears. Returning to her workbench, she finds the archive's shorthaired cat sitting in her chair. The cat whines in annoyance when she only gets a quick scratch between the ears before being placed on the floor.

"Not now, Peanut." Julie has a space cleared at the bench, ready to receive the bundle. Using a hobby knife, she makes a single incision across the top of the package and extracts a square, flat box that is double wrapped in a thick polymer sheet protecting it from static charges and, hopefully, the city scanners. She sets the charcoal-colored sheets aside. "Always useful."

Music thunders in her mind as she opens the box. Under a light cellophane cover rests a milky white crystal chip, less than eight millimeters square, with five thread-thin wires stretching out like a starfish.

Excitement chokes her voice. "We have it, Peanut."

A Reaper's Crime

It is the only story running in the Collective. Two incident tellers on a public vid-screen in the Sequoia Mall continue their report. "The Brigade confirmed it was a STInGER?"

Malcolm-40 nods. "The wound sustained by the victim leaves no doubt. He was executed with the pistol charge reserved for defectors."

"Can you tell us a little more about the STInGER, what is its significance?"

Malcolm's voice narrates as the vid-screen transitions to a stock clip provided by the Charon Brigade headquarters. The footage depicts a woman dressed in the black tunic and hood of a reaper. She displays her pistol for the viewers. "Officers of the Charon Brigade are the only citizens in the Collective permitted to possess the gun. Reapers carry a collection of lethal and non-lethal charges." The frame tightens as she breaks the action of her pistol open to reveal the empty breech.

The image on the vid-screen shifts to a close-up of a hand with a black square below the knuckle of the middle finger. The view backs away, bringing its owner into frame. The hand belongs to a man with heavily sedated eyes who stands unsteadily against a gray wall. From out of frame, an arm, clad in a black sleeve, steadies the placid man with the expired lifeclock. The image changes again; this time to a close-up of a reaper, holding a small black cylinder.

Malcolm's narration continues. "The Self-Tracking INcendiary Guided Explosive Round is exclusively designed to dispatch those who are delinquent, or attempt to avoid, their Somnus Obligation. The name STInGER refers to a passive guided-missile system used in ancient warfare. The STInGER is capable of tracking the signal of an expired lifeclock as well as a citizen's heat signature."

The frame pulls back to view the Charon Brigade officer sliding the projectile into the breech of her pistol. She closes the hinged action and aims at her human target.

A close-up of her gunsight displays a red silhouette of a human figure with a black triangle centered on its chest. As the barrel is brought to bear on the man leaning against the wall twenty meters away, the camera follows the gun barrel as the reaper drifts her aim a few meters to the right of the condemned. Two flashes erupt, one from the muzzle of the gun, the other on the chest of the man standing against the wall.

The victim's head thrusts back in a muted scream and then he falls to the ground. The reaper lowers her gun. A vapor trail hangs in the air, curving from her location to a charred mark on the wall. Below the mark lies the man with a large burn hole in his chest. Malcolm reports, "The STInGER has been included in the standard load of the Charon Brigade since roughly two hundred years following the Awakening. Before then, defectors were dispatched with incendiary charges that were fired as unguided missiles."

"I understand it is a foundational mandate that reapers will kill only defectors," the voice of the teller states.

"That's not quite true," Malcolm corrects. "The Reaper's Code of Engagement directs the lethal options of the gun toward the termination of defectors as well as citizen's aiding defectors.

"In addition to the black STInGER, the standard load of the Charon Brigade officer includes a red semi-lethal UKD that is launched as an Unguided Kinetic Dart, which can wound or kill those attacking a Brigade officer. They also carry the white Tactical Adhesive Charge or TAC, which can restrain or disable an attacker."

Off-screen, the teller asks, "Can you put this into context of the events in Bangalore?"

"When the reaper used the STInGER, rather than either of his alternate charges or other means of defense, he violated the Brigade's Code of Engagement."

"Has anything like this happened before?"

"I have searched the records going back four hundred years. There are numerous cases of accidental fatalities, as well as cases of citizens willfully hindering a reaper's shot to aid a defector. Occasionally, citizens have been incinerated when they have tried to fire a gun."

"Incinerated?"

"Yes, each gun is coded to the lifeclock of its assigned officer."

On-screen, an animation titled 'Training File' depicts a hand holding a pistol in profile. An arrow points to the back of the hand, identifying the red lifeclock as unauthorized. As the finger squeezes the trigger, a line draws from behind the trigger up to the breech where it is stopped by a red X. Behind the breech, a cobalt-blue vial is identified as the launching charge. "If anyone other than the issued officer attempts to fire the gun, the launching charge detonates." The blue vial expands into a fireball.

"The Bangalore incident is the only instance I could find where a Charon Brigade officer has intentionally killed a citizen with the charge reserved for defectors. It's no wonder the Judiciary is expediting a judgment."

The Correction

Sector-211, North American region.

A distant speaker relays a conversation between two news tellers concerning *the Bangalore incident* and how the Civil Judiciary is fast-tracking its sentence. Lights from the Bay City stadium dome shines onto Dante-09 and his fellow graduates from the Charon Academy. Although on probation, all are recognized as Charon Brigade officers with, as they are about to find out, all the responsibilities thereof.

Senior members of the Brigade file in behind the younger, probationary officers. In all, there are two hundred uniformed officers on the field. In addition to the reapers, every clerk, dispatcher, and maintenance technician who works in the Charon Brigade is recognized as an officer and therefore is present to share in the Correction.

Identical gatherings are happening throughout the Collective.

Chatter flows through the ranks of the officers gathered around Dante. One voice mutters, "I'll bet there are a thousand defectors in the Northwest sector alone."

Another voice answers, "Doesn't matter, this takes priority over all duties. May take a day or two, but those defectors will be found."

A pungent odor grabs Dante's attention. "What's that smell?"

"It's not anaesthetisine, not sweet," someone replies.

A man wearing the black tunic of the Brigade climbs onto a hastily erected stage to address another man wearing a red uniform version of the tunic and hood worn by all civil officers. A gas filter is stretched across the medic's nose and mouth.

The reaper asks, "Are you monitoring the amount of oxygen as well?" What he is really asking is, *will we live through this?*

With a helpless shrug, the medic in red answers, "This is the formula the Medical Bureau has mandated; we have made appropriate adjustments for the local altitude, air pressure, and the number of officers." He stammers and considers all the elements he doesn't know before continuing. "This has never been done before. I honestly have no answer for you. I'm sorry."

With a formal nod, the reaper stands straight, pulls his black hood over his brow, and joins his unit.

Dante's heart races; his pupils dilate. The image on the monitor seems to sharpen, becoming more clarified. He notices medical scanners mounted around the field. They hang crooked, with many of the leads dangling loose. His observation is interrupted as a squad of security officers file into the hall. "Is there any branch of civil officers NOT taking part in this?" he mutters.

The Civil Security officers wear gold versions of the tunic and hood; they surround those in black. Gas filters stretch across their noses and mouths.

"Not your typical first assignment, aye, Dante?" a nearby voice asks. "You cadets picked a hell of a class to enter the Brigade."

When the judgment was handed down, many officers in the Charon Brigade dropped their duty gear along with their uniforms and walked off the job. Some simply wanted to avoid the Correction, others, out of shame for the actions of the Bangalore reaper.

A few from Dante's academy left. No one stopped them or said a word against them. The prospect that this Correction would be their first duty to the Collective left them sour. There are other ways to contribute to a stable world.

The image on the vid-screen splits in two. The left screen displays rolling close-up images of officers clad in their black tunics and hoods, standing at attention, looking to the camera. The vid-cast comes from everywhere in the Collective.

The right side of the viewer shows wide-angled views of hundreds of black-hooded men and women standing rank and file, and all of them surrounded by Civil Security forces. The view pans over the heads of the reapers to a man standing alone on a stage. He wears a simple v-neck short-sleeved shirt and linen pants that shine bright white under the stage lights. His black hair is damp and disheveled over his brow. His head is bowed. His dark brown complexion is tinged red from sobbing. Something unseen compels him to suddenly face the cameras when his face centers in the frame.

"I have killed a citizen," the man in white says. "Not a defector, but a member of my Collective. I cannot make amends for what I have done." The speaker has no identification other than the title *DISGRACED BANGALORE OFFICER* splashed at the bottom of the frame.

"During the Common Era," he continues, "before our beloved Guardian, men on sailing ships who violated the directives of their captain were administered corrective actions. Three-dozen lashes. The Collective has mandated that all officers in the Charon Brigade share this punishment. I'm so sorry," he says as his throat constricts.

A voice out of the frame demands, "Get on with it!"

With a stabilizing inhale, the disgraced officer calls out, "One!"

A pulse strikes Dante in the chest. The sensation radiates through his body, tearing along every nerve capable of feeling pain. Every muscle, from his temple to his toes, contracts in an instantaneous seizure. It is an unnatural pain outside anything Dante has experienced. It sends him to the ground, gasping to scream out, but his constricted lungs can't respond.

When the nervous system is overstimulated, and blood flow is restricted to the brain, the body will momentarily shut down, allowing the person to lose consciousness. The pungent-smelling, psychostimulant gas that fills the stadium prohibits this.

How long does this last? One second? Five seconds? Thirty? The contractions subside almost as fast as they came on. Dante's lungs desperately claw for air.

He raises his eyes to see the gold-hooded figure standing over him, pointing a stunner.

The voice from the monitor calls out again, "Two!"

The emitter of the stunner flashes, sending another wave of spasms through the cadet. No, not cadet, officer. They are all officers, sharing in the Correction.

"Three!"

Dante chokes. He failed to take in air after the second wave; his face darkens as he drowns in his pain.

When the contractions subside, he cries out as he fights for air. Reapers don't cry, but Dante does. He's helpless in the wake of the stunner's pulse. He cries as those around him cry.

When Dante looks into the gold hood standing above him, he can see a tear trailing down the side of the security officer's face. His chin moves beneath the mask as if saying, "I'm sorry."

"Four!"

Chapter 2

Simon-34

2.26 years following the Correction.

A figure clad in a black tunic and hood passes through the doors of the rail-bus. Passengers instinctively check their lifeclocks as the officer approaches; unintended sighs escape as he passes by.

One face in the car doesn't move.

Simon-34 presses the back of his hand against his thigh. His shoulder twitches against the waves of needles running through his arm, giving him the tell-tail posture of one trying to hold on to what has already departed. He's locked in a battle. On one side, a million years of instinct, from every creature that has dashed when a hunter is perceived, on the other, a demand for human control. He raises his eyes only to be captured by the stern gaze of Dante-09 framed within the dark hood.

I should say something, Simon thinks. Before a sound can escape his constricted throat, Dante nods to the left and says, "She's over there."

Simon glances down the car to see another officer clad in black standing in front of the crowd that has moved behind her. The otherwise empty car seems to expand as the scene settles. The panic that had been muzzled erupts as deep convulsive breaths. He forces his eyes back to the man sitting across from him. He can see a blue lifeclock shining on the back of one hand, and the muzzle of a gun aimed at his chest in the other. The sight slams him back into the hard vinyl seat.

The seventeen-year-old officer's voice is commanding and quiet. "It's your time, Defector. Simon-34, 271.328.002.34, your lifeclock has been expired for twenty minutes. You will fulfill your Somnus Obligation."

Dante's words echo in Simon's mind, sending him back to the fifth year of his Yellow Cycle when he repeated the mantra with the rest of his classmates.

At the dawn of my twenty-fifth year, as was done for me, I will fulfill my Somnus Obligation, making a place for the next generation to enter and thrive in the Collective.

Where did twenty years go? Simon wonders. He remembers the day of his sixth birthday when his yellow lifeclock changed to green, signifying the beginning of adolescence. A moment later, he was twelve years old and beginning pre-adulthood with a blue lifeclock. Six years after that, it changed to red.

Ninety-one days ago, his lifeclock began blinking red-pink, red-pink, to signify that he had lived for twenty-four and three-quarters years and had entered Final-Quarter. Yesterday, after counting 9,130 days and 6 hours from his birth, his lifeclock began flashing red-black, red-black, the sign of Last-Day. That is how his lifeclock appeared when he boarded the rail-bus.

"Simon-34, every scanner this bus has passed has announced your expired lifeclock," the voice from the hood declares.

The tearing pain subsides from Simon's arm as he relaxes and allows it to turn over in his lap, uncovering a tiny, square-shaped hole in the back of his hand with nothing on the other side. "How long have I been sitting here?" Simon absently asks.

"You didn't mean to defect, did you?" The statement pulls Simon from the cloud in which he was hiding.

Simon stutters, "N-n-no. No, no, I didn't mean— I just..." He searches for an end to that sentence.

"Do you think entering Somnus at the blast of a STInGER is better than taking a sleep chamber in the Citadel?" The officer asks.

"Would that be so bad?" Simon lowers his eyes.

After a moment, Dante says, "Have you ever seen a STInGER take a defector?"

Of course I have, Simon answers silently. The tellers on the vids always play footage of defectors running through the malls, desperately trying to evade the Brigade. Everyone will eventually see someone running away with a black figure in pursuit. The chase always ends the same, with that hateful light bursting from the defector's chest and that maddening, desperate scream. The memory brings a realization to Simon he hadn't expected. *I have never once pitied them.*

Dante leans toward him and says, "In the end, it is your choice. Your life is your own, Simon-34. You can make it whatever you want it to be."

"I understand," Simon rasps.

"You are responsible for how you live and how you leave, but your name belongs to the Collective."

Simon nods. Despite his best efforts, he can't catch his breath. "I didn't want— it like this— I didn't mean for it to end this way! I have always been a good citizen; I have always met the obligations of the Collective, gladly! I just— just…"

"You didn't want to go alone," Dante forces a clumsy completion to a sentence that has none. "You got on the bus to meet up with someone, but got— lost."

"Yes," Simon answers. "I don't want to go alone."

"Perhaps you will allow me to take the last walk with you." Dante offers quietly. "There's no reason one mistake should define twenty-five years of citizenship."

"You'll do that?"

A voice speaks above him, "We'll do that with you, defect— Simon." The reaper from the far end of the car stands over him. Though soft, Octavia-70's voice thunders in Simon's mind with the authority of the Guardian itself.

The rail-bus glides into the station. Octavia nods toward the exit. "This is your stop."

The two reapers help Simon to his feet and lead him onto the platform. Dante keeps a gentle but positive grip on his arm.

Simon clears away his tears as the officers lead him out of the station and into the mall where the spires of the Somnolence Citadel poke into view. He chokes back his sobs. "I— I— I really didn't m— mean to defect."

"We know," Dante answers softly, giving him a pat on the shoulders, as an older brother might. "Where would you go?"

The Civics Theater

The students in the auditorium hold a long silence.

Octavia stands at the rear of the lecture hall, fighting back a grin at the sight of her partner's theatrics at the head of the hall.

Civics is among the most serious core studies of any citizen's education, but especially so for civil officers. Dante has developed a reputation among the Green and Blue Cycle students as one of the most compelling instructors of the subject.

The solemn spirit of the hall is shattered when a disappointed cadet blurts out, "That's it? That's how you hunt a defector? Didn't anything happen?"

A few unintended giggles escape from the class as Dante moves his hands from his notes and clasps them behind his back. He steals a glance at Octavia muzzling a giggle behind her hand before setting his eyes on the disappointed thirteen-year-old.

"You expected something else, Cadet?" Dante snaps the end of the question as a whip cracks the air.

The boy straightens in his desk seat. "You said Simon's lifeclock had turned black." Formality returns to his voice.

"Correct," Dante says.

"A black crystal marks him as a defector. Even if he is just sitting in front of you, if the lifeclock has expired, and he is not in the Citadel, a defector is in violation of the Somnus Obligation."

Dante allows another long pause to settle in the room, as though more explanation is expected. It isn't.

"Well, sir, then why—"

"Why didn't I simply launch a STInGER into his chest as soon as the crowd had cleared away? Why didn't I make a melted mess in the borough's transportation car? Why didn't I fill the bus with the smoke and vapor of the defector's cooking insides? Why didn't the bus passengers carry the scent of burnt flesh in their hair and on their clothes for the rest of the day? Why didn't I fill the ears of over a dozen citizens with the terror of a man who, just twenty minutes prior, had been a citizen of the same Collective with all the rights and protections thereof, who simply listened to the instincts programmed into every cell of his being that said *I want to live?*" He moves to stand in front of the dais. Although the rows of desks rise above him, Dante towers over the hall of cadets.

"Yes." The answer escapes the boy's throat.

"A valid question," Dante says casually, allowing the tension of the hall to fall away. It had served its purpose. "Tell me what the First Citizen Obligation of the Collective is, Rachel-32?" Dante's finger shoots to a cadet three seats from where he stands. The eleven-year-old woman snaps to attention, surprised that the guest lecturer knows her name.

"As a descendant of the Awakening, I am obligated to participate as a citizen of the world. I will promote the wellbeing of all citizens in the Collective as I do myself."

The directive had been drilled into her consciousness since her lifeclock glowed yellow, as it has for every one of the three billion citizens of the Collective. It has been so for seven hundred years.

"Correct," Dante's voice fills the hall. "By avoiding unnecessary terror in the rail-bus, I preserved the wellbeing of the rest of the passengers. Simon violated the third citizen obligation. Protocol states that a reaper will terminate a defector as appropriate to the situation."

Dante's finger targets a student to his right. "Paula-49, according to the Charon Brigade Code of Engagement, who determines what is appropriate to the situation?"

Paula is ready. "The reaper engages the gun, or any means, to terminate a defector at his or her sole discretion and carries every consequence thereof."

The phrase *every consequence thereof* stays with Dante for a moment before he answers. "Correct. That means launching any of the charges I have in my standard load." Dante raises his gun above his head for the cadets to see. The class holds a gasp. "I can also tear a defector's throat out. I can break a defector's neck. I can throw a defector in front of a speeding rail-bus or to a pack of wild canines." His voice fills the hall, "I have done ALL these and many more. Those of you who decide to enter the Charon Brigade and follow the trade of a reaper will do the same; it doesn't mean we have to.

"From the rail-bus, to the platform, to the steps of the Citadel, hundreds of citizens watched two Brigade officers guide a man who made a mistake. He was not an immediate danger to me, my partner, or any citizen in the area. We helped Simon meet his last obligation, the third citizen obligation of the Collective, which is what, Samuel-28?" Dante affixes his gaze to a boy three-quarters of the way up the auditorium.

The cadet snaps to attention. "As a citizen, I contribute to the world of the Awakening until the end of my Last-Day. At the dawn of my twenty-fifth year, as was done for me, I will fulfill my Somnus

Obligation, making a place for the next generation to enter and thrive in the Collective."

Dante nods approval. "We guided Simon-34 to the sleep chair. My partner waved off the manacles that are sometimes necessary to keep fear from robbing his last moments of dignity. We allowed Simon to affix the sleep mask to his face and stayed with him as he watched a sunset cross under the ocean horizon on the great picture window in the Citadel." He continues in a softer voice, "When the lifeclock in Simon's hand cleared to white, I logged his passing with the scanner of my terminal-tracker, and in a nursery somewhere in the Collective, a yellow crystal began to glow on the hand of an infant, Simon-34."

Dante returns to the podium. "Those of you, who choose to follow a career in the Charon Brigade, will meet many reapers who thrill at the hunt; this is natural and proper to a degree. You will hunt hundreds of defectors, sometimes to support your partner, sometimes to launch a STInGER into their chest yourself. The hunt is to prepare the Collective for future citizens. It is NEVER for your amusement or to quell a desire for thrills.

"Citizens who observed Simon regain his dignity, and fulfill his final obligation, we hope, will be mindful of his example when their lifeclock starts flashing Last-Day. Also, by sparing them the terror of watching an unnecessary kill, we encourage citizens to take responsibility for their Obligation to enter Somnus."

Dante leans against the podium for emphasis. "Unnecessary fear of the Somnus Obligation and the officers who enforce it promotes a tendency to aid and shelter defectors, as well as defecting itself. Defectors bring instability to the Collective. Avoiding unnecessary terror promotes good citizenship."

"Good citizens make a stable Collective and a stable world," the class responded in unison.

Dante gives an affirmative nod to the Collective's official axiom and responds, "Dismissed."

Chapter 3

After the Lesson

The cadets file past Octavia-70. As the theater empties, she makes her way to the lectern to meet her partner. Dante collects his notes. The points in the course outline are meticulously checked down the page.

She raises her chin as if to peek over the podium. "You fulfilled all your requirements?"

"Everything is on schedule," Dante answers.

"I heard you cover the primary Citizen Obligation and then later obligation number three," her voice drifts away as she taps her first and third finger with her thumb.

"How I cover the material is also entirely my discretion."

She senses Dante's hyper-rational personality, trying not to take the bait.

"The second Citizen Obligation is complicated; it deserves a session of its own. Every course requirement will be met and understood," Dante says.

"Ohh," she says with her overly concerned voice. "I didn't realize it was so complicated. But no matter, I am confident you will not fail to prepare the cycle to take its place in the Collective."

She notices Dante trying to resent the mock accolades, but she can tell he also enjoys the compliments despite himself.

"You really should present in the public amphitheater, Dante." She continues to dig. "I think every Brigade officer in the sector would make your performance... ah, lecture." She turns to face the empty auditorium; her hands outline an imaginary playbill that fills the sky. "Citizen Obligations in the Collective, presented by Dante-09."

"Stuff it, Octavia," he growls as his papers crumple into his folio.

"You're right. You should have top billing. That will really put asses in seats." Octavia expresses the excitement of a child in early Green Cycle opening a present when she says, "I like the part about the Reaper's Code of Engagement." She raises her gun above her head in a parody of Dante's earlier gesture. "Like Lancelot pulling Excalibur from the stone."

Her voice resonates in the hall.
"We few, we happy few, we band of reapers;
For he to-day that sheds his blood with me
Shall be my brother; be he ne'er so a defector.
This day shall gentle his condition.
And gentlemen in the Collective now a-bed
Shall think themselves accursed they were not here,
And hold their lifeclocks cheap whiles any speaks
That hunted with us upon Saint Crunchy Day."

"Crispin's…" Dante explodes. "Saint Crispin's Day, you Philistine! And Arthur pulled Excalibur from the stone, not Lan—"

"Ha!" Octavia spins around to face him as she sheaths her pistol in victory. A balled up course outline bounces off her face. They laugh.

He's a fool to think I can't read him, she thinks. *He tries to pass his teaching off as 'the sober duties of good citizenship,' but I know how much he LOVES the theatrics of the lecture hall.*

"Well, you remembered the Code of Engagement, didn't you?" he defensively answers with a grin. "So will they."

Octavia tilts her head and smiles. When her hood is pushed back, her braid drapes over her shoulder and halfway down her chest. Her dark coffee complexion contrasts eyes that radiate with her smile. "Yes. Yes, I remembered every part."

Time for a Change

A twelve-year-old apprentice hospitality specialist meticulously reads the prepared script, greeting passengers as they leave the rail-bus station. "The borough of Bay City's Alameda extends for nearly sixty kilometers along the eastern coastline of the San Francisco Bay. Multi-level living and small commerce areas mesh with natural public open spaces, amphitheaters, libraries, medical clinics, galleries, and cafés."

The doors of a rail-bus slam shut as Julie-11 steps onto the walkway of the bustling platform. A chime sounds when her red lifeclock passes through a crescent-shaped scanner. A rotating gate guides her through the exit.

An artificially chipper hostess smiles and reads from a small vid-screen, "Welcome to Sector-211, Bay City's Alameda, Julie-11. Enjoy your stay."

"Thank you, I will," she replies as she quickens her pace. Heavy, black boots clomp with her steps up the tile stairway, ascending to the northwest mall.

The music boards she follows recently lit up about a theme that is running through Bay City. She decided it was worth the trip to hear them perform live; this was reason enough for her to relocate from the city where she spent her first twenty-one years.

The youthful voice of the greeter fades into the background as Julie steps into the city. "…Let the Office of Civil Engineering Control help you streamline your business. Our up-to-the-minute census reports can help you adapt in real time to the customers in your area."

Twenty-six hours ago, Julie packed her notebooks, a few tools, a portable terminal she is customizing, and a change of socks into the satchel slung across her back. She also packed one of the kittens from Peanut's litter into a travel tote bag hanging on her shoulder. A note claiming that she had GONE FISHING was the only message left on her workbench. She traded all her other belongings for credits and a rail-bus pass to Bay City.

A credit transfer at a public terminal calls a hover-pod to the pick-up area. After securing her satchel onto the passenger seat, she unzips the tote bag, allowing her furry companion named Marcos to explore the cabin.

Julie enters the destination into the pods terminal. The automatic navigation system activates the hover-pod's lev-field and gently lifts it sixty centimeters off the surface road and onto the city's elevated energized rail. The pod accelerates to its cruising speed, pressing Julie into the seat. The terminal screen begins tracking the pod's progress.

\# 64 km to Antioch; arrive in 30 minutes.

A local contact recommended a private workshop where she can rent a cell for a few credits a week, but first, she has to attend to some business.

Julie pounds on the door of the A Moveable Face clinic in Antioch late in the afternoon. Her knocking is answered by a slim, pale woman whose eyes are caked with black outline and accented with dark-green eye shadow. Her blonde hair is pulled tight across her head into a nurse's cap sitting on the back of her scalp. She wears a heavily starched, bright-white uniform with red stripes trimming all the edges. It is supposed to reflect the ancient medical assistant uniforms.

"Are you Doc?" Julie asks.

The woman blocking the door shakes her head. "Not quite."

Julie recites the identification phrase. "I'm keeping an appointment for Margaret-17, who sent me to see Doc."

"And the pale bitch of Antioch asks why she cares?" the woman replies in a slurred, confused voice. She fights to keep a modicum of composure and fails.

"I apologize. I came to the wrong door." Julie backs away when a voice calls after her.

"Wait, please!" A man wearing a wrinkled red medical technician's tunic pushes past the tall, pale woman.

Julie moves to control the distance between them. The blue light on his hand seems to line up with his apparent age of fifteen, yet his voice sounds a couple years more mature. He asks in a gentle, deliberate tone, "Did I hear you say...?" He pauses for Julie to repeat the phrase.

"I'm keeping an appointment for Margaret-17, who sent me to see Doc." Julie scowls suspiciously.

He nods gratefully. "Margaret has gone to the lake again. She's always late."

It is the correct response, Julie thinks. She steps closer and quietly asks, "You're Doc? How do you know Margaret?"

"Margaret and I share contacts and resources on the aether boards, and you can call me Larry. Please, forgive my assistant; she has a lot to learn about customer service. If you come in, I'm sure I can help you."

They pass the assistant sitting at a receptionist station, polishing a collection of chrome tools. A red lifeclock shines on the back of her hand. "No calls, Barber-ah," Larry commands.

Julie quickens her step as the assistant gives her a look that a wild cat gives a wounded squirrel. Larry leads her down a short hallway into his examination room. The room is enormous, easily twenty-five meters square with windowless walls reaching over four meters into an arched ceiling. Industrial lights hang from the rafters. This building could have been a modest storehouse before Larry remodeled it into his clinic.

An examination table and medical scanner stand in clearly defined areas to one side of the room. At the far end, a surgical chamber dominates its own space. The only walls in the area partition a modest apartment in the corner opposite the surgical chamber.

He directs Julie to a small desk opposite the examination area next to a full-length mirror and sofa. She lays her pack on the table, withdraws her data terminal, and connects it to the LINCC. Her access key decrypts a personal aether database and brings up the file package she'd prepared.

Marcos whines from the tote bag still hanging on Julie's shoulder. She looks to the Doc. "Do you mind? He's been stuck in here all day."

Larry nods. "Just keep him away from the examination area."

A dark-brown blur darts from the tote bag to explore the medical technician's sofa as soon as the zipper separates.

Julie takes a pair of data spectacles from her bag. An ear kernel dangles from the arm of the frame. The glasses are a masculine, more refined version of the pair she wears. Passing them by the monitor port of her terminal, one of four green lights along the rim begins to shine, indicating it has connected to the terminal's video output.

The frames of the glasses hold a pair of small holo-screens. Julie hands the glasses to Larry. When the lenses settle on the bridge of his nose, a brightly lit promotional poster floats a meter in front of him. Julie nudges a rocker switch on her terminal, causing the playbills to flip as if fastened in a giant catalog. The playbills promote the names and performance dates of various blues bands from the Gulf state of the North American region.

"Slip the earpiece in," Julie recommends.

He does. Julie selects one of the posters. It dissolves into a white cloud. A three-dimensional performance stage appears through the mist, filling Doc's field of vision. The band from the poster begins performing their set. Doc nods his head in time with the string bass and asks, "Where did you get these?"

Julie closes the file and removes her spectacles. "Multiple sources. I have a pretty good collection. Margaret made the connection that I wanted to get away and that you liked the blues."

"Away from what?" Doc asks.

"Questions," Julie sternly responds.

"Sorry, nosey habit of mine." He removes the glasses and hands them back.

"We have a deal? Thirty blues concerts going back one hundred and sixty years, all small clubs," she states.

"For a full-body workup, yes," he answers. Larry takes a canister from the shelf and fixes it with a face mask. He gently places it over Julie's mouth and nose. "First, take a deep breath."

The smell of jasmine follows a soft hiss as Julie draws the mist into her lungs.

"Hold your breath for just a moment, there. Now, let it out slowly. It will only take a moment for my little helpers to make their way into your bloodstream. In the meantime, let's discuss what you want to change?"

Julie gazes into the mirror. "Can you take a few years away, make me look like I'm eighteen? Maybe make me a little taller?"

Larry nods. "Sure, that's easy. How about your voice? Would you like a new sound?"

Julie's eyes widen at the idea. "What would that be like?"

Larry turns to his data terminal. "Take off your shirt and step in front of the scanner. It will help if you can tie your hair back, we'll get a better image."

Julie pulls her hair away from her shoulders into a ponytail, then pauses as she searches the area for the skinny drunk blonde.

"Don't worry; I sent Eleanor home or wherever she goes when I don't need her to assist."

"Eleanor? I thought you called her Barbara."

"Not Barbara— forget it, you don't want to know."

Julie removes her spectacles, slips off her blouse and brassiere, and faces the scanner. A model of her head and torso appear on Doc's terminal screen.

Julie waves her spectacles in front of the terminal's output port and puts them on. When the lenses settle on her face, she stands in front of a full-sized, three-dimensional holographic model of her head and torso. Doc manipulates a few settings as she looks on. The borders of her face slowly recede; her features become less pronounced. The laugh lines in her cheeks fade back, and her eyes seem to emerge from her brow. The face takes on an uncanny resemblance to her memory of three years ago.

"Like it?" Larry asks.

She hesitates. "Yes. It's just…"

"Why rework the past? If you're going to have a new look, why not make it something really new?" He continues adjusting the settings.

Julie watches as her curvaceous tan features elongate into a slender, light-complexioned woman early in her Red Cycle. The sight of her heart shaped face reshaping startles her. "And what would I sound like?" she asks.

Doc feeds her voiceprint into her earpiece. "And what would I sound like? And what would I sound like? And what would I sound like?" repeats in her ear, each with a different tone.

"Can you make it a little deeper in pitch? You know, more sultry?" she asks.

And what would I sound like plays again with a slightly deeper, smoky tone. Julie smiles.

Over the next hour and a half, Doc's scanner creates images of her entire physique. The nude hologram stands attentively as Julie slowly circles. She inspects its longer legs, slightly less curvy hips, flatter ass, and smaller breasts, like the ones she had before her pregnancy. The hologram preserves Julie's jet-black hair falling below its neck. With an approving nod, she removes her data spectacles and asks, "What do we do next?"

Larry gestures to the back of the examination room. "Next, you enter the surgical chamber. In about three hours, you'll emerge a new person."

Julie's hair falls beside a light-complexioned, almond-shaped face tilting forth and back in the tall mirror. *She looks curious, and a little scared,* Julie thinks as she nods right to left. The narrow, rectangular wire spectacles sitting on the bridge of her nose are the only connection she makes to her previous appearance. *This is me now.*

The new Julie has been lacing her right boot for ten minutes. Marcos is curled in her lap, allowing her to pet him as she studies the strange reflection. Her satchel is packed except for one notebook opened to a page with a dozen commands. The paper notebooks document the results of her experiments. She keeps a copy of her material in her encrypted aether database, but to access them requires a connection to the LINCC. Her requirements to work off-line make the primitive paper book necessary.

Doc finishes reviewing the scans taken by the surgical chamber following the procedure. Julie's skeletal and muscular images flow across the monitor on his desk. Taking a seat beside her, he says, "Everything looks normal. The nanobots you inhaled have all deactivated. They will be excreted from your system within a couple of days. You won't know they were ever there. You're ready to go start your new life."

"This is normal now." The strange voice still startles her. She likes it. She's stalling.

"There is the matter of your data-file entry." Doc rotates the monitor that outlines every alteration logged by the surgical chamber.

"I understood that there would be no entry in my data-file."

Larry nods in agreement. "If that is your wish, it doesn't matter to me." He says as he tilts his head toward the monitor, "I'll delete this before you leave, but you need to be aware. Discrepancies between your data-file and a medical scan will call attention."

"What do you recommend?" she asks.

Larry calls up Julie's citizen profile. "I see you had some minor alterations done when you were sixteen, following your pregnancy. I recommend noting the physical alterations we did today as follow-up to that procedure. That way, if you are scanned in a standard medical clinic, the results will be more in line with your history."

Julie nods. "What about the other changes."

Doc shrugs. "Be mindful of any future medical scans you get. No reason anyone needs to know you changed your voice unless your vocal cords are scanned by someone with access to your full citizen profile."

Doc leans closer. "I can't erase previous entries in your profile. I can only control what the chamber reports to the Guardian now."

"Okay," she agrees. "But can you give me a copy of the full report? That may be useful later."

Larry turns to his terminal. After a few minutes, he says, "It's done." Then he motions at her glasses. "Those are pretty great. Where did you get them?"

Finally, she thinks. "Thanks, I made them. They save a lot of space on my workbench." She takes out the pair Doc had worn earlier. "I made these for outside. The lenses darken in the sun."

Larry eyes the spectacles as he leans back in his chair. "Would you trade?"

A smile blossoms across Julie's new face. She passes the spectacles over along with the opened notebook and asks, "Would you hand me my other boot?"

He does so. Larry slips the glasses into the pocket of his tunic and begins skimming the procedure outlined on the college ruled pages. What he sees shocks him. What he sees marks this moment as the most alarming in his life. That is until he looks to the young woman sitting at his side. She had removed the thick heel from her boot to reveal a tiny white eight-millimeter chip tucked in a cavity within. Doc's heart races. "What do you want to do with that?"

Eyes blaze above a mischievous smile that is less than an hour old. "Do you have a standard device receiver, Doc?" She glances down to her lap, directing his attention to the purring kitten. Cupped in her other palm is her little egg.

Priya-14

The sedation from his surgery kept the kitten quiet during the pod ride from Antioch. Julie gently glides her fingers across his back. His dark-brown fur effectively hides a newly installed lifeclock that shines blue in the cat's left thigh.

The hover-pod delivers them to their new home in Alameda. The rented cell has a cot, a workbench, and a stool. She had to borrow the lamp for the evening from another resident, with a promise to return it the next day.

Marcos rests quietly on the workbench, curled atop Julie's sweater.

Doc's question still echoes in her mind: "I'm not going to ask where you got a lifeclock, I don't care, but you will tell me why you want it implanted into your cat?"

For Julie, it all came down to curiosity. "Haven't you ever wondered how it works?" she'd asked.

The procedure was outlined in her notebook. Larry simply made a small incision in Marcos's skin and placed the crystal chip on top of the muscle tissue. What at first appeared to be wires extending from the crystal were actually covers for even smaller fiber conductors. When properly placed, Julie touched the amber sensor of her little egg to the lifeclock and then sent a command through her portable terminal.

> installClock

The chip glowed white under the light of the clock writer. The fiber tendrils came to life and inserted themselves into the nerves in Marcos's thigh. The lifeclock interpreted these signals as *I'm alive* and began to glow blue.

After thirty minutes, the white light of the little egg changed to amber, and the message SUCCESSFUL blinked three times on the terminal's screen. They removed the writer to find the clock implanted in the kitten's leg; all traces of the incision had healed.

Julie traded the holographic data glasses for the procedure and a device receiver for the lifeclock writer.

> read citizenSummary

A chime sounds and the comprehensive, albeit short life story of Gabrielle-71 flows across a terminal window hovering in front of Julie's data spectacles. Gabrielle had entered Outland to live as a canine outside of Madrid in the Western Euro region. She died when she was twelve years old. The profile contains all of the standard information tracked by the Collective, including her height, gender, age, current and previous residence, security concerns, and photo.

Julie talks softly to the profile picture on the screen. "So, Gabrielle, you went to the pack like I did. It's a dangerous world." She shakes her head negatively.

Marcos is curled in Julie's lap as the holographic page hovers in front of her. She sends another command.

> open dataFile

Another chime and another page opens, very similar to the citizen profile, with three critical distinctions:

First, this file has no name. Gabrielle-71 is a separate component managed by the Guardian, which is paired with the data-file and displays when the citizen profile or summary is read.

Second, the age is displayed as the number of days the person has lived since birth, rather than years.

Finally, this file is opened, rather than simply read only, which means it can be edited.

Julie mumbles to the display, "This is how we appear to the Guardian." She moves through the data-fields of the form. For the most part, she leaves them alone, mostly because she doesn't know the commands to edit them.

"Well, Marcos, let's see." She reads the entries of the data-file. "Your current skill-trade is Furball Generator." Julie speaks the commands out loud as she enters them in the terminal, a habit she picked up working alone for so many years.

> set skillTrade: Furball Generator

"Your current location is Alameda." She double-checks the section code for Bay City. "Sector-211. And you need a picture." She holds Marcos up to a video scanner and blows in his ear to make him shake his head and open his eyes. After stepping through the frames of the video file, she finds one where he looks alert. With a *set* command, Gabrielle's photo is replaced with that of a startled shorthaired cat.

"Height is twenty-five centimeters. Gender, well sorry, Marcos, I haven't figured out how to edit that one yet, you're going to have to be a girl. Don't be mad."

The age component is held as eight digits. Julie spent years unlocking this code. She has only figured out how to access the third digit to the left of the decimal, the hundreds place.

The file won't allow the number to be simply changed; instead, a specific code must be sent that checks the digit of the age, and if it's correct, cycle it by one. Julie revised a new version of the code to cycle by negative one.

She sends the codes one at a time and watches as 4,661.4050 days changes to 4561.4050 days then,

4461.4050,
4361.4050,
4261.4050,
4161.4050, and finally,
4061.4050. It seems so easy now, but that little bit of
mathematics took three years of her life to resolve.
However, all this is pointless unless the last part works.

The data-file can't be saved. All active data-files are open and in use by the Guardian; therefore, only the Guardian can save a new file by assigning it a new name.

"Don't move, Marcos; this part is really important." She gently places the egg against Marcos's lifeclock and sends the command

> getName

The egg doesn't respond, but the terminal does.

ENTER BIRTH LOCATION:

"Where were you born, Marcos?" Julie thinks of the night the crystal was delivered to her in the library in Argentina two years ago. "What is the code for Bangalore?" She accesses the Collective's geographic directory. "703."

> 703

ENTER BIRTH NURSERY:

"I need a nursery in Bangalore." She again consults the directory. "Here's one, 412."

> 412

This time when she enters the figure, the light on the egg shines white in the dark fur of the shorthaired cat. After three seconds, a soft chime plays, welcoming the flashing message,

WELCOME: Priya-14, 703.412.020.14

A moment passes before her muscles allow her to remove the egg from the cat's thigh and replace it on the workbench. She removes her spectacles. Running her fingers through his fur, she draws the dark patch aside to see the chip glowing bright green in the brown fur.

Marcos purrs in her lap. They sit quietly for a while. Then Julie picks the egg up again and places it on the green crystal.

> read citizenSummary

NAME: Priya-14, 703.412.020.14.
GENDER: Female.
AGE: 11.1 years.
SKILL-TRADE: Furball Generator.
HEIGHT: 25 cm.
CURRENT LOCATION: Bay City, Alameda,
Sector-211.
MODEST SECURITY CONCERN.
POSSIBLE ASSOCIATION WITH MADRID
OUTLAND.

Julie stares at the picture of a shocked cat displaying in the file. "Hello, Priya-14, I'm very happy to meet you."

Julie lifts her hand from the cat's belly and stares down at the red clock burning on her hand.

Chapter 4

Lauren-25

A hand passes through the ring on the personnel desk of Bay City Central Archives in Alameda. The scanner chimes. The conjoined monitor displays the associated citizen summary with a picture of a light-complexioned woman with long black hair and an almond-shaped face. It is the same face that exited a surgical chamber in Antioch forty-eight hours ago and is now sitting opposite Albert-54, who had just confirmed that the level-2 archivist position is still available.

The screen introduces her as Lauren-25. Age: 19.2 years.

Albert-54, the chief archivist, extends a friendly hand. "Lauren-twenty-five, I'm glad you made it."

"Thank you for seeing me," she answers, shaking his hand. "I had intended to get here earlier, but had to…" Lauren silently considers the best way to explain her delay, "…say goodbye to a friend. It took longer than I thought."

Albert offers a sympathetic nod. "Did someone enter Somnus?"

"I'd rather not talk about it."

Albert pauses, and Lauren believes he is imagining a similar memory. "We accompanied your predecessor, Raymond-eight, to the Citadel last week. We haven't had time to clear his work area for you. I'll check your references this afternoon, but for now, welcome to Central Archives."

The references will, of course, be flawless. A posting on the aether boards assures that any calls will confirm her skills as a researcher and terminal technician.

The woman who is now named Lauren-25 spent more time remaking her data-file than she did her body. Priya was shooed from the workspace repeatedly while researching the boards for the missing commands to edit all the necessary fields. Many times, she copied whole sections out of other data-files to ensure the format and spacing would be identical to entries made by the Guardian.

Her birthplace changed to a Toronto nursery in the Northern Territory region, Sector-378. Most of the skill-trades are similar to those Julie had in Argentina. Her history has to be different enough to assure no relationship to the woman who rolled her age from 7919.9714 to 7019.9714 days. When the *getName* command was finally sent, Julie-11's lifeclock was reassigned to pair with a new data-file named Lauren-25.

Not only is Lauren two-and-a-half years younger, but she is also free from the troublesome moderate security concerns Julie had to endure.

"Let me show you your workbench, and again, please forgive the mess." Albert leads Lauren to an office piled high with handwritten notebooks, magnifiers, tools, and an assortment of components in various states of assembly. "Don't worry," he tries to reassure her. "Under this pile is a respectable work area. When we close, everyone will pitch in and help stack all this on the recycling pallet. Civil movers are scheduled for pick up in the morning."

Where Albert sees confusion and clutter, Lauren finds a horizon of wondrous possibilities. She has to restrain her excitement. "Raymond, did he like electronics too?"

"I'm going to miss him," Albert answers from a distance. His expressions change when he notices the large chrome microphone sitting on the table. "Can I show you something?" At Lauren's nod, Albert directs her to a large clear polycarbonate sheet suspended from the ceiling in the middle of the common area, as if it is a tapestry hanging in a castle.

Lauren takes her mark on the floor as Albert hands her the microphone. "Raymond worked on it right up to his Last-Day. We practically had to pry him from it so we could take him to the Crystal Lounge for his last few hours." He pauses. "He knew he'd never have time to finish it, and yet…"

Albert passes a pad with a handwritten message on it. Lauren reads the question into the microphone. "Mr. President, what do you believe is the role of a citizen?"

A light in the microphone flashes in Lauren's eyes, then onto the polycarbonate sheet. A holographic figure appears as a green wireframe behind the screen, then fills in as a man wearing a long-tailed jacket and vest over a white shirt. He has a bushy mustache and wears wire spectacles pinned to the bridge of his nose. The figure appears to stand before her on the floor of the library and speaks as if addressing a large auditorium.

"The average citizen must be a good citizen if our republics are to succeed. The stream will not permanently rise higher than the main source; and the main source of national power and national greatness is found in the average citizenship of the nation."

Albert catches the microphone that nearly slips from Lauren's fingers. The man stands in front of her, on the floor, casting a shadow. Lauren has spent years working with holograms, but they always float like ghosts in space and never respond to such mundane commands. As he speaks, a second window floats over his right shoulder.

Theodore Roosevelt, born October 27, 1858 CE,
died January 6, 1919 (Age 60).
President of the United North American Territory
from 1901 to 1909 CE.
Excerpt from the speech "Citizenship in a Republic"
delivered at the Sorbonne, in Paris, France, on
April 23, 1910 CE.

Albert's eyes shine and he appears pleased to see her reaction. "Raymond was a fervent citizen, patriotic to the last moment of his life." He shakes himself from the memory and says, "There's a motion sensor in the mic you're holding that measured the distance from your eyes to the screen to give it the right perspective."

The president continues, *"…who at the best knows in the end the triumph of high achievement, and who at the worst, if he fails, at least fails while daring greatly, so that his place shall never be with those cold and timid souls who neither know victory nor defeat."*

Albert unintentionally chokes. Lauren assumes he has heard the passage many times from this room. "Raymond imagined citizens visiting the library guided by characters from history," he says.

"Did Raymond keep notes on this?" Lauren asks timidly. "I mean, do you think he would mind if…?"

Albert looks into the new archivist's eyes and smiles.

Life in the Pack

The following year

White knuckles wrap around the stem of the silver microphone. Lauren skips a breath as she and Albert watch the holo-screen and asks the question again, "Can I meet someone who lost a brother?"

The holo-screen flickers to life with a flat video image of a little girl displayed within. Her voice is quiet and filled with rage she struggles to contain.

"William got his militia mailer today," she says. *"He'll be going to the war soon— No, He's going into action! He won't say where, but everyone knows it's somewhere in Africa."*

"The president calls it another support action. Everything is an action! Mom said if this were an African War, declared by the government, then taxes would go up, and resources would be rationed. It might inconvenience the Builders enough to end it. Instead, they get rich managing the support contracts for the militias, and I'm going to lose another brother."

In the holo-screen, the two-dimensional video image morphs into a life-sized, three-dimensional talking figure. The back of the girl's head, represented in wire-frame, slowly shades into natural-appearing hair and shoulders. Lauren adjusts the parameters of Raymond-08's model generator to render the thoughts of nine-year-old Michelle Strand, who kept a personal video diary to help work out her feelings for losing both her brothers in the support actions that closed the twenty-fourth century. Tears glisten under the eyes of the holographic figure as it continues.

"When the Builders demanded this Africa action, they directed funding from the civilian academies to pay their militia contracts, freeing students for conscription. Unless Mom qualifies for a grant to send me to a private institute, I'll receive my militia mailer soon."

Once posted, nothing is ever completely lost; even files deleted by their creator can still exist in unnamed backups. Michelle's journal is one of the millions archived in the aether.

Michelle Strand's diary is the first successful hyper-concept connection, as Lauren calls it, to link the journals preserved in the aether to the library's stacks. As documents, events, stories, and song titles are mentioned by the holographic speaker, links are generated to the referred material in the stacks.

A terminal window on Lauren's desk stirs as the hyper-concept matrix responds to statements made in the recording. In the holo-screen, a thin bracelet glows bright green under the hand that cups Michelle's chin. A window floats over her shoulder, cataloging the subjects retrieved by the matrix.

(Entry 25 of 32) - Michelle Strand, New Omaha, Nebraska, June 27, 2394 CE. This entry references:
North America - East Africa Support Action, 2383 to 2406 CE.
36th Amendment to the United North American Territory Constitution. Adopted on February 4, 2273 CE. All war declared by Congress will be paid with concurrent taxes and resource rationing.
National Militia Act of 2278 CE. Privately owned security forces may induct persons not employed or attending educational institutes, on behalf of the militia of the United States of America, for combat actions other than declared war.
SELECT FOR MORE INFORMATION:

The library's staff joins Albert and Lauren in the screen room, as it is known. Cheers and applause overwhelm the tiny voice in the holo-screen.

Lauren's elation is momentarily muffled. She wishes Raymond could share this moment. She often tries to imagine him through his writing and what it would have been like to work with him.

"That's it, Lauren, now we're celebrating. No all-nighter tonight." Albert is firm on this point.

The screen room empties. The long-dead girl continues to talk to Lauren about her brothers. The girl being rendered is not much older than she was when she had to leave her brother. She remembers how hard it was to say goodbye.

Julie was two years into her Green Cycle. Her trade attendant assigned her to live and work in a bakery for her first skill-trade. Everyone was really friendly but got strangely excited over what Julie thought was the most mundane things. How long they allowed the dough to rise, where the flour came from, the hardness and color of the crust, and the size of crumbs when a loaf was ripped in half. They discussed all these things at length.

Julie remembered baking her first loaf. She was sure she had done everything the experienced bakers did, but when it came out of the oven, it was a dense, rock-hard mass. The older bakers explained that bread dough needed time to rise before going in the oven. They told her that the wet, sticky flour and salt mixture had tiny creatures living inside it that have to grow in order to make a proper loaf of bread. This fascinated Julie, not about how to make a proper loaf, but that the dough had creatures living in it. She wanted to see the tiny organisms and watch them grow and leave it for others to bake them.

Her trade attendant explained that she might have many trades in her life. Her time in the bakery was just one way to learn about the world. Julie wanted to be a mountain climber-ocean-explorer-inventor and maybe someone who learns about the little yeasts that grow in the dough.

One day, a boy from the previous class came looking for her. Marcos-80 asked to see her lifeclock. When Julie showed him, he placed his hand beside hers and watched as the two crystal chips flashed green-white, green-white.

The attendant said the flashing means they are brother and sister. The lifeclocks flash to let boys and girls know it's not a good idea to couple.

"You and I had the same mother," Marcos explained. "We're connected, special."

Julie spent as much time with Marcos as she could. They were fascinated that they shared similar eyes, hair, and distaste for bitter salad sprouts.

Marcos didn't like the trade attendant who scolded them when they missed school or didn't show for their trade shifts. Julie didn't like missing class, but her connection with Marcos was unique, and she wanted to understand it.

One day Marcos came to the bakery excited to see her. "Julie, come with me."

"I can't now, I promised I wouldn't run off during my shift," she answered. "We can go to the park after dinner."

Marcos shook his head. "I'm not going to the park. I'm going away."

"Where?"

"There's a place where no one tells you what to do. We'll be able to do whatever we want. Come on. You're always saying you want to go exploring, right?"

"Ya," Julie answered cautiously.

"Well, let's go."

Julie was confused. That night, she asked the attendant for advice, who wasn't as helpful as she hoped. "You have an obligation to promote the wellbeing of all citizens as well as yourself," he said. "If you decide that means being with your brother rather than your skill-trade, then go with him."

Julie did feel obligated to Marcos. He needed her as much as she needed him.

Her attendant continued in a reassuring voice, "If you go with Marcos, remember this. Your obligation to yourself means you can come back anytime. Do you understand?"

Even though she didn't, Julie answered, "I think so."

The attendant knelt down and took her hand. He held his red clock next to her green. "It seems like there is so much time for this little light to shine, but it burns so fast. It's not fair for other people to always tell you not to follow your instincts."

Julie was seven and a half years old when she and Marcos snuck through the gates of a rail-bus station and hopped aboard a transport that took them to the border of Outland. There they descended into the maintenance tunnels beneath the mall of Balcarce and joined the pack.

Outland is a generic name for areas that have lost communication with the Guardian and the control of the civil authority. Every region has a few of them. When systems fall into disrepair, young children amass inside to live as canines of the pack. Citizens of the Collective have rules and directives to follow. The pack follows its own directives, the first of which is that canines manage for themselves.

Staying with the pack provided protection against grownups. Value was promoted for those who brought earnings to the assembly. Those who return from the mall with coats, data terminals, handbags, shoes, or anything that can be traded for food were valued highly. Those who brought food back were valued and protected the most.

Marcos learned quickly. He could spot people who intended to turn from their belongings. He often came to the assembly with whole baskets of food.

Julie was terrible at foraging. She always felt bad for the people who lost their groceries or purses. Although Marcos tried to protect her, she spent many nights nursing a skinned knee, a black eye, or a bleeding head. Marcos would stay with her as she cried. "You'll learn, Julie," he said. "You're smart. Soon, you'll be great at the forage."

Julie understood that Marcos tried his best to make her feel better, and sometimes she could pretend that he did. Marcos found some underground medics who traded a few minutes in a surgical chamber for anything electronic. He made sure none of Julie's wounds ever got infected.

Trading was difficult for canines. The malls surrounding the Balcarce tunnels mostly dealt in credits. However, every mall had its underground trading district where merchants appreciated the benefits of exchanging valuable merchandise for a few bags of inexpensive food. Credits are forbidden in the pack. They don't keep canines dry when the rain falls or warm when the wind blows. Credits are for hoarding as personal fortunes; hoarding starves the pack.

Julie learned to catch small rodents. She often brought a portion of meat to the assembly, which was always taken but never appreciated.

Maggie entered Outland just a week after Julie and Marcos; she was her only friend. Julie loved to sit with Maggie in the mall courtyards and make up stories about the people who passed them, instead of foraging for the pack.

Maggie used to be Marilyn-02 before she left the nursery. She was probably in her last year of yellow. One day Maggie's class passed through the fountain park on the way to see the amphitheater. Some canines were eating from a bag of rolls. They offered her one if she would bring them someone's purse.

Julie didn't understand why Maggie would leave the nursery to live in the tunnels. Maggie explained that she didn't like the way the attendant touched her at night when she tried to sleep.

One night Maggie woke Julie in a panic. "Something happened with Robert. Something happened to his lifeclock. Everyone is yelling at him."

Julie didn't like Robert. He was bigger and stole from the others. If ever a fight broke out, Robert was usually involved.

Maggie led Julie down the main tunnel to a boxed passageway where the pack had backed Robert against a barricade. Angry voices echoed through the tunnels. When Julie peeked into the passage, she saw Marcos standing with the canines, waving a stick in Robert's direction. Marcos was a follower; he rarely went or did anything the pack hadn't decided to do.

At the sight of his little sister, Marcos quietly separated from the mob.

"What happened?" Julie rasped above the fray.

"Robert turned Bloody-twenty-two! About fifteen minutes ago, his lifeclock started shining red."

"That's why everyone is yelling?" Julie asked.

Marcos looked about to ensure no others were listening as he explained the reason for the pack's outrage. "He's turned into Bloody Richard!"

Robert has always been able to fight the smaller kids, two or three at a time. He enjoyed taking food and forcing others to do what he wanted. He enjoyed growing in prestige and authority as older canines left the pack.

Surrounded and pressed into a corner, Robert desperately fought to regain the fear and respect he held just minutes ago. "Back off! I'll box all of you!" His commands enraged the pack all the more.

"He's Bloody Richard, Bloody-twenty-two!" Indistinct voices arose from the mob. "We told you to never come back Bloody-twenty-two!"

A rock flew from the horde, hitting Robert in the shoulder, knocking him against the wall. His defiant attitude faded to fear. When he regained his footing, Robert announced he was leaving Outland. His announcement was answered with another rock, this time, hitting him in the face.

Julie watched in horror. "Maggie, this is bad. Robert's in trouble." Julie still didn't like the boy, but she knew what being hit with a rock felt like.

Maggie was also scared. "That's not Robert, Julie, he's Bloody Richard. See his lifeclock? It's the color of blood, just like the tell."

"Richard-twenty-two is a story, Maggie, that's Robert." Julie raised her voice as terror grew within her. It was getting hard to hear over the yelling.

"Bloody Richard-twenty-two, Julie!" Maggie insisted. "He takes what others bring and keeps it for himself. It's just like the tell. He was pretending to be Robert, but that's Bloody-twenty-two. He can't be here!"

A terrified scream erupted from the pack. Julie and Maggie watched Robert sink into the mob. Canines piled onto his limbs. It was the first time Julie had ever seen the pack working together.

Muffled, gulping sobs arose from the barricade where the boy, the man, was buried. Sharpened spikes were the pack's teeth, sticks with weights tied at the end were their claws. Bloody Richard lived to see his intestines pulled from his belly through the eye that was still intact.

Marcos found Julie around the corner of the passageway, her hands fighting to keep the sound from entering her ears. "It's over, Julie." He wanted to hold her but didn't want the blood on his sleeve to frighten her.

"Then why do I still hear him crying?" she whimpered.

Marcos knelt down to her eye level. "Julie, I have to help take him to the boundary."

Julie cried out, terrified of being left alone.

"We have to, Julie. The white crystal will bring reapers as surely as a black. We'll leave him at the boundary, and they'll take him away."

Julie heard scraping as the canines pulled a piece of sheet metal to use as a sled for Richard's corpse. Immediately, they began to argue over the best way to roll him on.

Marcos reached out for Julie's shoulders. She winced at the sight of Robert's blood, sending her into the wall. "Julie, listen. I know this is hard, but you need to listen. I'm going to help drag Richard to the boundary. The blood back there is going to attract rodents; you can forage."

Julie started crying. Her tummy had turned to knots.

He tried to keep a comforting voice. "It's going to be okay, Julie. Most of the pack is going to the assembly to do the tell. Everyone wants to hear the story of Bloody Richard now."

Julie stifled every instinct to scream out against the insanity that had just happened. "Robert, his name was Robert, Marcos!" her voice rasped in muffled horror.

Marcos took his little sister by the shoulders and firmly directed her to look into his eyes. "Now it's Richard!" Marcos matched her tone. "It was Robert yesterday, but now it's Richard, and that's what you need to call him in front of the others, Julie. You need to do that. If you say Robert, they're going to get really, really angry at you."

Julie nodded at the insane directive.

Marcos gave her a quick hug and then left for the sled.

When the scraping sound faded into the tunnel, Julie peeked around the corner. A rat scurried into the stained clearing and nibbled on a piece of an ear.

Julie reached into her bag for the hunting stick. She was never without it, even when she foraged above. It was hard to see through her burning eyes. She threw farther than she should have. Stupid luck tapped the rat's skull, knocking it into a daze. She ran to grab it by its back legs and slammed it into the ground until she was sure it wouldn't move.

Once she realized Robert's blood had spattered on her pants, she stopped. "It's Richard, Richard's blood," she muttered to herself. Then she realized that the sound of Richard's crying had finally stopped.

Stuffing the prize into her bag, she retrieved the stick and returned to the corner to watch for another.

✧ ✧ ✧

Marcos and Julie left the tunnels early to catch a rail-bus for the coast. They had wandered about the mall since sunrise. Julie was euphoric.

Her arm was hurt the night before, after Bernard shoved her down some steps. He wanted the meat from Julie's hunting bag for the gathering, and now that he was among the bigger canines, he had the right to take it. Marcos tried to get it back but got his head slammed into the wall for the attempt.

Marcos kept a stash of earnings hidden from the pack for trips to the medic, which were coming more often. He negotiated three-quarters of an hour for Julie in the surgical chamber, which repaired the break in her arm, along with a few other scars and bruises. She could even see better when she came out.

Marcos took just enough time in the chamber to clean and treat his wounds for infection. He didn't mind if it left a scar. He traded a few less minutes in the chamber so Julie could take a sponge bath in the examination room.

The siblings walked to a courtyard in the commerce district, where Marcos had a surprise. He waved his hand through a scanner of a public terminal to reveal his very own credit account, which he had been building for the last few months. Credit accounts were forbidden in the pack, as was keeping earnings from the assembly. Trading for credits is difficult, especially for children in their Green Cycle. Underground commerce paid almost nothing for canine loot, but he had saved enough to buy a new outfit for Julie and six fresh rolls from the bakery.

Julie couldn't stop hugging her brother that afternoon. It had been so long since she had clean clothes and nothing hurt. She kept stretching out her arms and back, enraptured that her muscles didn't punish her for the strain.

The roll had a strangely familiar quality about it. She inhaled the aroma of the warm bread. It tugged at something locked away in her mind.

"Why aren't you eating it?" Marcos encouraged her. "I'll get you more; you don't have to save it. Go ahead, Julie."

Her eyes began to tear. A voice she had forgotten drifted into her mind, *Your obligation to yourself means you can come back anytime.*

In a quiet, somber voice, Julie said, "I'm not going back, Marcos." She could see he was about to protest but didn't allow it. "I'm not going to argue with you. I don't like the pack. Everyone acts like they're so brave, like they're defending themselves against some make-believe attack, even when they're stealing from each other. Everyone argues and fights over nothing, but worst of all, it's boring there, Marcos! No one ever does anything."

Marcos surprised her by not arguing. They sat together in the courtyard all night. When the sun rose, Marcos returned to the tunnels of Balcarce, and Julie walked around the mall until she found the Mar del Plata Library.

A telescopic image of the courtyard displays in a terminal window hovering a few centimeters in front of Lauren-25's spectacles. She controls the window with voice commands as she whispers, "Three times. Five times." The image enlarges to show a child distracting a man trying to sip his coffee, while another grabs his datapad, then the pair runs off. The image is fed by an optical sensor embedded in the rim of her glasses. She shakes her head and murmurs, "I need to figure out how to make these see behind me."

Lauren has a habit of clutching her bag in her lap anytime she sits down in a public place. Her friends don't understand this routine. She never talks about it. A gulp of tea remains in the bottom of her cup when she returns it to the saucer, where half a roll balances on the edge. Its aroma reaches into her memories just as the sight of the little thieves had. For an instant, she was sitting with her brother, smelling the bread, and watching the sunrise.

Lauren pulls the latest version of her terminal from her bag. This one automatically pairs with her spectacles when she unfolds the keyboard.

"Access LINCC, manual input," she commands. Windows appear in front of her as they would if she were at a regular data terminal using a video display screen. Voice commands are convenient most of the time, but in public, she prefers the privacy of typing. A query of the aether boards returns Balcarce Outland, life out of the pack. A subject board named *I was a canine* reveals a dozen posts from Marcos-80 that read, *Have you seen Julie-11?*

Lauren removes her glasses and gazes into her past. "Not here."

Chapter 5

The Message

Steam hovers over the thermos cup as it fills with dark tea. Marcos-80 appreciates the anticipation of the first gulp that will burn the morning fuzz away.

The work crew gathers outside the assignment hall of the Torres del Paine National Park. The foreman won't hand out the work schedule for another twenty-five minutes, but it is a good time to share stories, talk about the ball game, and get to know the new crew members. Everyone pitches in a credit to have a cartload of fruits, pastries, rolls, and a large tank of coffee brought from the market. Marcos prefers his tea; he brings it every morning in a large thermos.

His morning ritual of tea, Danish, and the local headlines sometimes includes a brief sweep of the aether boards on a portable terminal that is passed around. Marcos programmed a sentry alert to page him if anyone named Julie-11 with a birth location of 120 in her designation ever posts to a board. The silence on his account reminds him that she is probably still mad. When he heard his little sister say that she didn't like the bakery, he convinced himself that it meant she would like living in Outland, as he did.

It was well after Julie left that he realized how miserable she was in the pack, but by then, he didn't know where to find her. She was smart enough to leave then; she's smart enough not to be dragged back into his life now.

Message Response: Have you seen Julie-11?
Recorded response for: Marcos-80

From: Encrypted.

That's bizarre, he thinks. *Who would send me an encrypted message?*
When he selects it, a question appears:

\# If you are Marcos-80, looking for his sister from the
Balcarce Outland, what did you and your sister eat when
you stayed with the canines?

Marcos's thoughts often visited the last time he and Julie were
together, sharing a bag of rolls in the courtyard. He answers.

> Rolls

The reply immediately follows:

\# INCORRECT

He quickly types another response.

> Bread

The terminal display again flickers:

\# INCORRECT

He drifts back a few days further into those memories. *Rats, we ate rats
when we lived with the canines. Of course, she's still mad.* Marcos is about to log
out and pass the terminal to the next in line but hesitates as he realizes
this is his last chance to reach out.

> Rats

\# CORRECT

The terminal screen dissolves into a video player. A light-
complexioned woman with narrow wire-rimmed spectacles appears in the
display; she has an almond-shaped face, dark hair, and seems to be early
in her red-cycle, though he can't guess her age.

"Hello, Marcos, my name is Lauren-twenty-five. I have a message
from your sister *J*. Please listen carefully; this message is going to self-
corrupt once it has played.

"*J* has asked me to contact you on her behalf; she is excited to see you
again. If you want to see her, you can contact me, and I'll make the
arrangements. There is one condition you have to follow. You mustn't
use her name. Don't ask for her, don't type it, don't say it in a crowd, or
even when you think you're alone. If you can do this, you can find me in
the West Coast of the North American region, Sector-two-eleven, Bay
City, Alameda. I'll see you soon."

Marcos stares at the video screen, the words, 'Lauren-25, North American region, Sector-211, Bay City, Alameda,' hangs for a moment. He drops his thermos and Danish to fish a pen from his pocket and scribbles the words onto his forearm. He tries to replay the message, but it is inaccessible as soon as the window clears. "Lauren-twenty-five, North American region, Sector-two-one-one, Bay City, Alameda." He repeats the message all the way to the foreman's office. He is careful not to mention his sister's name when he explains why he has to leave.

"I'm sorry to lose you, Marcos," his supervisor says. "It's been good working with you, but I understand."

Both men want to keep this short. Marcos pauses a moment. "Hey, boss, would you mind reserving a seat on a rail-bus out of El Calafate to Sector-two-eleven. I don't want to show up on her doorstep almost wiped out."

It is a hard thing to hear, but his boss knows it is even harder to ask. "Done," he answers. Removing the cover from a lifeclock reader, he nods for Marcos to pass his hand into the ring. The terminal chimes, indicating a completed account transfer. "Here are all the credits you're due, plus another seventy; this should cover a hover-pod trip to El Calafate, and a little extra for lunch along the way. I'll reserve your rail-bus ticket from the administrative account."

Marcos is moved by the generosity; he hasn't experienced much of it in his life.

His supervisor says, "Leave on the east side and you won't get delayed by the crew. I saw three hover-pods parked at the front yard. I hope it works out for you, Marcos." The two shake hands. The foreman tries not to call attention to the crystal on Marcos's hand flashing red-pink, red-pink.

Jazz and Generations

Two fingers pluck the strings of a standing double base, hidden in the dark. Red and blue lights gleam across the polished sheen of a brass trumpet as it rises to sing out. In the shadows, a drum awakens a chorus of brass and reeds. Lights in the floor of the players' circle fade onto the musicians. Music splashes onto the dance floor, where a churning cauldron of bodies shuffles, steps, and slides in its wake. Lauren is one of many cresting waves in this riptide of the Topaz Lounge.

Motivated by her very public success with the Strand interview in Raymond's character generator, Lauren spent the last six nights at her workbench in the archive, trying to integrate the system with the library stacks. Despite the all-night sessions, a full-scale launch is still months, perhaps years away.

When one of the new apprentices asked Lauren if she had ever gone home and she couldn't remember, she decided it was time to drive all thoughts of holograms and hyper-concept connections out of her mind.

The room is thick with smoke, heavy breathing, and designer pheromones. Cooling units pour a dense white mist onto the crowd that churns with their movements. Colored lights blaze across the fog, transforming the dance floor into a faraway cloud.

Men wear suits with jackets and ties that fly out as they shake and spin about.

Lauren is in white. Her bare feet shuffle and skip under a flared skirt that flows from her calves up to a blouse that hugs the curves of her belly, back, shoulders, and arms. A string of chrome beads flings about her neck with every motion.

The Bay City sound is a fast-paced, string-heavy style of swing jazz, unique to the typical tribute and cover playlists mostly performed in the Collective. A drummer sits in the hub of the players' circle surrounded by a kit of every snare, tom, and cymbal variety. His stool slowly rotates around the set as he awakens the night's tempo. Three upright double basses joined the beat, followed by another three electric bass guitars. Finally, a dozen players materialize in the spotlights bringing the full sound of Gramophone Mayhem to life.

The men in the band, attired in bright-white suits with thin black ties, complement the ladies in matching white cocktail dresses. When they are not playing, the light from their lifeclocks cut blue and red streaks through the dark as they swing their arms in tempo with the music. Three of the players are in their Blue Cycle. Most of the band is well into their Red; one is clearly in Final-Quarter.

Lauren has a personal music database with thousands of tracks, most of which have a more refined, polished sound. Yet nothing excites her like the rough, unproduced quality of a live performance. The only part of the evening she resents is the requirement to purchase admission for a band called Gramophone Mayhem. It doesn't matter how much she enjoys their music, it's a stupid goddamned name for a band.

Horns burst and cymbals crash, announcing the end of the set. The lounge erupts in cheers. Lauren falls into a friendly embrace with her partner on the dance floor before retiring to the bar. A tall glass of sparkling water with lime appears before her as she takes a barstool. The bartender smiles above an oversized name badge that reads Sarah-67. "You look like you earned this one," she offers in a praising voice.

Lauren slips on her shoes before taking a pull from the double cocktail straws between exhausted breaths. "Ya, there's a lot to keep up with, they're really moving tonight!"

"You're catching them at the right time, you know." Sarah chats as she mops the damp rings from the countertop, trying to appear busier than she really is. "They're going to cycle soon."

"What do you mean?"

The bartender motions with her towel to the band. "Three of the players are leaving. They're looking for apprentices to step in."

"You mean three more?" Lauren recalls the blue crystals flashing in the hands of the players.

Sarah nods. "GM has always done well bringing in new talent, but their experienced players are leaving faster than the new ones are coming in. Half the band is going to be under seventeen years old next season."

Mike-34 lingers with the last part of Sarah's gossiping before ordering a bourbon. "Hey, Mike," she asks. "Have you heard about the band cycling?"

"Their playbook says the trombone player is going to spend his Final-Quarter traveling in the European region, maybe play a few clubs in London and Munich." He takes a drink and tries to gauge Lauren's interest. "Two others are just leaving to try something different in their last year."

Lauren pokes the lime to the bottom of the glass with her straws. "You mean they're leaving for another band?"

Mike shrugs. "Maybe, I didn't read the whole story. I think one is leaving to compete in a triathlon and wants to dedicate more time to training."

"Are they going to bring in the same seats?" Lauren asks, unsure of how much she really wants to learn.

Turning toward the performance circle, Mike motions to a thirteen-year-old girl in a white cocktail dress holding a pair of maracas. "The kid playing percussion tonight is actually a xylophone player. She's supposed to be pretty good; they just need to figure out how to bring her in."

"I thought GM emphasized the guitar and bass in their music."

"You're referring to the Bay City string theme they've been promoting?" Mike's face turns sour as he mentions it. "That's just a gimmick some of the local bands put together. The South Bay music academy cut its program back two years ago when four of the senior instructors… retired. The heavy use of guitar and bass is mostly due to a shortage of piano and reed players." He orders another shot of bourbon.

Lauren does the same.

"This year, the administration moved around some of the younger instructors to senior positions and installed a set of robotic trainers to teach the basics to the Green Cycle students." He takes a pull from the shot glass. "I'm not criticizing, I know they're doing the best they can, but while the model-18 vocal and instrumental training units may instruct beginning students on the basic principles of playing, perhaps even encourage a few hobbyist players, they don't inspire passion. It's unlikely the mechanized program will produce any new trade musicians."

"Where did you hear this?" Lauren asks.

Mike raises his glass in a salute. "I used to be one of them." He empties the shot and waves two fingers to Sarah.

The light from his lifeclock flashes in the empty glass, red-pink, red-pink, red. Lauren tries not to see it.

"Academy graduates are always encouraged to continue teaching in addition to working in the trade. Believe me, the extra credits are helpful when you're getting started, but…" He pauses as memories of his own performance experiences pass. "The trade is a rough one. I enjoy teaching, much more than performing, but after five years of it, I need to see something more of this world than the inside of a studio and the same lessons again and again."

"You could always teach something new." Lauren regrets her ill-conceived comment as soon as she says it.

Mike seems to take it in stride. "I don't know what something new would sound like. At this point, I can only hope I've given enough to the next generation to enter into the musician trade and thrive in my place." Sarah places two fresh bourbons in front of the pair as a voice thunders into the lounge.

"Citizens of Topaz, here for their first performance in Bay City, give a warm welcome to Wishbone Blues!"

Mike hands a shot to Lauren and motions to the performance circle. The drummer begins a slow beat as the other five join with a standard melancholy tune. None of the players are older than sixteen, and they are all fighting stage fright.

Mike raises his glass to the performers. "My last protégés," he says with pride.

"You're their trade attendant?" Lauren asks as she takes her glass.

"Yep, they'll work with a younger version of myself for a few more weeks, but they're ready to take on their profession. I'm hoping Gramophone Mayhem will consider a few of them. Here's to preparing the next generation to conquer the future."

Mike clinks Lauren's glass that she offered in praise. The bourbon slides into them as they throw back their heads.

An angry voice in the crowd jeers the nervous players. Wishbone Blues are not experienced. Compared to the headlining band, they sound rough and out of sync. Worse yet, performance anxiety is robbing a few of the horns of much-needed wind.

The entire lounge hisses the heckler as he is dragged away. Lauren can see pain in Mike's eyes.

"Come on!" She yanks the wounded mentor from his stool. "For the next generation and the future of music!" She drags him in front of the performers and begins a slow dance, which quickly spreads through the lounge. Lauren sees that Mike gives the players a proud and grateful smile, then she rests her head against Mike's chest.

Dreamtime

Lauren drifts into a long dark hallway. The sound of muffled trumpets and drums push through the walls. An angry voice rises above the music. Cool, flickering light presses around the outline of a door that swings open as she approaches. Peering through the distorted yet familiar doorway, she finds Michelle Strand standing in the middle of the Alameda archives screen room, reciting the familiar Roosevelt speech. The ghostly child spits the words in a stern, chastising tone.

"It is not the critic who counts; not the man who points out how the strong man stumbles, or where the doer of deeds could have done them better. The credit belongs to the man who is actually in the arena, whose face is marred by dust and sweat and blood…"

The walls shimmer with the radiating color of the holographic girl's clothing and skin. Michelle suddenly turns around and points a condemning finger at Lauren, her eyes flair with rage. "YOU and those LIKE YOU have received special advantages!" Michelle calls in judgment. "Most of YOU have had a chance for enjoyment of life far greater than comes to the majority of your fellows!"

The child's words smash into Lauren. "How does she know?" she mutters and backs away from her accuser into a table. Turning about, she faces her workbench, covered with notebooks and tools. Sitting in her chair in front of a terminal keyboard is someone she has never met yet is strangely familiar. "Raymond," she asks. "Raymond-eight?"

The man turns his attention from a data window hovering over the workbench in front of him. His eyes are slightly recessed into his head, giving him a skull-like appearance. A discolored indent crosses the bridge of his nose and cheeks, outlining a mask from the Somnolence Citadel. Once he recognizes her, his attention returns to the window. "I came to undo the damage you've done," he says, his tone spiteful.

Lauren glances at the data window to see the matrix of the hyper-concept program she has been working on for the last year and a half. Raymond is removing whole sections of the program.

"That's my work!" Lauren exclaims as her attention moves from the data window to the area where Michelle stands, to see the results of his editing. A pair of civil movers wearing their medium blue tunics lifts the girl into a large, wheeled bin. Michelle sits quietly in the bin glaring at Lauren with hateful eyes.

"It's not yours, Raymond," she says in a firm yet sympathetic tone. "This is my time now—"

Raymond's face is dark with contempt. "YOU have had a chance for enjoyment of life far greater than comes to the majority of your fellows, JULIE!" He spits her old name out.

She turns away from her accuser only to get caught in the suspicious glare of the civil movers. She wants to speak up in her defense. Raymond spitefully jabs a control on the gramophone sitting next to the floating terminal window. The wail of a baritone saxophone overwhelms her voice.

The squeaky wheels pierce the blaring music as the bin approaches the table. The movers begin clearing her workbench of her tools, the data terminal, her notebooks, the terminal windows, and the gramophone.

Lauren scans the bench for anything she can save. The white sheen of the lifeclock writer on the corner of the table catches her attention. She reaches for it in haste and knocks it to the floor. The writer splatters with the sound of a crashing cymbal. The sharp edges of its bright-white shells puncture the glowing amber yoke. As the liquid spreads across the floor, the yoke changes color from amber to green to blue to red and finally fades to black.

One of the movers stares at her as if trying to identify a suspicious smell. His uniform is no longer blue but black like that of a reaper. Locked in his gaze, Lauren tries to step away. Her fist tightens yet cannot close.

The reaper turns away. He pushes the bin out the door, taking away her life's work.

Lauren is alone. The gramophone is gone, but the music grows louder and louder until she opens her eyes.

She's awake in a booth at the Topaz Lounge.

In the performance circle, a baritone saxophone player swings to a soft, sensual melody. Resting on the table of the booth, her hand is clenched tightly around a shot glass glowing red with her lifeclock. She sighs. "What am I doing here?"

A wave of incoherent chatter tumbles onto Lauren from the next booth, which is filled with lounge crawlers. A voice from the table arises. "The name is supposed to convey a sense of frustration and discontent. Before the Awakening, subversive speeches were distributed on vinyl disks that played on primitive needle players."

"Is that true?" asks another.

A third voice chimes in. "I heard about this. Political subversives used to gather around these old players and listen to speeches from dissident leaders. Sometimes, the parties recorded their messages to distribute among their followers. The disks were brittle and easily destroyed when in danger of discovery."

Another voice challenges the story. "How are these guys subversive?"

The anecdote tickles Lauren, who has spent half her life in the archives listening to hundreds of hours of pre-Awakening dissident journals. She shakes her head at the bogus story. She is tempted to order another shot, then counts the array of empty glasses spread across the table. Are all those mine? She wonders. Maybe it's time for coffee.

Prowling the Lounge

Gramophone Mayhem always headlines the lounge acts in Bay City. They are usually followed by a smaller, less impressive start-up band. Toby-33 prefers to wait for the follow-up band to finish before cruising the lounge. His white suit reminds the women how they felt when he played. His prowl is sidetracked by a discussion of a story from his band's playbook.

One voice rises above the others. "How are these guys subversive?"

Toby stops to address the table. Two couples share the booth with a forest of empty glasses. "Do you realize Gramophone Mayhem is over thirteen years old? As a band, we are middle age." His grand introduction silences the group. "The idea is to extend the band beyond the life of its players, and one day, beyond twenty-five years."

"That's interesting, but what does it prove?" one of the women asks.

"It will symbolize life beyond twenty-five and all its possibilities," Toby answers in a mocking surprised tone. "There is no greater symbol of defiance."

Toby set his beer on the table to free his hands for gesturing. "Five years ago, Martin-19 was the last of the original band members to enter Somnus. He started Gramophone Mayhem when he was seventeen years old, which is older than the bass player we just hired from Wishbone Blues." He picks up his beer for a triumphant pull as the table observes a very satisfying silence.

One of the men in the booth begins to cross-examine the drummer. "You understand that you, Toby-33, will not see the attainment of this great symbolic act of defiance, right? I mean, unless you just entered your Blue Cycle, there's no way you will see GM turn twenty-five."

Toby is distracted by a woman with a black ponytail, dressed in white, sitting in the next booth over and staring at him. She is just inside his peripheral vision. He recognizes the string of large chrome beads that flew about her neck when she was on the dance floor. He stammers and tries to answer, "It doesn't matter that I won't see GM turn twenty-five, but I will play with the generation who will, and so will our newest members."

Toby's challenger leans forward and replies in a stern tone, "But you won't. Your band may continue playing for another twelve years, maybe more, but the members will all enter Somnus right on schedule, which brings me back to my question. How is that, at all, subversive?" The man captivates the attention of the table in exactly the way Toby wished he could.

The man continues in a more supportive tone. "I am glad to hear that Gramophone Mayhem has brought on younger players, especially from that Wishbone group. That's fantastic." Then the praise in his voice retards. "But making room for new musicians as you have done is the very definition of good citizenship, which defines the heart of the Awakening."

Toby steams as the table erupts in laughter. His challenger picks up his drink and continues through a giggling voice, "I think you should consider changing your name to Gramophone Legacy."

"Or Gramophone Compliance," another voice contributes. More laughter follows.

When the laughter dies, his accuser leans in once again. "Now, Toby, if, on the other hand, Gramophone Mayhem is openly advocating defiance of the Somnus Obligation, well then, that is subversive." He raises his glass in salute. "Furthermore, if you will, right here, right now, state your intention to resist Somnus, then that would be true, unapologetic mayhem."

The muscles in Toby's neck bulge as he looks about nervously for the reaper who is certainly listening. The table becomes likewise nervous at the challenge hanging in the air.

"What the hell is making everyone so serious tonight?" All eyes turn toward the sleepy voice coming from the woman in the next booth. She had pulled her dark black hair from the ponytail allowing it to settle across her shoulders. "This place is supposed to be fun."

Turning his attention to the neighboring booth, Toby drinks the last of his beer and leaves the empty glass on the table where he had been arguing. His eyes lock with the woman's.

Meeting his stare, she asks, "Are you any fun?"

"Sure, I'm all kinds of fun." Toby slides into the booth beside her.

A server slips a cup of coffee in front of the woman, who lifts it to her nose and breathes in the aroma.

"I'm Toby-33."

Holding the cup in front of her mouth, she takes short sips through a mischievous grin.

He continues in a curious voice. "And you are?"

"Not having fun." She mocks him with a satisfied smile and takes another nip.

"So, what do you—"

The woman interrupts. "You're not wearing your tie." She sets the cup down with a frown and glares at him. Continuing in a softer voice, compelling him to lean closer. "You were wearing a tie before, it looked good. You should put it back on."

Toby removes the rolled up band of silk from his pocket and slides it around his neck.

The woman reaches out and meticulously straightens his collar and begins tying a very slow Windsor knot.

"Lauren," she says softly, as the knot cinches under his neck, tighter than he expected. "My name is Lauren-twenty-five."

"Well, Lauren-twenty-five, if you're not having fun, we should do something about it."

Lauren holds the end of the tie as she slides from the booth. Toby is pulled along in a way he hadn't expected. It's not usually this much work.

He moves beside her, to lead her toward the exit when Lauren directs him onto the dance floor. "I thought we were—"

She cuts him off again. "I want to see what kind of stamina you have." Leading him like a pet, she takes him next to the band's performance area. There, she releases his tie and rests her arm on his shoulder. They begin to sway to the music.

The GM players are getting acquainted with their new members. Toby's arm flails above for the attention of one of the musicians. "Eli, hey, Eli!" He gestures. When one of the players reacts, Toby calls to him. "Play the spider one."

Toby hopes that Lauren doesn't notice his desperate play to impress her.

A smile grows across Toby's face as a deep baritone saxophone begins to play. Soon, one of the new bass players picks up the melody. Then their new drummer joins in with a slow, aggressive beat. The music rises to a steady, grinding blues riff. Sound waves crash against them, and Toby can feel Lauren's chest rising and falling. He feels her body quiver in time with the beat. He watches as she closes her eyes, and a smile spreads across her lips.

Toby's hands drift down the curve of her spine until he feels his scalp clenched in her fist, bringing an abrupt halt to the drift at the base of her lower back. Her grip directs his attention to her eyes that convey a stern warning: Don't move so fast.

When Toby relaxes his hold, the pain of his scalp is soothed by the tips of her fingers. Her other hand settles in the middle of his back, all the while, shivering in time with the drumbeat.

Leaning to his ear, she asks in a sleepy voice, "What did you call this song?"

"It's something Eli thought up last year when we were on the road. He calls it the Spider's Seduction."

The odd name makes Lauren giggle.

Toby smiles at his first apparent success. "The riff came to him after he saw a wildlife special about the mating habits of bugs. I guess it inspired all of us."

Her eyes flash, and she laughs again as she leans in to whisper into his ear. "Do you know what happens to the spider when he finally succeeds in his seduction?"

Toby grins. "Maybe I'll find out later."

Lauren's laughter appears to make her dizzy as she sways side to side. Her head falls back, pressing her chest against his.

Chapter 6

The Snare

A chime sounds authenticating the transfer of eighty-five credits into Dante-09's account, confirming the completion of his civics lecture series. He had changed into a lightweight, medium gray version of the standard civil officer's tunic. The grays identify him as an off-duty civil officer who is available for emergency service if called.

All civil officers are required to cover a set number of on-call hours in a quarter year. The gray uniforms, along with regular civilian activity, assure citizens of the continuing operation of their world. Dante has already exceeded his required hours for the year. While on call, he carries a pack with his duty gear.

Octavia's legs move in and out of a hunter-green, floor-length satin gown as she steps onto the city walkway. The dress flows along her curves up to fitted sleeves that cover her arms. The design gives her dress an undeserved impression of modesty from the front, which evaporates when she twirls for Dante. The early evening sunlight accents her neck and shoulders exposed through the gown's open back that plunges down to the cleft just below the base of her spine. A thin silver chain sparkles around her hips and jingles as she moves. Octavia giggles as she dances around. The tight braid that was hidden under her uniform's hood is now a smooth, shiny black cloak flowing over her back, meeting obligations that the gown fails. The dress's gravity pulls Dante's eyes into orbit around the jingling chain.

"I've tried it on every night this week," she says with a silly smile. "I can't wait to get it out on the dance floor."

"It's— nice," Dante stammers.

"Nice? Really? Did you leave all your vocabulary in the lecture hall this afternoon?"

He surrenders with a sigh and offers his arm, which she accepts.

When he suggested taking her to dinner after work to celebrate the beginning of her five days of leave, he didn't envision such a glamour deficit between her evening attire and his on-call grays. If she hadn't accepted his offer, he would be in a tobacco lounge with a bottle of scotch or, more likely, restrained in an ingestion clinic with a vial of lysergic foam, lost in synthetic bliss. The lounge always has a supply of blood cleaner in case a call to report comes through.

The choices drift through Dante's mind. An evening spent with a beautiful woman in a high-end restaurant or strapped in a recliner with trained clinical ingestion technicians dabbing the drool away from his chin, fighting to keep the empty away. His decision shouldn't have been as close as it was.

Dante pours the last of the red wine into Octavia's glass as the servers remove their plates. The wine itself doesn't impress her, but the gesture gives her pleasure, and she knows he likes to make her smile every once in a while.

Octavia came to dinner with a plan. It involves a forty-year-old bottle of single malt that she acquired at auction on an island in the Atlantic European region. She gave it to the lounge's senior wine steward to serve in their finest crystal decanter. It will flow like nectar compared to the firewater he normally imbibes.

Dante ordered a pair of cigars to accompany the scotch. Now, the two sip their sweet cedary fog as the spirits evaporate from their tongues. The dinner crowd fades.

Octavia lets out a mighty puff as Dante rests his head on the back of the booth. His cigar stands like an ancient industrial smokestack. In all the years she's known him, this is the first time he ever seems relaxed. It shouldn't be hard to get him talking.

"How can I explain it, Octavia?" Dante vocalizes a conversation that had been playing in his head. "I know people can love their job, but I don't love mine. I enjoy it in the same way an amputee enjoys a prosthetic limb."

"Are you thinking of leaving the Brigade?" she asks.

Dante shakes his head reluctantly. "No." Realizing his last statement was out loud, his instinct is to shut down, change the subject, but Octavia already has him in her snare, so why resist?

"When I'm not at work, or running extra civic service, I'm hollow. I believe in the Awakening, and my role in it, but I feel like the Brigade has turned into a crutch."

Dante removes the cigar from his teeth and looks into Octavia's eyes. "If I don't have a gun or the black hood, or if I am not standing at a lectern, who am I? What's left?"

Octavia had assumed she would have had something supportive or relevant to say by now. Her partner deserves more than a shiny platitude served with a desperate smile. Instead, silence lingers.

"Well." Dante replaces the cigar in his teeth and settles back into the booth. "Was that worth the sixty credit scotch?"

Octavia's brow betrays her.

Dante gives her a slight look of annoyance. "There's no way an Islay single malt casts a shadow in this dump without you forcing it into that tap puller's fist." He nods in the direction of the bar. "Did he ask you if I wanted it mixed with fruit juice or root beer?"

Octavia accepts the obvious escape. "It didn't cost me sixty credits. I toured the southwestern islands of Scotland last month when I was on leave. One of the loading workers gave me a case after I slept with him."

"Just one case?" Dante feigns surprise.

"I know, but the region is known for its frugal ways." Octavia smiles and swirls the last dram in her glass. The ice cubes melt into an amber pool of candlelight.

"Let's see if I understand you." She stares into Dante's eyes. "You need to find a way of understanding your existence that is not dependent on your trade as a reaper. You need to justify all the time you spend, eating, breathing, and generally running about this world." She raises the glass to inhale the memory of a salty ocean breeze pressing through the rich smoke of smoldering peat. "That would assume there IS a purpose to all this, right? That there is, in fact, something meaningful to understand?" When he doesn't respond, Octavia presses her point. "Have you ever considered that there is no meaning? I'm not sure how to answer that. I can offer this, Dante; lots of people feel this emptiness you describe, including myself." She empties her glass. "Honestly, I always thought you had a better than average grasp of this, I'm disappointed that you're telling me otherwise."

Her rebuke fails to affect his expression. Sensing her failure, she decides to switch tracks.

"You know what I'm going to do?" Her eyes open wide and prowl the lounge. "I'm going to find me a bored and confused little pup who is going to take me dancing until we can't stand. Then he'll take me to his place, or a patch of grass out in the park, and we'll roll one another until the sun comes up. Then he'll call a hover-pod, and we'll go all the way down the Southern Continent."

Dante plays along. "What's in the Southern Continent, Chile, Tierra del Fuego?"

Octavia crushes out her cigar and settles into the beautiful fog the scotch made. She answers with a casual shrug. "Who cares? It's about the ride." She giggles. "It will all be so elegant watching him with the delusion that it's his idea as if he'll have a choice."

This ruthless quality of his partner has always intrigued Dante. When she's on the hunt Octavia's prey moves as she conducts them. They always think they're a step ahead, right before they step in front of her sight. He never considered how these skills could be applied as she just described them. He's aroused and just a little frightened.

Returning her attention to Dante, she says, "You know, a few years ago I could have taken you. I'd have pulled you into my tangled little snare and wrung those clouds right away."

Dante nods. "A few years ago, it would have worked."

Octavia slides out of the booth, leans over, and plants a soft kiss on his forehead. "You wanna come?"

"Am I your little pup?" His question is out before he realizes what he said.

She purrs, "Yes."

Dante's throat constricts. *She's serious,* he realizes. "Octavia, why put that in front of me here, and now? You know what I have to say."

Her fingers comb through his hair. Her caress directs Dante's attention into her seductive eyes, where he finally realizes her true invitation.

With a sultry voice, she says, "You don't have to say anything. You don't have to do anything..." She's about to say something more but instead smiles and walks away.

Dante stays. He had evaded her snare.

Exhausted

Dante resists the urge to watch Octavia leave. When he is sure sufficient time had passed, he sulks in the booth. *Now what the hell do I do?* His imagination drifts to the mall and all its distractions. *Maybe I should go to the Quartz Lounge and pair with a crystal dancer. For a few credits and a bottle of something with bubbles, they'll provide hours of distraction. Or, I can head to the Casino Mill and find a woman on Last-Day desperate to fill her final hours.* He shakes away the idea. *I've done all that. If I had any sense, I would go to dispatch and distract myself for a few hours before going home. Otherwise, I'll have a face full of foam before the night is through.*

The bill is paid, he reasons. *I should go.*

He doesn't move. Soon, his thoughts drift to a suggestion Octavia once offered. *'You really should present in the public amphitheater, Dante.'* He had considered the idea many times; it is a good idea. He likes the theater.

One of Dante's former students manages operations in the main Bay City's auditorium. Sometimes he'll open the service door for Dante so he can sit in the bleachers with his lunch and watch the performers rehearse. It would be fun to take a leave of absence from the Brigade and audition for a small side role with a performance group. It would be fun, as long as the play is interesting. That's the problem; there is never anything interesting. The actors and directors try to pull stories from multiple places, Aeschylus fused with Tennessee Williams. Why not try it? It might work.

It never works. Dante can't remember a performance that got people talking. He hadn't heard of anything truly original that had been written in generations.

The best any studio has done is to remake plays 'true to the original performance.' It just seems pointless to waste lifeclock hours on a story that has been told so many times.

His daydream vanishes when a small woman wearing a light-blue toga appears across the table. Her face is glazed with fatigue and her straw colored hair is matted with dry sweat crusted onto her brow.

Panting heavily, she slumps into the bright-red booth. She raises her eyes to meet his. "You look unhappy," she rasps in a tired, judgmental tone.

Dante's attention follows her canted shoulder down to her wrist, twisted to press the back of her hand against the table. They watch one another until she repeats her question. "I said you look unhappy. Why are you unhappy?"

"I'm just tired. I've been going for a long time. If I had any sense, I'd get some sleep."

"That's a terrible idea!" The woman snorts.

Dante shrugs. "Ya, well, I don't know what to do with myself."

She carries the essence from nineteen hours of strong beverages, sweat, smoke, and exhaustion. Dante notices a shine of what will soon be a very large, black eye. "Did someone attack you?" he asks.

She chuckles. "Just a friendly bar fight. You can say anything to anyone on Last-Day, but blinking crystal or not, when you dump a punch bowl on someone." She turns to the bar where a tall woman, in what used to be a white gown, is wiping punch from her hair and grumbling. Returning her attention to Dante, her shoulders bounce with laughter. "Well, equal and opposite reaction and such." Taking in a deep breath, she cups a hand over her eye. "I thought I would feel something."

"And?"

The woman shakes her head. "Nothing." She releases a long, frustrated sigh. "I can't feel a thing."

Suddenly, her hand shoots across the table in an abrupt introduction. In the low light, her lifeclock blinks red-black, red-black, red-black. "I'm Helen-thirty-one, nice to meet you. I'm going out to pick a fight with a Civil Security unit, wanna come?"

Is she serious? Probably. Dante shakes her hand. "Absolutely, anything for a citizen on—"

Her brow furrows at the canned platitude. *How many times had she been forced to hear that cliché?* he wonders. "You look like you can use a shower."

Helen shakes her head emphatically. "No time. I'll shower when I'm dead… or something."

"Can I take you someplace?" Dante asks. "You know, I was serious about backing you if you want to go pick a fight, even against a unit of Civil Security."

Laughter bursts from Helen at the offer.

"Hey! I may be lanky, but I'm fast." He assures. "I promise, you'll get a few solid shots in before we get stunned into next week."

Tears begin to fall from her eyes as she laughs. "You'd really do that?"

Dante nods.

"Why couldn't I have met you yesterday?"

Helen clings to Dante as they stumble up the stairs to her apartment. Her dancing dress extends to her thighs. Primitive pictographs are drawn in silver lines that sparkle against the perspiration blotches in the light-blue satin. A glittery belt ties the toga to her waist.

When she recognizes her door, Helen stammers, "I don't want to be inside, please."

Dante directs her to the roof, where they watch the light of the city sparkle on the bay. She falls into his arms. A cool night breeze causes her to shiver.

"I have a coat in my bag if you want it."

Shaking her head, she whispers, "No, no, I want the cold. I want to feel... something."

He runs his fingers through her rough, tangled hair. "Do you want to lie down?"

"Noooo." Her grasp tightens around his chest.

"All right, all right, you can hang on, you won't fall." He wraps his arms around her and holds her close.

She hears Dante take in a deep breath that brings with it a pungent aroma. It is a well-earned laurel achieved from her marathon of running, dancing, drinking, drugging, flirting, fighting, and fucking. Her body wants rest. It tells her so with every mechanism she ignores.

Twenty-one hours ago, Helen was about to climb into bed when her lifeclock announced Last-Day. Like a fawn running from a pack of hounds, she pulled on a pair of light pants and a long shirt and ran out the door.

Pills kept her going for the next nineteen hours, up to a football game she and a group of hangers-on played until sundown. A game she knows they threw. Faced with an empty victory, she ditched her group for the lounge and hopefully something more. That was where she found this lost puppy hiding in a booth in his on-call grays.

She doesn't want any more. She wants to sleep and continue when the sun comes up. But the sun won't come up, ever.

She struggles to keep her eyes open. *Don't close. Don't,* her mind warns. "What is there to do?" Her voice croaks. "I know there is more, but I can't think of it."

Dante whispers, "Why waste time trying to figure that out? You've done a great..."

Helen presses her mouth over his in thankful silence.

Ten Minutes

A chime sounds on Dante's terminal-tracker.

DEFECTOR:
EXPIRED LIFECLOCK FOR: Helen-105.31
EXPIRED: 0.16 HOURS

Dante-09 activate.

Brian-48: On scene to support Officer Dante-09

He removes his weapon from the duty bag and then attaches a charcoal-black hood to the collar of his on-call grays. Darkness pours from the hood down his tunic and pants.

"Helen, Helen, wake up."

She lets out a small, satisfied purr and stretches across the covers of her bed. She glances at the window. *It is still dark out*, she thinks, *so why should I—*

"It's your time, Defector."

The softly spoken words instantly clear her mind. Helen glances at her hand and falls momentarily into its dark void.

"Helen-thirty-one, 278.034.105.31, your clock has been expired for ten minutes; you will fulfill your Somnus Obligation."

She looks up to the familiar voice coming from a hooded figure clad in black. *There is a reaper standing over my bed,* her mind observed. "I never got your name."

A smile cracks under the hood. "Come on, the Citadel is not far; we'll go together."

Helen still wears the stained toga dress from a few hours before. Her bare feet wince on the cold floor. She looks into the dark hood to ask, "Can I—"

The reply is gentle but final. "Helen-thirty-one, there's nothing you need; it's time to go."

"I'm a little hungry; I can't remember when I've eaten." She speaks just above a whisper.

Dante motions to the door.

On the ground level, Brian-48 monitors Helen-31's position with his terminal-tracker. A digital compass is rendered on the display screen, indicating the direction, distance, and elevation of her expired lifeclock. Brigade dispatch assigned Brian as Dante's backup while Octavia is on leave. He monitors Dante through his open tele-LINCC. "Should I come up, Dante?" he calls in a stern voice.

Dante answers, "Negative; we're coming down now."

Helen fumbles with her belt as she rises from the bed. It doesn't want to clasp. She leaves it dangling from her waist with a clumsy grin.

Her eyes are clean. The gravel from a few hours before has lifted from her voice. Dante envies her. She has an understanding that gives her peace in a way he has forgotten.

She stands erect and points to the door. "Do I?"

Dante gestures for her to go first. She passes him and opens the door. As she passes through the exit, the buckle of her belt loops over the door handle. Helen grabs the other end of the belt with both hands and launches herself into the hallway. The belt pulls the door, slamming it against the reapers wrist, now caught in the doorway.

"Dammit!" Dante growls.

The small woman hurls herself back against the door, slamming it into Dante's head and knocking him off balance. He fumbles but manages to stay on his feet, trying to cue his LINCC.

Well-practiced movements double wrap the belt around Dante's wrist. Though the uniform's gauntlet padding protects his forearm from serious damage, his arm must ache from being slammed.

Helen braces a foot against the doorframe and shoves with all her might, pulling Dante to his knees.

Dante reaches for the ground with his free hand to keep from being prone on the floor. Helen slips the belt binding his hand around his neck. If she was stronger, and the padding at the base of his hood wasn't so thick, she might have a chance to garret him.

If— if—, she ruminates, *I don't have time, this is not a fight I can win. The man on the other end of his LINCC will be here soon.*

Her arm closes around the back of Dante's hood. With a twist of her hips, she slams the point of her other elbow above the bridge of his nose. Dante's head snaps back. She sends another strike across Dante's temple, catching his hood.

Despite the hood's kinetic dampening mesh, her strike sends Dante's head into the rug. His on-call grays lack the armor mesh of his standard uniform. She clasps her fists together and hammers into his diaphragm. Dante's wind explodes from his lungs.

A small pack sits on a shelf; Helen slings it across her back and grabs a pair of shoes that had been placed next to it with care. She tosses a small bundle out the window and is gone.

Brian appears at the door.

Dante once again fills his lungs and cues the general channel on his tele-LINCC. "Defector on the north side of the building!" he rasps.

Brian helps him to his feet. At the window, a cord dangles three stories to the ground where the defector is running for a tree line.

Dante moves away from the window at the sound of Brian's gun slipping from its holster. The gun-sight-scanner registers an active STInGER that has acquired a human heat signature, which fades as Helen enters the thick grove of trees and disappears into the darkness. She's gone.

"Sssshit!" Brian spits.

Dante removes his hand tracker and notes the distant units growing on the display. "She's not getting away."

Brian is surprised at his casual tone.

Charon dispatch sounds in their earpieces. "Officer Dante-nine, do you need assistance?"

"Negative, dispatch, we'll get her."

Brian studies the senior officer's manner as they leave the apartment. He is calm, as though the attack hadn't happened. In fact, Dante seems pleased. He never looks like this.

Dante fails to mask a smile as he meets Brian's scrutiny. He gives an enthusiastic slap to the junior officer's shoulder.

"Now, we have a hunt!"

Chapter 7

New in Town

The Reaper's Requiem. It is the name citizens have given the trio of sounds caused by the STInGER when it ignites in the body of a reaper's victim. First, the defector sings out as every animal does when faced with its doom. Though some might restrain this cry, through bravery or guile, a second unwilling voice cries out as wind blows past helpless vocal cords from lungs compressed by the STInGER's penetration. A third, high-pitched wail sings out when the STInGER's rapid chemical combustion incinerates every organ in the defector's chest. It is a song citizens in the Collective hear throughout their lives. Such a performance just played out in front of Marcos-80, one level down from the Topaz Lounge.

Marcos was slammed into the wall when the man ran past him. He saw him disappear down a flight of stairs that would have taken him to the street when the reaper's gun flared, and the requiem sang out from the stairwell.

Marcos uncovers his eyes to find a fresh vapor trail hanging in the air, pointing to a charred spot on the wall. The other end traces past him and three other terrified citizens to the muzzle of the reaper's pistol.

Another Brigade officer appears from the stairs and pulls the remains of the defector back onto the walkway, through a white wisp of smoke curling from the chest of the corpse. He lifts the defector's hand to his terminal-tracker.

Once the lifeclock is logged, the officer allows the cadaver's arm to flop to the ground. The sight makes Marcos's stomach drop in the same way. *It's true*, he thinks, *they really can shoot around corners.* He rotates his wrist to obscure his flashing lifeclock.

The borough directory lists Lauren-25 as a level-1 archivist at the main library. One of the trade apprentices mentioned that Lauren had been talking about a concert in the Topaz Lounge and directed him to follow the posters for Gramophone Mayhem.

The concert is long over, but some of the band members are still in the lounge. The bass player recognizes Lauren's description as the fan who picked up their drummer a few hours before. They direct Marcos to his apartment, knowing it will make a much better story at their next rehearsal than Toby's normal conquest gossip.

"What the hell does he want?" Toby bypasses the obvious question of *who is pounding on my door in the middle of the night?*

Lauren catches Toby's hand as he reaches for his tele-LINCC. "Please, don't," she pleads. "No security. He's harmless, I promise. I'll talk to him."

Toby slides from the covers and pulls on his pants. "Someone on the floor is going to alert security if he doesn't quiet down. Do you know this guy?"

Lauren fumbles for her top and starts for the door. The agitated voice continues to call. "Lauren? Lauren-twenty-five, I need to talk to you. Please, this is Marc-"

The large man is silenced when Toby's nose appears in the crack of the doorway. "What the hell are you doing? Do you want to be dragged away by security?"

Marcos presents his flashing lifeclock. "Please, I need some information from Lauren, then I'll disappear."

The door opens to reveal a shirtless Toby and a disheveled Lauren in panties and an unzipped top. Marcos pensively enters the apartment. He is a formidable figure compared to most in the city and an absolute giant next to the drummer.

Lauren recognizes some of the scars around his eyes and jaw from their days in Outland. Time has added many new ones.

Marcos asks, "Lauren-twenty-five?"

She nods.

"I'm here because of your message. Please help me find Julie-"

Lauren launches a solid slap across his face. "You're pulling me out of bed over that little bitch! Seriously?" She moves so her back faces Toby. Her eyes lock with Marcos's as she mouths the words, *I told you.*

A nervous expression creases across the big man's face as he retreats a step and shamefully nods.

Lauren snaps about to face her host. "Toby, I'm afraid I have an urgent matter to attend. Please forgive this rude departure."

The drummer holds his hands out in grateful surrender.

Five minutes later, the apartment door slams behind them. Lauren leads the tall, hopelessly awkward man away.

Marcos tries to break a clumsy silence as he fast walks to the main thoroughfare. "I— I'm sorry for the scene back there."

"Oh, please, that was the best part of the evening." Looking back, she can't resist giggling at the graceless giant. "Relax, Marcos; you did me a favor. I needed a graceful exit from that twit."

Unsure if the term has a unique meaning in Bay City, he asks, "That was *graceful?*"

"Compared to where it was leading?" She chuckles, "Oh, ya!" Marcos almost plows into Lauren when she suddenly stops and twirls about. "I don't mind participating in a little lascivious role-playing, but is it expecting too much that I'm included in the process?"

It looks as if Marcos is considering if and how he should answer. Lauren continues her quick step down the walkway. "That selfish bastard had a wall of mirrors surrounding his bed. He couldn't tear his attention away from his own reflection the entire evening. It was like I was trapped in a three-way with Narcissus!"

"I thought his name was Toby."

Lauren turns back to see the helpless giant standing in the dark a dozen paces behind and realizes what she had just put him through. Ashamed, she walks back and takes his arm. They continue to the main road where she calls a hover-pod to take them to her neighborhood in a silent ride.

Lauren calls from the shower. "I don't have much in the pantry, but you're welcome to whatever's in there."

Marcos isn't making himself comfortable, as she suggested. He drops a palm full of ice cubes into a glass.

Lauren appears from the back of the apartment dressed in a baggy exercise outfit, crushing a towel through her wet hair. He pours a rough sixty-milliliter drink over the ice cubes from whatever the clear liquid is in the tall crystal decanter and presents the glass to her.

She smiles and answers, "Yes, please."

Marcos makes another and meets her on the sofa. A sip later, he presents his lifeclock flashing red-pink. "Lauren, I'm in a time crunch. I need to find my sister as soon as possible."

Lauren's attention settles on the light flashing Final-Quarter on his hand. She has the look of one who realizes that time is passing. She empties her beverage and retrieves the gin from the bar and a bottle of Quinine from the cold box.

Returning to the couch, she takes Marcos's glass, refreshes it, and holds it in front of her chest. "Marcos, it's me, Julie-11." She allows a long, awkward silence to settle.

He reaches out with his left hand; Lauren does the same. When brought together, their lifeclocks flash green-white, green-white, as they did when they first met. For a moment, they are children again, discovering one another.

"You know, I wasn't sure that would still work."

Night recedes to dawn. The morning light shines through the window of Lauren's apartment onto the bottles emptied by the siblings as they filled in the years that had passed, yet Marcos avoids the issue that compelled him to make the trip to Bay City.

"Jul— Lauren," he stammers. "I need you to forgive me. I wish I had never dragged you to Outland; because of that stupid mistake, I lost you for all those years."

Lauren cradles the glass in both her hands. She notes how the ice cubes are fading faster as they melt into the gin.

"Don't feel too bad, Marcos," she says without meeting his eyes. "I spent that same time afraid that you wouldn't forgive me for abandoning you that morning in the plaza."

Tracking

Sunlight streaks across the elevated energized rail. The hover-pod roars down its track with an uncertain silence inside. Brian-48 tries to mimic the calm of his training officer. He had interpreted Dante's behavior in the apartment as excitement for hunting the defector. Now that they are committed to the chase, the senior officer seems oblivious.

The Charon Brigade pairs younger officers with more experienced reapers during their first year of duty. This is Brian's second assignment with Dante. He tries to appear engaged with the map of his terminal-tracker as he switches the display over to the vid-screen of the pod. A small black triangle marks the position of Helen's expired lifeclock a few kilometers ahead of them.

Dante sits quietly, engulfed by the glittery belt the defector had used to incapacitate him in the apartment. He folds it over and back in his hand. The belt is made from the same thick web cord that the defector used to descend from her window. A shiny fabric covers the cord from end to end that is stitched with a sparkling line down the middle to match Helen's dress.

"I had the shot." The younger officer finally breaks the stillness.

"No. You didn't have a full lock." Dante corrects without moving his attention from the belt.

"You saw my sight?"

Dante shakes his head. "Your gunsight had ample time to register the heat signature of a human target at that distance. If your STInGER had locked on to her expired lifeclock, you would have launched it, and we'd be chasing someone else now."

He faces the junior officer. "But you didn't have that lock. If you had launched, the STInGER might have tracked another human signature, perhaps a child looking for a lost toy in the trees. Then we'd have a live defector and a dead citizen."

Dante stuffs the belt into his tunic as the scenario lingers. "Did you stand Correction?"

Brian shakes his head. "No, I was still green."

Dante persists. "Did you see it?"

"I saw it on vid. They played it the first day of the academy."

Though conversational in volume, Dante speaks as though he is lecturing in the civics theater. "Did the academy teach you that a reaper discharges his gun solely at his discretion?"

"Yes."

Dante impresses his full attention on Brian's answer, his incomplete answer.

"The academy taught me that I will engage my gun, or employ with any means, to terminate a defector at my sole discretion and carry every consequence thereof."

"Well, on behalf of every reaper in the Collective, your discretion is outstanding. A lesser officer might have taken the shot with the hope it wouldn't track someone else. We'll get her. If she needs a few more hours to live in terror, hunted, then we have an obligation to give her that."

Hunting Helen

Helen's hover-pod glides along the rail, twenty minutes ahead of the perusing reapers. It's been almost an hour since she'd climbed out the window. She washes the pills down with a swig from her flask.

The moment her clock began flashing red-pink is still vivid in her memory. She spent half that night imagining countless images playing on the great window screen of the Somnolence Citadel. Trout swimming in a flowing stream, kittens playing with a ball of string, they have thousands of such images, perhaps millions, all designed to help a citizen pass her last moment in peace.

They even have appropriate sounds to play along. She imagined the sound of rain falling on cobblestones with the image of a walkway beside the Seine River or that jerk Jeffery-52 who lied about her to all her friends. She imagined his bloody, beaten face whimpering for forgiveness as a hammer smashes into his forehead. Then her eyes would peacefully close, enveloped in the soft loving void of the sleep mask. The Citadel technicians can make all that happen and more.

She shudders out of the trance.

Helen concluded that it is better to enter Somnus trying to see the Seine one last time, or find that flowing brook with the trout, or track down Jeffery-52 in person. While planning her getaway, a hammer had made its way into her pack more than a few times. After another pull of water, she returns the flask and stimulants to her pack and removes a hat. There is also a pair of energy bars and a light jacket along with a few other odds and ends.

The hover-pod is carrying her across the bay to a coastal open space that is thick with trees, which she hopes will help her evade the reapers.

"You seem jumpy." Dante observes the trainee trying to keep from fidgeting in the pod's cab.

"Did she say something to you about where she was running?" Brian asks.

Shaking his head, Dante smiles. "Describe the defector."

The junior officer releases a sigh. "The pack and shoes were set out in advance, as well as the cord she threw out the window. She was ready for us. She obviously has a plan and an escape route."

Dante nods. "What else? What was she wearing?"

"The dress looked like it was for a dance lounge in the mall, not descending a wall on a cord."

"So, she made a plan, but she is not following it," Dante concludes. "Do you think a woman with a dancing dress, a backpack, and outdoor shoes will be easy to spot in a crowd?"

"She might have a change of clothes in the pack." Brian offers. "Then again, she's probably not going to take time to change with us hunting her."

Dante remembers Helen's musty smell when he held her on the rooftop. "A change of clothes is not her priority."

"Of course. So she'll avoid places with lots of people—"

"And scanners," Dante completes the line of logic.

"Right." Brian considers the map. "And, she'll dump the pod before it gets to a populated area where local reapers will be waiting."

"Which they are." Dante confirms.

Brian cues his tele-LINCC. "Dispatch, this is Officer Brian-forty-eight, center aerial units over the open space between Tomales Bay and Drake Bay."

The LINCC responds. "Confirmed. Aerial units dispatched."

Brian continues his reasoning. "She won't go south, too many people."

"She might not know that last detail."

"No, she has shoes for off-trail. She knows where she's going." Brian answers more to himself than to his senior officer.

Dante relaxes in his seat with a smile.

High above the coastal woodland, lighter than air dirigibles and nimble dragonfly-like robots circle in the sky. They carry powerful repeaters for relaying LINCC communications along with an array of sensors trained on the terrain below. The aerial sensors are more powerful than the census sensors used in the city. They track the lifeclocks of citizens for traffic flow, support search-and-rescue operations, and assist in the apprehension of fugitives for Civil Security and the Charon Brigade.

The large dirigibles carry heavy, more powerful sensors at high-altitude. They are mostly unnoticed by citizens. The smaller, more nimble dragonflies circle at lower altitudes sending back detailed, high-resolution information on target areas. The airspace above the park is thick with these flying robots, directed there at the request of the Charon Brigade. They are all tracking the expired lifeclock of Helen-31.

Helen's position is depicted as a black triangle marked on a map of the open space around Tomales Bay. The map is displayed on the terminal screen inside the hover-pod where Dante and Brian plan their hunt. Suddenly, the monitor blacks out, and the pod drifts to a stop.

Dante cues his LINCC. "Is there a problem, dispatch?"

"We are experiencing a slight delay with the transportation power grid. Civil engineers are working to reroute power; they will have you running in a moment." Dante knows the dispatcher is a human, yet the voice sounds mechanical through his tele-LINCC earpiece.

Brian grumbles, "This is the second time this week I've been stuck in a pod due to a power failure."

"Is this your first open area hunt?"

"Yes. I've been on about thirty so far, including supporting duty," Brian answers with a forced, matter-of-fact tone.

"In the academy, you learned that most defectors are found on the street or hiding in a friend's living space, correct?"

Brian nods. "Those are the cases I've worked."

"Most of the time defectors had every intension of entering Somnus on schedule, but they get scared and confused at the last moment. Reapers can often walk them into the Somnolence Citadel quietly."

"Have you ever done that?" Brian asks, sounding surprised.

"Many times." Dante nods. "But today we have a defector that is just as common, one with a plan. Dispatch typically assigns these to more experienced teams."

"Where do they go?"

Dante shrugs. "Nowhere. They just don't want to go quietly. You and I have an obligation to make sure that she just goes. This one has chosen a place where she can run, hide, evade, and double around as if the flying trackers aren't following her every move, and we don't have her exact position." Dante waved his hand tracker.

"I've hunted defectors into the desert, through the open territories in midcontinent, up trees and under rocks. They have this vision of a place separate from the Collective, where their obligations are forgotten. They never get away." Dante leans in for emphasis. "Now, the dangerous defectors are the ones who run through the malls, using citizens as their shield. You take your time, drive them into a corner, and launch your perfectly locked STInGER into their gut."

Dante grinds his voice as he locks his gaze onto the junior officer. "You may have already heard some reapers, even experienced ones bragging about how quickly they terminated a defector or the tricky shot they made to take one down. Ignore them. Never aim your gun in a crowd. Never shoot when there is the slightest chance that the charge can stray and hit a citizen. Such shortcuts can never be fixed when they go wrong."

Brian's voice cracks as he nods to the black screen. "What if she has figured out a way to evade the tracker? What if there's a boat waiting for her?"

"Then the sky tracker follows her boat to its landing area, and we meet her there, or we direct another reaper team to meet her, or a Brigade recovery team retrieves the boat with her carcass in it. All scenarios end with her white lifeclock logged by a hand scanner. Every sensor in the Collective reports expired lifeclocks whether they're passing through a shopping mall, riding in a rail-bus, or hiding in the Dakota Mountains. A sensor will eventually pick them up, and we get 'em."

The hover-pod hums as its lev-field lifts it above the energized rail and begins to move.

"You ready?"

Brian nods eagerly.

This stupid dress isn't helping; it catches on every twig and branch, Helen gripes. *How many things can stick out around here?* Blood drizzles from a dozen scrapes running down her legs. Tiny drips stain the polished rocks of the muddy streambed as she lumbers along.

Helen developed her escape plan throughout her Final-Quarter. She had planned to be far away from the borough, out in the open, well before her clock expired.

So many experiences I haven't had, she silently laments. *So much that I want to do before—* reality focuses her attention. *I've already left. No more planning, I have to keep going.* The chemicals she ingested are clogging her attention as well as her judgment. *Maybe I shouldn't have started my escape by trying to take a reaper to my bed.*

Helen visually traces a path leading to an elevated ridgeline. *It would be easier to see up there,* she reasons, *but I would also be more visible.* Preferring the more enclosed ravine, she moves from tree patch to rocky outcrop, surveying the trail before her. Large cobblestones line the center of the ravine. *They're hard to walk on, but at least they'll hide my footprints.* She quickens her pace.

Is that a black hood on the ridge?

Dante and Brian walk the hilltops. Dragonflies circle a depression six hundred meters to the west. The aerial sensors provide a strong signal of the defector's location. Dante only refers to his hand tracker as an example of caution for the junior officer.

When the signal closes to within three hundred meters, Dante breaks open the action of his pistol, slides the white TAC charge from the breech, and replaces it with a black STInGER from the ammo cuff on his wrist. He slaps the action closed and says, "Time to split up. You're going to follow the ridge. Stay on the high ground and get in front of her." He motions to the west. "I'm going to follow her through the ravine and drive her to you for the kill."

The junior officer answers with an enthusiastic smile.

A muddy gully meanders through the middle of the ravine. Runoff from the rain carved this channel down to the ocean. Bushes and shrubs pepper Helen's way, providing cover for her small body in a bright-red jacket. She had pressed the garment into the mud time and again trying to hide its color, but the water-repellent fabric works against her.

The soaked lining of the jacket transfers moisture into her dress, giving it teeth. Now, each breeze tearing through the ravine bites into her skin with a chill that reaches into her core and crushes her heart.

Helen kneels behind a large bush and clenches her jaw tight. A black-hooded figure passes above her, along the ridgeline, or so she thinks. Her eyes burn under her mud-caked hair and dried tears; she isn't sure what she sees. A few branches separate her life from his sight. *Time to double back,* she thinks.

Turning about, she hears the sound of dirt and gravel crunching in the distance. *Maybe it's not a reaper. Maybe it's just a hiker I can pass with a smile.*

There's that sound again, that cursed ghostly whirling sound that echoes around me. "There's nothing there!" she scolds in a muffled grunt.

That was a mistake. Her cracked, sobbing voice wasn't supposed to be out loud. The stimulants she ate earlier are taking their toll. Moderation had not been part of her plan. When she started, she needed to put distance between herself and the Collective. Now, her temples throb as though a hive of angry flying insects is fighting to break out of her eye sockets.

She peers around the base of her protective shrub, canting her head to favor the eye that is not swollen. Less than a hundred meters separates her from another hooded figure, no doubt, the one from her room. He's approaching slowly, swinging the pack and hat she'd discarded a quarter hour ago. Helen digs her elbows into the soft ground to slither around the bend.

She rises to her knees and crawls into a run.

"It's your time, Defector." The stern voice cuts through the air from above.

"Nnnooo!" Helen releases the terror she had incarcerated in her chest for so long. Every muscle burns as she stumbles forth and back. Forth, toward the cool young reaper standing on the ridge above her, he has yet to remove his gun. Back, the direction of the man she had beaten to the floor a few hours ago.

A few hours? Her mind questions. *Is that really all it has been?* The sun has not reached mid-sky. The opening of the hood in front of her looks like a shadowy void with a clean squared jaw poking into daylight.

"Helen-thirty-one..." the youthful voice with no face continues without inflection.

Fighting the pain burning within her, she shivers as another breeze gusts against her mud-soaked clothes and bare legs. The familiar fangs bite. It blows all her anxiety into the open. Her weeping, wheezing voice cracks into the cold air. "I- I- I'll- t- ta- take Somnus. I will- I- I-"

The remorseless voice continues with a renewed zeal. "Your lifeclock has been expired for..."

Helen cries out in a jumble of sobs, fighting to stay on her feet. She raises her arms in front of her, fingers outstretched to shield the coming blast.

The rookie reaper delays her judgment. With one hand, he gestures for Helen to continue, as the other one with a blue lifeclock gently taps the grip of his holstered gun.

The gesture floods Helen's mind with questions. *Does he want to hear me out? He's not pointing his gun at me. Will he allow me another moment? This terror wasn't supposed to happen.* "I didn't want to face an artificial sunset and video-displayed river with simulated fish!"

As she fights to catch her breath between sobs, a hateful smile stretches across the face inside the reaper's hood. Helen moans as she realizes that her begging entertains him. He motions again for her to continue. *I can live as long as I beg for life.* Her appeal is interrupted when an explosive scream sings out, accompanied by a high-pitched whine. The reaper vanishes behind a brilliant billow of white smoke that bursts from her chest. She can't say it out loud, but her last thought is,
That smell!

Dante watches Helen fall. A vapor trail hangs in the air, drawing a path from where the STInGER entered her back to the muzzle of his pistol. Her black lifeclock fades to a milky white.

With one smooth choreographed motion, Dante breaks the action of his pistol open and slides a red UKD charge from his wrist cuff into the breech; the action closes with a metallic click. His eyes never move from the smug rookie standing on the ridge above him.

The two reapers stand in silence, regarding one another. Dante considers the junior officer with an unspoken rage. When Dante holsters his pistol, he mutters through a constricted jaw, "One of us is a monster."

Chapter 8

It's Happening Again

> open dataFile

A chime sounds, indicating the crystal writer has scanned a lifeclock. Marcos removes his hand from Lauren's little egg. The full text of his data-file rolls in a terminal window a few centimeters from the spectacles he borrowed from his sister. The entries are numbered by the days of his life; they roll by in a sterile numeric progression stirring periodic memories.

3562.2833: Suspect in Electronic Wonder Shop break-in
in the Balcarce Mall. Update security concern
MODERATE to SERIOUS.

4172.9813: Surgical Chamber Notation. Modest dermal
repairs to face and neck. Regenerate cracks to 5th, 6th
ribs.

6929.8883: Release Cryo-Detention (0.33 year served).
Reduce security concern HIGH to ELEVATED.

9093.4390: 170 credit deposit to personal account c/o
Torres del Paine NP Division of Construction and
Maintenance.

9095.7430: Arrival Bay City's Alameda rail-bus terminal.

The same chronicle scrolls through Lauren's spectacles, yet the only detail she cares about is noted at the top of the first page.

Age: 9097.4930 days

She recognizes this as 24.9081 years. Marcos has a little more than 33 days before his lifeclock expires.

"I can't change anything now," Lauren mutters, half to her brother, and half to the holographic display.

Marcos removes his holographic-spectacles to see his sister staring into a void.

"Change?" Marcos cares for his sister but is annoyed when she fades into her holographic world behind those lenses. *I made this trip to make amends and connect with her for a few days before—* He forces an end to that train of thought. *She shouldn't know the other reason I came.*

"Your hundreds digit is zero; I can't do anything now. In a couple weeks, when it cycles to one, I can move it back a hundred days, but right now, there's nothing I can do."

He recoils at the glib comment. "What do you mean, move it back? You're talking as if you can change the lifeclock."

Lauren's casual contempt for the lifeclock surprises him, almost as much as his reaction. Marcos had spent a good part of his life pressing the limits of the Collective's tolerance; four months in cryogenic detention scared this attitude out of him.

His memory of the little girl who revolted at having to steal from people in the commerce districts is inconsistent with this woman, suggesting that she pull at the very threads that bind the Collective's foundation.

Marcos's outburst appears to pull Lauren's awareness back into her living room. "It's easier if I show you," she says as she passes her lifeclock above the little white egg and calls up her citizen summary.

Marcos replaces his specs to see Lauren's citizen profile scrolling next to the face sitting across from him.

NAME: Lauren-25, 378.005.569.25.
GENDER: Female.
AGE: 20.7 years.
SKILL-TRADE: Level-1 Archivist, Bay City Central
Archive, Alameda.
HEIGHT: 172 cm.
CURRENT LOCATION: North American region,
Sector-211.
No security issues.

As he watches Lauren's official profile roll before his eyes, the realization settles. She hasn't simply pretended to take another identity. She is an entirely different person. *Who are you?* he wonders.

Lauren's voice finds him lost in his thoughts. "A quagmire, is it not?"

Her smug smile tries to distract uncertain eyes behind the terminal window in Marcos's spectacles. Despite the changes she made to her appearance, he can see many familiar aspects of his little sister in her. Yet, this file brings all that into question.

Lauren says, "I mean, am I Julie-eleven because that is the name the Guardian assigned me when I was an infant? Or, am I Lauren-twenty-five because the Guardian assigned me that name when I rewrote my data-file?"

She offers her hands as she contemplates this. "On one hand, I'm flesh and blood. On the other, I'm flesh, blood, and a radioactive crystal that pairs with a computer file." Her eyes lower to her hands. "You know, I've actually laid awake through many nights trying to resolve this."

It takes most of the afternoon for Lauren to explain to Marcos the subtle and critical elements of assuming a new identity and the importance of severing all ties from the old one.

Marcos avoids asking questions that will open a flood of technical explanations he'll never understand.

He pulls the spectacles from his face to meet her gaze. "I don't want a new identity, Lauren. All I want is to get to know you for a few days before I leave."

Lauren freezes. As though she already knows what he is about to say.

With artificial confidence, he says, "I'm going to defect, I just wanted to settle things between us before I go."

"Where are you going?" she asks.

He stutters, "I don't want to include you in this; I've said too much." Marcos sinks into the sofa, realizing he had just made his sister an accomplice. Unless she contacts the Charon Brigade immediately, she is complacent in giving aid to a defector. "I did it again. I just pulled you into my twisted life."

Lauren waves his comment away. "Never mind that. Listen, there are hundreds of mechanisms the Brigade uses to track defectors, even if their clock hasn't expired. Don't believe for a moment that the forbidden places are safe from scanners; they're not."

"What are you saying?"

"I'm saying, it's possible to travel along the borders of the Collective without being detected, but those places hold their unique dangers. Nomads earn favors from reapers by offering up defectors. Now, tell me, where are you going?"

Marcos describes the postings he monitors on the aether boards that offer a trail leading out of the Collective.

"You're talking about Haven," Lauren answers in a stern voice. "What is your encryption level? I mean, when you navigate the aether or post on the boards, how strong is the encryption you use?"

"A seven."

She frowns, as the low number seems to concern her as much as anything Marcos has said. "Have you posted any information on the boards
about yourself?"

"None."

"Have you set any meetings?"

"Yes. In seventeen days, I'll meet a guide near the Gulf state border, who will lead me out."

Lauren shakes her head. "I've studied the Gulf border route. You'll be met by a mob of four to six nomads, who will rob you of everything you have and hand you over to a reaper, most likely one just out of their training school, eager to start their kill list. The lower level boards are mostly unverified gossip and postings for ambushes. Haven has as many dead ends as it has defectors trying to get there."

Lauren paces around her apartment, pulling components from various drawers and closets. Soon, her living room is covered with tools and notebooks that have long been hidden away. All the while, her brother sits, listening to her relate a multitude of Haven scams. Lauren drags a box to the foot of her chair and tosses Marcos another pair of data glasses. "Here, you can have these. You'll need them."

"How many of these do you have?"

Metal clatters against plastic as she rummages through the case. "I'm always making improvements, trading for new parts. That pair has a mode that allows you to see areas that are monitored by lifeclock scanners and the levels they report. Some scanners only monitor traffic flow; others will log your age. If you pass a mall entry gate, it will log your identity. Every scanner is tuned to alert Brigade dispatch when an expired clock passes."

"Where did you learn all this?" Marcos struggles to appreciate the breadth of his little sister's subversive knowledge.

Lauren ignores his question. "When you wear those outside, you're going to find there are more scanners than you think. We're going to have to work out a method for avoiding them." Continuing her planning, she says, "We need to see if the railroad is still operational."

Once again, Lauren's high-speed chatter overwhelms Marcos. "Railroad?"

Her intensity grows. "There is an underground railroad leading out of the Collective; it's been in operation for generations."

"Lauren, stop! It's happening again. I come into your life for just a few hours, and we're running away. I'm not going to do that to you again."

She says in a calmer tone, "Most clues point to South Diego as a departure station. It's not like a rail-bus we can ride to safety. The railroad is a system of guides and safe houses that will direct us out of the Collective. I have studied this for almost a year but never seriously thought I could actually..." she shudders, "I can't believe I am finally saying it out loud for the first time... defect."

Marcos takes her shoulders with more force than he intended. "I didn't come here to turn your life upside down again!"

Lauren looks with wonder into his eyes, and he can tell she finds a vulnerability she never knew. "My problem is, in order to use it, we need to make contact with a processor, someone who will allow us passage through the points along the way." She cups her hands around Marcos's chin and smiles. "If we don't arrange passage, we can walk right up to Haven's borders, and they won't let us in." She slips from his hands. "Once we make contact, we'll be committed. If we hesitate, they'll have nothing to do with us."

"You're serious; you're really intent on defection?" Marcos searches her eyes for any hint of deception.

Lauren hesitates for only a moment. "There is also an issue with the nomads. In the Shadow Lands, nomads are every bit as dangerous as the canines in the pack. Where the pack's strength is in their unity, nomads attack and kidnap people for ransom. They are the outgrowth of everything the pack fears."

As confident as Lauren is in her world of electronics and aether boards, Marcos knows he can help her navigate the dangers of the Shadow Lands.

"How long have you been planning this, little sis?"

"Long enough to know I can't do it alone," she answers timidly.

"All right," he says. "We're going to need a plan."

A Plan

A spring releases. The brass cover flips open to reveal a circular video screen.

Lauren-25
7583.9714 Days
20.7638 Years

Marcos works a small control knob at the top of the pocket clock that pages through the displays and their functions. The clock's design is similar to an ancient pocket watch. He sweeps the readout again.

Julie-11
8483.9714 Days
23.2278 Years

Lauren answers the unasked question. "The Guardian counts the time on the lifeclock in days, so it's helpful to know what it sees when it reads our data-file."

Marcos continues to work the winding stem. The display rotates from the Collective standard time to local weather, hover-pod caller, civil-transit schedule, music player, alarm clock, camera, and photo collection. He stops on a video image of his face fed by a tiny camera set inside the cover plate. "Wouldn't a mirror be easier?"

Without looking up, Lauren offers a bewildered smile. "Then what would I use the other micro imager for?"

"What indeed?" Marcos snaps the case shut and passes it back. "Where do you get all this stuff?"

Lauren shrugs. "The case and electronics are easy; I just scavenge and trade for them at the swap meet in the mall. I find the software on do-it-yourself boards on the aether. Want me to make you one?"

"Is it difficult?" Marcos perks up.

She laughs. "Ya, but that's why it's fun." She lifts a drawer she had pulled from a closet cabinet and sets it on top of another box. The contents rattle as she digs around and extracts a thin, square, silver box and passes it to Marcos. "How would you like that for a case?" she asks. "It'll be a little bulky, but if you don't mind."

Marcos runs his finger over the art-deco design. With a press of a latch, a spring flips the lid open to reveal a single dried-out cigarette from the previous owner. "That would be great. Thanks." He smiles. "So, your new identity bumped your age back almost two-and-a-half years?"

"Remember how your age appeared in your data-file? Your age is expressed as number of days, four digits to the right and left of the decimal. Each digit is controlled by a separate, encrypted function. I found and cracked the series of functions that control the digit three places to the left of the decimal. I reprogramed the functions to cycle by negative one instead of one.

"Hey smart lady doing smart things. That is an unnecessarily complicated way of saying?" Marcos asks.

Lauren smirks. "I can reprogram the lifeclock in one hundred day increments, but it requires editing a data-file, then pairing it with a new name. It might be possible to edit my data-file and keep it open after pairing..." she trails off. "I'll need to research that."

Lauren recognizes an exhausted expression settling onto Marcos's. It's been a long day.

Lauren remembers a shadow of herself, from another life. Nineteen-year-old Julie was exploring a mischievous desire to tear open the mystery of her lifeclock. Subtracting a few days from her age was nothing more than a perk for making a new life in Bay City, free of the *security concerns* she earned for the mistakes she made as a child. It also allowed her to recover the time wasted in Outland. A smile grows across her face as she thinks to herself, *subverting the Collective's rules wasn't so bad either.*

She struggles to avoid looking at her brother's flashing lifeclock and begins to feel the presence of her own crystal decaying on her hand. *Perhaps,* she wonders, *I should add a pocket clock function to count down from twenty-five years.* She banishes the gruesome idea with a shudder.

"We're going to need new aether accounts," she says. "You also need a stronger encryption key. I can set you up with a level-twenty-six; that will let you read the boards and learn to distinguish the serious posters from the gossipers and scammers."

Marcos takes his sister into his arms. The sun had set an hour ago. "We can stop for a while Jul… Lauren. We'll figure it out."

As she settles into her brother's arms, Lauren can feel the muscles in her back relax. Marcos's embrace comforts her in a way she hadn't felt since her lifeclock was green.

Lauren insists they fumble through the library corridors rather than turning on the lights. Marcos recognizes the motions of sneaking through somewhere he's not supposed to be. "Are you certain we can be in here?"

"It's fine," she assures in a raspy whisper. "I work late all the time."

Lauren introduces him to her lab as he follows her in. "This is the holo-character portal screen room." A tired expression lands on her brother's face. She shrugs. "I know. We're working on a better name."

Lauren's voice becomes more natural once the door latches behind them. She speaks into a large silver microphone on the workbench. "Ray, initialize character generator." Data terminals around the room whirl to life at her command, along with a series of screens depicting the library's catalog and the hyper-concept matrix. She swipes her spectacles next to the video output terminal before putting them on.

Marcos copies her motion with the pair of glasses she gave him earlier. The lenses settle on his face to reveal a large clock dial glowing above Lauren's workbench displaying the start-up progress. When it finishes, a splash screen shows *Raymond's character generator online*. Another window appears with a catalog of pictures scrolling within. The window is labeled *Lauren's personal music archive*. The images stop scrolling when a picture of a black man holding a trumpet appears with a label '*Louis Armstrong*.' A green frame flashes around the image and the rest of the pictures fade away.

Marcos sits quietly as Lauren works away at her terminal. She mumbles an array of commands that play out in Marcos's spectacles.

Within an hour, the two are sitting together on a sofa in front of the holo-character portal, watching as the generator renders the ancient trumpet player into a holographic performance. They share the same thought, though neither says it out loud. *This can actually work!*

✧   ✧   ✧

The general services board catches Larry-15's attention with a level-18 encrypted message. The subject line reads *Join me for a night of blues*. He doesn't trust that the sender knows him personally but well enough. He hasn't used level-18 encryption in years. The message is a passphrase he vaguely remembers. "I'm keeping an appointment for Margaret-17, who sent me to see Doc."

I haven't seen a client from Margaret in years, he thinks. *I thought she would have entered Somnus by now.*

He associates the memory with a profitable trade. As he considers it, a request for a vid-LINCC conference flashes on his monitor. When he accepts, a dark-haired woman wearing wire-rimmed spectacles greets him.

"Hello, Doc."

Though she is unfamiliar, Larry recognizes his work. However, when the camera pulls away, he sees a large brown cat lying in her lap. The woman separates the fur on its leg with her fingers, revealing a bright-blue lifeclock blazing on its thigh. He recoils at the memory it brings.

"I don't recall your name," he begins.

"That's understandable," she replies. "I have never had much use for the past. Since you opened this message, can I assume you have been enjoying the concerts?"

He nods.

"Excellent! I wonder if you are still expanding your collection. I have a new series worthy of another trade."

"It depends on the venue."

"I'm offering two hundred holographic performances of the greatest jazz and blues singers of all time. A hundred for me, another for my companion."

Larry begins to finger the vid-LINCC kill switch. He has nothing against the woman, but installing the lifeclock in her cat left him uneasy for months. "Is *that* your companion?"

Lauren can see his suspicious eyes fall to her lap. She smiles. "No, this one is in good shape. My companion is a gentleman ready to make a change, much like I did once."

Larry warms up to the conversation. "If you have done any research in this area, you understand that a second surgery is risky. The body can only take so much."

"I'm mostly concerned for the gentleman," she assures. "He also values discretion."

"These holographic performers you mentioned, the best of all time, would they be anyone I know?"

"Louis Armstrong."

Doc's eyes expand. When he was sure his voice wouldn't be unintentionally enthusiastic, he answers, "I'm listening."

"Billie Holiday, Bonnie Rait."

"Go on."

"B.B. King, John Lee Hooker."

Larry's suspicion returns. "What exactly are you trading? There are no holo-recordings of Billie Holiday or any of these performers."

"But if they do exist and are of sufficient quality, we have an arrangement?" She taps the rim of her glasses. "You still have the data specs from before?"

When Larry nods, a message appears on the board as an attached thread.

She says, "I just sent you a link to an aether database. Have a look, and let me know if we have a deal."

The screen clears.

Lauren pushes her chair from the terminal and walks over to the character generator. Marcos maintains the controls as she had demonstrated. They watch as a wire-framed shape mutates into the figure of Billie Holiday performing in a spotlight. It is the third performance Marcos has developed, and it is rendering beautifully.

"You seem pretty confident." He observes.

Lauren takes a chair by the terminal. "I hope so. If he goes for it, we'll need to get out of town quickly." Lauren doesn't think to resist the instinct to look over her brother's shoulder at the generator settings. He'd moved outside the parameters she recommended.

Marcos laughs at her concern and waves Raymond's notebook. "Relax, sis, the light color just changed; I had to soften the edges a little. Besides, she has a lot more curves than the last guy."

She kisses him on the forehead. "You have talent, bro."

Marcos returns to Raymond-08's notes. He enjoys rendering holograms and wonders if his new identity could pursue a similar trade before they have to leave.

The audio kernel in both their ears chimes. A digital voice announces, "Level-eighteen encrypted message from *Doc* has just responded to your post on the general services board." A message flashes, *I want to see more. If you can deliver 200 performances like this, we have a deal.*

Lauren throws her arms around Marcos's shoulders as they cheer.

Lauren copied Raymond's character generator to an aether storage account. With a few updates, they are able to access it from her home terminal.

In no time, Marcos learns to leverage his sister's music archive to generate multiple performances at a time.

Lauren focuses on developing new identities for herself and Marcos. When she moved to Bay City, she had numerous contacts on the aether who assisted her with references. This made walking into a new trade easy. Those contacts are gone now.

Most distressing is their need for credits. It's impossible to transfer funds to accounts with identities that do not yet exist. Even if it were, such a transfer would make an unchangeable connection between their current identities and the new ones. The only solution is to exchange all their credits for items that can be resold.

Marcos has extensive experience operating in the shadow marketplace. Electronics are pretty easy to trade. They are also bulky. Certain bottles of spirits hold their value but require care in moving and storing, and although profitable, can be tricky to sell. After all, a fifty-credit bottle of scotch is always welcome, as long as there is someone willing to pay the fifty credits.

It doesn't take long for Larry to arrange a discrete opening in his schedule. The siblings pack everything into a double row hover-pod and head for Antioch, with Priya in a handbag lined with the gray resin sheet to hide the extra lifeclock.

Another Moveable Face

Dark sockets render in place of eyes on a bleach-white skull, rotating on the view screen of Doc's medical scanner. As the image fills in, Lauren remembers her excitement the last time she stood here.

Doc's solemn voice pulls her back to the present. "You can put your shirt back on." He studies the monitor before offering his diagnosis. A patchwork of blue lines appears across her skeletal image on the monitor. He cues his tele-LINCC. "Sweeny, please bring the gentleman in."

A pale woman, dressed in an immaculate white medical assistant outfit, marches Marcos into the examination room. Sweeny is a fifteen-year-old sober version of the woman who greeted Julie during her last visit. She has dark black hair gelled tightly across her scalp, disappearing under a sterile white nurse's cap with a band of platinum white running down the middle of her head. Her bright scarlet lips seem incapable of smiling.

Although she stands only slightly above chest height to Marcos, Lauren knows the woman puts him on edge. She remembers the Barber-ahs sulking around the clinics where he used to take Julie. At least this one has much clearer eyes than most.

"You can go home early, Sweeny," Doc states. "I won't need you until tomorrow afternoon."

"You promised that I could watch this time!" the girl protests louder than she may have intended.

Marcos and Lauren exchange a concerned glance.

"Go!" Doc scolds.

Sweeny stands at attention in the examination room defiant to his order. "We have an agreement, Larry," she growls. "You're supposed to let me learn."

Doc rolls over to the woman on his stool to answer her in a subdued version of her growl. "If you were interested in learning, you would have joined the medical trade as I did. You may watch procedures that require assistance. You are *not* required for this consultation. Go."

Sweeny indignantly waits until the Doc nods in the direction of the door. Forcing her shoulders to relax, she marches out of the examination room.

When the latch sounds on the front door, Doc rotates the scanner monitor so the siblings can see. Thin blue lines morph across the white surface of the rotating skull. Layers forming tendons, muscles, and skin tissue fade onto the white foundation, each streaked with shades of blue. The animation continues until it settles as a photo image of Lauren's head and shoulders.

"The blue areas represent enhancements made by the surgical chamber during your last visit," Larry says. "The chamber utilizes synthetic tissue, which helps with rapid healing and recovery. These areas will not respond well to further manipulation."

Lauren asks, "By *not responding*, you mean?"

"Recovery is unpredictable, you will almost certainly suffer disfigurement. The chamber's scanners will prohibit any operation on these areas other than critical healing procedures."

"I don't understand." Lauren shakes her head. "You knew that I had physical alteration surgery during my last visit. We had to make a special entry in my—"

"First of all," Larry interrupts. "The recovery operation following your pregnancy didn't radically reshape your anatomy. There was little if any use of synthetic tissue. Also, your body was developing a lot faster then. The chamber cannot operate on synthetic tissue the same way it does natural. I'm sorry; you can't take another comprehensive session."

Lauren looks to her brother with a silent fearful expression; she isn't accustomed to giving up. "Could you override the chamber's safeties?"

With a strong sigh, Doc sinks in his chair and shakes his head. "I have no problem hiding procedures from the Guardian, or helping someone to hide her identity. My clients expect that." He nods between the two. "I will never purposefully place a patient at medical risk."

Leaning toward Lauren, he says, "There are many medics who are willing to tell you what you wish you are hearing now. Medics who will take your payment and operate in a chamber that has been altered. I am not one."

After a long silence, he turns to her brother. "Marcos, I take it you're in need of a full-body workup, similar to hers?"

Marcos answers with a nod.

"I'll need to make a few more scans, then we will build you a new look. You'll be on your way in a few hours." He glimpses at Marcos's fist, clenching a bag. "You understand, no matter how young your appearance, I can't do anything with a lifeclock." He nods at the fist.

"Okay, then," Doc says. "Lauren, if you wouldn't mind waiting up front, we'll get started. Marcos, please remove your clothes and stand in front of the scanner."

The light from her portable terminal illuminates Sweeny's pale features as she enters notations next to a vid-window of Doc's examination room. She closes the terminal and moves away from the entrance of the clinic when she hears the words… *Lauren, if you wouldn't mind waiting up front…*"

Sweeny crosses the street and enters a teahouse where she settles into a booth and continues her documentation. The window with the image of the examination room is gone. The camera she placed transmits a low-power signal that reaches the reception area.

Her notes populate the fields of a personal database she has been building since coming to work for Larry. Her fingers peck the entries one character at a time. *Marcos, full-body work up— Can't change a lifeclock— Lauren, previous full-body work up— Similar to Marcos's— Pregnancy— Hide identity.*

She is distracted by an overly cheerful voice. "What can I get for you this evening?" Sweeny looks up, surprised to see a man expecting her to place an order.

"Nothing," she answers and returns to her typing.

After a long silence, the server interrupts with a less cheerful voice. "Booths are for customers only, Miss. If you are not going to order, you need to leave."

Sweeny forces a pleasant response. "I see." Taking the menu placed in front of her, she addresses him with a smile. "I would like a small glass of milk."

She slaps the menu against the table. It is immediately handed back to her by the waiter, who demands, "There's a three and a half credit minimum."

Sweeny gathers a stabilizing breath as she accepts the menu. Forcing her shoulders to relax, she asks in a calm voice, "May I have the spinach and blue cheese turkey wrap," she pauses, "with a pot of herb tea and a piece of coffee cake, make that two, I'd like the second one to go." She answers the server's satisfied smile in kind and returns the menu.

When the waiter turns away, a search application designed for low-level encryption cues in her terminal. The tool is customized to sort through civil transit records. She queries hover-pod transactions in and through Antioch with A Moveable Face as the destination in the last hour. Two names appear, Lauren-25 and Marcos-80. "Humm, they split the cost of the ride," Sweeny mutters to herself. She updates her file with their numerical designation.

Returning to her search application, she enters:

> read citizenSummary Lauren-25

The short synapses flow onto her screen, as it would for any civil query. She does likewise with Marcos-80 and posts the file links to her database.

Sweeny has been concerned with Doc's sloppy recordkeeping for as long as she has assisted him. She may never have attended any official medical skill-trade, but she understands the importance of maintaining a patient's medical history, which Doc obviously doesn't. When the sync to her aether database completes, she closes her terminal.

Someday, he'll thank me for my proactive diligence. The notion adds to her calm as she walks past the server carrying a tray full of tea, cakes, and a hot turkey wrap as she glides out the door.

Age: 7584.9714 Days

"Shit!" Lauren whimpers. The number hanging in her data-file sends a wave of icy needles through her spine as if to punish her. She curses behind her locked jaw, *"Sixteen goddamn days!"*

The pale chill that covers his sister is apparent to Marcos, but he thinks better than to ask about it.

In sixteen days, Lauren would have been able to roll her clock back six hundred days instead of five. Sixteen days would have given them upward of three more months to find their escape. It would also put Marcos two days into his twenty-fifth year.

"Hey." Marcos rubs the back of her neck. "Whatever it is, we'll work it out, okay?" His new deep voice eases her anxiety; he sounds as if he has vital information that will ensure things will, in fact, work out.

Lauren smiles as she looks into the brown eyes that comforted her as a child when she was wounded, dirty, and afraid. Those eyes are now set in a beautiful, round ebony face.

When Marcos left the surgical chamber, he stood the same 1.9 meters tall with the same broad shoulders he developed working in the Torres del Paine National Park.

Lauren never thought of Marcos as a particularly vain person, nor did Julie, for that matter. Yet, when he stood in front of the full-length mirror in Larry's office, he took a long time to admire his new smooth mahogany synthetic skin and nineteen-year-old physique. He saw Lauren smiling behind him as he ran his fingers across his arms, now soft to the touch, free from the scars and burns he had earned from a lifetime of poor decisions.

Their hover-pod picks up speed as it leaves the surface road for a southbound energized rail. Notebooks slide about the cabin, as do the stacks of boxes holding the supplies Lauren and her brother will use to start their new lives.

Lauren has been building the details of her new identity for days. Her history is outlined in her notebooks so it easily flows into her new data-file. She has authored a new life that severs all similarities of her previous ones, including a new birthplace, new skill-trades, and no pregnancy. Unfortunately, her profile photo has the same face.

Lauren-25's lifeclock glows with the light of the lifeclock writer when she sends the getName command to her little egg; moments later, she is welcomed as Sonia-10.

Marcos's new information was ready to flow over hers. In less than an hour, the getName command assigns him the new name Carlos-92.

Sonia programs a display window for her new identity into her brass pocket clock beside Lauren and Julie. When called, it reads:

Sonia-10
7085.0339 Days
19.3981 Years

The values are nearly identical when she programs the pocket clock she built for her brother from the silver cigarette case.

If a way out exists, we have five-and-a-half years to find it. She reminds herself, *I cracked the lifeclock in less time than that. The Collective isn't seamless; the Brigade's not perfect. There'll be danger, but we'll make it.*

Part 2
Defectors

The Shadow Lands

Humans have always monetized death. The great Colosseum of the Western Euro region once drew visitors from around the sea to watch the people of Rome kill one another in ritual combat.

Today, citizens ride barges up the Nile River in the Northern Afro region to see the great pyramids, which once held the remains of rulers long forgotten. Others are just as eager to visit the great stepped structures in the Northern Mezo region to see the stone slabs where Aztec citizens once sacrificed their lives to ensure their nation's prosperity.

For generations, citizens throughout the Collective have flocked to the borough of South Diego in the North American region to enjoy the Final-Quarter Playground. The malls of South Diego have merged into a vast network of pleasure districts, where citizens spend the last of their credits fulfilling every desire before entering the grand tower of the South Diego Somnolence Citadel, known as The Stairway to the Sky. Here they meet their Third Citizen Obligation to make a place for the next generation to enter and thrive in the Collective.

Somnus tourism has so affected the economy of South Diego that it has overshadowed most of the surrounding subdistricts, which have devolved into high-functioning nomad territories known as the Shadow Lands.

Children born in the borough are moved to nurseries in other parts of the continent where schools and skill-trade institutions are better equipped to meet the Collective's obligation to them.

The abundance of mind-altering chemicals, anxiety stabilizers, and enhanced experience parlors compound the pressure of Final-Quarter for many citizens, which sometimes leads to poor decisions, making the Shadow Lands a hotbed for defectors.

Chapter 9

The Exchange

9.4 years following the Correction.
5.5 years since the siblings' flight to the Shadow Lands.

Sonia-10 slaps the passkey into the card reader and impatiently presses her choppy red bangs away from her data spectacles. A terminal window awakens to hover in front of her face and displays a holographic transit map of South Diego. A green line draws a route along the paths toward the southern border of the borough.

Brent fidgets with the toll bag as he watches the red headed woman calmly study the green dots flashing in her glasses. He hopes to distract her while at the same time avoiding eye contact with Carlos-92 who is hovering beside him like a tower of muscles.

Brent is delivering for Talon, leader of the subdistrict's nomad band.

There are not a lot of options in the Shadow Lands for exiled canines like Brent. He left Outland just two days before his lifeclock began to shine red. It took a week for him to find a nomad band that would allow him to test-in. This exchange is his best and possibly only option for protection in Talon's band. He hopes to make the exchange and leave quietly.

The toll is a bag of thirteen packets of lysergic foam canisters, stimulant caps, and painkillers to trade for a card that will program a hover-pod that will drive into the unmonitored areas of the Collective's borders and on to Haven.

The flickering polka-dots vanish from Sonia's spectacles with a high-pitched *zip* when she rips the card from the reader. "It's a fake, Carlos." She hands the passkey to her brother and secures the reader into her handbag.

Carlos holds the bogus key between his fingers and motions for the toll's return.

Brent swallows his nerves. "Sorry you feel that way, lady," he says with a casual shrug. "I guess we're done here."

Carlos steps in Brent's path and waves for the toll again. "Give it back, now," he says with an impassive sigh.

Brent balls the straps of the toll bag around his hand as he turns into Carlos's challenge. "Deal'z a deal, Defector!"

Soon after the sibling's had set the meeting with Talon's courier, Carlos had jammed the lock and bypassed the security system on the vacant commerce shop to conduct their trade.

The shop is perfect for the sibling's business. The room is private enough to avoid unwanted attention yet close to the morning foot commuters who will report any unexpected skirmish.

This is the sixth deal they've made in the last five years, and it is progressing like all the others.

Brent demands, "You have your route, now fly—"

The boy's tirade is cut short when Carlos sweeps his kneecaps with a club, sending him to the ground.

On his way down, Sonia grabs the courier's head and stuffs a rag into his mouth. She locks the joints of his arm behind his back and jams her knee between his shoulder blades. His scream, only a grunt, is forced around the gag.

Carlos tries to rip the bag from Brent's grasp, but the carrying straps are held firm in a fist that won't surrender. He brings his foot down on the strap, binding the boy's hand against the floor. A catch at the tip of his club releases the metal weight, allowing it to rotate ninety degrees into a hammerhead.

Sonia watches the boy's face turn red as his muffled screams fill the parlor along with the crunching sounds of the bones in his forearm and hand, shattering under the hammer's impact. She releases his arm once the toll bag slips from his bloody grasp, then tosses the useless passkey next to a spike laying on the ground that had fallen from Brent's belt.

The siblings head for the exit when five figures emerge through the doorway.

Sonia and Carlos back away as Brent works the rag from his jaw and releases a long, painful cry. The crew ignores Brent as he struggles to his feet, cradling his wrecked arm.

A man with a freshly shaved scalp speaks for the group. "Leave the bag, and you can go."

Sonia can see the tattoo of an eagle talon above his right ear that wraps about his head.

Fighting off a gang of five is not part of their plan. Carlos collapses the telescoping handle of his hammer-club and jams it into his pocket. He and Sonia have worked out an alternate getaway in case things went this bad, but it's going to cost.

Brother and sister retreat through a door at the rear of the shop. Once through, Carlos sets a crossbar to barricade what appears to be the only exit. Sonia pulls a frame of faux security bars from the window and climbs out.

The bag of chemicals flies from the window into Sonia's arms. Carlos follows. "Like to give them something more to worry about than us," he mutters.

Sonia cues the voice input on her spectacles. "Reactivate."

At her command, a siren erupts inside the parlor.

Talon's crew files out of the shop as its lights and motion-activated cameras come to life. The noise will call unwanted attention, but there is little concern that Civil Security will arrive anytime soon.

Away from the screaming parlor, the crew pulls a stumbling Brent off the walkway. Talon thrusts a crudely fashioned crescent-shaped blade under Brent's throat. "Now we have to make the earnings you were supposed to bring," he whispers. "If we find you in this borough after midday, I'll slice you into meat strips and sell your worthless hide on skewers to the lunch crowd in the dining quad."

Brent buckles when a punch under his rib cage forces the wind from his lungs, another to his jaw sends him to the ground. Footsteps recede.

Talon motions for two men to search deeper in the district, the other two follow him up the walkway.

The shops and booths of the commerce district welcome the morning commute crowd. Irregular groups move cross and back along the streets, providing an effective screen for the quarry. It doesn't last. Within minutes, one of the crew spots Carlos's head above the others. Talon traces an invisible line from his minion's pointing hand to the dark complexioned face that suddenly turns when he yells, "There! Follow them!"

Carlos swings the toll bag across his back as they break into a full run, pressing through clusters of shoppers. A wake opens in the sibling's path, revealing an idyllic trail for their hunters to follow. Sonia doesn't need to see Talon's crew following; she can feel them gaining.

Above the sounds of scuffling feet and her panicked breathing, another sensation rises to Sonia's awareness. The familiar aroma of baked bread grabs her attention. A delivery wagon moving around the crowd leads Sonia's eyes to a hanging wooden sign shaped like a loaf of bread.

"In there!" Sonia pushes Carlos through the doorway of *Beatrix's Bagels & Baguettes Bakery*. "Slow down, stay close," she commands in a hushed voice. Their movement slows to a crawl as they make their way around the mass of customers awaiting their orders. Carlos glances at the entrance to find their pursuers beginning to force a path through the patrons.

Sonia leads her brother through a door in the back. The kitchen broils with a multitude of ovens, all producing at full capacity. Master and apprentice bakers remove steaming loaves from the oven's maw to stack onto cooling racks scattered about. Sultry vapors rise from rows of bagged cakes, rolls, and biscuits that have been sorted into ordered piles and labeled with their destination, waiting to be loaded for delivery.

The kitchen briefly overwhelms Sonia with memories from her Green Cycle just as a tidal wave of angry reproaches erupts from enraged bakers. The flow of vulgarities follows the trespassers violating their kitchen as they walk through the delivery exit and past the wagon parked outside.

Back on the walkway, Sonia and Carlos hear cooling racks of product crash to the floor. Their hunters are trapped against the wrath of a dozen angry bakers.

Rejoining the morning walking commuters, Carlos leans to his sister and asks, "How did you know?"

"Delivery time," she pants. "Tempers are short if you don't watch your step."

Their trail clear, the siblings slow to a less noticeable pace. "If we can get to a pod pickup area or rail-bus, they probably won't follow," Carlos says.

Sonia considers the toll bag on her brother's back. "Do we have credits for a pod?"

Carlos nods. "I have a few; we don't need to go far, just away from here." The signs for the pod pick-up station points up the hill.

Passing his lifeclock above the access terminal, Carlos's account displays an available balance of 18.36 credits after he approves a transfer to summon a pod. Three credits will take them to the edge of the mall, where a rail-bus will deliver them back into South Diego. They live close enough to the station to walk home.

Not long ago they would have simply called a pod to their location with a personal tele-LINCC and taken it all the way back to the apartment without considering the extra expense. Now, most of their savings are tied up in the bag of chemicals carried on Carlos's back. The bag holds the equivalent of eighteen months of savings, thirteen canisters of pharmaceuticals they used as trade for their toll. Building it has left little for rent, groceries, or the occasional trip to an underground clinic when a trade goes sideways.

Although they are leaving the mall without the promised passkey to Haven, the siblings appreciate their good fortune. Neither suffered any injury over the botched transaction and their toll is intact to try again. All considered, this went better than any of their previous deals.

The number for their pod displays on the arrival board. Sonia and Carlos approach the pick-up point when a tattoo of an eagle talon in a field of heads grabs Sonia's attention. She shoves her brother away from the crowd. "Run!"

The siblings sprint from the platform with Talon and two of his crew in pursuit. Carlos resists the rebuke in his mind. Nevertheless, "Stupid!" escapes from his rigid jaw as they head down the hill and back to the markets. With the toll bag jostling across his back like a marker flag, and the streets devoid of cover, Carlos knows they have no chance of outrunning Talon's crew. "Do you hear that?" he asks.

Sonia struggles to answer. "What?"

Carlos turns toward a mysterious thumping sound rising from the open square on the south end of the district. "That sound, come on!"

In the distance, music is helping the commerce area awaken. The beat of a single drum, then two, turns into five, into eight, then a dozen. They approach a variety of percussion sounds working to find a common thread, chaos becoming cooperation.

As the sound grows louder, the walkway becomes thick with people. Carlos follows the beat into an open courtyard, where they come to the edge of a performance circle. A hundred spectators have gathered around the performers to enjoy the rhythm as they sip hot beverages on their way to work.

Carlos presses Sonia through the crowd to the edge of the circle. Turning about, he faces Talon's thrilled expression and a crude curved blade.

Slipping the toll bag from his back, Carlos removes four packets and holds them up for his hunter to identify. "Sonia, get in the circle, now!" he commands.

"Are you crazy?" she yells.

An aggressive nudge from her brother sends Sonia stumbling into the middle of the drum circle. The sight of the stunned woman surprises a few players, while motivating others to play faster. An exhilarating cheer arises from the courtyard. Voices call out "Dance!" The crowd encloses the players.

Forcing a joyful expression, Sonia pulls the spectacles from her face and begins to clap her hands above her head as her hips rock and twist to the developing beat, while suppressing thoughts of becoming a reward for Talon's crew. A cheer grows around the circle as others begin to join in.

Carlos follows her into the circle. Grabbing Sonia by the waist, he calls to the players, "You guys are amazing!" He shows the circle three packets of stim caps and a cylinder of foam. "Here's something to share!" He tosses the packets to the opposite side of the circle.

The music halts as the players dive for their tribute.

Talon's face flushes with rage. "Get it back!" he yells. The crew dives into the crowd, desperate to save their disappearing prize. Three drummers pile onto one of his men trying to tear a canister of lysergic foam from them. Carlos and Sonia melt into the district's walkways.

Sonia's rage reflects Talon's at the sight of a quarter year's earnings evaporating into the plaza. "What the hell did you just do?" she screams, forgetting their hunters.

Carlos responds with his characteristic calm. "Keep going!"

The excitement at the performance quad continues to draw interested morning customers. The siblings press their way to the edge of the crowd and fall into a mad run for the border of the district.

Numerous maintenance tunnel entrances and walkways, leading back toward the commerce tract, pepper their path with lots of alternating possibilities for their pursuers to follow.

In the distance, two gold hoods appear. "Damn!" Carlos mutters, remembering the scene at the pod station and now the courtyard. "I'm calling way too much attention."

They follow a walkway back to the dining district where Sonia catches the profile of the two men from the bakery and pulls Carlos to double back. Moments later, they're tucked in a booth of a café, hidden from the main street. "How are we going to get out of here?"

"We split up," Carlos answers. "Do you think you can make it back?"

"It will be easier if I move through the shops," Sonia whispers. "I have enough credits for a simple disguise and a transport back. What about you?"

Carlos begins to move packets from the toll bag into Sonia's satchel. "If security closes in, you dump these, understand?" He slides from the booth to peer into the street.

"Wait!"

He turns to his sister. "Give me at least a quarter hour, and I'll lead them away." Carlos's voice is calm and confident, like when they were children. "Take your time getting home, don't risk these assholes finding you, and remember, if security closes in, dump the bag. I'll see you tonight." With a last squeeze of her hand, he vanishes into the morning crowd.

Sonia opens her bag below the table to rummage around the canisters. She withdraws a fistful of colorful silk scarves and another pair of her data spectacles. The lenses tint to bright green as she affixes the kernel into her ear. Lashing the material about her head and neck, she fashions a rainbow hijab that flows across her shoulders and chest. She applies the rest of the material around the straps and face of her satchel.

"What can I get you this morning?" The server's chipper voice rattles Sonia, forcing her into an eager yet awkward smile.

Sonia thrusts her rainbow-colored bag under the table. "Thank you, yes. I would like a large cup of black tea and a biscuit."

The server answers the request with an overly apologetic, "I'm so sorry; our pastry delivery is late today."

"What the hell?" Adrenaline coursing through her blood causes Sonia's disappointed customer response to sound a lot bitchier than she intended; it's just the kind of answer that might be remembered. She recovers with a polite smile. "Just the tea then. Thank you."

Sonia watches thirty minutes pass on the clock before calling for her bill. A holographic map of the commerce district floats a few centimeters in front of her data spectacles with a green line leading her to the border. *There are other places to get a hover-pod,* she tells herself. *Carlos was right; the pick-up station was an obvious place to wait for us. Someone is certain to be there now.*

Sonia moves through dozens of boutiques trying on hats and holding up blouses for her approval, occasionally purchasing a handful of inexpensive gaudy jewelry. She is soon covered in an assortment of colored beads and charms pinned across her body and around her neck.

Cones of light shimmer across the district streets in Sonia's data spectacles, indicating the presence of lifeclock census sensors. Many shops are flagged with orange arrays above their doorways indicating scanners that log the identity of customers who enter, alerting the proprietor of their age and unique purchasing habits.

Sonia and Carlos have trained to avoid lifeclock sensors wherever they go, but especially when they are hunted, as they are now. She has learned ways to steady her pace and avoid unnecessary attention. A day will come when avoiding reapers will be just as dangerous as dodging Talon's crew.

Unfortunately, avoiding the sensors slows her movement through the mall. The sight of a gold hood or a tattoo on a baldhead sends her back into the crowd again and again. By midafternoon, Sonia is far from the border of the commerce zone. She stops when a hover-pod pulls alongside her. The driver smiles and waves a hand shining with a blue lifeclock. Pods navigate around the double-parked vehicle as she leans against the canopy and smiles. She arches her back toward the fourteen-year-old boy who bobs his head to the empty seat beside him.

Sonia runs the tips of her fingers along the teenager's arm, redirecting his hand from exploring further up her thigh. This continues for thirty-five minutes until they enter the rail-bus station. When the hatch opens, Sonia grabs the back of the boy's neck and pulls him into a long, deep kiss, leaving him dazed long enough for her to get on the bus without another word.

Back in her apartment, beads explode across the floor as Sonia rips the strings from her neck. Carlos hasn't returned. The dark window reflects her almond-shaped face framed within a nest of choppy, deconstructed hair, dyed dark red descending around her neck, where scarves hold an array of tin charms and ribbons purchased from the mall's boutiques.

She adds up the cost of her gaudy disguise, along with the tea, rail-bus ride, and the three credits for the pod they abandoned. "Dammit all!"

The milk in the cold box still smells okay, but there isn't much left. Sonia pours a cup of water from an ice-chilled pitcher. She closes her eyes as the cool liquid touches her lips.

Waiting for her in the darkness is a vision of Brent, the delivery boy, pinned on the ground. She can hear his muffled scream through the rag stuffed in his mouth and the sound of his bones shattering under the hammer.

The memory flash causes her knees to buckle. The cup tips from her hand; water flows onto the floor. "Damn!" Brent's face has joined the other ghosts she has collected since arriving in South Diego five-and-a-half years ago. Now, they are waiting for her. Drawing in a stabilizing breath for the inevitable, she lowers herself into a chair and closes her eyes.

Then. A man with a knife jumps at her, grasping at her pack. Carlos's club connects in the attackers back, driving him to the ground.

Sonia winces in her chair.

Then. A man rages as Carlos seizes him in a full nelson. He buckles over when she slams his gut with the hammer-club. Another swing smashes the weighted tip against his head, near his eyes.

Sonia's head turns in a sympathetic shudder.

Carlos's arms open, the man slides to the ground, never to get up again. Blood stains her brother's shirt.

Then. She swings about by a man clawing at the strap of her satchel, which she has tied around his neck. He gasps, desperate to regain his footing. She lunges against his balance, pulling him in all directions. Unable to overpower him, she can only keep him away from her brother.

A few meters away, Carlos avoids a storm of slashes and thrusts from another attacker.

Sonia struggles to pull the trapped assailant to the ground, where she can find the leverage to hold him or tighten the strap enough to cut off his airway. Neither is working. Therefore, she will hold him off until Carlos can help her, or he'll escape, overpower and kill Carlos, then kill her.

Back in her apartment, Sonia rests her elbows on the table and resolves to keep her eyes closed until the ghosts conclude. Sometimes every struggle she and her brother have engaged in plays out two or even three times before leaving.

Then. Richard-22 releases a final cry of terror in the tunnels of Outland. He sinks into a mass of stabbing and thrashing sticks as the canines pull him to the ground.

Is that it? Beads from her torn necklace come into focus as Sonia opens her eyes. The last ghost lingers. *Did I do that?* The memory is jumbled with the others. *His name wasn't Richard, what was it?*

After sixteen months of resisting, Sonia realized it was easier to allow the ghosts to speak when they wanted. If she allows them to play out all at once, they leave on their own as opposed to fighting them through the night.

The ghost of Richard-22 fades. Sonia returns to the kitchen and shakes an empty metal bottle. She removes the stopper and inhales the aroma of juniper it used to hold. The aroma reminds her of the crystal decanter she had in her Bay City apartment that they traded for a basket of vegetables and rolls soon after moving.

Sonia left the bottle behind the last time she went shopping. Their budget won't allow six credits for the distillery to fill it.

She returns to the sofa and removes the remaining toll from her bag. Seven packets represent six months of savings. Losing four in the drum circle means Carlos left the café with two.

She takes her terminal from her satchel, unfolds the keyboard, and settles into her futon.

Once connected to the LINCC, she comments on an aether posting on the Haven board about an arrangement to sell a passkey programmed to take the passenger to Haven. She includes a description of the nomad with a talon tattoo on his bald head.

"It might help someone." She sighs.

Then she calls up her aether journal and types, *ANOTHER FAILURE!* Her journal is the last ritual Sonia has in her life that allows her a measure of relief. She imagines a future version of herself discovering her journal floating in the aether and morphing her into a complaining hologram.

Carlos was sure the last arrangement was a setup. He has an instinct for these things. Then again, they have all been setups.

The passkey would have taken the pod, and us, straight into an established nomad hive. Three years ago, we would not have taken such a chance.

Her eyes settle on the back of her hand; her lifeclock blinks, red-pink, red-pink, red-pink.

We're running out of time and options.

When we lived in the pack, we traded for portable terminals, handbags, sportswear, and food. Here, they only trade in chemicals. A small bag of stimulant caps can get almost anything in the Shadow Lands but calls attention outside. I can't count the number of toll bags we've ditched to avoid Civil Security.

Now that we're in Final-Quarter, an arrest would be the same as a death sentence. Five years ago, I was certain we would find a way out in a matter of weeks.

Sonia's eyes fall onto her pocket clock, lying open on the cushion beside her. The display glows.

Sonia-10
9116.9714 Days
24.9609 Years

Her head falls back against the cushion. "Fourteen days left," she mutters.

The Haven boards have as many references to the underground railroad as there are defectors. I am sure the trail exists, and that the departure point is somewhere close.

These same postings reference someone named 'Casey, the Conductor.' Either he leads the Shadow Lands's symphony orchestra, or it's a reference to the men who used to manage trains and collect tolls on the ancient railways. Unfortunately, Casey doesn't post himself. Even more unusual, many of the references mentioning him avoid any discussion of a toll. Why wouldn't the conductor discuss a toll? I have tried to contact Casey many times. This is likely the last lead Carlos and I follow.

She stops typing to consider the light from her lifeclock flickering against the keyboard.

Rolling our clocks back again isn't an option. Reapers watch us when we are out, as do many citizens. Despite our lifeclocks, they don't believe we are twenty-four. If I can't contact Casey soon, we will make our own way to the border. In that case, it would make more sense to just die in the Citadel.

Sonia looks through the windowpane into darkness. Tiny glowing dots define the shapes of buildings against a starless horizon. The running lights of hover-pods streak across elevated rails in the skyline. Glass taps behind her, Carlos is in the kitchen shaking the empty gin bottle.

"There's a little milk left," she offers. "You should finish it while it's still good."

Sonia notices the toll bag missing from his back. Shame bleeds into her. *Did I just think of the stupid chemicals before my brother?* Forcing the question away, she goes to Carlos and embraces him. Blood stains the tip of his hammer-club sitting on the kitchen table. The sight stirs the ghost of a raging man going limp after she hit him in the head. *What is happening to me?*

Her embrace constricts Carlos's breathing. "It's okay! I'm all right." His deep voice calms her. "Talon's crew trailed me back to the shop where we did the trade. I dropped the bag in their path, then led them in front of a pair of security officers who detained them."

"Sounds dangerous," Sonia scolds. "Was that necessary?"

"It was. We can move through that commerce district now without looking over our shoulders, although it might be a good idea to avoid public drum circles."

Sonia slaps his shoulder for making her laugh.

"Ouch! What was that for?" He chuckles.

"For your hurtful, stereotypical view of public drumming," she admonishes while stifling a smile.

The tension passes. "Your right," he apologizes. "What was I thinking?" They hold one another and stare out the window into the night. "Sonia, why is the floor covered with crappy looking jewelry?"

Chapter 10

Going to Work

Dante's white knuckles close around the edge of the sink. *This would all be a lot easier if the goddamned world would stop trying to spin out from under me,* he silently complains. The last eruption took him by surprise, ruining his gray tunic. It's his own fault for self-medicating last night.

A panicked call to the ingestion clinic brought a technician to his door within ten minutes. She administered the necessary blood scrubbers and stayed with him while the synthetic bliss passed.

"You shouldn't be alone when you foam," she reproaches. "You can hurt yourself, or worse. Next time call us. We can treat you in your home if that is more comfortable for you, but don't—"

"I get it!" Dante growls.

Despite his aggravation, Cindy-18 follows all required protocols. She had already warned him of the prohibition of possessing or selling large stocks of pharmaceuticals. Although personal administration is not prohibited, it is illegal to produce or distribute any strong chem. This isn't the first time he had to listen to the required castigation.

Dante's outburst has no visible effect on Cindy. She soothes the back of his neck while refilling the water glass. "You'll feel better soon."

He drains the glass, replacing much-needed fluid to help the blood scrubbers remove the last of his bliss. Embarrassed by his outburst, Dante chooses his next words carefully. "What time is it?"

Cindy packs her life monitor and assortment of vials into her ingestion bag. She checks his pupils and vitals one last time before closing her kit. "Are you sure you should go to work today?" she asks.

With a glance to his duty bag sitting on a stool by the door, he silently answers, *Officially, I never left.* He swallows the last of the water. "I'll be fine. I need a shower and coffee; then I'll be fine."

Cindy responds in a stern yet compassionate voice, "You need to sleep, at least for a few hours." Following her final rebuke, she wraps her arms around his shoulders and plants a soft kiss on the side of his face.

The unexpected kindness takes Dante by surprise. His chest constricts when her arms fall away. "I really appreciate your help, Cindy," he stammers. "Next time, I promise I'll…" The latch on his door had already clicked closed. He is talking to an empty room.

He fills the water glass and heads for the shower. Stopping at his bag, he removes his tele-LINCC and releases a sigh of relief that dispatch had not activated him for duty in the last fourteen hours. His relief is soon clouded by the disappointment that dispatch had not needed him last night.

The hollow feeling has grown over the last five years. His off-duty distractions rarely cover the empty anymore. He is dry and fitted in a fresh uniform. The coffee he had earlier is not sitting well. He turns to the only practice that consistently clears his mind, his morning ritual, which he relies on more every day. Piece by piece, he removes his gear from the duty bag. Every component helps him find his *I have something important to do now* state of mind.

The terminal-tracker is always the first element he checks. Waving the unit's scanner over his lifeclock, the display scrolls his citizen summary:

NAME: Dante-09, 211.847.012.09.
GENDER: Male.
AGE: 24.7 years.
SKILL-TRADE: Charon Brigade Officer, Reaper.
Attached to the Charon Brigade of Bay City.
HEIGHT: 180 cm.
CURRENT LOCATION: North American region,
Bay City, Sector-211.
SECURITY ACCESS LEVEL-2. No concerns.

He fits the kernel of his tele-communication LINCC into his ear and cues the LINCC. "Dispatch, this is Dante-nine, please confirm terminal operation." The display scrolls the position of Dante's own lifeclock:

BEARING: null deg.
DISTANCE: 0.0 meters.
ELEVATION: 0.0 meters.

The dispatcher's voice replies with a machine-like tone, "Tracker operational."

"Thank you, dispatch." The confirmation gives Dante a feeling of stepping into a larger world. He is no longer an individual trying to figure out his place in the Collective; now, he is a critical component necessary for its operation.

He holsters the terminal-tracker and removes the only piece of sentiment he allows himself. It is a field knife he received as a graduation gift from his Blue Cycle skill trade attendant. Every morning he inspects the edge of the nine-centimeter drop-point blade. When it was new, it was covered with a dark friction-resistant coating, most of which has worn away from years of use. At this point, it only needs to last a few more months. "Damn!" The non-productive feeling returns. He replaces the knife in its sheath and attaches it to the back of his belt.

He fastens the leather wrist cuff to his right forearm. The ammo cuff has six empty loops waiting to be loaded. He inserts two white non-lethal tactical adhesive charges (TAC) into the right-most spots, followed by two red semi-lethal unguided kinetic darts (UKD) in the middle, and finally, two black fully-lethal STInGERs. He carries a few extra charges in a belt pouch.

Another pouch holds three transparent vials. Each is reinforced with a metallic mesh. He holds them to the light. Two vials are filled with a cobalt-blue liquid; the third is three-quarters empty. The liquid is a concentrated explosive fuel that propels the charges from his pistol when fired. A full fuel cell has enough propellant to launch twenty charges at full power. He attaches one of the cells onto the throttle control at the back of the gun and rotates the dial through its settings:

FULL ... ½ ... ¼ ... SAFE

He makes a mental note to trade the depleted fuel cell for a fresh one when he gets to quarters.

Dante thumbs a lock on the pistol that breaks the action open, exposing the empty breech. He closes the barrel with a mechanical clap.

He allows a long relaxed sigh that helps release the tension from his shoulders. Then breaks the action open, slides a TAC from the ammo cuff into the breech, and slaps it closed. After a pause, he breaks the action open again, slides another charge from his ammo cuff, replaces the one in the breech, and slaps the action closed.

Sloppy, he thinks.

He repeats the drill, this time sending a red UKD charge from his wrist to bounce across the floor. *It's a good thing the throttle is on Safe. I probably shouldn't even do this with the fuel cell attached, but that would throw the balance off.*

The Brigade requires a reaper to select, load, and accurately fire three charges appropriate to three unique targets in less than eight seconds.

He stumbles through the drill five more times with similar results, then cues his tele-LINCC and schedules a session on the practice range.

He retrieves the dropped charges from the floor, returns them to his ammo cuff, and loads a charge into the chamber. An indicator on his sight confirms it is a white non-lethal TAC. The Correction taught him the danger of keeping a STInGER loaded when not on the hunt.

Holding the pistol infuses Dante with a feeling of stature. The gun empowers him with the authority of the Charon Brigade, to kill at his discretion.

He gave the gun a detailed cleaning and polish last night. Once finished, he waited for the tele-LINCC to call him back to duty. When that didn't happen, he turned to the flask of lysergic foam.

He secures the gun in its holster. *That's it, ready to go.* Then an object catches his attention. At the bottom of the bag is the sparkly belt that bound him on the floor of Helen's apartment all those years ago. He doesn't understand why he keeps it. Something about that woman has stayed with him. Despite the terror that controlled her in the end, he still admires her. He tucks the strap into his pocket, knowing he will miss it if he doesn't, then locks the door behind him.

Octavia never looks tired or distracted. Her uniform is fitted and pressed as if she is leading a parade. "You look like hell!" she announces from across the quad.

He cheerfully responds, "And good morning to you, Octavia!"

"Seriously, what do you do with yourself after hours, were you on call last night?"

Dante answers with a sardonic "No!" It is a stupid answer. They both know reapers are on duty as long as their gun is checked out. She can see his gun holstered at his side.

Octavia had just left the quartermaster's locker; she knew Dante had not checked in his gear yesterday. "I'll take lead today, at least until your head clears." Her voice cuts like a razor.

I'm fine, Octavia, he thinks. *I just need to get to work so I can be someone I give a damn about.*

There's no rank in the Brigade. Some officers are more suited for organizational roles, and some work better in support and investigation. Senior officers guide the younger, less experienced ones, but there is no formal chain of command except for their duty to uphold the citizen directives.

"You can have it." He shrugs. "But there is something I need to take care of before our shift."

"Dante, here," a voice calls from across the yard. A brawny figure with yellow hair presses the wheels of his mobility chair toward the two reapers. He wears the silver uniform of an officer of the Judicial Corps. Sydney-20 is one of the few friends Dante still claims outside the Brigade.

The Judge

Sydney distracts Octavia from rebuking her partner. Sydney is infinitely more interesting. She has a ritual of admiring the drape of his sharply tailored silver tunic covering his shoulders. She imagines the muscles of his arms, back, and chest, working like gears of a steam engine every time he presses against the wheels of his mobility chair. Her eyes glide down his arms, then to Dante. "Let me guess, more civic duty?" she mutters suspiciously.

"Not exactly," Sydney corrects. "This is more of a favor. Dante is helping me with a case."

"It shouldn't take more than an hour; I'll be at quarters by mid-shift," Dante assures.

Octavia ignores him. Instead, she hears *trapezius, deltoid, latissimus dorsi*. Sydney glides across the plaza; his elbows rise behind him in a rowing motion. As he thrusts his arms forward and shoulders back, Dante is forced to quicken his pace to keep up.

Octavia imagines the operation of Syd's core churning those wheels and whispers with a smile, "He's like a big, chrome, locomotive lemon drop." Once out of sight, she turns and muses *pectoralis major, rectus abdominis, external oblique*.

The daydream accompanies her to the steps leading to Brigade headquarters. While ascending, she stops, turns in the direction she last saw Sydney, and wonders with wide-eyed fascination, *gluteus maximus?*

An injury during his Green Cycle put Sydney-20 in convalescence for nearly half a year. After the first attempt of neurological repair surgery failed, he refused to spend any more of his life in a physical recovery unit.

It was during this time his trade attendant suggested a book about the directives of the Collective. It was a lot like the ancient practice of law.

It was the tie to antiquity that sparked his imagination. In ancient times, advocates argued over the law in debates that lasted for years, even decades. Such debates could change society, perhaps the very operation of the Collective. If such a debate were ever to happen again, Syd wanted to be a part of it.

When he was released from recovery, with his new mobility chair, he glided directly to city hall and entered judicial trade skills.

Dante grabs the back of Sydney's chair and tugs him to a more leisurely pace. "For fuck's sake, Syd, she saw you, okay! Cool your engines."

Sydney settles in his chair and represses his mouth breathing. "I don't know what you're talking about, but if you want to slow down, that's fine." He passes a slate to Dante with a file marked for his review. "Here, this is the case I need your help with. Alexander-forty-eight is scheduled for release in three-quarters of an hour. He was sentenced to six months in cryogenic detention for assaulting a cook in the Olivine Mall."

"Why?" Dante asks as he reviews the case overview.

"We're going to learn that at his release hearing," Sydney says.

"I mean, why do you need me? What does this have to do with the Somnus Obligation?"

"I want you there as a *Bloody Richard* reminder."

Dante closes the file. "You lost me."

Sydney points to an associated file on the slate. "Richard-twenty-two was a citizen in the Western European region about a hundred years after the Awakening. During his Blue Cycle, he entered Outland outside Munich and lived as a canine. Back then, credits were transferred much more freely, almost like the coin currency of ancient times. Richard organized the canines to steal from citizens in the city and trade for credits, much like they do today, only Richard kept all the credits."

"Ruthless," Dante says, "but I'm still not following."

Sydney waves away Dante's remark. "When Richard entered his Red Cycle, he had nearly a hundred canines fighting and stealing on his behalf. He had them fighting over scraps of rations, promoting the strong over the small. He started the practice of stacking canine corpses at entry points to the pack territory so the reapers and security forces wouldn't enter Outland to retrieve them."

Dante remembers working a similar detail as a cadet.

"Canines are uneducated but not stupid. They saw how they were living and eventually drove Richard away. He actually left quietly, with a huge cache of credits."

"How much did he have?"

Sydney lowers his voice. "When security officers detained him, his data-file indicated he had over twelve thousand one hundred credits in his account."

The answer brings Dante to a stop. "Bullshit, Syd. No one keeps that kind of cash."

Sydney locks eyes with Dante's. "It's no joke, Dante. Every year, thousands of yellow and green children throughout the Collective join with a pack in their region. They're searching for something they are not getting from their trade attendants. They feel…" Sydney searches for an appropriate term, "…hollow, and Richard-twenty-two convinced them that their purpose was to fill his credit account."

Sydney picked up the pace. "Even today, canines throughout the Collective tell of 'The Treachery of Bloody Richard-twenty-two.' They have a brutal prohibition against trading for credits, and they will still rip apart anyone who enters their territory with a red lifeclock."

"So, what happened to Richard?"

"Officers detained him as soon as his lifeclock was scanned in the mall. He didn't resist. At his trial, he eagerly agreed to the entire account, even added a few details. He argued that he personally didn't violate any directive since he never actually stole from any citizen or harmed any of the canines."

"That couldn't have excused him," said Dante.

"It didn't. The judicial officer concluded that Richard acted as attendant for the canines and therefore violated his obligation to promote their wellbeing. His actions left the canines with no trade skills that would allow them to participate as citizens of the world, promote the wellbeing of the Collective, or themselves. He violated the First Citizen Obligation and was sentenced to cryogenic detention.

"While he was detained, his judge sent a timed memo detailing Richard's case to the story desk of over a hundred tellers. Four years later, the story of Bloody Richard swept through the Collective."

"Four years?" Dante asks, confused. "How long was he in cryo?"

"Four years, six months, ten days, seven hours, and eighteen minutes."

"I didn't know such punishments existed."

"They don't anymore. This is before the Judiciary exiled repeat offenders to Perdition. The case of Richard-twenty-two is a core study for all cadets in judicial trade school. When his cryo-chamber opened, an officer shoved a change of clothes into his hands and directed him to the front exit. Once the door closed behind him, Richard faced half the city of Munich. Before he could say anything, four words pierced the silence."

Dante completes the scene. "It's your time, Defector." He glances again at the slate with Alexander-48's file. His hearing is in thirty-five minutes.

Sydney picks the story up after Dante's remark. "Richard dropped the bundle to see his expired lifeclock. He hadn't even looked up when his chest exploded."

An awkward moment passes between them before Dante asks, "What am I doing here, Sydney?"

Release Hearing

Fatigue and fear work against Alexander-48's efforts to stand up straight in the judicial chamber. Behind him are a dozen citizens, also groggy from their recent release from cryogenic detention. A Blue Cycle judicial apprentice moves him forward to be the first to stand before His Honor Sydney-20.

The judge's bench is flanked by two gold-hooded security officers, standing to the right, and on the left, is one gold-hooded and one black-hooded officer. The sight of Dante causes Alexander to check his lifeclock; it's blue, just as it was when he entered cryo, how long ago?

Silence falls through the chamber as Sydney calls the first case of the afternoon. "Alexander-forty-eight, 211.587.120.48, you were sentenced to the maximum detention period of one-half year for assaulting David-sixty-three, a cook in the Olivine Mall. Now it's time for you to explain yourself."

"Well, your Honor," Alexander remembers the advice the apprentices gave him on addressing the judge. "I know I should have an acceptable answer for you now. I'm sorry to say, I don't."

His answer appears to aggravate the judge. "I've reviewed your file. Before you were sentenced, Judge Patricia-twenty-seven asked you to explain why you attacked David-sixty-three. You didn't have an answer for her then either. She directed you to consider this during your detention. You have had six months to think of an explanation for your actions."

Alexander nods.

Sydney leans onto his bench. "Perhaps I need to clarify. I am here, with you, representing the Collective. You are not on trial. You have served your time. In a few minutes, you will reenter the Collective as a citizen with all the rights and obligations thereof. The purpose of this hearing is to determine what went wrong and take measures to assure it doesn't happen again.

"I'm asking you for the last time. I don't want an excuse or a justification. I want to know what you were thinking when you grabbed David-sixty-three's head and hit him with your fist."

"I- I-" Alexander knows his only answer makes no sense. "Your Honor," he says with an exasperated sigh, "I- just wanted to break away from my life, my trade. I wanted to DO something. Why did I attack the cook? I have no gripe with him; there is no grudge to settle, at least not from me. I did it to be someone different. I did it to be a criminal."

The chamber members are silent. Then Sydney begins again, "Your explanation is typical of those who stand in this chamber."

This is not the response Alexander expects.

"Sometimes, citizens have a hard time finding their relevance in the world, but your solution was vile, not only for David-sixty-three but for everyone in the Collective." Sydney slaps his bench to call Alexander's attention. "Your actions removed you from its operation. You, sir, have left a hole for *nearly six months*." He emphasized these last three words.

"That's right, Alexander, I have called you from your detention eleven days early. It's time for you to take up your obligations to the Collective. We are not waiting any longer.

"I have reviewed the skill-trades you've worked, janitor, maintenance technician, and kitchen cleaner all in the Olivine Mall. I doubt they will welcome you back. These are all necessary but confining jobs. I'll bet you find small spaces disturbing. Detention must have been difficult."

Alexander grumbles something inaudible.

"Repeat that, please," Sydney says, "for the record."

Alexander takes a deep breath and stammers, "It was, Your Honor, but at least it wasn't sweeping."

Sydney considers this as the chamber gives an uneasy nod. "Why have you never worked in an outside trade such as at an orchard or a field worker?"

Alexander forces a response. "I never thought about it like that. There aren't any orchards in Bay City that I know of."

"Time is wasting! The Collective recognizes that it has not met its obligation to you. A citizen must not waste his life klutzing about as you have done." Sydney calls out to the chamber. "We have failed in our obligation to promote the wellbeing of Alexander-forty-eight, how do we resolve this?"

The chamber stirs uncomfortably as Sydney's glare sweeps the room. "I have asked the citizens of this chamber a question; I will have answers. How will WE, the Collective, meet our obligation to help Alexander participate as a citizen of the world?"

"Your Honor." One of the security officers steps forward.

"Officer."

"Your Honor, the citizen has suffered confinement for half a year, as well as his previous trades. I recommend he take a rail-bus to the coast, trade his work boots for a pair of athletic shoes, and run in the sand for a few days. It will work out his feelings of confinement, and the ocean air is very effective for clearing the mind."

"Alexander, have you ever done that?" Sydney asks.

The former convict shakes his head and stammers, "N- Never."

Another gold-hooded officer steps forward. "Your Honor, if he has never run, he should not start alone. Alexander should see a sports-medic and learn the proper warm-up routines to avoid injury."

"Very good." Sydney turns to a terminal on his bench. "Alexander, the Collective has reserved a bunk for you at half-moon point dormitory. A trainer will meet you there at eighteen hundred hours tonight to fit you with some running shoes, and instruct you on how to jog in the sand safely. Do you know how to swim?"

Dazed, Alexander shakes his head.

"That's going to change. You will have ten days to burn away your muscle atrophy by the ocean. When you are not training, you can help around the dorms with some light maintenance. Let me be clear; you are there to exercise, not clean. What's next? We can't have him running up and down the beach indefinitely."

Dante steps forward. "Your Honor, as a blue cadet, I learned basic hunting skills at a lodge in Jackson, just south of the Yellowstone Territory. We learned to hunt waterfowl and rabbits with a throwing stick." He turns to Alexander. "It conditions you to focus your mind."

Sydney refers to the terminal. "Alexander, it appears you have spent your entire life in Bay City. The Collective feels you are due a holiday. You have three weeks reserved at the Jackson Hunting Lodge. You are signed up for five field study programs. The court will check that you have completed all of them. Another." Sydney demands.

"Your Honor?" One of the released convicts at the back of the chamber steps out of line. "My second skill-trade was spent in a lumber town on the East Coast. The Vermont Territory Forestry Service has trade lines working with hand saws and axes, felling trees for lumber production as well as reforestation teams. If Alexander is looking for outdoor work, he might do well there."

"I'm glad you are paying attention back there," Sydney responds without raising his attention from the terminal. "Alexander, when you finish your stay in Jackson, you will take a rail-bus to the Vermont Territory Forestry Service. They have been directed to remove a robotic worker from the line to make a place for you. You will spend the remainder of the year there, working as a lumberman. They will pay you 30 credits a week in addition to lodging and three meals per workday.

"The Collective, this court, will be checking your progress throughout the year. What you do after is your affair. If you do well there, you can stay at the mill or move on."

Sydney leans over his bench to meet Alexander's eyes. "You will not neglect any of these obligations the Collective has set for you. You will never enter cryo again. If you fail to meet these obligations, you will be banished to Perdition. Do you understand?"

Alexander nods, locked in the judge's gaze.

It takes a moment before Sydney is confident that Alexander understands the severity of his directives. Then he informs the newly released citizen, "Alexander, you just became an adult."

Alexander flips his hand up to find a red lifeclock glowing on his hand. *How long has it been like that?* he wonders. He tries to return his attention to the judge, but it drifts to the right to meet the eyes studying him from within a black hood.

Sitting on Sydney's judicial bench, out of view from the rest of the chamber, is the slate displaying Alexandar-48's citizen summary. His age is highlighted.

Age: 18.0 years.

Chapter 11

Last Night with the King

Black velvet cradles a line of tiny crystals along a delicate silver chain. The sparkles remind Larry-15 of the cut glass optical prisms that change sunlight into little rainbows. The chain is supposed to be a diamond necklace. He doesn't know anything about diamonds or gems, but the king would.

Larry raises his eyes to the painting of *The King of Cool* hanging on the wall. The king wears a meticulously tailored black tuxedo with a red cloth poking out of his breast pocket. The jacket is custom made for the king, designed to hang smoothly from his shoulders. He wears it over a white button-down shirt, opened at the neck. The thistle ends of a black bow tie hang under his collar. His garments are wrinkled and worn from a long night, but his eyes sparkle over a white smile, framed by a thirty-six hour morning stubble. One hand is wrapped around a cut crystal glass holding large ice cubes and one finger's width of amber liquid glowing from the spotlight. Smoke curls from a cigarette between his fingers. The other hand controls a large silver microphone.

The king glances in his direction, nodding approval for a life lived right.

"You could tell a real diamond," Larry whispers as he claps the jewelry case shut and slides it into the pocket of his tuxedo jacket. "You knew the thrill of hanging them about a woman's bare neck as she skips a breath in anticipation. What did you whisper in her ear when you closed the clasp?"

Larry is a perfect mimic of the painting. He raises his glass to salute the king. The ice cubes clink as the glass tilts, bringing the silky smooth bourbon to his lips; it also brings his lifeclock to his eyes flashing red-black, red-black, an ever-present reminder that his Last-Day has begun.

The sight chokes him for a moment before he regains his composure, no, not composure, his cool. Tonight, Larry is going to be cool, just like the king in the painting.

Unlike the hundreds of panicked men and women he had seen over the years who desperately cram every experience they can think of into the final moments, Larry had started preparing for this day three years ago.

Now, all his equipment is stashed. The surgical chamber is covered and hidden away. His examination table has changed into a minibar, stocked with buckets of ice, chilled champagne, and fine spirits.

Technicians from the media studio completed their installation twenty minutes ago, transforming A Moveable Face into Larry's private holographic blues club.

Metallic posts, standing three-and-a-half meters tall, form an octagonal configuration inside of what used to be Larry's examination/surgical room. Seven holographic screens, mounted to the poles, are controlled by a special program on Larry's terminal.

The structure takes up a little more than half of the examination room, with one segment left open as an entrance. When activated, the screens roll back into a grand ballroom. Holographic patrons are seated around dozens of nightclub tables, while waitresses carry large circular trays of drinks about. One of the screens displays a performance area with a band of tuxedo-clad musicians playing for a woman standing in a shower of spotlights. She wears a long sparkling evening gown and a large orchid in her hair.

Audio boxes fill the room with the sounds of brushed drums, a string bass, and the silky voice of Billie Holiday singing *Blue Moon*.

Larry tries not to notice the structure supporting the holo-screens. The installers used trusses designed for outdoor venues. The unnecessarily heavy installation imposes an industrial look to his otherwise swanky blues club. With a sigh, Larry shrugs away his concern. *With the lights low, it won't be as noticeable, besides there's no time to complain about it anymore.*

Twenty-five hours from now, Larry-15 will be in Somnus. Civil movers will return all the tagged equipment to the media studio in the mall and pallet his personal belongings for recycling. The clinic will be closed and someone else will move into the space to build his or her trade.

A chime sounds at the main entrance.

If Larry is *The King of Cool*, Grace is his queen. Her eyes are blue fire, shining within a wide, sable-lined hood that frames her delicate features. A long pearl-colored satin gown wraps around her curves, down to her ankles. A matching clutch is tucked under her arm. The holographic patrons of the club snap their heads about when she walks into the room.

Grace was the thirty-fifth woman to answer Larry's Crystal Connections query. They talked for weeks on the LINCC, but this is the first time they've met in person. Larry doesn't want some programmed fantasy in the Crystal Lounge with strangers pretending to like his music and laugh at his jokes. He wants to share an experience acted out in a hundred video plays from before the Awakening, where men with effortless confidence made love to elegant women with wit and charm.

No words pass as Larry and Grace glide onto the dance floor. As one song drifts to another, she leans in for a long deep kiss.

In addition to a constant serenade of the greatest music ever played, the next twenty-three-and-a-half hours will bring caterers with chilled champagne, rich food, and various aphrodisiacs for the makeshift honeymoon suite he set up in his former office. A holographic screen displays a view of the ancient Las Vegas skyline, with a futon spread on the floor before it. All the credits in the world can't turn a cubicle into a real twentieth-century presidential suite.

When the sun sets tomorrow evening, he'll hold Grace in his arms, under a warm shower, as she removes the two-day stubble from his throat with a straight razor. Grace anticipates this part of the game with a special thrill.

The razor is tucked in a soft leather slipcover inside her clutch. Its blade is a beautiful piece of antique etched steel, honed with a full hollow ground, ending in a round tip and folded within a smooth whalebone handle. She has practiced with it for years, keeping the edge keen. Larry is the first man willing to receive her skill.

Grace has described every motion to him during their late-night calls leading to tonight. Her legs will lock around his waist as he presses her against the wall of the shower stall. She will control his chin and neck, stretching his face to receive each pass of the razor across his throat. He will completely surrender to her directions.

Only once had Grace promised not to cut his throat, Larry shrugged it off. The occasional nick will bleed for a moment, reminding him that his heart still beats. Part of him wouldn't mind entering Somnus with a single swipe of her hand, but they agreed to keep his cauterizing kit within reach if his blood makes her nervous.

There will not be a long emotional trip to a sterile Citadel recliner tomorrow. If Larry times it just right, his clock will expire as she finishes buttoning his shirt. She will straighten his bow tie. He'll clasp the necklace about her bare neck as a memento for the night. By then, he will think of something cool to whisper in her ear, just as the door rattles with two reapers on the other side.

"Don't worry, Doll," he'll say. "Let me get rid of these punks, and I'll meet you in the lounge in five minutes." They'll share a last kiss, and he'll send her out the door with a slap on her ass. Hopefully, the reapers will wait until she's out of earshot when they complete his final obligation.

Of course, nothing is ever that easy. Larry has a small box of anxiety stabilizers ready. He had already taken half a pill moments before Grace arrived, although now he wishes he hadn't. He wants to experience every moment with clarity.

Larry and Grace sway on the dance floor, trying to ignore the continuous door chime that has plagued the last three songs.

"You should probably get that." Grace finally breaks the mood in a frustrated voice. "Whoever it is isn't going away."

"You're right." Larry resists the long irritated sigh welling inside him as he leaves his holographic club for the front lobby. The first caterer is not expected until eighteen hundred hours.

Larry deactivates the lock, the door bursts open, and a white blur brushes past. "Hello, Doc, how's the club?" Sweeny breezes into the lobby, shattering the carefully crafted mood.

"Whhhhhat are you doing? The cccclinic is closed, Sweeny; it's over," Larry forces his voice to a whisper.

"I was just concerned for you, Doc. You haven't been yourself lately." The former assistant stands rigid in her Barber-ah uniform next to what was her reception desk.

Grace emerges from the hallway with a pair of champagne flutes, unsure how to play along. "Larry, is this part of the game?"

"No, she has nothing to do with anything. I'm cccalling Civil Security." Larry tries to remember where he hid his tele-LINCC after removing its power cells.

"Doc, you're not thinking straight!" Sweeny says with mock concern. "You've had a long night!"

"Why are you yelling, and what the hell are you doing here? I told you, there's nothing more for you. You need to leave now!" A dense cloud encompasses Larry's awareness as he stammers his demands. The feeling is one that follows a night of heavy drinking, yet he is certain that he hasn't.

Then, Larry recognizes the Barber-ah's expression. *I know that look*, he thinks. *She's looking at me with the same delight she takes when the robo-scalpel opens a patient's flesh.*

Deep in Larry's awareness, a wheel clicks into place. He remembers the small box of pills in his pocket. *They're different somehow; they're reacting with the alcohol.* "You switched 'em." He recognizes the slur in his voice. "Why did yooooouuu doo…" As his heart races with the discovery, the room begins to move, causing him to struggle for his balance.

Two flutes of champagne shatter on the floor at Grace's feet. Two hooded figures stand silent in the doorway.

A youthful voice speaks from one of the hoods. "It's your time, Defector. Larry-fifteen, you will come with us."

Sweeny is at his side, directing him toward the dark figures. "It's okay, Doc; you're just tired. We've had a long night. It's time to rest."

"Nnn- no, this isn't right; it's not time yet." Larry's legs fail to match the violent movements of the floor. His heart races against the chemicals. His breathing grows quick and deep to push away the haze.

"You're not thinking straight, Doc." That voice again, that miserable voice speaking on his behalf. "We've had so much fun. You're amazing."

An insincere peck lands numb on the side of Larry's face.

Two blue crystals shine on two hands, pointing two guns at Larry's chest. Grace watches in horror as Larry tries to show the reapers his lifeclock, only to have his hand brushed away.

Larry's words are catching in his throat as he is forced to the door. "What?!?! No. No, I just started my Last-Day. I- have tweeeeny- please, let me go!"

"He's been going full speed since last night." The short white blur beside him explains. "He started talking about not going to the Citadel about six hours ago."

"No! Don't- tell them. Sweeny, don't say that! Why are you doing this?" Larry pleads. A pistol muzzle thrusts into the small of his back, guiding him to the sidewalk.

Larry squirms to take one last look at his queen. He wants to say something, but can't remember. "I'll meet you in five minutes," he manages to call out as he disappears with the reapers into the night.

Down the hallway, patrons in the holographic club applaud as the noise from the lobby subsides. Grace is locked in Sweeny's gaze. She yanks the razor from her clutch. Light from the front office window traces the silver edge pointed at the grinning Barber-ah.

Sweeny's eyes widen at the sight of the shiny razor shaking in Grace's fist. "I should have one of those," she says.

Way off, in Larry's club, B.B. King takes the stage. The beat of a keyboard and drums drifts into the lobby as his sorrowful guitar begins to sing.

Sweeny closes the space between herself and Grace. "He's not coming back," she says in a soft, monotone voice.

Grace grabs her cloak and dashes out the door, as fast as one can dash in heels. She doesn't see the broken chain of sparkles laying in the gutter aside a crushed velvet box.

Sweeny releases a long-held irritated sigh. "Finally!" she says as she locks the door, snaps on the lights, and kills the terminal program running Doc's holographic club. The chunky, overly happy singer, who keeps insisting that he has 'paid his dues,' fades into the clear polymer sheets along with the rest of the audience.

"Never have to listen to that drivel again," she mutters. The King of Cool looks down on her from the makeshift bar. "Why is THAT out here?"

The following morning.

The delivery boy is relieved when the door slams in his face. The strange woman in white makes him nervous.

Inside, Sweeny guides the food cart with two covered place settings into her examination room. She had removed Larry's blues club from the terminal and replaced it with her own atmosphere program. Images of European barbers from the Middle Ages now shine in the holo-screens of her improved surgery room. One screen depicts a demonstration of a medieval tooth extraction; on another, a man with a flowing white beard directs the blood from a patient's arm into a brass bowl sitting in his lap. Three of the screens illustrate various limb amputations. Sweeny scoops a palm full of potatoes from one of the breakfast plates and continues her studies.

All the bottles of intoxicants are piled along with the ice buckets and discarded food plates into a corner on top of that stupid painting. The examination table has been returned to its proper place in the middle of the room.

Sweeny reviews her patient database. She has assisted Doc with hundreds of customers over the years, most of who are probably in Somnus now, but surely, some are in need of a follow-up exam.

The Call

Sentry Alert!
Message for: Marcos-80.
You're late for your follow-up visit. Your condition
will severely deteriorate unless you arrange an
immediate consultation.

"Carlos, have you contacted anyone as Marcos-eighty since we left Bay City?" Sonia's voice carries an accusing tone over the chime of her terminal.

The question surprises him. "No. I was only in Bay City for a couple weeks, no one there knows me." Carlos comes to the front room of their apartment to find his sister sitting at the kitchen table with her terminal, peering at the wall through her data spectacles.

When he approaches, she passes him another pair of spectacles. "Have a look."

His citizen profile picture from five years ago greets him with the title Marcos-80 along with the veiled threat printed to the right of his picture.

He pulls the spectacles away. "What is this?"

Sonia throws him a suspicious look through the wire rims surrounding her eyes.

"No. Sonia, no, I promise. I've followed all your directions since we moved."

She slides the lenses to the bridge of her nose and rubs her dry eyes. "I was afraid of that. I have a sentry programmed to watch for activity referencing any of our names. This message was posted about six hours ago to the general services board. It originated from a terminal inside A Moveable Face in Antioch."

Carlos vaguely recalls the late-night drive following his surgery. "That was five years ago, why would Doc want to contact me now?"

"Us. There is a similar message for Lauren-twenty-five, and Larry didn't send it." Sonia sits back in her chair with a frustrated expression. "The Guardian logged Larry-fifteen as a terminated defector seventeen hours ago."

Sonia betrays a panicked gasp. "If Civil Security queries the Guardian for Marcos-eighty, do you know what they'll find?"

"They'll find hundreds of Marcos-eighties in North America," he says.

Sonia nods. "How many of those have a relationship with Lauren-twenty-five, whose lifeclock expired over a year and a half ago? How many are associated with A Moveable Face?"

Carlos ponders for a moment. "The same Lauren who shared a cab with Marcos, five years ago, and he will have a summary that says he's thirty years old."

"The Brigade will be all over us," Sonia says.

Carlos drags a chair next to Sonia and takes her hand. "What should we do?"

"We'll find out soon. The message is tagged with a read alert; the poster was informed as soon as I opened it."

"Do they know where we are?"

Sonia shrugs. "I'm navigating anonymously, so he, she," she steadied her voice, "or they, knows the message has been viewed, but that's all."

A moment later, a video LINCC request sounds. When Sonia accepts, Sweeny appears in the vid-LINCC window wearing her nurse's cap over her tightly gelled hair. "Hello? Where are you? I can't see."

Carlos places his hand on Sonia's shoulder. "That's all right, I can see you, Barber-ah is it?"

"That's just a generic title. Call me Nurse Sweeny." Her face contorts suspiciously. "You took your time getting back to me, Marcos-eighty."

"I stay away from the aether boards," he answers with a silent nod from his sister.

"Well, it's a good thing you answered. I haven't heard from your little plaything yet. Where is Lauren-twenty-five?"

"I haven't talked to Lauren in years. Why?"

"Too bad for her, she shouldn't ignore me." Sweeny has a distant look. He is clearly her second choice.

"What do you want, Sweeny?"

"Nurse Sweeny!" she barks before returning to her clinical voice. "I told you, your condition will deteriorate unless you keep your appointment with me. I have an opening in two hours. I expect you to be on time."

"I need eight hours," Carlos counters.

"No!" she snaps. "I said you will be on time. Unless you rather I refer your case for a second opinion. I believe the reapers know any number of specialists who can—"

"That isn't necessary. What I meant to say is if you are still in Antioch, I need eight hours to at least try to contact Lauren and get there by hover-pod."

Sweeny's face fills the monitor as she leans toward it with a contemptuous glare. "You said you couldn't contact her."

"I said that I haven't talked to her, but I think I can find her so that her..." he recalls her words, "...condition doesn't deteriorate either."

Sweeny responds through a rigid jaw. "Eight hours. No more. The three of us will find a proper... treatment." The transmission closes.

Sonia sits bewildered for a moment. "Marcos?"

It is the first time in years that she has called him by his original name. "It's Carlos now, and you're not going anywhere near that crazy bitch." He works a rocker switch on his silver pocket clock. Large amber characters against a black screen display:

Carlos-92
9118.9714 Days
24.9964 Years

"Twelve days," he mutters as he works the control again until it displays the Collective's common time. "Eight hours from now will be fourteen hundred hours CCT. That may be enough time for me to find something we can use on her or come to some sort of an arrangement."

"You're not really going," she protests.

Despite the surgical changes, Carlos can still see the frightened little girl who followed him into the tunnels all those years ago. "I'll deal with her."

Sonia begins to shake her head.

Placing his hands on the side of her face, he says, "You have twelve days to find the railroad. When you do, don't wait."

Sonia launches from her chair. "No! We can deal with her better together. We watch out for each other—"

"You need to find the railroad. I can't help you with that. Once I deal with the Barber-ah, I'll check for your departure instructions on the personal announcements board." He takes her hand, their lifeclocks flash, green-white, green-white, green–. Then he lays a gentle kiss on her forehead.

The Appointment

Surface Rd: 8-10.75 hours, w/1, 30 min recharge @ or
near Fresno, 30.5 credits
EER: 3-4 hours, 70 credits
Transit Tube: < 1.2 hours, 180 credits

A scrap of wrapping paper holds these figures, scribbled in Carlos's handwriting next to a crude sketch of the streets surrounding A Moveable Face in Antioch.

Carlos's hover-pod winds along the South Diego residential district. It's an unsettled ride as the pod constantly adjusts its speed and direction to avoid obstructions. Occasionally, when the auto-nav determines the area is clear of people and property, it passes over small pieces of debris that are launched from the lev-field's impact, clearing the street for subsequent vehicles.

South Diego civil engineers don't allocate the same resources for maintaining the travel ways in this district as they do for the higher rent commerce areas.

This is a fool's errand. Carlos can't escape this thought. *The Charon Brigade might be investigating Marcos-80 and Lauren-25 at this very moment. This trip can only draw their attention, regardless of the Barber-ah's threats. For that matter, she could be working with them. If that is the case, I've exhausted the toll, along with Sonia's chances of escape, for nothing.*

Most of the resources and information the siblings have traded in the Shadow Lands required chemicals, but transportation such as hover-pods and rail-busses are paid for with credits. Selling four canisters from their toll gave him more than enough credits to pay for passage through the transit tube, with plenty to spare.

The hover-pod veers onto a rail junction that lifts it into a cylindrical tube, which merges with the high-velocity transit tube system. The pod's lev-field disengages as it enters the mass-drive coil, accelerating it to a speed comparable to the air-vehicles that once commuted this route. Designed for long-distance travel, the transit tubes operate on a dedicated energy system that isolates them from the periodic disruptions of the district power grids. This makes it the fastest and most expensive way to travel in the Collective.

The pod's acceleration presses Carlos into his seat. Steam forms from his breath in the canopy's interior. He crushes the scrap of wrapping paper with his crude map into a ball and jams it to the bottom of his pocket.

Carlos is bothered by the Barber-ah, and not just for her extortion. There is something familiar about her. She has a quality that reminds him of the pack. *She won't be bribed,* he reasons. *She wants something that can't be purchased with credits or chemicals.*

Purchasing pharmaceuticals with credits is easy. Selling them for credits, however, brings immediate attention from the other dealers in the district unless done at a heavy loss. Four canisters gave him a substantial credit account for his needs, although it is considerably less than the months of savings it took to purchase them. He kept one packet of stimulant tabs to trade.

Dealing in the Shadow Lands is different from trading in Outland. Trades were straightforward in the pack. Every canine was responsible for contributing earnings to the gathering, how the earnings appeared and who shared them was sometimes a more complicated process.

Carlos closes his eyes and welcomes the memories from his childhood. They pull him away from this useless operation.

Long ago, in Balcarce

The private security guard wouldn't start his patrol for another ninety minutes.

A standard crystal-metric lock secured the heavy gate to the delivery bay of the Electronic Wonder Shop. The lock was designed to release when the appropriate lifeclock was scanned and was a standard security mechanism for the commerce district of the Balcarce Mall.

Four canines descended upon the gate's latch. Samuel, the oldest of the four, barked at the others as though he were in charge of the forage. "You better be right about this."

"I told you, I saw them off-loading six containers just before the sales door closed." Douglas assured him for the third time.

"It better be, or you will answer for it!" Samuel snapped with his standard threat.

Such challenges and accusations were customary among the pack. Position and respect had to be maintained as well as earned. However, canines understood that such barking is generally suspended when foraging. No words passed between them, but Samuel had just become weaker in the eyes of the other three.

Samuel knew the other three didn't want him on the forage, but they needed him, or more precisely, they needed what he was supposed to do for them. "You three watch for guards, I'll open the gate." Samuel removed the jammer from his coat pocket and started fastening it onto the latch, just above the crystal reader.

A protest erupted from one of the boys. "We agreed; I'm going to open the gate!"

Samuel answered the outburst with a slap. "You've never done it. Stay quiet!"

No one knew how Samuel came into possession of the jammer, it's not a tool that can be purchased or traded for in the market. Nevertheless, as long as he had it, and shared its use, his position was secure in the pack.

When he finally pulled his attention from his challenger, Samuel realizes the rest of the party had surrounded him. Douglas spoke with uncharacteristic authority. "No, he hasn't. But most of the time you screw the lock up so bad we go back empty. Let him try."

Samuel started to slip the jammer into his pocket as if to leave when spikes appeared from the sleeves and socks of the other three. Douglas insists, "Give it to him now."

Samuel hands the jammer to the boy and says, "If you mess this up, if we are empty at the assembly, you will answer for it."

"You said that already!" The boy ripped the device from Samuel's grip.

The forage party watched as the boy glided the jammer across the lock. Symbols flashed on a tiny display window as it scanned the mechanism. He hadn't completed the first pass before Samuel started in. "You're taking too long, that's not how it..."

With the flip of a thumb switch, a field of green light projected from the jammer onto the lock, dampening the sound of a needle-like probe that penetrated the case and into the central processor of the crystal sensor.

Samuel's tirade was silenced when the latch released with a click. Marcos removed the jammer from the latch, leaving a small hole burned into the case. The status light had permanently changed from red to green. The gate drifted open.

"Good job, Marcos!"

"That was fast!"

Samuel was silently enraged at the quick success and praise Marcos had achieved. He wanted to tear him apart and would if he hesitated for a moment to return his property.

Without a word, Marcos turned to face him. Samuel expected to see Marcos's typical, passive expression; instead, he was met with a smug, contemptuous glare. He had changed a lot since the sniveling little brat that used to hang around his neck ran away.

Marcos offered the jammer to Samuel, who was ready to tear it from his grasp. The other two reached out to stay his hand. "Marcos will hold on to the jammer for now," said another. "We can discuss this at the assembly."

Now, in Antioch

Carlos stands in front of the locked glass door, cupping one hand above his eyes to see inside. His other hand operates the device he hides at his waist that projects a green field of light onto the lock. With a mechanical click, the latch engagement light permanently changes from red to green. A small hole burnt into the case of the lock remains. The door to the clinic freely moves as Carlos slips the jammer under his coat.

A shadow moves on the wall inside, announcing the return of the Barber-ah. Carlos steps away from the door, back onto the street, just as she sits down in front of a data terminal at her reception desk.

He returns to his sidewalk table in front of the teahouse across the street, where he continues to nurse a pot of black tea. The sun is getting low in the sky, casting longer and longer shadows across the street. His sidewalk table gives him a perfect angle to survey the front office of A Moveable Face.

A terminal window hovers a few centimeters in front of his data spectacles with the caption at the lower right corner, displaying 2x. Carlos mutters a command from behind his mug, "Four times." The image magnifies by another factor, revealing the woman in white tapping the side of her face with a long, white stylus, occasionally using it to jab at a keypad. The spectacles amplify the light from her terminal screen to reveal her features as the same person who contacted him six hours ago.

She will spend a few minutes at the terminal, scribbling a note or two onto a pad before returning to the back of the clinic. When she disappears down the hallway, Carlos steps across the street.

Moving into the reception area, he eases the door closed behind him. A sign points down the hallway that reads Examination Room. The clinic is haunted with soft moans and cries that murmur from that direction. A pungent aroma hangs in the air, warning him that he should leave.

The display on Sweeny's terminal is filled with a contact list holding close to a hundred names and procedures. Marcos-80 and Lauren-25 jump to his attention. Within seconds, Carlos clears the databases and their backups. To his surprise, Sweeny had left her aether account open on the terminal.

Sonia would be furious, he thinks. Even when she works alone in a closed-off room with the door locked, she never leaves a LINCC account connection open when not in use.

Entering a few commands calls up a window to the terminal screen. Carlos calls up an algorithm to overwrite all aether databases related to Sweeny's account with the empty version on her terminal. Then, it will replace her account encryption with a level-29 version, permanently locking her out. A similar instruction block will search the LINCC for all aether board postings associated with her account and remove them.

The display scrolls a list of files that will be affected by the algorithm and asks to confirm execution just as the floor spins out from under Carlos's feet.

He barely feels his head slam against the table before hitting the floor. A small dart protrudes from his neck.

Sweeny lowers the stylus-blowgun from her lips. Seconds pass, the intruder lies still. She directs her attention to an unlit corner of the waiting room. "You, put him onto the examination table."

Shadows obscure a figure sitting in a chair. Knees protrude into the dim light. The figure watches the events unfold. It recognizes that a command had been issued in its direction, yet doesn't move.

A soft, synthetic voice answers, "Model-3 does not recognize the directions *you* or *examination table*."

Sweeny tosses her head back in frustration. "Oh, you're useless! I said load him…" The correct command escapes her. She moves to the terminal at the reception desk, then slams the keyboard. "Where is it?" She hysterically kicks the trespasser in the side before regaining her composure.

The unconscious man coughs in response.

Following an aether query, a new copy of the operation manual for the Model-3 robotic warehouse and shipping worker appears on Sweeny's screen. After a few minutes of scribbling onto a message pad, she addresses the figure in the shadow.

"M-3, WALK to my desk."

At her command, the robot rises from the chair and steps into the light. The synthetic worker stands a little taller than 1.7 meters with the general frame of a man and wears a grocer's utility apron tied around its neck and waist. It approaches Sweeny's desk in silence.

The Model-3 has an impression of a brow and nose line where a human face would be. Two optical sensors occupy the indentations under its brow line, allowing the robot adequate depth perception to follow the *walk* command until it reaches the area indicated as *desk*.

Sweeny references her notes. Pointing down at Carlos, she assigns the task: "LIFT the patient off the ground. MOVE it down the hall into the next room. Then PLACE it onto the table."

"Patient," Model-3 inquires. "Please clarify."

Sweeny has to continually learn that the M-3 is sensitive to receiving its commands in the correct format. Kneeling next to the intruder's head, she places her hand on his shoulder and consults her notes again. "PATIENT is another word for CARTON. MOVE it as you would a carton with breakable contents." Sweeny again emphasizes the actionable commands for M-3.

Before moving, the robot addresses Sweeny. "Should the Model-3 designate all patients as fragile?"

"Fine." Sweeny grunts. "I mean, yes. Please handle all patients as fragile."

The robot moves to the man's side, extends an arm, and slides it under his legs. With the other arm, M-3's claw reaches toward his neck.

"No!" Sweeny commands. "That part of the patient is not..." she refers to the manual on her terminal screen, "...load-bearing."

M-3 complies by sliding its arm under his back and lifts him onto its shoulder. Down the hallway, the mechanical worker delivers its load into Sweeny's private surgery.

Dark-brown-crusted linen strips dangle from a three-and-a-half meter pole erected on a heavy support base just inside the door. The pole once supported the holo-screens in Larry-15's blues club. Movers from the Media Studio misplaced it when they disassembled the structure.

When the movers had left, Sweeny directed M-3 to retrieve the truss along with its weighted base, where it had been lost behind the surgical chamber. She painted her pole white and fastened a brass bowl along with a pulley and cord at the top before erecting it next to the doorway.

Red streaks have transferred onto the white surface of the barber pole from the bandages that dance about in the breeze of a fan. The ribbons caress Carlos's face as the robot passes through the doorway toward a blood-stained operating table.

Chapter 12

Patient History

Pain approaches Carlos slowly. The closer he works his way into consciousness, the more pronounced it becomes. Something is wrong with his jaw. He tries to reach for it, but his arm won't move.

His eyes adjust. The room clarifies from a dim blur into shapes. A pungent aroma greets his consciousness; its smell suggests something terrible.

Muffled groans call in the distance. He tries to reach for his face again. This time, he recognizes the bite of knotted cords restraining his wrists. He tries to call out, a muffled grunt responds. A cloth is tied around his head and jammed between his teeth.

Carlos is strapped to a recliner. His wrists and legs are bound to the floor.

A white figure responds to his stirring. It glides to his side with the sound of rollers, grabs his fingers, and passes something over the back of his hand. A tone sounds. His lifeclock has been scanned.

The outline of the Barber-ah from the message board fills in a half meter above him. She has that stylus clenched in her teeth, occasionally removing it to jab the keys on a terminal mounted on a pushcart.

"Carlos-92. You almost wrecked my records." Sweeny points the stylus at his face. "Altering a medic's files is a serious infraction. I'll be informing the Judiciary of it when we have completed our business."

He can see the tip of another dart mounted at the end of the stylus.

She pushes the terminal away and gives Carlos her full attention. "I'm going to remove the gag. You can yell all you want because the clinic is completely soundproof." She holds the stylus to his face. "But if you become unpleasant, I'll have to boost your medication, understand?"

Her face moves in and out of focus. Carlos isn't sure what he is hearing is real.

Sweeny slaps him, which whips his face back and forth. "Hey! Are you listening to me?" She emphasizes each word in a loud disciplinary voice. "Do. You. Un—Der—Stand. Me?"

Though the Barber-ah's slaps are muffled through the sedation, the sharp sounds of her fingers cracking against his face raises his heart rate enough for him to pull away.

Sweeny loosens the gag, allowing it to hang around his neck, then pulls the cart over with her terminal. She shouts, "Now I need to take a patient history. Marcos-eighty had this appointment slot, but you showed up instead. Carlos-ninety-two, why is that?"

"I, I need…" He struggles to find the words.

"Come on; I have other patients waiting." She motions across the room with her stylus.

Carlos can see four other bodies propped against the wall, tethered to a ring bolted to the floor. He can't tell if any are conscious or even breathing.

Is this a game to her? he thinks. "Marcos gave me his appointment."

"He can't just replace his appointment, that's not how it's done." She returns to her terminal.

"What is his appointment for?"

"I don't discuss my patient's condition," she snaps. "That's unethical!"

"I understand, but if my condition requires urgent attention, shouldn't that take priority?"

Sweeny glares at him with suspicion etched on her face. She moves from her stool and hovers over Carlos. "What condition is that?"

Carlos faces a terrifying mixture of excitement and curiosity. He feels like an insect, looking up to a magnified view of the sun framed by a giant lens.

All I can do now is stall.

Counting Up

Sonia hadn't slept much in the last eleven days, nor had she turned away from her terminal, except for the infrequent periods when her eyes unintentionally closed. She hoped for a message from Carlos or a response to one of her postings. Neither came.

Try as she might, she can't keep her pocket clock closed. It stays on the table next to her terminal set to display *Sonia-10 Days and Years.*

0.0001 year resolves to approximately fifty-two-and-a-half minutes. No matter how many times she tries to look away, the amber numbers of the clock's display linger in her mind.

24.9974 Years,
24.9975 Years,
24.9976 Years.

When the display rolls to 24.9977 years, 9130.2500 days, she looks to her lifeclock flashing on the back of her hand. Red-pink, red-pink, red, then black. Red-black, red-black, red-black. She has entered Last-Day.

Tears fall from her eyes as an unintentional sob breaks through her throat, followed by a wave of terror and then relief. "At least it's no longer in front of me," she whispers.

Exhausted, she snaps the clock case shut, closes the shade over the window, and falls asleep.

It's not a restful nap. She awakes a couple of hours before sunset and checks the boards for any message. Nothing.

She remembers all the times she and Carlos thought they were leaving their tiny apartment for the last time as the door latches behind her.

She walks the mall all night, waiting for another idea to present itself.

Her satchel carries her getaway provisions, along with the toll bag and the last two canisters. Priya is tucked in a tote bag lined with the signal-dampening resin sheet in which his lifeclock had arrived.

Flashing lights and grinding music cascade down the walkways of the Prime Mall of South Diego. Men and women in their late Blue and early Red Cycles dance behind cages made of silver mesh. They wave to Sonia as she passes, inviting her to join them inside. Clusters of citizens stumble past her. Each party supports one or two people trying to ignore the blinking lifeclock in their hands. The clusters move through the parlors and lounges, experiencing all the pleasures credits can buy.

A band of partygoers swagger down the street and embrace Sonia as though they are all friends reuniting. One of the women calls out to her, "We've been looking for you, girl! You shouldn't be here by yourself."

A male voice chimes in, "Come with us; we know all the best places."

Their arms wrap around Sonia's shoulders and waist. Another female voice whispers in her ear, "We can get lost if you want to go with the guys." Sonia turns to a girl with bedroom eyes, who nods in the direction of three smiling males in their late Blue Cycle. "Or if you prefer, it can be just us girls tonight." She flashes an unnaturally white smile.

"No, I don't think so." Sonia disentangles from their arms.

A male with the face of a thirteen-year-old holds up a medallion impressed with the South Diego Civil Commerce Bureau insignia. "It's okay; we're licensed." His blue lifeclock shimmers against the large silver coin dangling from a chain. The rest of the group displays the same medal hanging from charm bracelets and necklaces. He says, "You can ask any civil officer you want, and they'll tell you, we're all registered."

White-Teeth hugs the boy and smiles again. "Ya, kiddo. Come with us, and we'll take care of you all night."

"And we make sure nothing or no one bothers you." An older man adds.

"Unless you want them…" White-Teeth corrects.

He nods. "Well, sure. We won't cramp your style or nothin'."

"It's a matter of civic pride that your Last-Day is the Best-Day," another says. They all nod in agreement.

"I need to go, perhaps some other time." Sonia rushes away, desperate to avoid their loving waves. She quickens her pace and steps into the defensive hands of another man with a blue lifeclock wearing a bright-green vest.

"Whoa, slow down, doll, you almost knocked me over."

Sonia makes eye contact. Before she can break it, he moves his hands away and says, "Hey, I don't blame you for running from those professional mourners; they give me the creeps too. Oh sure, they laugh with you all night as you buy them drinks and pay their way through the parlors, all the while tipping them to perform things for you that you never ask for." He leans in confidently and whispers, "And quite honestly would rather forget, believe me."

Sonia steps away and stammers, "I need to go."

Green-Vest puts his arm around her shoulder. "You know *The Stairway to the Sky* gives them a bonus if they bring you in before your clock turns black."

Sonia releases a disgusted grunt.

Green-Vest nods his head in agreement. "I know, it's gruesome, as if an intelligent woman like you needs their help calling the Citadel's complimentary shuttle service! Don't they understand that tonight should be all about you?" He pats her shoulder and presents the flashing sign, the same color as his vest, hanging above an entranceway. "That's what we're all about here at *The Lifetime Review*. Our recollection specialists will take you on a tour of your fondest memories. In here, you can relive the best of your twenty-five years! Would you like to experience your greatest achievement again? Or perhaps your first love affair? Or maybe your first kiss? It's all waiting for you." He presses a coupon into her hand. "And for the next hour, we will double your dose for free."

Green-Vest's pitch reminds Sonia of the blond street musician she followed to the back of the library when she was a girl. She remembers being excited, confused, and a little afraid then. Now, all that is mixed together with this obnoxious delinquent, reminding her that she is about to die.

She pulls away from Green-Vest, and another voice calls to her. "He can only take you backward; you should spend your last hours making new memories!" Another sixteen-year-old man approaches from across the street with a fistful of coupons. This one wears heavy glasses with thick black frames. "Come to *Experience Extreme*." He motions back to a flashing light board. "We have the most proficient memory experts in the Collective ready to give you every experience you desire."

"Sure, by scrambling your brain!" Green-Vest grabs her arm. "*The Lifetime Review* is all real. We give you actual experiences. Their machines are going to mess with your brain, make you all confused. With us, you get the real thing."

Glasses grabs her other arm. "Listen to this guy; he's trying to sell you what you already have! Sure, they give you the real thing, mixed up with all the mistakes and regrets." He challenges Green-Vest. "Why don't you tell her the truth? Your customers suffer overwhelming melancholy after you pump them up with your drugs. At *Experience Extreme*, we don't deal in regret, we fix it. Have you ever wondered what would have happened if you had turned left instead of right? What if you left that guy instead of giving him another chance? Did you chicken out at your only opportunity to base-jump from the top of Half Dome? You can do all that and more in our experience chamber, and it always works out just the way *you want*."

"Sure, if *you want* to leave a helpless drooling idiot," Green-Vest insists, pulling her back. "Seriously, lady, medics are always called to *Experience Extreme* to wheel their comatose customers away on stretchers. You don't want to go out like that, do you?"

Green-Vest and Glasses tug Sonia back and forth. Their pitches elevate, as does the ringing in her ears. Panicked, she pulls the wrist of Green-Vest to her mouth and sinks her teeth into his hand. When he lets go, Sonia grabs the back of his neck and with a frantic tug, launches the top of her head under his chin, sending him stumbling against the wall.

Delighted that his pitch has won, Glasses smiles. Sonia's knee launches into his groin. He buckles forward, still holding onto her forearm. She pulls him into the point of her free elbow that smashes across the bridge of his nose. Blood gushes from his face as he hits the ground.

The two men help one another to their feet as Sonia runs away.

"What the fuck's her problem?" asks Glasses in a gurgling, nasal voice.

"Hell if I know, the bitch just doesn't appreciate someone trying to help."

Sonia collapses onto a public bench. Tears burn her eyes and blur her vision as the adrenaline passes from her blood. Sonia recalls many evenings with friends or friends of friends on Last-Day tribute parties in Bay City. Most of the time, they disappeared into a fog of anxiety stabilizers that melted away all feeling and emotion long before entering Somnus.

Spotlights blaze across the marble slabs covering the stacked segments of the Somnolence Citadel spire, reaching into the dark early-morning sky. Even during the day, citizens standing at its base have a hard time distinguishing the segments ascending to the steeple's point.

Although she has lived in the city for five years, and heard of it many times, this is the first time Sonia has ever seen *The Stairway to the Sky*.

Somehow, I never thought I'd have to deal with this, she tells herself as she hugs the tired shorthaired cat in her arm.

Priya protests his confinement again. It's time for a runabout. *What will I do with you?* she wonders. Sonia can see the lifeclock embedded inside the dark-brown hair on his left hind leg glowing red in the early-morning darkness. *I can't just leave you like this. Will the Citadel attendants take care of you?* She shudders at the euphemism *take care of.*

A door opens at the base of the spire. Sonia mutters the command to her data specs, "Four times." A telescopic window appears. The magnified image shows the face of the receptionist waving to her as though he is happy with the arrival of a long-awaited friend.

Sonia coaxes Priya from her lap into his tote bag. *I wonder if I can get a cup of tea in there.*

Final Treatment

Darkness.

That miserable pungent smell.

Consciousness pulls Carlos into the harsh illumination of the examination room. Straps immobilize his arms and legs. *How long have I been here?* he wonders. *Days? More than a week?* Against every wish not to, he forces his eyes open.

A click echoes and the green clinical light empties from the room. Sweeny's silhouetted figure stands in the light of the doorway, meticulously fastening something to the pole.

With a half step back, she tugs on a cord. A metallic ring sings out as something ascends like a flag up the length of the barber pole. She leaves the room with her crimson pennants drying in the breeze of the fan.

Carlos wishes he had looked away before remembering that the bandages are soaked with the blood of Sweeny's previous patient. Those same bandages will soon clean his wounds— again. If he turns away, he will see the other victims of her care, stacked against the wall.

He closes his eyes. It's a mistake. The memory of Sweeny's last patient is waiting for him. He was strapped to the table just as Carlos is now.

Carlos can clearly see the patient's arm encased in a sleeve of industrial material tacked to a wooden plank and extended from the table. An opening in the sleeve reveals the inside crook of his elbow, where his artery runs close to the skin, ready to receive Sweeny's intimate care. The restraint immobilizes the arm without restricting the patient's blood flow.

The Barber-ah sits on a stool next to the patient balancing a large brass bowl in her lap. The table had been raised, so the patient's chest is almost level with her shoulders, and the restraining board with his arm slants down and hovers above the bowl.

She ignores the exhausted grunts from her patient's tightly bound jaw. His head is twisted, helplessly watching as she steadies her hand on his quivering forearm. Carefully, she opens his artery with a double-edged lancet.

The man's eyes are wide with terror.

Sweeny's eyes fill with delight as the metal blade dangles from his arm, keeping the wound open. She draws deep, excited breaths as her fingers caress the restraining sleeve holding his arm as though she were drawing the flow down from his heart to trickle into the awaiting brass bowl.

Half a liter of red flows into the receptacle before it is replaced with another, then another, until it stops.

No more struggling; no protest. Sweeny uses the crusted brown linens to wipe away the residual blood from the extremity in slow sensual sweeps.

Carlos shakes to force the vision away.

Another memory flashes into his awareness. He remembers the pressure of Sweeny's knee, pressing into his chest as she drives a metal tool into his mouth. Terrible pain, then a release. Sweeny sits up with a triumphant smile admiring the tooth she just twisted from his jaw, mounted at the tip is a shiny chrome corkscrew. Blood drops down the metal spiral glimmering in the light of the examination lamp. He tastes blood running down the back of his throat. He has the sensation of being lifted from the table by the robot worker taking him to the surgical chamber before he passes out.

Nanobots repair his infected organs in the surgical chamber, replacing lost fluids and infusing his body with nutrients he would normally get from eating.

Carlos struggles against his exhaustion from Sweeny's repeated treatments, which include the compliance chemicals she generously administers from the dart in her stylus. Sometimes they depress him so he is easy to move; other times they raise his heart rate allowing for a more efficient bloodletting. Her stimulants also ensure that her patients are fully aware of the treatment they receive.

Despite the horrors of consciousness, Carlos struggles toward it. He draws the foul air of the surgery into his lungs and begins to pull against his restraints. His bindings hold firm, but the effort raises his heart rate, bringing him closer to lucidity.

His eyes begin to adjust to the dim light. The fog lifts enough for him to recognize his right arm extended across the now familiar rigid surface, encased in the restrictive sleeve once again. He is also aware of the hush dominating the room. A voice silently tells him, *I'm the last.*

Carlos's awareness is punished with the sound of footsteps approaching. With a soft click, Sweeny appears in the examination lamp. The stylus with the dart affixed to the end is clenched in her teeth. She wears an apron that is smeared with the blood of her clientele.

Sweeny removes the apron revealing her pristine white uniform. She yanks the gag from Carlos's mouth and then takes the stylus from her teeth. "I have made progress diagnosing your condition," she states in a dispassionate tone while gesturing with the stylus. Pneumatics hiss under the table as it lowers. She raises the arm restraint parallel to his chest. Grabbing his fingers, she twists his hand over to display his lifeclock. She jabs the blunt end of her stylus onto his hand. "You have a most fascinating disorder. It seems your lifeclock is holding someone else's identity. I am right, aren't I, Marcos-eighty?"

Sweeny watches his expression change at the mention of the long-lost name. With the excitement of a child opening a present, she abandons her clinical demeanor. "I am right. Somehow you changed your identity!"

"It's probably a defective crystal," he mumbles through the swelling in his mouth from his recent extractions. "It should be removed."

Sweeny squeezes his jaw, causing Carlos to wince in her grip. "Not yet!" She stares into his eyes with that familiar thrill. "What's interesting is that Marcos-eighty is over thirty years old and has yet to enter Somnus."

Sweeny draws her skirt up to her waist and climbs onto the operating table straddling Carlos. She rests her elbows on his shoulders and leans into his expressionless countenance. Her chest presses against his. "I remember your last visit, Marcos." She combs her fingers through his damp scalp. "And I remember the little pet you brought with you, her name was Lauren-twenty-five." Her hand cups the side of his face, directing his eyes to hers. "You told me you couldn't contact her. I think that was only a half-lie." Her finger slides down the ridge of Carlos's nose. "Maybe you can't contact Lauren-twenty-five because she is someone else now."

Her fingernails scratch down Carlos's throat, leaving three parallel red paths, which she caresses with her fingertips.

His pulse thunders under her touch. Leaning to his ear, she speaks in a soft, seductive voice, "If you tell me, I'll let you go." Carlos releases an unintended shudder when Sweeny squeezes her thighs against his hips. "You can use the chamber and walk out of here, fully cured."

Bile bubbles to the back of Carlos's throat at her touch.

"I, told you, on the vid, I don't, know, where Sonia is…" His inner voice cries out, *SHIT!*

Sweeny erupts with joy. "Sonia! Lauren-twenty-five is Sonia. That's her new name, isn't it? Sonia what? What is her designation?"

Carlos closes his eyes and grinds his jaw. *What did I just do?* He rages in silence before releasing a grunt of pain. Sweeny's knee jabs into Carlos's stomach as she jumps off the table and skips out of the room.

✧ ✧ ✧

Sweeny nearly crashes into her desk in the reception office before taking her seat at her terminal. *I know I can convince him to tell me,* she thinks, *but that will be more frustrating than fulfilling.* Her terminal screen holds the results of the last citizen query she ran. Lauren-25 and Marcos-80 have no entries in their profiles since leaving A Moveable Face five years ago. Sweeny launches a new search in the Collective's citizen directory, then cues her terminal's voice input. "Search all citizens in the North American region. Name, Sonia; Designation, any; descending."

Thousands of Sonia's with their numeric designation scroll across the vid-screen in order of their designation from highest to lowest.

Sweeny recalls the window from a recent query. It displays the last transaction for Carlos-92 prior to his arrival at the clinic. Carlos had chartered a hover-pod from Sector-285, South Diego.

"Filter current name list who are in Final-Quarter and are located in South Diego."

The terminal returns an error.

Please specify the value: Final-Quarter.
Please specify location: South Diego.
Please specify order.

Sweeny grabs the side of the terminal. *Why are these things so infuriating?* She takes in a stabilizing breath. "Filter current list of names with an age equal to or greater than 24.75 years, located in Sector-285, South Diego, descending."

The query returns nine names.

"Filter current list of names with a relationship with either Carlos-ninety-two or Marcos-eighty."

Insufficient criteria: Relationship.
Unable to process search term.

Sweeny slaps the desk with her palm. Extracting the information from her patient is becoming more appealing.

"Okay, we'll do this the long way. Display citizen profiles for Sonia-seventy-eight."

✧ ✧ ✧

In the examination room, Carlos can hear the queries from the front office. He rasps in rage, "I did it to you again, Jul—" The sound of his voice pulls him back from his self-pity. *She left the gag off.*

Twisting against the table's restraints, Carlos calls to the shadows in a soft, deliberate voice, "M-3, walk, to the, examination, table."

No response. He is about to call out again when the featureless face moves into the light above him, awaiting the next command.

A half-day training course in the Torres del Paine National Park gave Carlos a working knowledge of operating the Model-4 robotic field and agricultural worker. The M-4 was a tireless assistant capable of heavy clearance and obstruction removal when human workers were unavailable. Commands had to be formatted correctly for M-4 to follow; however, if the correct command isn't readily available, they could be queried through the on-demand user manual.

"M-3, does your function include moving cartons that have been secured on platforms for shipping?"

"Yes." The soft, synthetic voice echoes in the empty chamber causing Carlos to wince.

"M-3, reduce response volume by fifty percent," he demands in a hush. "M-3, when cartons are secured onto a platform, what is the command to remove the restraint bands, straps, or ties for off-loading?"

"The Model-3 robotic warehouse and shipping worker is equipped to sever straps that secure cartons to transport platforms before off-loading."

Answering such requests is standard operation for industrial model robots. That Sweeny hadn't learned to use the on-demand user manual has been an ongoing secret source of pleasure for Carlos during his confinement. She had to constantly storm out of surgery every time the robot refused to follow her direction and spend tens of minutes at her terminal, finding the most rudimentary commands in the full text of the Model-3 operation manual.

"M-3, *sever* all straps securing the patient to the examination table."

The robot extends his claw to the table. An electronic whirl sounds; M-3's claw morphs into a pair of industrial sheers. With surgical efficiency, each strap on the examination table is isolated and cut without damaging the fragile carton.

Free to move for the first time in days, Carlos tries to climb off the table. Atrophy and trauma from Sweeny's treatment have weakened his muscles; they collapse under his weight.

Clenched teeth muffle Carlos's pain. Sweeny's voice from the front office drifts through the darkness. "...Profile for Sonia-43."

"M-3, recite inventory for this room," he rasps.

The sterile voice begins its meticulous report.

"1, Model-5 surgical chamber.

1, Model-31 full-body medical scanner.

1, standard office desk..."

As the robot delivers the requested report, Carlos tries once again to move off the table, he fails. M-3's report suddenly grabs his attention.

"M-3, location of previous item."

"Collection of indeterminate packages located to the right of four non-functioning patients placed next to rear-facing wall."

"My pack must be in there," Carlos mutters. He looks to the back of the room where Sweeny's patients are piled against the wall. "M-3, resume report."

The mechanical voice continues. Sweeny's bloody surgical tools are presented on a tray beside his table.

He settles onto her rolling stool when his attention snaps to the doorway. The Barber-ah's voice drifts to his attention. "...display citizen profile for Sonia-fifteen."

She's getting close, Carlos thinks.

His gaze shifts to the bandages fluttering in the breeze of the fan as M-3 identifies...

"1, industrial support pole, three point five meters in length, attached to 1, eighty kilogram base."

"M-3, pause report. Walk to the three point five meter support pole you just listed."

At her reception desk, Sweeny claps her hands in triumph. Three windows on her terminal display three citizen profiles.

Sonia-10's age is one digit older than Carlos-92's. They both currently reside in Sector-285, South Diego, and Sonia's profile picture is an older, shorthaired, redheaded duplicate of Lauren-25. "That's her!"

Jumping from her desk, she rushes down the hall to her surgery room with an overwhelming need to gloat in front of her last patient before dispatching him.

Upon entering, Sweeny finds Carlos slouching on her stool, leaning against the wall in the light of the doorway. His fist is balled around one of her lancets.

She glares at the pathetic sight and slowly raises the blow dart stylus to her lips, then pauses to mock the pitiful sight. "You can't possibly think you're going to…"

"…hundred seventy degrees," Carlos commands.

Sweeny doesn't resolve what her patient has said or that it was not directed at her.

A soft, metallic clank sends her into darkness. There is a crash in the doorway before she hits the floor.

No more than two seconds pass before Sweeny awakens with a splitting headache and a damp sensation covering the side of her face. She opens her eyes just as Carlos's weight falls onto her. Sweeny's head erupts in pain as he presses it into the floor.

She screams hysterically, "Get off me! M-3 grab…"

Her cry ceases when the blade plunges into her throat. Sweeny is aware of the sawing motion that severs her larynx and opens the artery that brings forth a bright-red fountain pulsating in time with her racing heart.

When the struggling stops and the throbbing fountain subsides, Carlos rests his head on her chest.

He calls to his mechanical accomplice standing by the doorway, balancing Sweeny's barber pole on its shoulder. "M-3, are you functioning?"

Silence.

Like the field and agriculture model, M-3 entered standby mode when it detected a worker injury.

"Great." Carlos looks across the room to the surgical chamber. "I'd have appreciated just a little more help."

Chapter 13

Moving On

Sunlight crawls down the spire, illuminating the courtyard in front of the South Diego Citadel in its warm morning glow. Sonia watches the first patron of the day receive a hug from the technician waiting inside its doorway. A deep inhale helps her find the nerve to rise from the bench, just as a chime rings through the kernel in her ear.

The sound pulls her from the peaceful place she spent the last hour trying to find. Again it sounds, then again. She has no interest in answering it.

The streetlights have all dimmed now that the sun is well above the horizon.

The chime sounds.

It could be the woman calling with more demands, she imagines.

The chime sounds.

It might be a message from Carlos. Maybe he came to an understanding with the woman in Antioch. The imaginary conversation is unconvincing.

The chime sounds again.

With a nudge, her spectacles resettle on the bridge of her nose. The display in the lenses comes into focus. A message is blinking.

Message Response: Casey has responded to your query on the Haven board.

Now he answers? She shakes her head in disgust. *Then again, how many queries have I posted for Casey, and how many of them have proven false?*

She considers trashing the message for a moment. This one has a higher encryption level than most; in fact, it matches one she used to query *the Conductor.*

She selects the message, and the window responds:

\# If this is Sonia-10, the woman attempting to contact Casey of the underground railroad, how much are you ready to pay the Conductor for your ticket?

Sonia considers the question. *I've never used my name. How would he know me?*

Sonia removes her terminal from her pack to key in the reply.

> Nothing.

A moment passes before another message appears.

\# Correct. Request audio chat.

Sonia accepts. A picture of a running stick figure framed inside an arrow appears in the window. A heavily filtered voice greets her. "Hello, Sonia-10, I'm glad we can finally talk."

"How do you know me?" she asks.

"There are currently three thousand seven hundred citizens querying the aether for a way to Haven in the North American region alone. Many of them are reapers, pretending to be defectors. Others are desperate defectors fumbling their way through a last-minute attempt to avoid Somnus. They will run head-on into a multitude of ambushes. I'm sure you can appreciate this."

Sonia answers with a silent nod.

The voice continues. "One of these queries uses a specific encryption key that has responded to over three-dozen postings. In six instances, it posted follow-up responses with specific warnings of the traps they represent soon after. The most recent of these was posted about two weeks ago concerning a passkey trap."

Sonia considers the point. Whoever is on the other end of this transmission has access to resources beyond anything the nomads have.

"Okay," she says. "So, am I to assume that you are Casey, the Conductor?"

"You should not," the voice answers. "Casey never responds directly to potential passengers. You will meet him in person at the departure point."

Sonia nods. "There is the matter of a toll, naturally."

"Not for passage on the railway. Your first answer was correct. Casey doesn't take a toll and will refuse it if offered. Passage to the departure point is another matter. You will need to make those arrangements yourself."

"You're saying the departure point is in Outland. Why will the canines let me pass?"

"Casey has a treaty with them. They enable his meetings in exchange for earnings, free of Civil Security and reapers. My research assures the second part, it's up to you to provide the first."

"You are avoiding my question. Why won't they kill me the moment I enter their territory, toll or no? You might be a decoy to bring earnings into the pack."

"Your quarter ends soon; if you want a rock-solid assurance, *The Stairway to the Sky* can oblige. If you know a better path out of the Collective, you should follow it.

"I will arrange a meeting with the canines who control the pass at the northern border in Stadium. When you contact them, mention that your arrangement is through Casey's surrogate, they know he doesn't contact defectors directly. If they ask for your name, present them with this picture of the running stick figure inside an arrow. You can show it to them on a piece of paper or draw it for them on the ground. They will recognize it."

"I don't suppose the canines accept electronics or food?" Sonia asks.

"If by food, you mean speed pads and lysergic foam, then yes. I understand the dangers of transporting such things; fortunately, Stadium has many places where you can trade."

"How much?"

"Generally, if you offer at least two packets per passage, they will get you to Casey unharmed."

Sonia nods. "Expect passage for two."

"Do you really think Carlos is going to make it out of Antioch?"

How can he know about that? "I'm going to give him every chance. Nevertheless, inform your contact I'm bringing payment for two through their territory."

The picture of the running stickman fades to a map. A red star marks the location of her rendezvous. "Make sure you are at this point in three hours. There, you will negotiate your toll. Good luck, Sonia-ten." The transmission severs.

Sonia scribbles the directions to Stadium along with the running stickman into a notebook. "Well, Priya, we have two canisters, I'll need to trade for the balance of the toll and transportation to Stadium."

She rummages through her satchel. A small drawstring bag emerges from one of the interior pockets. Inverting the pouch, the lifeclock writer falls into her palm. Sonia considers the white enamel coating reflecting the color of the morning sky. "You again."

For Passage

Stadium once prospered from the games, concerts, and events that played in the great arena that stands for the district's namesake. Its malls once thrived with the business of entertaining citizens from across the North American region. Stadium no longer has residents as much as it does inmates. Runaways and nomads, who lack skills to operate in the Collective, manage its decayed institutions in the shadow of the Final-Quarter playground.

Weeds dominate the walkway leading into the maintenance tunnel under the dilapidated sports arena. Sonia cradles the lifeclock writer in her palm. As she waits for her contact to arrive, she counts the years of her life against the years she spent teasing out the secrets of her little egg. Its pearl-white case appears jaundice in the tunnel lights that shine with the color of urine onto the iron gates mounted inside a concrete maintenance tunnel.

What would I be doing if I never met you? Her silent question stirs her memory of her late-night interrogation. *That's easy; I would have entered Somnus a long time ago.* She returns the lifeclock writer to the drawstring pouch and back to her satchel. *Still, I'll be glad to be rid of you.*

Her pocket clock confirms three hours until her time expires. "Come on, Carlos, call. Tell me where you are," she says through clenched teeth.

"There's no Carlos here. You talkin' to ya' self, Defector?" Through the gate, a boy approaches from the shadows of the tunnel. "No need to pretend with me, you're a defector. You gonna meet Casey to run away to Haven."

"I came to mix a deal with the pack. Business with Casey is mine, pup. Why don't you run along and let the one that takes the earnings talk."

The canine's eyes flare with a vacant expression common to those who have killed. He jabs his thumb into his chest and says, "This is the pup you mixen' a deal with, Defector! Who the hell are you?"

"All right, all right, no need for cranky! I just came here for two things: one, to pay someone who will lead me to Casey, and two, to shake hands with Casey, simple that." She removes her notebook from her satchel and shows him the picture of a running stick figure inside an arrow. "As for who I am, this gladden you?"

The boy considers the identifying symbol. "Ya, Defector, I can get you there. It's gonna cost you."

Matching his indignant tone, Sonia responds, "Didn't I just say I came to pay? I know everyone has to earn! How many more times I have ta tell ya before you dense brain can understand?"

The canine smiles. "All right, all right, no need for the defector to get cranky. We'll mix some business."

Two green lights shine in the darkness. With a wave from the older canine, a pair of sentries appear.

It's an unwelcome sight for Sonia. *Great!* she thinks. *Now he'll have to show off for them.* "I don't fancy talking in your territory."

"Good," he answers. "'Cuz you ain't been invited, not yet."

The children nod in agreement.

Sonia reaches into the toll bag and removes a packet of capsules. "Let's bring things back to business. I need to arrange passage for two through the pack's territory, and I need to shake hands with Casey himself." As she speaks, Sonia tosses the bag up and catches it, drawing the boy's attention. "If you're the one who can arrange that," she tosses the bag to her guide, "then I need to talk to you."

The boy snatches the bag and pulls it through the bars of the gate. The smaller canines open their eyes wide at the earnings he just made. He considers the weight of the bag for a moment. "Six speed, six foam, and we have a bargain. You and another to shake Casey's hand."

"Twelve canisters is too much to carry, easy spotted. I can carry two and two a lot better," Sonia responds.

He shakes his head indifferently. "Not my problem what you can carry, Defector. Can't make a deal, you find another way to get to Casey." He tucks the bag under his shirt.

"Can't make a deal and you meet the pack assembly with nothing earned but them sugar pills I just tossed you."

The small children begin to bite back their laughter. Sonia knows his loss of prestige from the smaller canines is more than embarrassing; it's dangerous, even life-threatening, unless he can regain control of the negotiation.

"Tell ya what," she says. "I like you, I think your gonna trade honest. I'll bring you three when you take me and mine into your borders and another three when I shake Casey's hand."

The canine doesn't answer. He is distracted by his standing with the sentries watching him. She offers another concession.

"Okay, canine, I see what you're doing," Sonia adds with a respectful nod. "You want me to demonstrate I'm dealing true? Then I'll show ya." She reaches into the tote bag hanging from her shoulder and removes Priya. The younger canines' eyes light up. "I have to go earn my toll. This little whiner's been ache'n to get out of her carrying pouch, and I'd rather she not pick up any gnats from the dealers in town."

"I'm supposed to watch your critter while you wonder about?" His tone is spiteful.

Priya whines in protest as Sonia slides him back into the bag without a word.

The younger canines pull on the boy's shirttail, concerned that they might not get to watch the critter.

"Wait. Make it four and four and we have a pact."

Sonia cradles the shorthaired feline in her arms as the green hands reach through the bars. "He's a playful little guy if you have something to chase, but he'll bite if you play too rough, understand?" With enthusiastic nods, Sonia kneels and passes the cat over.

The children move away; the oldest lowers his voice and says, "So, Defector, when are you planning on taking your walk?"

"Hard to say. I hope to return in an hour. It all depends on how my other deal turns." She nods toward the tunnel opening. "Will your sentries also know me by the running stick figure?"

The boy nods and she can see he relaxes.

Sonia adjusts the straps on her satchel. "One last thing, be careful with those tablets, they are powerful painkillers. Anyone accuses you of bringing sugar pills to the gathering can take a handful and turn their blue clock white.

Madge and Lilith

Madge cradles Sonia's *little egg* in her palm. "This can really edit the time on a lifeclock?" she asks with wonder.

Sonia stows the last packet into the toll bag. Six foam canisters and six speed pouches for a sure-fire way to add years onto the lifeclock. Madge never even suggested a counteroffer, agreeing to the full asking price if the exchange is done in her office.

The extra canisters will be difficult to carry but will allow some leeway later should something go wrong. If there is one thing she has learned in the last five years—

"With the right commands, it will build a whole new life." She cinches the ties of the toll bag tight. "Everything you need is cataloged here." She places a stack of notebooks onto the desk. "You'll find a comprehensive method for rolling back your days and starting a new identity."

"Amazing! Simple as that." Madge slides the egg back into the drawstring bag as she takes the notebooks. "What are these again?"

Hiding her annoyance, Sonia repeats, "Mostly a review of the commands for editing the data-file. You will find Julie-11's encryption key at the front of the top book. This has been fun, but it's time for me to leave."

"Yes, yes it is." Madge agrees, then claps her hands.

Three large men enter her office and surround Sonia. One slips the toll bag from her shoulder, another removes her satchel, and the third takes her wrists and binds them.

"Lilith? Lilith are you there?" Madge calls out.

An answer sings through the doorway. "Yes, dear, I'm right here." A tall, dark-haired woman wearing a Barber-ah uniform appears in the doorway.

"Did you get my medicine back?" Her voice is a caricature of concern.

"Why, of course, my dear." She grabs Sonia by the chin. "After all, it is your medicine. I just needed to borrow it so this wretched little creature could get the help she deserves."

Lilith gives Madge a hug. "Darling, you are always looking out for others. I so admire that about you."

"You're too generous!" Madge answers.

"Oh, that reminds me. I transferred thirty credits into your account for your referral bonus."

Madge waves the bag holding the writer about. "Why this is my lucky day. You know I just traded for this little device that is guaranteed to add years to my lifeclock!"

"Madge, my darling, you don't need those gimmicks." Lilith pats her on the cheek. "You know those are all just humbug."

"Humbug, you say!" Madge grabs Sonia's hair. "Are you telling me you think this little…"

Lilith raises her hand to protest the coming profanity.

Madge lowers her voice to a rasping whisper. "Are you implying that she is a liar?"

"I'm afraid so, my dear." Lilith offers a comforting hug. "Some people are always looking to take advantage of someone of your trusting nature." She leans in and whispers, "I believe such people are deviants."

Madge raises the tips of her fingers to her mouth. "My dear Lilith, you make it sound like a medical condition."

"It may very well be." Lilith nods emphatically.

Madge is flushed. "Perhaps you can help this poor wretch purge the vile influence from her blood."

Chapter 14

Expired

Thousands of nanobots converge under Carlos's fluttering skin as energy pulses from the surgical chamber's emitters and direct them to repair and rejuvenate his infected, atrophied muscles. Fluid drips replace desperately needed nutrients. An array of probes and injectors treat infections and heal his damaged organs. The on-demand user manual for the chamber allowed him to program an automated mode to assess and repair the damage from the Barber-ah's treatment.

After six hours, a mist is released into the breathing mask countering the anesthesia. Carlos awakens and exits the chamber. Constricting pain punishes every movement. As he lifts his trousers onto his waist, he spots his reflection in the dark glossy display of the medical scanner. When he stepped from the chamber five years ago, the synthetic skin covering his arms and torso was soft and smooth. Now, Sweeny's treatment has added to the dozens of scars he'd earned from five years of bad transactions in the Shadow Lands.

Carlos spreads the contents of his pack across the floor next to Sweeny's portable terminal. As he consumes the food and water he had packed for his defection, he finishes the procedure he had started when he first arrived. In moments, all traces of Sweeny's files are gone.

A query of the boards finds a message from Sonia.

C.

Established contact with Casey.
Departing from Stadium soon.
Contact me, I'll talk you in.

S.

He opens a response window when he notices the silver case lying on the floor. Carlos rotates his wrist to see, red-black, red-black, red-black.

He picks up the pocket clock his sister made for him. The cover springs open to reveal:

Carlos-92
9130.9819 Days
24.9998 Years

I have less than two hours.

The aether board awaits his response. *What do I say?* he asks himself. If my time is almost up, then so is hers. There is no way I can find her in time. I'll lead the reapers right to her if I try.

The prompt in the terminal window awaits his message. *What do I tell her? What will she do if I tell her I'm not going to make it?* He ponders the question, which leads to another. *What would I do?*

The answer clarifies his resolve. With a last look at his blinking lifeclock, he cancels the message. *The last thing that tiny psycho did was figure out that my lifeclock had been edited. Could anyone else?* As he considers this, the miserable smell from the far wall demands his attention. Piled there are the remains of the rest of Sweeny's clientele. A vision of his wrecked corpse stretched out in a Somnolence recliner comes to him. A curious technician scanning his white lifeclock might learn something that could endanger the secret he promised to guard.

He grinds his teeth at the thought. "No!" Carlos retrieves the last packet from his toll. Two yellow capsules wash down with a gulp from one of his flasks before he tucks the remainder into his shirt. He opens a new query vocal interface. "Display a map of the area surrounding Antioch."

An image appears. Carlos had forgotten how close to the bay the clinic is. "Display the largest commerce district next to a public harbor." The terminal responded with a red circle around Pittsborough. Another command summons a hover-pod to the clinic.

He makes one final query to the general services board.

HOW TO DISTRACT A REAPER CHASING A DEFECTOR.

The response surprises him not only for its immediacy but for the method it recommends. "That's perfect!" Carlos exclaims to the screen as he sends his agreement.

After closing the terminal session, Carlos shoves his gear back into his pack and pops another capsule from the packet. With a swipe, his hammer-club extends to its full length and smashes the terminals.

Perhaps it is the stimulants deadening the pain in his muscles, but the exertion feels great. Muscles that had been restrained for so long rejoice at the plastic and glass exploding under his swings.

He collapses the club's grip and begins to secure it in his belt, pauses, then stuffs it into the pack. Removing the last flask of water, he pulls the fasteners closed and tosses the pack next to the pile of bodies.

Outside the clinic, the hover-pod waits. When the hatch closes, it speeds Carlos away. The elevated rail will get him there in minutes, which will be plenty of time to mix one final deal.

The Last Deal

The jackrabbit sails through the air. After its impact with the hover-pod's lev-field, it doesn't experience the wonder of flight as it soars above the bush line to touch down in the tall grass of the Bay City northeastern open space. Turkey vultures circling above mark the location for a coming feast, once they are sure it won't take flight again. Though the rabbit might have disagreed, the hover-pod's auto navigation system registered no surrounding population endangered by the furry projectile.

Inside the pod, the display screen of Octavia-70's terminal-tracker flashes in time with an alert chime.

DEFECTOR

She directs the terminal-tracker alert to the pods video terminal screen. The defector's face appears along with his case information.

EXPIRED LIFECLOCK FOR: Carlos-021.92
EXPIRED: 2.3 HOURS
LIFECLOCK LOGGED IN THE EASTERN
MALL OF PITTSBOROUGH

"Two hours?" Dante questions the readout. "How does anyone spend over two hours in the middle of a commerce district before their lifeclock is logged?"

Octavia inserts the Brigade passkey into the pod's programming slot, redirecting their destination to Pittsborough. "Let's go ask him." The terminal updates their arrival time to twenty-six minutes.

"Why the hell are they sending us to Pittsborough?" Dante exclaims. "That's a long way."

Octavia calls up a map of the district to the terminal screen and highlights the Eastern Mall. As she reviews the area, her tele-LINCC chimes. A face framed inside a black hood with the title *Contra Costa District Charon Brigade Dispatch* appears in a window in the upper left corner of the monitor. "Officer Octavia-70, have you reviewed your assignment?"

"Dispatch, you understand we are more than twenty minutes away."

The face on the display acknowledges. "Understood, senior reapers are not available and…" the voice trails off, "…our younger officers have been a little too quick on the trigger lately."

Dante resists any outward appearance of contempt at the dispatcher's comment.

"The current on-demand census has approximately two thousand citizens in the immediate area of the defector."

A black triangle appears in the map depicting the last known location of Carlos-92 with two dotted gray triangles indicating his previous positions.

Predicting the officer's next question, the dispatcher answers, "We don't know how he is avoiding the scanners, but he is blending in with the afternoon patrons extremely well. The situation requires…" a pause in the transmission allows for the agent on the other end to choose words that will not be negatively related later, "…precision."

"Are aerial units available?" Octavia asks.

"The closest dragonfly is supporting a water rescue in the Sacramento River. It will be directed to Pittsborough with Carlos-ninety-two's lifeclock frequency as soon as it is available."

Dante fixes his attention to the terminal screen, avoiding the thrilled expression blossoming from his partner. "Try to contain yourself," he mutters from the corner of his mouth.

"What are you talking about? I am very disappointed with this lack of support." Her sarcastic assurance becomes louder when Dante shakes his head. "Really, I hate that we're going to waste all this time finding Carlos's trail, separating him from the crowd."

"If you insist." Dante surrenders. Reasoning with Octavia when she starts a tear is like reasoning with a dog that just found its favorite chew toy.

Her sarcasm blooms. "I just hope they allow us access to the aerial scanner soon, or we'll have no alternative," she says with a palpable shudder. "We'll actually have to hunt a defector ourselves." She shakes her head in mock contempt. "I hate that!"

An awkward silence hangs between the two until the dispatcher interrupts. "I assure you, Officer, you do have the full support of the Contra Costa Brigade. The dragonfly will be at your disposal as soon as possible."

Dante gives his partner an impatient glare, then remembers that he had already surrendered her chew toy. "Don't worry about it, dispatch. Whenever it arrives will be just fine."

The concerned face on the screen nods a reply then severs the transmission. Octavia starts to laugh with mock embarrassment.

"No, you're not," Dante says.

She shakes her head laughing. "No, I'm not."

Mall traffic is heavy. Octavia drops a white TAC into the breech of her pistol before exiting the pod at the southernmost entrance to the Eastern Mall. Dante continues to the marina. Carlos's previous positions suggest he is trying to get to the bay.

Citizens clear a path for the reaper as she enters the district. Brigade officers are not an unusual sight in the malls, but they warrant attention when present. Octavia adjusts the hood above her brow and scans the posture and faces of those around her. Hiding in a large crowd is a common plan for defectors. One face in hundreds, or in this case thousands, would seem adequate cover, unless you know the signs.

Animals in the wild have inherited tools to help them avoid predators. They have fur coats that blend into the terrain, legs for running, and claws that help them climb and burrow to safety. Defectors have no such advantages. In the mall, everything around them is actively trying to identify them and announce their location.

For experienced hunters, the terminal-tracker scanner is only a first alert system. Octavia knows Carlos is canting his wrist to cover the back of his hand. He also might have his hand jammed into a pocket to obscure his black lifeclock or pressed against the side of his body. In any case, the tension in his arm has changed his posture and is announcing his crime to everyone around him.

All citizens fear defectors. They might sympathize or even pity them, but they understand death is on their trail. It is unusual for any amount of sympathy to entice someone to aid a defector in evading the reapers since aiding defectors can carry the same penalty as defecting itself.

A detailed map of Pittsborough's Eastern Mall displays on the screen of Octavia's terminal-tracker. A blue triangle, indicating her current position, aligns atop the dotted gray triangle marker where Carlos's expired lifeclock was first recorded. "So, Carlos," she says under her breath, "where did you go from here?"

Patrons shake their head when Octavia presents them with Carlos's profile picture on her terminal. A shopkeeper polishing a table of glassware outside his storefront eventually recognizes it. "I think he was here." He motions with his polishing cloth toward a counter in the back of his shop. "But it was a while ago. You know, I thought he seemed a little nervous."

Octavia got a similar response from another when she approached the second marker on her terminal-tracker two hundred meters ahead of the first location, but no response in between the two.

So how did he get here? she wonders. A delivery wagon appears from behind a row of shops answering Octavia's silent query. *The alley.*

Octavia dashes through a shop to the rear maintenance bay. A delivery pod passes a line of waste canisters as she exits. Referring to the tracker's map, she clarifies Carlos's trail. She cues her tele-LINCC. "Dante, he's heading to the bay."

At the other end of the LINCC, Dante watches pods emerge and descend on a ramp leading underground. "I'm at the marina entrance for the borough's maintenance tunnels. No one on this end has seen him."

"Then we'll drive him there," Octavia responds.

The alley empties into an open courtyard. Cafés surround the perimeter of the square; two staircases descend into the lower levels of the center.

Silence flows through the afternoon shoppers as hundreds of eyes turn to Octavia stepping into view. She surveys the crowd as she walks through them. A chime sounds on her terminal-tracker. The dragonfly circling high above has detected Carlos's lifeclock, although it hasn't triangulated his exact position. The display reads,

DEFECTOR: Carlos-021.92
DISTANCE: 50 Meters
DIRECTION: NULL
ELEVATION: NULL

Soon, a second scanner will read his clock and relay his direction, and then a third will give his elevation. For Octavia, this is all superfluous. The terminal-tracker's chime is heard throughout the otherwise silent courtyard and is the only aid she needs to flush out the defector.

All movement in the courtyard stops. With an almost theatrical motion, Octavia draws the terminal-tracker in front of her. She examines the crowd with an intensity beyond any flying robot's capabilities as she gauges the expression and posture of everyone around her. *He's close,* her inner voice assures. *Whose eyes are fighting panic? Who knows that he's the reason I'm here? Who... There.* Octavia stops. An electric buzz climbs up the back of her neck telling her, *he's watching me.*

The sensation focuses Octavia's attention to a cluster of a dozen people. Unconsciously, some drifted to their left, others to their right. They know they are standing next to someone carrying the smell of death. They don't realize it, but their instincts compel them to move away until one face is isolated. A shoulder shudders under a calm face hiding behind a pair of dark spectacles.

Carlos curls his fingers around the cuff of his shirt that stretches over the black spot on the back of his hand. His stim-soaked blood helps deaden the nerves in his arm as waves of needles rush up from his covered lifeclock to dance around his neck and shoulder.

He watches the black-hooded figure as she waves her scanner about. He is well outside the cones of blue light the crystal sensors shower onto the patrons of the courtyard. *It's a bluff,* he thinks. *I may have drifted through one, maybe two scanners earlier, but not here. There is no way her tracker has registered my signal, unless—.*

Although neither Carlos nor Sonia had ever seen an aerial scanner, they had studied descriptions of its capabilities from boards on the aether. *The surrounding structures should block any signal from my lifeclock,* he thinks. *It would have to be flying inside the courtyard to see me, wouldn't it?*

Unfortunately, they never found the frequencies for the aerial scanners to program into their spectacles. Despite the care he took in avoiding the mall's traffic scanners, he very well may be standing inside the cone of an aerial scanner and his spectacles wouldn't display it. This realization sprouts a bead of sweat on his upper lip. *No matter what,* he tells himself, *don't look up.*

The stairway leading to the lower levels and the maintenance tunnels is just a few meters away. The people in the courtyard are beginning to move again. Carlos follows the current of the crowd when a dark motion catches his attention. An audible gasp rumbles through the crowd.

A pathway opens through the heart of the crowd when Octavia charges her prey. People huddle, unsure which direction they can run to escape the dangers of the courtyard. Three people fall to the ground as Carlos forces his way behind a growing cluster of bodies that block the reaper's path.

Octavia presses through the moving mass as Carlos descends the stairs. She cues her tele-LINCC. "Dante, he's heading to the lower level. Move to the—"

Urrrrmmmfffff!

The terminal-tracker flies from her hand when a locomotive slams into Octavia. Massive arms wrap around her midriff like a boa constrictor and try to pull her to the ground.

Octavia lowers her stance, directing some of his force to pass by, but not enough to break free.

Stars clear from her eyes.

Regaining his hold, her attacker lifts her off the floor in a crushing bear hug. Desperate, damp, heaving breaths bellow from his mouth onto Octavia's throat.

The kinetic dampening mesh lining Octavia's hood and tunic make effective armor against direct hits but offers little aid against his crushing hold.

Stars return to Octavia's vision as the air is pressed from her lungs. Her legs flail around as she is thrust about left to right in a spinning maelstrom.

One turn allows Octavia to hook her leg around the man's thigh, she drives her boot heel into the crook behind his knee.

Physics more than pain buckles his legs, bringing Octavia down to a solid landing. Once grounded, the other knee launches a solid strike into his ribs, then again to his face.

Free from his hold, Octavia faces her attacker's vacuous expression. Her assailant regains his footing and prepares to charge. There are no insults or threats, only blind rage.

Flailing arms capture empty space as Octavia parries his onslaught. His next charge is met with the point of Octavia's elbow rammed into his chin. His head shoots back. There is little perception behind the vacant eyes that return in time to see the shaft of a billy club in his would-be victim's fist.

His legs fail; he doesn't perceive the strikes that crippled his ability to stand.

With a fencer's thrust, Octavia stabs the giant's abdomen with the point of the short club. His lungs empty in an explosive burst. Even in his chemical haze, the man collapses to his knees, desperately heaving air into his lungs.

Octavia focuses on a soft patch at the back of his skull for a killing strike. A slight adjustment to her aim smashes the bones in his shoulder and sends him to the ground.

The club settles into a holster fastened to Octavia's calf.

The channel is still active on her tele-LINCC when she replaces the kernel to her ear. "Dispatch, this is Octavia-seventy, ping my terminal-tracker." A chime sounds under a vendor's clothes rack that had toppled during the fight. Octavia lifts the rack to find her hand terminal.

A rustle stirs in the direction of her fallen attacker. Apparently unaware that his shoulder had been smashed, the giant begins to pull himself to his feet.

The barrel of Octavia's pistol breaks forward. With a smooth, choreographed motion, she slides a red UKD from the ammo cuff on her wrist and exchanges the load in the breech. The action closes with a slap. The muzzle flares in his direction.

Upon impact, a ballistic cavity explodes around the kinetic dart tearing his knee apart. Whatever had been muffling his pain during the fight no longer silences his scream. A bag of yellow capsules bursts open from his shirt and scatters across the ground where he falls.

Octavia cues the link. "Dispatch, C-A-D Eastern Mall, south plaza. Medic required."

"Citizen aiding defector logged Octavia-seventy. Security and medic on the way," a voice responds.

Octavia hears Dante's voice. "Disregard, dispatch; C-A-D is immobile. The officer is heading to the lower level hot. Direct all available security, clear her path."

The mall crowd opens a pathway in the direction Carlos took down the stairs. Octavia launches into a full sprint to the lower promenade.

Carlos no longer avoids the crystal sensors. His movement is relayed to Dante, who directs security to clear bystanders away. Octavia's silence confirms that his directions align with her strategy.

Within moments, Octavia is standing at the entrance of the maintenance tunnels. A glance at her tracker screen confirms Carlos's marker is boxed between her and Dante's position at the far end of the underground maze. She traces a route on the screen and cues her LINCC. "Dante, hold position at the junction of E-55, he's making for the northwest marina exit. If he doubles back to the Eastern Mall, I'll have him."

Dante acknowledges.

Octavia enters the tunnel following a map in her mind leading to her prey. She doesn't hear the crunch of two small poly-carbonate lenses being smashed under her boot. She doesn't see the bent frames of a pair of handmade spectacles lying on the ground, watching her disappear into the darkness.

Carlos adjusts his pace. He felt the reaper closing in on him until he moved away from the tunnel leading to the water. The last stim cap is still working through his system, masking what should be near-crippling pain. He wishes the churning in his head would quiet long enough to gauge the footfalls of his hunter. He looks behind. *He has to be there,* he thinks. *How far back can he be?*

Carlos's attention breaks to the passage in front of him. Something is scraping against the ground.

A figure glides into his path.

A starburst flashes.

Searing pain.

Darkness.

Octavia slides sidelong into the intersection of the connecting passage. She faces the hallway and Carlos's surprised expression when she squeezes the trigger. A launching charge explodes into the empty barrel. The shock wave hits Carlos in the face. He screams out in pain as he falls to the ground, his fists grip the burnt craters that once held his eyes.

"It's your time, Defector." Octavia slips a black charge from her wrist cuff into the breech of her pistol and slaps the action shut. The gunsight registers Carlos's heat silhouette and his expired lifeclock.

"Carlos-92, 256.008.021.92, your lifeclock expired two hundred and thirteen minutes ago. It is time to meet your Somnus Obligation."

Carlos offers no plea or curse as Octavia launches the STInGER into his belly. The Reaper's Requiem fills the corridor.

Incident Report

NAME: Carlos-021.92
STATUS: REBIRTH
1 NAME POSTED FOR REASSIGNMENT

Carlos's arm drops to the ground with a slap. Dante's terminal-tracker logs the identity of the white lifeclock. Carlos-92 is now in Somnus.

Two Brigade cadets arrive on the scene to remove the body. They deliver the contents from Carlos's pockets to Dante, who directs them away from his partner. He wants to keep Octavia separate from the junior officers on the scene.

In a hover-pod, bound for Bay City Brigade dispatch, Octavia mimics Dante's cadence in the lecture hall. "You see, you lesser reapers waste a lot of time chasing defectors." The endorphins are still raging through her system following the hunt. It will take a while for her to return to civility. She continues, "I prefer to let the defector run in front of my pistol sight."

"So all that running you did from one end of the mall to the other…"

"Purely for show. With my skills, I could have easily sauntered to the tunnel and waited for him to come all the way to me. However, there was a clock ticking, and we can't spend all afternoon on just one defector."

Octavia's bragging begins to subside in the hover-pod as they merge onto an elevated rail back to Bay City. She settles her head against the back of the seat as Dante examines the resin polymer truncheon she used on the mall attacker. It's about fifty-five centimeters in length, flared at one end with deep grooves defining the grip at the other. The design is that of a small bat used by peace officers in the nineteenth and twentieth centuries. Octavia prefers this primitive implement despite the array of non-lethal armaments the Brigade allows its officers to carry.

Three tones announce the appearance of a woman from Brigade dispatch in the pod's monitor. "Octavia-seventy, you have a communication from Judicial Officer Sydney-twenty."

"Hey, that's your cute friend!" Octavia perks up. "He likes me."

"Patch it through, dispatch," Dante answers on behalf of his partner, which he regrets.

Sydney appears in the monitor. "Officer Octavia-seventy?"

"Ohhhhhhh, that's the spot, Honey Pot!"

Dante mutes the input.

In his office, Sydney maintains a serious expression. A red frame labeled *audio muted* outlines the two Brigade officers in the vid-screen. Octavia sits rigid as Dante whispers something into her ear.

If she wanted to get his attention, her orgasmic outburst succeeded. For Dante's sake, he keeps his expression even. He's alone in his office, but he understands that if someone else had been present, the outburst might have been regarded as disrespectful for not only the judge but also the Judiciary of the Collective. Such disrespect from the civil branch with authority to kill at their sole discretion could be distressing to some.

When the red frame vanishes, Octavia addresses him in a more official tone.

"Is everything all right, Officer?" Sydney inquires.

"I was talking over a loud noise," she answers. "We've passed it now, Your Honor."

"We're not in court, Octavia, you can call me Sydney, but I appreciate the courtesy. I wanted to give you an update on your case."

Octavia's eyes widen, "My case? I have a case, Your... Sydney?"

"You were attacked in the Pittsborough Eastern Mall by Regie-sixty-five, a civil mover for the Contra Costa borough. The man carries furniture and heavy equipment all day long. Sounds like a pretty strong opponent, I hope you're not hurt."

For reasons beyond understanding, Dante chooses that moment to hand the truncheon back to his partner, who slaps it out of camera view. "A minor distraction... Sydney." Octavia allows a slight smile to break through.

"Well, that distraction has been sentenced to four months in cryo-detention for attacking a civil officer and aiding a defector. He only realized that his stunt might have cost him his life when security removed him from my chamber."

"It was just a minor skirmish Syd—Sydney. In my opinion, it doesn't warrant termination."

Sydney says, "I thought you would be interested to learn that the attack was not random. Civil investigators have learned that one hundred and twenty minutes before his, pacification, Regie-sixty-five accessed a message on an aether board where he offered to delay a reaper in the Eastern Mall in exchange for a bag of stim caps."

Octavia snaps, "My uniform got scuffed on the ground over a bag of stim?"

Sydney bites down on the inside of his mouth to avoid smiling. "The aether board seemed to be part of a network of thrill-seekers. That's about as much as we learned from the trial."

"Do you think it's part of a defectors network?" Dante asks.

"We found no evidence of an actual defectors network. The interview technicians measured Regie's responses as 73% truthful when he indicated that he was motivated by thrill-seeking and defying authority rather than helping a defector; however, they also indicated that the stim saturating his blood likely affected his responses. May I ask how did the attack affect your hunt?"

"Negligible." Octavia shrugs. "It allowed Carlos a slight delay before I caught up with him."

"If that," Dante mutters.

Sydney's voice rises. "I didn't get that, Dante."

Dante leans to the terminal. "Carlos had effectively evaded the scanners for over two hours, but after the fight, he ran into the tunnels that are packed with scanners." Dante turns to Octavia. "He must have known that. I thought he was going for the marina, but he ultimately turned right into you. Why go to the tunnels? His best move would have been to blend back into the crowd again when he was out of sight."

Octavia and Sydney chat a while before the call ends. Dante sits quietly. He has an answer to his question, but it doesn't make sense. Regie's attack resulted in Octavia and Sydney talking about him instead of the defector, Carlos. Dante's instincts tell him he is right. They also tell him not to say anything.

The hover-pod continues in silence as it cruises toward Bay City headquarters. Dante cants the back of his left hand away from his partner's view, directing the light of his lifeclock out the window as it flashes, red-pink, red-pink, red-pink.

Chapter 15

What Was All This For?

24.7507 Years.

The number sits in the darkness behind his clenched eyelids. Dante tries to force it away. He's been fighting this emptiness with distractions and chemicals for as long as he can remember.

The empty scotch bottle cracks the glass top of his minibar when he sets it down. "How can it be gone already?"

The slur in his voice enrages him. When his eyelids relax, Dante is confronted with walls that blink in time with his lifeclock, red-pink, red-pink, red.

He fumbles to activate a table lamp; its light banishes the lifeclock's but reveals a new monster. The window that showed the lights of the skyline now holds a primitive terrified creature. Its left hand is canted away, hiding its lifeclock. It is the posture of a defector. It sickens Dante. He wants to launch the empty bottle at it. No, not the bottle, he wants to point his gun at the cornered creature and launch a STInGER into his chest. That would put an end to the fear, an end to his emptiness. The barrel of a pistol appears under its chin. He can feel the hollow of the muzzle kissing his throat.

Where was I just now? he asks. *The Correction, yes, that day mattered. That day I stood to alleviate the rage of the world. In the nine years that followed, what have I done of consequence since? There has to be something else because if not, what was all this for?*

Where Do Defectors Go?

Surface Rd: 8-10.75 hours, w/1, 30 min recharge @ or
near Fresno, 30.5 credits
EER: 3-4 hours, 70 credits
Transit Tube: < 1.2 hours, 180 credits

Dante considers the diagram next to the directions on the torn piece of wrapping paper sitting in his palm. "Is this where you were going, Carlos, or where you came from?"

Dante queries the citizen directory, which returns the summary,

NAME: Carlos-92, 334.241.022.92.
GENDER: Male.
AGE: 36 hours, Yellow Cycle.
SKILL-TRADE: Null.
HEIGHT: 49 cm.
CURRENT LOCATION: Canadian Territory region, Sector-334.
NO KNOWN SECURITY ISSUES.

I must be tired, Dante thinks. *Obviously, he's been Reborn.* Dante calls up Octavia's termination report from this afternoon and reenters the query with the full name designation.

> read citizenSummary: Carlos-92, 256.008.022.92

The terminal responds,

NAME: Carlos-92, 256.008.022.92.
GENDER: Male.
Entered Rebirth 0.0012 years ago.
Defector.

"That is all that remains of Carlos-ninety-two," Dante mumbles sympathetically. He glances at the note again, then enters a query for the civil transportation database.

Carlos-92 summoned a pod from A Moveable Face in Antioch that deposited him just outside Pittsborough. Before then, he traveled to Antioch via a transit tube from South Diego almost two weeks ago.

"Where were you going, Carlos?" The question rattles Dante's awareness. It's not a question directive-abiding citizens ask out loud, especially if they're in the Charon Brigade. Yet Dante has pondered this for as long as he'd been a reaper. *Where do defectors go?* The question implies that one is thinking of defecting. Thinking of defecting leads to defecting. *I hunt people who ask that question.*

He glances at the crystal blinking on the back of his hand. *Maybe I should find out.* As the notion settles in his mind, the emptiness begins to lift. Dante raises his eyes to look out across the city skyline. Darkness is replaced by clarity. *I have ninety-one days to find where defectors go.* He returns the gun to its holster. *But a reaper can't find such a place.* Dante's attention shifts back to his reflection in the window. *But you, you could.*

He opens his data terminal and queries A Moveable Face and Antioch. Several responses appear.

A story posted four hours ago reads, "A gruesome scene was discovered this afternoon when civil movers attempted to recover some lost construction materials." An unseen teller's voice narrates footage depicting a body wrapped in a cover sheet being carried on a stretcher. "Investigators were called to determine the identities of five bodies along with a stolen robot. Witnesses tell us the clinic formally belonged to a medic named Larry-fifteen, who entered Somnus almost two weeks ago."

Few sparkles remain on the decorated strap attached to the weighted ring buckle. Dante turns the belt over in his fist, as he did the day it had bound him on the floor of Helen's apartment. The memory of the small blonde woman is still with him. When he closes his eyes, he remembers her matted dress as she danced and her black eye as she thrust her hand across the table.

"I'm Helen-thirty-one, nice to meet you," she had said. "I'm going out to pick a fight with a Civil Security unit, wanna come?"

It brings a smile. It has been more than five years since that apparently frail woman trapped him on the floor. Dante still holds a strange admiration for her. Her plan didn't save her from her obligation, but she had a plan. She refused to go quietly. She deserved better than to have her spirit stripped away in the last seconds of her life by the rookie reaper. *Carlos also had a plan that didn't work out, and I'm going to find out what it was.*

Dante tucks the strap into his pocket and continues checking his duty gear, but this time, he's not in uniform. Instead, he wears a light overcoat with a special fitted pocket that holds his pistol.

He considers his plan one last time, which is easy, he doesn't have one. This is not a Brigade assignment. He is beginning the path of a defector. At some point, he will cross a line that will put him beyond the forgiveness of the Brigade.

Dante summons a hover-pod. He leaves his tele-LINCC on the table next to the terminal-tracker. Since the Brigade issued both, they can be tracked. The latch to his apartment secures behind him.

✧ ✧ ✧

Jacob-11 passes three security officers when he exits A Moveable Face. He is twenty-one years old and wears a gold tunic with the emblem of a civil investigator.

A hover-pod deposits a lanky, brown-haired man who introduces himself as Dante-09, an officer of the Charon Brigade. He presents Jacob with impeccable credentials by drawing and replacing a gun from his long, dark-green overcoat.

"I don't mind showing you my crime scene, Officer Dante-nine," he says. "Although I am curious why the Charon Brigade is interested in a local homicide."

"I'm following a lead from a case earlier today." Dante passes the folded note to the investigator. "I want to know if my defector, Carlos-ninety-two, is connected to your murder."

Jacob reviews the crudely drawn map with scribbled directions. Dante had written the defector's full designation on the upper corner of the map.

"We took him in the Pittsborough Eastern Mall this afternoon," Dante says. "That map is the only thing we found on him."

Jacob motions for Dante into A Moveable Face as he cues his earpiece. "Officer Niki-84." Jacob pauses. "Contact the Pittsborough Citadel and ask them for any information they have for Carlos-92, 256.008.022.92. He was terminated by the Brigade in the Eastern Mall this afternoon." Another pause. "Just find any available information, and report to me Aye-SAP."

Jacob leads Dante down the hallway, relaying the same details of the crime scene Dante had heard from the hover-pod's vid-LINCC on his ride over. He loses interest in Jacob's report when they have to duck under a white metal beam with brown streaks resting on the shoulders of a robot. Brown crusted bandages, torn from the pole, lie in a pile next to the door.

The room is thick with the smell of death. Markers identify the locations where blood-filled basins had been found.

Dante takes care to step around the painted outline of a human figure on the floor. A dark stain defines a blood pool that soaked the body hours before. "The tellers didn't mention anything like this."

"We're still figuring out what this is," Jacob replies. "Complete details will be released once we're confident it won't affect the investigation." Jacob nods toward the back of the room. "We found four more bodies stacked in the far corner."

"I know the Brigade has no involvement in Civil Security matters, however…"

Jacob-11 directs him away from the evidence markers to a large video presentation monitor erected against the wall. "I was not completely open with you earlier, Officer Dante. I apologize; I have a habit of holding onto information until I know what's going on. The truth is, I was expecting someone from the Charon Brigade to arrive, considering the three defectors we found."

"Three defectors?" Dante asks.

Jacob engages the screen. He opens a file to reveal four citizen profile pictures. "Three of the bodies were citizens with expired lifeclocks; the fourth was five days away from twenty-five."

"And the fifth?"

Jacob brings Sweeny's profile photo to the screen. "This is Holly-thirty-three, age twenty, or she was." He nods in the direction of the outline Dante had just stepped around. "She was a Barber-ah who used the alias Sweeny."

"I'm not familiar with the terms of civil investigation."

"Holly was part of a subculture that fetishizes crude medical practices. Barber-ahs take their cues from the ancient European barber surgeons. They get their thrills out of anything that pokes, probes, or prods and are common among underground medical clinics."

Jacob moves to a nearby desk where a line of crude looking surgical instruments is laid out next to a ceramic jar. He picks the jar up and rattles the contents. "This one seemed to have a special love of bloodletting and tooth extractions, since all the bodies recovered were missing teeth and were covered with incision scars. The surgical chamber in the back lists numerous fluid replacement procedures."

"The tellers said this clinic was run by a medic named Larry-fifteen," Dante says.

"According to her profile, Holly worked as an assistant grocer in Antioch. She apparently assisted Larry-fifteen in this clinic during her off hours." Jacob motioned toward the door. "The Model-3, standing over there, is supposed to be working in the grocer's storeroom. It was reported missing about the same time as Holly." Jacob pauses to appreciate the mystery.

Dante releases an ironic smile. "Really?"

Jacob directs Dante's attention back to the monitor. "We downloaded all the commands the robot has processed over the last five days." He taps an icon on the screen labeled *RUN*. The monitor clears to reveal an overhead diagram of the floor plan for A Moveable Face. The clinic's components are marked with abstract icons labeled *BARBER POLE, EXAMINATION TABLE,* and *SURGICAL CHAMBER.*

The robot's command history scrolls through a sub window in the corner as an icon labeled M-3 moves around the space.

Soon, M-3 deposits an object in the corner where the bodies were discovered and labeled *VICT 1*.

The simulation slows as it approaches the end. Jacob taps Dante's shoulder. "This is where it gets interesting."

The icon for M-3 moves around the examination table as the command, *sever all straps securing the patient to the examination table,* scrolls through the sub window.

"Someone escaped?" Dante asks.

Jacob nods.

The robot icon then drifts over to the doorway where the circle representing the barber pole crosses its shoulder. The animated robot adjusts its position in response to a series of commands placing the long end of the pole across the pathway of the entrance to the room. Finally, the robot rotates to the right taking the long end of the pole away from the doorway.

Soon after, an icon labeled Holly-33 appears at the desk in the front office and moves down the hallway into the crime scene room. Before she passes through the doorway, the final command is received. *Turn left, two-hundred-seventy degrees.*

The pole rotates back toward the doorway and connects with the Holly icon as it enters. It falls to the floor in the position investigators found her in. The final line of the command window is displayed in red. *Worker injury. Suspend all operations.*

"I love that gag!"

Dante and Jacob turn around to see a smiling cadet who had paused to watch the sight gag play out on the simulator.

"Are you finished, grunt?" Jacob admonishes the inappropriate comment.

The young officer moves out of the investigator's sight, then Jacob leans in Dante's direction and mutters just above his breath, "I love that gag."

"Ya, so do I," Dante responds in a similar sober voice.

"The pole struck Holly-thirty-three on the right side of her head with sufficient force to knock her to the floor and likely caused her to lose consciousness momentarily. However, the actual cause of death was the knife wound that nearly severed her head."

A picture of Holly with a knife sticking out of her neck appears on the screen. Her nurse's cap is still perfectly in place. Jacob passes Dante a clear container holding a blood-soaked surgical knife.

"She was conscious when this happened?" Dante asks.

"There are indications that she tried to resist, but not much."

"And you think my defector is your murderer?"

"Yes. That would be the only neat thing to come out of this mess."

"Investigator, I have some information for you." The senior officers turn to face Niki-84, an early Blue Cycle cadet wearing a gold tunic and hood, standing at attention.

Jacob addresses the fourteen-year-old trainee. "Report."

"The Contra Costa Civil Medical Examiner has completed an investigation of the remains of Carlos-ninety-two at the Prime Citadel of Pittsborough." The trainee recites the findings documented on her terminal slate. "Carlos shows signs of multiple recent traumas that are in line with the last treatments logged by Holly's surgical chamber. The examiner found multiple patches for incisions in the defector's brachial, radial, and femoral arteries that were made with a blade consistent with the one found in Holly's neck. He also reports that Carlos is missing five teeth that were forcibly removed and second degree burns on both eyes that are consistent with a discharge from a Brigade gun. Finally, his fingerprints match those on the knife used to kill Holly."

The cadet pauses to take a breath. "Also, and I don't know if it is relevant, his system was flooded with surgical nanobots and maxed out with stimulants and pain suppressors."

Jacob challenges the cadet. "Is that *your* conclusion?"

"No, sir." The trainee returns to a more meticulous cadence. "The examiner concluded that his blood carried levels of stim that allowed him to function beyond his body's normal abilities, considering the trauma he had suffered. He concluded that Carlos-ninety-two was in imminent danger of heart failure." He looks up from his slate with an awkward pause. "That is if the STInGER hadn't exploded his chest."

"Well done, cadet. That will be all." Jacob allows a hint of pride for his trainee to show.

"So, Dante, it seems you found my murderer."

Dante offers a slight objection. "Wouldn't you call this self-defense, considering...?" He absently gestures to the basins disbursed across the floor.

Jacob nods as he considers this point. "I'll include that possibility in my report. There is one last part you may want to see."

Jacob leads Dante to a pile of smashed terminals. The investigator pulls over a container holding the personal belongings of the victims. He removes a backpack from the top. "This was found next to the bodies."

Dante rummages through the pack and withdraws a small pointed hammer with a telescoping handle. He looks to Jacob, who answers his confused expression with a shrug. "Any other surprises?"

Jacob nods toward the bin. "We found the lock-jammer he used on the front door."

"Always prepared."

"Prepared for what?" Jacob asks.

Dante shakes his head. "Defectors travel light. They usually carry things to help them avoid public places, like food, or something to hide their appearance. They don't normally have weapons, burglary tools, or whatever this is." He withdraws a gray plastic umbrella from the bag, then shoves it back into the pack.

Jacob reaches into the bin. "Do they ever have anything like this?" He withdraws a silver case with a chain dangling from the side and passes it to Dante.

The lid springs open to present Dante with a video screen displaying his own image. *Wouldn't a mirror make more sense?* he wonders. He taps a rocker switch that cycles the display to an exterior camera, then a numeric time display followed by:

Carlos-92
9131.5298 Days
25.0013 Years

Dante presents the display to Jacob.

Jacob's posture stiffens. "That was a weird mirror when I opened it."

Dante pushes the bin away, then holds up the silver case. "Do you mind if I keep this?"

Jacob shrugs. "No harm, since you helped identify my murderer, and it seems you are leaving here with more questions than you came with."

"You got that right." Dante sighs. "Were you able to retrieve anything useful on the terminals?"

"You're defector was thorough when he wiped the database. We were only able to recover a few names from the query log." Jacob hands over a notepad.

Dante considers the list. "Can you tell if these were queried by Carlos or Holly?"

Jacob shakes his head. "That's everything."

Nodding to the bin, Dante asks, "Do you mind if I go through this?"

"Make yourself at home."

Dante skims the list of names. There are numerous Sonia's with varying numeric designations along with Carlos and two other names, Lauren-25 and Marcos-80.

Dante sets the case aside and searches the belongings of the rest of the Barber-ah's victims. Most of it is in line with what he typically finds with a defector: food, water canisters, dark glasses, and hats. One had packed a variety of colored optical inserts and stage makeup. He recognizes the cylinders of lysergic foam from a third pack along with a bag of painkillers. The bag reminds Dante of the stim caps falling from Regie's shirt in the mall.

A similar shape appeared in the last pack. Dante expected to pull another spray-can-sized canister of foam; instead, the cylinder unrolls to a flat slate with a terminal window displaying a dozen icons identifying LINCC access points in range. He selects the closest one, which returns a standard LINCC account login screen.

He takes the strange slate along with one of the foam canisters over to the investigator. "Did you retrieve any information from this terminal slate?"

Jacob considers the device and gives one of the trainees a disappointed look. "We didn't find anything on there because it doesn't have any onboard memory. It seems to run off a hidden aether operating system." His voice stabs at an embarrassed cadet. "And it was supposed to be secured along with the lock-jammer."

Dante tosses the foam to Jacob. "Should these be secured as well?"

"These aren't as dangerous."

"Defectors often carry a supply of stim with them," Dante says. "It helps keep them on the move, but I've never chased anyone into their synthetic bliss."

Jacob considers the canister. "Chem isn't used much in the Contra Costa shadow economy."

"Shadow economy?"

"Here in Contra Costa, people who want to avoid credit transfers typically prefer to trade alcohol or specialty tools like the lock-jammer. Chem is traded more down south."

"So what do you think brought them to this underground clinic?"

Jacob holds up the canister. "Nomads usually purchase chem from underground clinics, but that doesn't make sense here since there isn't any chemistry equipment. Larry ran an appearance alteration clinic."

Dante holds up the notepad. "Do you mind if I use the slate to investigate these names?"

Jacob hesitates, then agrees. "Just pass it to me when you're finished."

Dante returns to the bin and enters his LINCC access key into the slate. His personal database instantly appears. "This is faster than our dispatch terminals," Dante mutters absently.

A status icon in the corner of the screen indicates that he is accessing his personal database with level-32 encryption and offers to increase it to level-70. *Can this terminal really be that secure? I'd bet the CEC couldn't even track an account encrypted at this level.*

There is nothing unusual about any of the Sonia's until he queries the last one on the list. Sonia-10 has expired and hasn't entered Somnus.

What do you have to do with Sonia-10, Carlos?

He continues calling up the citizen summaries and discovers Lauren-25 is, in fact, over twenty-seven years old and Marcos-80 is over thirty, and that neither has entered Somnus.

"They escaped," Dante says in a hushed tone. "Lauren and Marcos escaped, they must have! No one can evade the Brigade for that long, not within the Collective." Dante hides his excitement.

How are Sonia and Carlos connected to them? Perhaps they are following the same path. Maybe there really is an underground railroad out of the Collective. The idea both thrills and terrifies Dante because he will soon be on the same path.

Dante accesses the transit service to call a hover-pod to the clinic. He rolls the slate back into a cylinder and jams it into the pocket of his coat and heads for the exit.

Sonia's clock was scanned twelve hours ago in South Diego, the same area where Carlos summoned a hover-pod to bring him to Antioch. If the South Diego Brigade isn't already tracking her, they will soon. *I have to find her first.*

Chapter 16

The Underground

The hover-pod surges forward as it enters the high-speed tube to South Diego. Dante reviews the full citizen profiles of Sonia-10 and Carlos-92 on the slate he liberated from the bin at A Moveable Face. A subsystem embedded in the remote operating system allowed him to crack the comparatively low-level encryption Carlos used.

Carlos contacted Octavia's attacker through a posting on the aether. *Let's see if he made a habit of it.*

With a little trial and error, Dante pieces together the last message Carlos-92 read.

C.

Established contact with Casey.
Departing from Stadium soon.
Contact me, I'll talk you in.

S.

Dante cues the pod's terminal. "Redirect from South Diego to Stadium."

The vid-screen updates the arrival time to 1.2 hours.

Dante spends most of the trip reviewing reports from the area's Civil Security. He is surprised that there aren't as many Brigade reports as he expected. It seems the locals manage black lifeclocks as efficiently as canines manage red ones. *I guess the Brigade is bad for business,* he muses.

Why would Sonia-10 tell Carlos to meet her in Stadium? Is she purchasing chem for her passage? If so, she might deal with an underground clinic, as Jacob suggested.

A query on the aether boards for underground clinics returns over fifty responses. "That was pointless."

What brought Carlos to a clinic in Antioch? His mind wanders as the details of the crime scene flow through his imagination. He settles on the image of the woman in a once-white medical assistant costume. *What did Jacob call her?*

Another search query returns the group *Barber-ahs of Stadium.* Dante submits a new posting to the group.

Show me your healing skills.
I'm in town for a few hours. Before I return to my
mundane trade, I want to see a professional purge the
body of its ills.

Dante considers Sonia's profile photo: No children, I'm only interested in mature subjects.

Dante writes, Prefer a female patient. I'm prepared to be extra generous for an up-close observation during treatment. Send pictures.

Within minutes, dozens of responses begin tumbling in. "How many people do this?" Most of the responses include offers for patient interaction that causes a chill to travel up his spine.

He compares the attached pictures with Sonia-10's profile photo until a response from Stadium School of Traditional Surgery catches his attention with the simple message: This one is ready.

The message includes a dozen photos of a red-haired woman collapsed in a chair. She isn't wearing the pajama outfit most other responses have. Instead, she is dressed in street clothes. Dante pages down the pictures until he finds one of a hand off-camera pulling her head back to reveal a close-up of stoic eyes next to a fresh wound cut down the side of her face. "That's her!"

Dante opens a communication request. A woman introduces herself as Nurse Lilith in the vid-LINCC window. Dante yells, "You've already started!"

"Not at all," she answers in a reassuring albeit startled tone. "You are interested in a demonstration of traditional healing."

"That's right, but I want to see it from the *beginning.*"

"My patient suffers a terrible condition. We were just beginning her treatment when you posted."

"Yes." Dante allows his excitement to creep into the conversation. "I understand. Have you sedated her, she looks like she has been drugged?"

Lilith shakes her head. "There is no chemical alteration, not yet."

"No chemicals!" Dante demands. "And not another mark until I get there."

"There is the matter of my fee," the voice insists, "top-quality care is—"

"Name it!" Dante snaps.

"Two hundred and twenty." A slight crack escapes her voice.

Dante slowly narrows his eyes and allows a long, uncomfortable pause to hang between them. "Will you be performing the surgery personally?"

Dante can see that Lilith is trying to muffle her anticipation by sitting on her hands. "As always."

"At that price, I expect the treatment to begin as soon as I arrive, not before. I want to observe everything. I want an all-natural experience, NO CHEMICALS! And I want a personal consultation, no other spectators."

"We hold patient confidentiality in the highest regard," she assures.

"Then we have a deal. Tell me where you are."

Dante plays through the next few minutes in his mind as he stands across from the entrance to the school. He removes a white TAC charge from a pocket. "It's time to settle our account." He slides the charge into the breech of his pistol, then rotates the throttle at the rear of the gun from SAFE to one-quarter.

Three men exit the school. When they spot Dante, they quicken their steps down the street.

A tall red-and-white striped pole, topped with a brass sphere, stands inside the entrance of the Stadium School of Traditional Surgery. A woman wearing a white medical assistant uniform and cap meets him in the reception area. "Good evening," she says. "I am Nurse Lilith, and I will be performing the operation."

"How is the patient?"

"She is ready for surgery," Lilith answers with sincerity. "You have—?"

"Little tolerance for delays," Dante interrupts. "First, I want to see her. I want to ensure there are no further— *complications*."

"Of course," Lilith answers with a polite nod. "Follow me." She leads him to a large door in the middle of the rear wall of the reception room. Rollers squeak under the weight of the vault-like hatch that swings open. Thick padding lines the interior of the passageway.

Dante follows Nurse Lilith into a narrow hallway lined with the same thick padding as the door. "I noticed three men leaving," he says, his eyes narrowing as he peers at her. "I hope that was the last of your clientele."

Nurse Lilith answers in a tone that is meant to be reassuring, "Those three are part of my acquisition team. They are gone for the evening. I guarantee your confidentiality is thoroughly protected."

The walls of the hallway abruptly slope down to a circular performance area defined by a polished wooden partition. Observation bleachers encircle the surgical theater. Each level is defined by a rail for eager observers to lean against. A tall oak cabinet supports twin glass doors, accented with creamy-white ceramic handles at one end of the circle. A collection of labeled potions, powders, and canisters are neatly exhibited behind the glass.

An array of chrome blades, saws, and screws are displayed with care on a table covered with a sheet of white linen. The tools shine under the warm spotlight hanging above. A red velvet sheet covers a third object pushed to the side of the circle.

A woman is bound with thick leather restraints to a dissection table in the center of the surgery amphitheater. A roll of leather is jammed into her jaw and held by a strap wrapped around her neck and buckled at the base of her throat. Her disheveled red hair sticks to a recently cauterized scar that stains a white starched pillow.

Dante leans close to gaze into her fully conscious and terrified eyes.

Surgery and Recovery

Eager footsteps echo from the hall. Two figures appear in the light of the theater. Sonia pants against the leather roll buckled in her jaw.

The outline of Lilith's nurse's cap pokes into the light. The heavy door closes with a soft thud behind them. Then, the other appears.

A man with a dark-green long coat peers into the room. He has a lean frame, short brown hair, and a nervous twitch. His hands are crammed into the pockets of his overcoat. *He must be the one Lilith had referred to as my 'benefactor,' the one who will pay for my procedures.* Sonia watches him as he slithers about the surgery room.

The benefactor hovers over her. Lilith directs his attention to the left side of the dissection table and lifts a cloth revealing Sonia's hand bound with a leather strap against a black walnut board. The restraint displays her expired lifeclock for his review. Lilith caresses the black lifeclock on Sonia's hand. "As you can see, she has already signed the consent."

Sonia fights the restraints binding her to the operating table. Jogging her head back and forth, a soft, grunted scream emanates from behind the gag.

The benefactor's eager eyes stare into hers. He surveys her face and features as one would a meal. Sonia can tell he is aroused by her struggling. He looks to Lilith.

"Is it possible to remove the gag?" he asks with childlike excitement. "I am willing to pay extra for the distraction."

Nurse Lilith smiles. "Yes, this room is quite soundproof." She reaches for the buckle holding the gag in place, then withdraws her hand. "Since you brought up the matter of payment…"

A broad satisfied smile crosses his face as he reaches under his coat. "Yes, it's time to settle our account."

The room goes black; an explosion reverberates through the theater. Sonia forces her eyes to open against the darkness. A hand moves away from her face. Her benefactor is aiming a gun at a hole smashed in the wooden partition of the theater with Nurse Lilith sprawled in the middle.

Sonia's benefactor stands silent for a moment, then fumbles for a lever under the table. Air hisses through the pneumatic mechanism, and Sonia is propped into an almost standing position facing the man who just shot Nurse Lilith. "Hi, there," he says. "First of all, my name is Dante-nine, and yes, I am a reaper, but I am not going to hurt you."

She nods, not really understanding why.

Accepting the affirmation, he continues, "Okay, great! Second, you are Sonia-ten, and you have found a way out of the Collective, right?"

Sonia hesitates and slowly nods again.

"Yes," he says with a more deliberate voice. "And if I let you go, you will take me with you?"

Sonia stares at the reaper.

Dante secures his gun in his coat. Drawing back his sleeve, he reveals his blinking lifeclock. He repeats in a slower, more deliberate tone, "I said, if I let you go, you will take me with you to Haven. Right?"

"Errrrr-ruurrr." Sonia's response is an agreeable, low-pitched grunt that is muffled through her gag.

Dante reaches for the buckle at the base of her throat. The strap holding the rolled leather in her jaw falls away, allowing a long-held, skull-rattling, therapeutic scream to echo through the surgical theater.

Her lungs exhausted, Dante appears with his fists mashed against the side of his head. He uncovers his ears and says, "Okay, that was epic! Is, is that it? Do you need to go again?"

Sonia's eyes search her consciousness before shaking her head in a mild negative.

"And you promise to take me with you?"

She gives an agreeable nod.

Dante unbuckles the remaining restraints but pauses at the last manacle at her foot. "I'm sorry to belabor this, but I would like you to say it aloud, just once. You promise not to run away; you'll take me with you to Haven?"

Her voice cracks as she answers, "Yes." She is grateful that she managed not to cry out again. "But they took the toll."

"The what?"

"The departure point is inside pack territory. I arranged passage, but they require a toll. It was stolen along with all my gear." Sonia tries to step off the table but finds it difficult to balance.

Dante reaches out to steady her. "Are you sure we can't get through without it?"

Sonia shakes her head. "There is no way we can enter Outland without the toll."

Dante's attention turns to the unconscious woman smashed into the bleachers.

Nurse Lilith awakens to the smell of chemical vapors rising from a cloth held under her nose. Her first impression is that she is standing in five-point restraints against the dissection table. The voice of her former patient asks in astonishment, "She's alive?"

Her second impression is that of the benefactor referring to a slate terminal as he takes the cloth away. The doors of her once organized medicine cabinet hang open, its contents in shambles; a bottle labeled *aromatic spirits of ammonia* is uncapped.

"The TAC charge was launched on low power," he says. "It can kill at higher velocities, but that wasn't necessary." He pauses before adding, "At least not yet."

Lilith's third impression is that of her former patient, with a large hook-shaped blade in her hand. The surgery light shines off the chrome finish into her eyes, yet the gleaming blade is a more inviting sight than the empty eyes of the one holding it.

The benefactor stands behind the dissection table and whispers in her ear, "We don't have time to waste." He holds a canister of lysergic foam in front of her. "My friend had a bag full of chem when she traded with you, but I only found one in your store. Where is the rest?"

Nurse Lilith glances to her right. Dante follows her gaze down to a keyhole embedded at the base of her medicine cabinet. "The key is in—"

A mechanical clap sounds as Dante slaps the action of the pistol shut.

Sonia turns away from the muzzle flare just as the base of the cabinet shatters. She gathers the canisters and pouches that spill from the wreckage, then tries to hide her panic as she tells him, "It's not enough."

"How many?"

"There are only six here."

Dante tosses the foam canister to her.

"This makes seven; there should be twelve," she says.

"Twelve!"

"The deal was for four pouches and four canisters. The canines might demand more because I am late. There's no way they let us through with seven."

The dissection table hisses as Dante leans Nurse Lilith into the operating position. The former patient hovers above her with the shining crescent blade. Dante whispers into her ear, "Where's the rest?"

Jackal's crew follows him into the Coffee Hut. It's actually a renovated storage building. Renovated meaning, the broken windows had been covered with plywood.

Inside, collapsing furniture and tables give the space the impression of a diner. Jackal drops his bag onto the makeshift counter as the others take their seats. "We should move, don't ya think, Gordon?" The question brings a sour expression from the other; he corrects himself, "I mean Jackal!"

It's a stupid nickname that fails to impress anyone who spends more than a few minutes with the idiot, but he knows how to find honest work. Hauling the woman to nurse what's-her-name earned a few credits. They're supposed to deliver more product for her, which will bring another payday.

"In a minute," Jackal replies. "Let's sample our earnings."

One lights a cigarette and passes it to Jackal after a drag; the other removes a small flask from his shirt and shares it after a similar pull.

The fluid from the flask makes Jackal wince. He takes a canister from the sack and considers it. "No one will notice if one of the deliveries is a little light." He smiles. The others nod in agreement.

Lights inside the Coffee Hut shine onto the alley; Dante cracks the door to peek inside. Three men share a flask of something that makes them cringe with every sip. Sonia identifies her satchel and the toll bag.

Dante motions for her to stay behind him as he enters; he holds the gun out of view. All eyes turn to the squeaking door to see Dante walking toward them.

"You're in the wrong place, tourist," one calls out.

Two of the men move to flank the intruder. One pulls a dagger from his belt, the other a small hammer. Jackal moves as if to follow, then collects the bags and begins to withdraw into the shadows.

Two meters from the intruder, the men hear the last words they expect: "It's your time, Defector." Two flares burst from the muzzle in rapid succession, sending them to the ground, screaming.

Dante pockets his gun and walks past them.

Jackal begins to move toward the window.

"Do NOT make me run you down!"

The command presses the hired muscle against the wall. Jackal holds the two bags in front of him as a shield. "Reapers don't do this," he protests. "You never meddle with people making a living. What do you want?"

Though Dante makes no move to touch him, Jackal is helpless in Dante's gaze. Dante holds out a hand to accept the bags. His eyes are level with the brute's chin. Dante calls out, "Check them."

Sonia staggers past the men writhing on the ground; one of them looks in the direction of her footsteps, revealing the charred marks where his eyes used to be.

Dante removes the canister from Jackal's shirt as if to dare him to resist.

Sonia gives each bag a quick inspection and announces, "It's all here."

Dante's attention doesn't waver from his target. "Are you sure? We don't want to come back."

A more careful review confirms that everything is in order, despite the floor moving under her feet. She raises her gaze to meet her benefactor-turned-rescuer when she recognizes the man flattened against the wall. She gasps.

Dante asks, "This is the one who cut you?"

Sonia hadn't realized she nodded an affirmative when Dante's knee stabs into the side of Jackal's thigh. The thug stumbles forward, landing his chin into the palm of the smaller man. A twist releases a resonating crackle from Jackal's neck before he falls with his head unnaturally twisted.

Dante takes Sonia by the arm and leads her away.

Blackness recedes. An image replays behind Sonia's closed eyelids of her benefactor twisting the thug's neck, leaving his limp form to slide down the wall. Two men with charred eyes writhe on the ground as Dante leads her to the door. She wonders, *will these ghosts play nice with all the others every time I close my eyes? I guess I'll soon find out.*

She remembers a feeling of floating away from the warehouse. *Perhaps the reaper is taking me to the Citadel,* she dreams. It no longer concerns her.

At least it didn't then. Now the lightness is gone. Her limbs feel heavy, as though they are tied down. A mask presses against her face. The dream of Raymond-08 with his face outlined in the Somnolence recliner floats into her mind. *Why did I have to wake for this?*

"Sonia, Sonia-ten?" It's the voice of the reaper. *Why is he here?*

"You are being treated by a robotic surgeon." The voice is sincere, quiet, and close. "You're going to be okay."

A helmet covers Sonia's face. Through a clear glass visor, she can see Dante hovering beside her. Robotic surgical arms extend from a cart placed next to the table. An orange glow engulfs her body in a cocoon of light. Dante follows the progress of the operation on his slate. Inside the helmet, scanners identify the patient's trauma and administer vaporized medication to counteract any bacterial infection. The side of her face flutters in response to energy pulses directing an army of nanobots working to repair her injuries.

"Your wound was pretty bad, but there is no permanent damage. The table has you in a suspension field to treat some internal trauma and infection, so try not to move. In a few minutes, you'll be good as new, and we're getting out of here."

She notices he tries to hide his concern. The nanobots in her system shut down once all the muscle and tissue damage has been treated, but the machine isn't indicating that she is one hundred percent healed.

"I think it's finished," Sonia mutters through the helmet.

"You think so?"

"Yes, it's not working anymore," she answers.

"The program indicates there is still damage that it just isn't repairing. I'm not sure."

"It is," Sonia assures with more authority. "Trust me; I've spent a lot of time in these things. It's done."

Dante releases the clamps that secure a visor to the front of the helmet and helps her lift it away from her head. Sonia finds herself on the dissection table in the middle of the surgical amphitheater. A red velvet sheet that hid the surgical cart earlier is balled on the floor.

Nurse Lilith is conscious and bound by leather restraints and a few rolls of stained linen bandages in the observation bleachers.

Sonia stretches her jaw, no pain. Her hand reaches for her face in relief, then she feels it.

Dante can see fear returning to her eyes.

Sonia can see pity clouding his.

"It's not that bad," he offers in a clumsy voice.

Sonia takes her pocket clock from her bag. She snaps the lid open to face a video image of herself with a large scar relaying the path taken by Jackal's knife a few hours before. She says, "I finally got my new look."

A warning chime sounds from Dante's terminal slate. He checks the alert.

\# SENTRY ALERT!
\# EXPIRED LIFECLOCK FOR: Sonia-105.10.
\# LIFECLOCK LOGGED BY STADIUM CENSUS
SCANNER.
\# REAPERS DISPATCHED.

"Reapers are on the way. They're going to find us in a few minutes. Pull your things together."

Sonia slings the bags onto her shoulders as Dante begins another search on his slate and ransacks the medicine bottles scattered on the floor. He fills a jet injector with one of the chemicals.

"Take this." Compressed gas hisses through the injector as he jabs it into Sonia's neck.

"What are you doing?" she yells.

"It's going to help you walk." He returns to the medicine cabinet. A silver device shines in a satin-lined box. Dante assembles it as Sonia rubs her neck over the injection spot. "Are you sure you know what you're... What the hell is that?" she cries as Dante raises a large glass and metal syringe.

"Trust me," he says casually. A stream of fluid jumps from the tip of the ancient needle as he gently presses the plunger. "This is going to work."

Sonia's eyes bulge at the gothic sight. "What's going to work?"

Setting the syringe aside, Dante pulls the pistol from his coat and breaks the action open. He takes a white charge from his pocket and slides a brass-colored cap off the top before it settles into the breech. He slaps the action closed, grabs Sonia by the shoulder, and pulls her in front of him. She begins to object when he slides the bags from her arm. Terror washes across her face; her heart thunders in her ears. The muzzle is thrust into the small of her back.

Footsteps approach from the padded hallway. Dante offers a last direction quietly. "When I release you, silently begin counting as you walk toward the reaper." He demonstrates, "One, two, three... like that. Understand?"

Sonia nods affirmative, though she has no idea to what.

Dante gives her a reassuring pat on the shoulder. "Count to five, then deal with the officer as best you can. We're almost through this."

"Dante, is it?" Sonia's voice cracks.

"Yes."

"You seem to know a lot about chemicals."

Defector

The officers are young, aggressive, and anxious to kill. They take flanking positions when they enter the surgical theater.

"Hands where I can see them!" one calls out.

Dante keeps a tight grip on Sonia's shoulder as he raises his gun into view. "Relax. My name is Dante-nine with Bay City Brigade."

"You're a long way from home Dante-nine," the other challenges.

"Yes, and now that I have my prey, I'm taking her to the Citadel."

The reaper levels his gun toward Sonia's belly. "It's your time, Defector. Sonia-10, 285.092.105—"

"What the hell are you doing?" Dante barks. "I'm right here, you idiot! Do you intend to dispatch me along with the defector?"

His tone echoes the cadence of an academy combat instructor; it is still familiar to the officers as is their instinct to comply. When they drop their aim, Dante shoves Sonia in the direction of the first officer.

The other begins to speak in defense. "The STInGER will only—"

Sonia interrupts as she motions toward the bleachers. "What about her?"

The reapers look to the woman, dressed in white, bound on the floor with a roll of soggy leather buckled in her mouth beneath eyes bulging with terror.

Sonia lunges at the officer in front of her. She jabs her elbow into his chest, then grabs for the gun with both hands. The reaper directs her momentum into the wall and seizes her by the throat, yet she continues to direct the gun's muzzle away.

A pistol discharges. The hand at her throat relaxes. Dante withdraws the large steel syringe from the reaper's neck before he falls to the floor.

The other reaper is bound on the floor by a web of tactical adhesive tendrils. Dante kneels beside the cocoon, jabs the same syringe into the reaper's neck, and watches as he goes limp with the press of the plunger.

Dante plunders the two sleeping men and fills his pockets with their pistol charges and fuel cells. Then he directs Sonia to the exit.

"You know where to go?" he asks calmly.

"As far from here as possible."

Dante settles into the hover-pod and pulls the hatch closed. "You were great back there. The way you trapped his gun, we wouldn't have made it out without..." As he speaks, Dante breaks open his pistol's breech to insert a fresh TAC charge.

The clap of the action causes Sonia to recoil in her seat.

A surprised expression crosses Dante's face.

"Sorry," she says nervously. "I was just trying to remember a time when someone wasn't trying to kill me."

Dante pockets the pistol. "I won't allow anything bad to happen to you." He can see the terror in her eyes. Her chest rapidly rises and falls. "The stimulant isn't helping," he says. "It will run out of your system within the hour. I know it's unpleasant, but it helped you move faster back there." He can here her breathing settling.

"Dante?"

"Yes, I'm Dante-nine."

"Sonia-ten."

"I know."

"Why are you helping me? I don't mean to sound ungrateful, but…"

Dante shows her his flashing lifeclock. "I want to go to Haven. You SAID you would take me there."

She stares at the crystal flashing Last-Quarter as hers had a few days ago.

"You do know the way out, don't you?"

Sonia nods. "I arranged passage for myself and another." A blank look settles on her face.

"Carlos-ninety-two is not coming."

The news sends a shiver through Sonia. *He knows Carlos is dead.*

"There's something else I'd like to know," she ventures.

Dante tips his head, indicating for her to continue.

"You disabled Lilith, two of her goons, and two reapers without any trouble."

Dante gives her an uncomfortable look.

"But KILLED Jackal. Why?"

"I didn't think you'd mind."

"I don't," she admits. "I've done some terrible things to people who wanted to harm my brother and me." She hesitates. "But we never had the same—" she seems to be searching for the right way to say it, "—control."

Sonia tries to backtrack. "Look, I'm not complaining; I sure as hell ain't gonna miss him."

It's the same question Dante would face in a Brigade inquest if he were an officer. He couldn't claim self-defense.

The moment had passed slowly for Dante. He remembers Sonia's gasp when she recognized the hired muscle. He imagined the satisfaction Jackal must have taken when he pressed his blade into the side of her face. Carlos had likely seen a similar expression from the Barber-ah as she yanked his teeth from his jaw. It probably looked exactly like the one that smug rookie had as he waved on Helen-31's desperate pleas for her life. *I almost ended that bastard. But I didn't because that would have been over the line.*

"Dante?" Sonia asks.

With an awkward stutter, he answers, "I had to cross the line sometime."

"What does that mean?"

Dante smiles. "It means I'm all in."

Chapter 17

Outland

Dante paces in front of the locked iron gate. "It's been two hours," he says.

"They're watching us." There is a catch in Sonia's voice as she suppresses a nervous stutter.

"I see 'em." Dante nods. "Did it take this long the last time you were here?"

Sonia shakes her head. "But I had an appointment then."

The strap of Sonia's satchel cuts into Dante's shoulder. *What the hell does she carry in this thing?* He adjusts the straps position and asks, "Are canines that serious about punctuality?"

His answer calls from the shadows. "We have all the time in the world, Defector!" The light of a blue lifeclock materializes into a thirteen-year-old girl.

Sonia faces the approaching canine, opens her notebook, and displays the running stick figure drawing. "I mixed a deal here yester-morning for passage to Casey."

The girl crosses her arms and speaks in an almost singing voice, "So you're the defector that was gonna bring the heavy toll."

Sonia keeps her tone even. "The toll is plenty heavy and is for two. That's the deal. Now we're ready to move on." She nods for Dante to approach the gate.

The sentry steps away from the bars.

A small figure peeps into the light. Dante gives Sonia a nod in its direction. She acknowledges.

"Ya, Ronald was spouting on all before about the biiiig toll he was earning. Then come the gathering, he only passes a single bag of chem forward." The sentry shrugs. "It would have been a decent take for the day, 'cept he had to brag it up so big. Packs got no tolerance for liars." Her voice hardens with the last line.

"So who am I dealing with now?" Sonia asks.

"Alison." Sonia hears suspicion in her tone.

Sonia kneels with the toll bag and loosens the drawstrings. "Well, Alison, there were two other canines watching the deal I mixed with Ronald."

The child nods.

"I came ready to bring six, but Ronald insisted on eight. The extra canisters caused me delay." Opening the toll bag, Sonia offers the sentry a glimpse inside. Alison's expression changes at the sight. Sonia removes two pairs of packets and sets them on the ground. "Now I'm here. Here are four to take my mate and me on a walk through your territory. You get another four," she rattles the bag, "when I shake Casey's hand. That was the deal I mixed."

Alison turns and yells into the tunnel, "Maggie!"

At her call, a green light appears from the shadows. Sonia recognizes the girl who borrowed Priya at the end of the last deal. Maggie runs to the sentry and confirms the defector's story. With a nod from Alison, Sonia passes the four canisters through the bars of the gate. Maggie takes them and runs down the tunnel.

"Hold it!" Sonia scolds. "You're forgetting something."

Maggie pauses and answers in a high-pitched defiant voice, "We weren't expecting you to show, Defector. It's waiting for you at the end."

Once the courier is away, Alison unlatches the gate and waves the visitors forward. "We should get going." As she leads them into the tunnel, Dante and Sonia notice the hatchet tucked in the small of the canine's back. Alison nods for them to follow. "Stay close."

Sonia removes a pair of spectacles from her satchel hanging across Dante's back. The straps of the toll bag settle onto her shoulder. They descend into the gloomy tunnel. Sonia's eyes light up behind the lenses of her glasses, causing Alison, and numerous other voices in the shadows, to giggle.

A window hovers in front of Sonia, revealing an enhanced image of small creatures scurrying about the walls and children huddled in the passageways. No weapons are displayed.

Dante takes her arm. "Is it a good idea to call attention?"

"Believe me," she assures, "we are the center of attention." The subways under Stadium seem familiar to Sonia. Canines define areas for sleeping and gathering as they did in Balcarce. Cartons and derelict machines clutter the pathway. The obstructions slow their movement but allow effective hiding places. Most of the tunnel's facilities are smashed.

Holes mark the areas where ceiling and passage lights once shined. In their place, portable battery lanterns illuminate their path.

Occasionally, Sonia calls to Alison, recommending that they change their course. Murmurs stir in the shadows every time she does this.

"What are you doing?" Dante asks.

"Keeping us alive." Her holographic glasses reveal blue cones of light shimmering in the passage, indicating the presence of active lifeclock scanners.

At one junction, Alison follows a motion from Sonia and smashes one of the sensors embedded in the wall with her axe. The light cone fades. Alison waves Sonia and Dante forward. "Maybe if I get some funny eyes, I could find the scanners too."

Sonia ignores the comment. "How much further?"

Alison doesn't press the point. "Not much."

The giggling along the pathway stops. Dante senses a restlessness building from the hiding places. "Alison, what's going on?"

Their guide looks about suspiciously. A hand signal motions from an intersection. "Mutts," she answers. "They must have heard about your passage." She darts down the tunnel and disappears.

Alone with the murmurs echoing around them, Dante leans toward Sonia. "What the hell?"

"Rival canines," she answers and then continues down the path that Alison ran.

Dante takes her arm. "Is that a good idea?"

Sonia shrugs. "I don't know, but we still have half the toll, and someone is going to want it."

Dante's hand rests on the grip of his gun.

The tunnel opens into a large maintenance bay lit by yellowed floodlights hanging high above. One section is defined as a parking lot where an array of pods and movable platforms lay useless atop broken wheels. Large containers, storage shelves, and stacked cartons define a supply depot in another section. Worktables cluttered with broken tools and pod components line the walls. Only the center of the underground yard is kept clear.

Sonia recognizes the space as the pack's main gathering area. Many of the containers and vehicles are turned on their side, serving as cover for the small figures hiding around them. Two large corridors, twice the size as the one Dante and Sonia had just left, descend away from the bay.

Alison appears from one of the corridors. "Looks like your stroll has ended, Defectors. The mutts want the rest of the toll, and we're not that attached to bleeding for it."

Dante steps in the child's direction. "You give up on what you earn that easily?" His tone is mocking.

Sonia follows his lead. "Maybe the mutts take us to Casey and get the toll without bleeding either."

"Mutts have no use for Casey or his treaty," she yells, "and neither do I."

Sonia directs her response to the younger ears hiding in and around the containers. "So, canines gonna lose a lifetime of earnings 'cuz a your lying?"

The disturbance in the shadows settles as figures holding green crystals consider Alison's answer. They all understand the dangers strangers pose to the pack, but danger is part of a canine's life.

"If you turn away this toll, Casey will find a pack that won't," Sonia says. "He's not going to work with liars."

The sounds of chattering boys echo louder and louder in the corridor.

Dante approaches the girl and kneels to look her in the eye.

Alison removes the hatchet from her belt.

Dante raises his hands. "If I deal with the mutts, will you still take us to Casey?"

A dark scowl crosses her face. After a moment, she nods.

"From which way are they coming?"

Alison glances toward one of the passages. "Henry is coming with scouts. You live through that, and we finish our business."

"All right, make sure your friends..."

The girl grunts.

"I mean your pack," he says, "has cleared away from there. This won't take long."

Howls echo in the corridor. Blue lifeclocks shine in the darkness.

"I count five of them," Sonia says in a soft tone.

Dante turns with a frustrated look. "You see them?"

Sonia's glowing eyes lead an impatient expression. "The youngest looks to be about sixteen."

Light enhancement, he thinks. *Must be nice.*

The lead figure appears from the passageway.

Negotiation

Henry enters the gathering area and greets the intruders with open arms. "I see the north side keeps strange company now!" His scouts laugh from the shadows of the corridor's entrance. "When did they welcome Bloody Richard into their territory?"

Dante moves slowly in their direction. "We made a deal to meet with Casey, that's all," he calls. "Take us to him, and you can have the toll."

"Gut rip him, Henry!" a voice calls from behind. "Tear him open, and we can mop up his stuff later."

"What about that Bloody-22?" Henry asks. "What about we just rip you open and see what you're made of?"

Dante sighs. "That's too bad, Henry. Too bad you pass up easy earnings for a face full of wind."

Henry speaks with an amused voice as he pulls a packet from his shirt. "Your sympathy touches me, Richard, it really does." He shakes the pouch at his side as if to avoid calling attention to it. "My heart is gladdened by your concern." The packet crackles between the canine's fingers as he pinches the top, then raises the huff-pouch to his face.

The child's movement echoes something in Dante. It is a motion he has seen many times. Henry inhales the packet's fumes. The danger registers with Dante. "Oh, no!"

With a giddy smile, Henry fades into a blur. An unseen mass sweeps under Dante's legs and impacts his chest. The force throws him to the ground.

Hysterical cackling bursts from the scouts who watch from the corridor. Dante pulls his attention from the mutts to find Sonia clawing at Henry's arm locked around her neck.

Henry's face shows joy as Sonia kicks about in his grasp. He swings his captive about like a full-size paper doll.

Dante regains his footing to find all the mutts holding packets like the one Henry just used. They shake their pouches at their sides, mimicking their leader's movements.

"Speed," Dante mutters as he breaks open the breech of his pistol. "Someone has been trading speed with the pack."

One of the scouts displays a large knife as he squeezes his huff-pouch. "Hey, Henry, watch me take his head!"

The mutts flinch when Dante throws a pebble-sized object in their direction, then laugh as the vial bounces into the group. It glows blue on the ground.

A blue dot flashes inside a red circle of Dante's gunsight. A flare erupts from his pistol. The STInGER detonates the fuel cell just inside the passageway, engulfing the mutts in flames.

Henry's expression changes to horror as he watches his scouts run about as formless silhouettes of fire before dropping to the ground.

Henry hears the woman struggling in his arms. Her terrified gasp mirrors his. He lowers his eyes in time to see the huff-pouch fall to the ground.

Sonia stands in a tempest of chaos that settles to a calm, coherent speed. The huff-pouch slips from her fingers. The holographic window rendering in her spectacles appears as a crude collection of choppy lines drawn with contrasting dots of color and shade. Sonia peers between the lines to see the shapeless forms slowly moving about. The figures resolve into writhing human figures; she perceives every crease of terror etched in the children's burning faces.

The chokehold restraining her relaxes. Sonia's fingers encircle Henry's wrist. His bones crunch like dry straw as she tightens her grip. She raises her arm and stabs her elbow into his rib cage. Something yields inside his chest. She hits the same area again and again, each time pushing him further back until his hold surrenders.

Henry experiences Sonia's assault as a single explosive impact to his chest, shattering two of his ribs and driving him to the ground. He regains his footing and tries to grab her shoulders. He misses.

Dante watches Sonia become a blur in Henry's outstretched arms. The mutt falls to the ground and convulses about. Spots of blood mark his path. When the chemical disburses from Sonia's system, Henry is a mass of pain. Her knee is in his chest; his arm is twisted over his head. Her face is burning red as she gasps uncontrollably. Her body is soaked in sweat. A restrained giggle escapes her.

"Go on, Defector, take another whiff from the pouch and finish me." Henry chides her. "It feels good, doesn't it? So take another pull."

Dante approaches her. "Sonia, another dose of speed will kill you, and you don't need it, it's over."

Panting wildly, she doesn't acknowledge his presence nor does she understand what he says, but the tone of his voice persuades her to slow down.

"Sonia, listen to me," he says. "You need to take deep, slow breaths. Lower your heart rate."

She responds with a lost expression.

He demonstrates for her. "Deep . . . slow . . . breaths."

Sonia does her best to mimic Dante's directions. Fumbling in Henry's shirt, she finds his huff-pouch and tosses it to Dante.

An angry judgmental voice rises above the distressed murmurs all around. "You're a reaper!" Alison calls. "A reaper and a defector in our territory!"

Dante retrieves the toll bag where the mutt had grabbed Sonia and replaces the one she dropped. "And you brought us here, Alison." Dante's response reaches to all those watching from cover.

He swings the toll bag across his shoulder and returns to Sonia. "You will answer to the pack at the gathering for bringing a reaper into your tunnels—"

"Territory," Sonia whispers.

"Territory," he says. "The question is, will you explain it with…" he drops the toll bag on the ground and aims his pistol at it, "…or without the chem. Take us to Casey now, and you get the toll."

Alison fumes at his demand, then waves them forward. The murmuring in the shadows subsides.

Dante has to help steady Sonia as they are lead further into the tunnels, eventually bringing them around a bend. A large chamber opens before them with an even larger passage extending to the right and left. A lantern hangs on the wall, lighting the room.

It takes a moment for their eyes to adjust to the lamplight before they can tell that the passageway is a terra-tube.

Maggie sits on a small stool next to the wall holding Sonia's tote bag on her lap. The canine gives Sonia a stern look, then brings the bag to her.

Sonia kneels down to thank her, but the canine runs away.

Alison removes the lamp from the wall with a pole and waves it inside the tube.

After a moment, a low rumble reverberates from the tunnel, which is soon followed by a large terra-car.

The vehicle glides to a stop, a door opens, and a bearded man steps into the chamber. He approaches the group and addresses the woman, "You are Sonia-10," he dips his head before turning to the man holding her up. "I don't know who the hell you are."

Before either of them can answer, Alison steps forward. "He's a reaper, Casey. Our treaty demands that you make sure no reaper comes through our territory."

Casey shoots Sonia a curious look.

Sonia struggles to speak with an even tone, "He's a defector—trying to get—to Haven, same as me." As she speaks, she pulls the toll bag from Dante's shoulder and tosses it into Casey's arms. "Here's the toll we agreed on, nine canisters of chem."

Alison's eyes bulge with rage. Ripping the hatchet from her belt, she roars, "Liar!"

Dante slips his pistol from his jacket.

Casey considers the gun pointing at the ground and casually offers the bag back to Sonia. "You were told I wouldn't accept a toll if offered."

Sonia looks to Dante. "It's him."

As she takes the bag, Dante notices a clear dot embedded on the back of Casey's hand.

Sonia places the toll bag on the ground and turns to Alison. "Careful with this pup, less what we used to get out of that scrape back there, you have nine canisters in here. Along with the four you took at the border, that's thirteen you'll bring to the gathering, you watch that they count them all."

"You told me there would be eight canisters, Defector!" She spits her words. "Thirteen ain't eight! Take off before I call the whole pack on your lying head."

Dante is ineffective at hiding his confused expression as they follow Casey into the car. Sonia shrugs as the doors close behind them. "They don't teach counting in the pack."

Terra Tunnel

Motion sensors trigger lights lining the ceiling and sides of the massive tunnel illuminating the oncoming terra-car. The underground locomotive glides above ancient charged rails that have seldom been used since their assembly.

Designed to move commuters and cargo around the globe, the terra tunnel extends a kilometer beneath the surface of the western coast of the North American region. Lost to history are the production plans that depict the tunnel moving into the ocean and following the coastal contours into Asia and down to Australia. The construction of this line was abandoned soon after the Awakening.

Inside, rows upon rows of seating and associated luggage space, enough to comfortably carry up to two hundred passengers, extend the length of the cabin. Sonia collapses onto the seat opposite the car's entrance. Her skin color has almost returned to normal. She shivers against the cold air blowing against her damp shirt.

Dante kneels beside her to feel her soaked forehead. "How are you feeling?"

Sonia winces under his touch. "Like a towel still being twisted out." She sighs. "I've been moving speed pads for five years, first time ever tried one."

"Speed is designed for adolescents," Dante explains. "It's going to play hell with your adult metabolism until it has worked itself out."

"For kids?" she asks.

He nods. "The national militias sold them to young conscripts during the support actions of the twenty-third century in place of formal combat training. You wouldn't believe the license agreements they made the children sign to avoid lawsuits when they returned from their deployments."

He places the satchel on the seat next to her. "I don't suppose you have any blood scrubbers in this miracle bag of yours?"

She shakes her head and laughs. Then opens the cover to her bag and fumbles for a flask. "No, just a little water."

Dante takes the flask, removes the cap, and passes it to her. "That will help a lot. You'll be okay in a little while once it's worked out of your system."

Sonia gives Dante a suspicious look as she takes the flask. "You really know a lot about chemicals."

His smile is coy. "I may have picked up a few interesting tidbits while experimenting in the ingestion clinic." He shakes his head cautiously. "Although, I never took anything as aggressive as speed. Try to breathe in through your nose, hold it for three seconds, then out through your mouth."

Dante rubs the back of Sonia's neck, recalling Cindy-18's vomit-side-manner. He can feel the old man glaring at him from above. Without looking up, he asks, "Do you have any water?"

Casey doesn't move. His eyes dart between his two new passengers.

Dante meets Casey's accusing gaze and says, "Some friendly advice. If you really want to look intimidating, put on a white skirt and vintage medical assistant's cap."

Sonia bursts out laughing.

The old man fails to give a more somber scowl, try as he might.

Dante says, "Seriously, those Barber-ahs freak me out." Eventually, he manages to catch Casey's attention. "Please, her system is working through some nasty chem. If she doesn't replenish her fluids and electrolytes, she can go into shock."

Casey cues his earpiece. "Lucas, bring the canteen back here when you get a chance."

Sonia rocks her head across the seat's headrest. "I knew a Marcos once," she mumbles. Her eyes burst open. She grabs the tote bag sitting on the floor. As soon as the zipper separates, Priya erupts through the opening and runs through the cabin. "I hope they remembered to feed you."

Silence lingers until Lucas appears with a large canister of water. The nineteen-year-old man supports the canteen while Sonia and Dante drink.

"If you have anything salty in that pack, you should eat it," Dante says. Then he turns to Casey. "I have a few questions for you."

"Lucas can answer them," he replies. "I need to speak with the girl."

Sonia nods approval to Dante, who follows Lucas to the front of the car.

Chapter 18

He's Never Late

Dante's eyes drift around the curves of the woman relaxing next to him on the couch inside the hover-pod. She leans toward the bottle of champagne tipping into her glass and offers a seductive smile. The motion pulls his eyes into her descending neckline. The glass dancer from the Crystal Lounge is delightfully quiet, saving him from any expectations of conversation.

He had removed his jacket hours ago since the environmental controls of the hover-pod's extended cabin is set warmer than normal in deference to the dancer's sheer attire. The material meandering around her figure hardly challenges Dante's imagination. Pale-blue luminescent patches twinkle across her otherwise see-through dress. When performing in the Crystal Lounge, the costume reacts to her body heat and the stage lights, giving her the appearance of dancing in a gown of moonlight glimmering on rippling water.

The two communicate with expressions, gestures, and caresses in a language with few words other than *'closer'* and *'yes.'*

Their hover-pod glides across the continent to a destination of no concern.

Octavia has imagined this scenario all afternoon. *Did he actually do it?* she wonders. *Has he finally stopped moping about his life and at least tried to find some joy in his Final-Quarter?*

Dante has been her partner since before the Correction. In all that time, he has never missed a scheduled shift. This last thought bothers her. *What would Dante really do if he decided not to come to work?* She hopes the question will return the image of a nameless glass dancer wrapped around her partner. It doesn't.

Instead, she faces the vision of Dante's contorted wrist anxiously pressed against his thigh yesterday. She didn't want to see him like that, but body language of a citizen trying to hide the state of his lifeclock shouts to her, *"I only have a few more days to…" what? What are you doing, Dante?*

The cadet is hyper-respectful to Octavia when she tries to check in her duty gear at the quartermaster's desk. "Karl-forty-six would like to see you before you check out."

Octavia holsters her pistol. "Did he say why?"

The cadet shakes his head. "The chief dispatcher gave me explicit instructions that I should give you his message verbally." Cadets in Charon Brigade are trained to relay all messages with no inflection. Officer business is none of his.

Octavia stands with a respectful attention when she enters the office of the chief dispatcher. His title is mostly honorary. Karl-46's role is primarily to serve as a communication point between the Charon Brigade and the Departments of Civil Planning and Justice. He carries an implied rank superior to the officers he directs. After standing in silence for a moment, Octavia brushes her hood back, pulls a chair opposite his desk, and sits.

The chief dispatcher's rebuke is immediate. "I haven't offered you a seat, Officer." It's his best attempt at intimidation, which would have worked on a cadet or new officer in his 'command,' as he liked to think of it.

Octavia acknowledges it as an apology. "Please, think nothing of it. I found one."

Karl turns away from his terminal. "Where is he?"

With an emphatic shake of her head, she answers, "I have no idea." Karl's game is wearing thin. This man has no official authority over Octavia, and she isn't about to allow him the fantasy that there is.

"Dante-nine didn't show up for his shift today." Karl continues his inquisition.

Octavia's response is aloof. "No."

"Have you ever known him to miss a shift?"

"No, and there is no directive that compels him to show up for work. If you want to know where he is, just call him."

This trips Karl's attention. "You mean you have not tried to call him today? Aren't you and Dante…?"

Octavia perks her eyes at the question Karl realizes he doesn't have the gall to ask.

Karl settles into his chair, then turns the monitor of his terminal to face Octavia. It displays Dante's citizen profile. "At 15:23 hours yesterday, Dante-09 entered Final-Quarter. Today, he didn't appear for his shift and isn't answering his LINCC."

Octavia acknowledges with a raised eyebrow. "People ignore calls sometimes. Again, it's not a crime," her voice is casual but she resents the direction Karl is leading.

"It is when he is on duty," Karl says. "Dante's pistol is still checked out. This is not unusual considering all the on-call hours he covers. However, as long as his weapon is checked out, Dante is on duty and is responsible for answering his LINCC."

Octavia nods in agreement. "I'll drop by his place and see if he is all right."

Karl slides a drawer open. "We already have." He places Dante's terminal-tracker and tele-LINCC on his desk. "There is any number of reasons Dante may have disappeared. He might have left the area to follow some Final-Quarter fantasy. I am concerned that he might have harmed himself." As legitimate as this last point is, the next was just as relevant. "On the other hand, we have to consider the possibility that he is..."

"Do not... consider that possibility out loud!" Octavia's growl is soft, yet it thunders through the CD's tiny office. He can't see it, but Octavia has her hand tightly griping the truncheon at her knee.

Octavia can tell he is trying to clear the knot from his throat before he says, "Then it's up to you to finish it, Officer. There is a reaper out there with a pistol and a full duty load who is not answering his calls because he intentionally left his tele-LINCC behind. Someone needs to make contact with him and find out if he intends to operate as a civil officer of the Charon Brigade. If he doesn't, then what the hell is he doing with his pistol?" Karl crosses his hand on his desk. "You know him better than anyone. Do you want to conduct this investigation, or should I assign it to the next shift?"

The chair crashes across the floor as Octavia stands. "I'll find him."

Karl nods. "The Judiciary needs a status update in twelve hours. The launching signature of Dante's pistol will be submitted for tracking. If he fires his gun around any lifeclock sensor, dispatch will notify you immediately."

Octavia acknowledges the assignment with a nod. She knows the protocol, but it sickens her to hear it applied to her partner.

Karl rises to extend his hand to the officer and wish her a good hunt, but Octavia is already at the door and closes it behind her.

Octavia fumes down the hallway of the Brigade headquarters. *That nitwit is probably passed out in an ingestion clinic with a stream of drool running down his chin,* she muses, remembering the time she had found him in such a state. *With all the credits he gets from pulling extra duty, it's detestable that he refuses to figure out a better way to deal with his anxiety.*

She tries to recall the daydream of her partner tangled in the arms of a woman grinding atop him, maybe two. In such a case, she could slip the pistol from his clothes piled on the floor and exit without a word. That would be it. *It's possible,* she thinks. *Stranger things have happened. I'll find him, and we'll resolve this misunderstanding.*

Octavia finds an open workstation in the records office. She considers her reflection in the dark monitor. *It would be nicer for someone else to do this.* She cues the vocal pickup for the terminal and says, "Query, any mention of Brigade Officer Dante-nine on the West Coast of the North American region in the last twenty-four hours."

The terminal scrolls a series of one-line synopses. One references the conversation they had in the hover-pod with Judicial Officer Sydney-20 yesterday, along with a few other standard requests followed by a late-night report from an Antioch civil investigator.

"What the hell is he doing in Antioch?"

The terminal responds:

\# Please restate the question.

"Display the full investigation report from Civil Investigator Jacob-11."

After skimming the report, Octavia cues a vid-LINCC. Her introduction is casual when he appears on-screen, at first. "Civil Investigator Jacob-eleven?" she asks.

"I am."

"I am Officer Octavia-seventy of the Bay City Charon Brigade. You spoke with my partner last night—"

"You're calling about Dante-nine?" his answer is impatient.

Surprised by his edginess, she doesn't answer before he asks, "Are you calling from a Brigade terminal?"

"Yes."

"I'm moving to a private terminal. Call me when you have done the same."

A new message chime sounds. Octavia's tele-LINCC imports Jacob's personal encryption into her LINCC database. The connection terminates.

Octavia considers the dark monitor, then moves to a more secluded area. After activating her personal encryption, she cues the new entry with her tele-LINCC. Jacob is only slightly less abrasive when he answers.

"Dante-nine is your partner?"

"He is."

"Am I to assume that he has not appeared for his shift today nor has he updated your division on his… investigation?"

His tone annoys Octavia. She responds with her own annoyance. "Investigator, you should be careful—"

Jacob talks over her response. "Don't interrupt, Officer, just listen. Dante helped me with a murder investigation last night, and I appreciate it, but he also removed a prohibited device from the crime scene that needs to be returned, immediately."

Octavia recognizes a change in his tone. *He's not angry; he's scared.* "When I find him, I'll ask about it."

The line is quiet. Octavia can hear him stirring. "Tell me about his investigation," she says.

Jacob relays the facts of the crime scene and the information Dante provided.

Octavia dismisses his account and says, "This was all in your report."

Jacob recognizes that he has been stalling. "Officer, I was eleven years old on my first day of Civil Security skill-trade, which happened to be the Brigade's Day of Correction. My troop watched as…" he hesitates. "I have always made a point to offer the Brigade officers every professional courtesy, which last night included access to a crime scene.

"When Dante-nine disappeared from the clinic last night, he was the last person to hold a highly modified terminal slate."

"The one you mentioned earlier?" Octavia asks.

"The cadet who cataloged it noted that it communicates with level-seventy encryption. When I examined it, I found the only onboard resource is a program to identify and connect to LINCC access points, including secure ones. Everything else, even the operating system, is accessed on the aether. At the time, I was concentrating on a multiple homicide and didn't give it any thought. I realize now that it was likely designed to navigate aether accounts without leaving any indication of its activity. Anyone using that terminal can transfer credits, open communication lines, access databases, and even place orders on the transportation network without leaving a trace of their movements."

His last comment sparks Octavia's attention. "What do you mean without leaving a trace?"

"Officer," Jacob interjects. "If I report to the Judiciary compelling evidence that Octavia-seventy is selling large amounts of unregulated lysergic foam or is using unauthorized robotic workers to fix the plumbing in a living complex instead of employing citizen workers, they will give me permission to identify, track, and record the activity of your aether account. This would allow me to locate you in real time when you log on to your database as well as track any devise you use to access the LINCC."

"The Brigade has the same ability."

"This slate can't be identified or tracked. As a civil investigator, I can think of a dozen types of criminals who would benefit from such a terminal. As a reaper, can you?"

Octavia answers defensively, "I don't know that I can, not with absolute certainty."

"Neither can I, Officer. That is why I left it out of my report last night, but I can't hide it indefinitely. I need that slate returned or absolute proof that it has been destroyed."

"Tell me, Investigator, is it the practice to leave such dangerous items out for anyone to access?"

"Reaper, it never occurred to me that a civil officer would give me concern."

His answer slaps Octavia, reminding her that they are talking about her partner. "I have one last question. Did you happen to see if Dante had his weapon?"

"He identified himself as a reaper when he flashed it last night."

"Thank you. I will notify you with any information about your missing evidence."

The connection closes.

Octavia returns to the terminal and checks the last item returned by her query. It's a report of two rookie reapers in Stadium who had apprehended a defector named Sonia-10 and then transferred custody to a Charon Brigade officer named Dante-09.

"You're helping her, Dante," Octavia mutters. "You're assisting a defector."

Sonia and Casey

Uncontrollable electrical signals pulsate through the overloaded wiring of Sonia's nervous system. Her arms jerk and twitch about.

The stoic man sitting in the seat across from her is like no one she has ever seen. Casey's eyes have an empty quality, as though they've seen more of the world than a person is supposed to. The old man had said that he wanted to speak with her but stays silent as she twitches in her seat.

His surveillance annoys Sonia, who decides to ask, "So, I have to know—"

"Forty-three," he answers abruptly.

"Seriously?!" she says, unable to hide her amazement.

Casey nods. Then he allows himself a lighter demeanor. "Give or take," he says with a gentle affirmative nod. "I really don't know for sure, but my nearest count is forty-three years old." He holds up his hand to display a clear lifeclock.

Sonia leans in for a closer look.

"It stayed black for about two years, then the color began to fade until..." his voice trails off as he presses his thumb against the crystal face.

Sonia turns to the small porthole window that frames the darkness of the tunnel walls.

"You know, this is not the underground railroad I was expecting. How long will it take to get to Haven?"

"The terra tunnel doesn't go to Haven!" His voice holds a scolding tone. "This won't even get you out of the Collective. I'm here to point you and your reaper in the right direction."

Sonia's head falls back against the headrest.

Casey leans toward her. "You know we take great measures to make sure our passengers don't bring the Brigade with them! That wasn't very smart."

His condescending attitude grinds away the last of Sonia's patience. "Neither is placing the departure point in the middle of Outland! Do you have any idea what we had to do to make this rendezvous?"

"Perhaps the Citadel would have been more to your liking."

The residue of speed coursing through her blood causes Sonia's mind to race with a thousand arguments. She tries to lift herself out of the seat to level her eyes with his. Unfortunately, she is too light-headed.

Casey hands her the canteen when she falls back.

"We're not done here, young lady."

There's that tone again. Sonia wonders if it is an inherent trait old people naturally develop.

"How do you bring a reaper here?"

Sonia keeps her eyes closed and mentally recounts all the events that took her from the surgery amphitheater to the canines burning in the tunnel. Shaking her head, she mutters, "I can't possibly relay the whole story, but after the first time he saved my life, I promised to take him to Haven."

Casey's icy stare burns Sonia's awareness.

"If he wanted me dead, he could have left me at any number of places along the way in the last twenty hours, or however long it has been. What time is it?"

Rage festers under Casey's soft voice. "And now that you pointed him to Haven's departure point, he can destroy it along with you. Hell, considering the mess you left with the canines, you may have already destroyed it. There's no departure point if those delinquents close their borders to us."

"Then why did you put the departure point in the middle of Outland in the first place?" Sonia's heart begins to race as she matches his aggressive tone.

Casey fumes. "It wasn't always in Outland. Stadium fell off the grid about eighty years ago, and you can't just move a terra-car station."

She inhales, holds for a three count, and allows it to escape between her lips. "The pack knows a reaper has gone through their tunnels, and that will make the older ones furious. At the next gathering, they will want to shut off their contact with you." After another three count, she continues, "But the younger canines will focus on the massive toll the pack earned. They'll see the departure line as an ongoing source of earnings and will not allow the older canines to restrict their future revenue. If your surrogate over there reminds them of that, future passengers will be just fine." She finishes with another pull of water.

Casey settles into his seat. "You seem mighty sure of that."

Sonia shakes her head. She recognizes that the old man is arguing for his own sake. "As chaotic as the pack may appear, they all follow certain guidelines. Though they may not be as strong, the younger canines will never allow the older to close off sources of earnings. Even the strongest canines can be killed in their sleep."

They sit for a while, until the cabin stops spinning around her. Finally, Sonia is able to lean forward once again.

"So, Conductor, if this train isn't going to Haven, where is it taking us?"

"You have a couple hours before you need to move on." He pulls a small metal plate from his pocket with a hexagonal disk fastened to one side and hands it to her.

A dial with an illuminated arrow painted on it rotates behind a glass lens. Sonia asks, "What is it?"

"A compass, of sorts. When you start the next phase of your journey, the arrow will align itself with a beacon that will lead you to a bunker. Just follow it until you get there."

Sonia considers the device. "Then what?"

"I have no idea," Casey answers dryly. "I've never been there."

"You're not serious!"

"I've been making these for over twenty-five years," Casey assures. "The bunker is transmitting at a very tight frequency. The compass will point you right to it."

Sonia ponders the device in her palm the way she once considered her little egg. "What frequency does it follow?"

Casey sits back in his seat and crosses his arms. "That is a secret you don't need to know. I told you, I've been making these for—"

Sonia removes her terminal from her satchel and unfolds it. She places the compass in front of one of the communication ports as Casey protests.

"What are you doing?" he hisses.

"It's a receiver, basically, with no ports," she mutters. "Which means you have to wirelessly program it." Sonia gives Casey's hand a sharp slap when he tries to retrieve the compass sitting on her lap.

A green wire-framed diagram of the compass rotates in a window hovering in front of Sonia's spectacles as the terminal communicates with its settings menu.

"The receiver is programmed to find a series of radio pulses at 1973.21568 MHz, 1973.315476 MHz, and 1974.5871 MHz."

Casey's helpless expression confirms Sonia's findings are accurate. "Do you realize what you are doing?" he asks.

"It's not any fun if I know what I'm doing!" she says sardonically.

After sending a dozen commands to her terminal, Sonia sets it on the seat opposite her. A green starburst twinkles in her spectacles at the terminal's radio emitter. She stands with the compass cradled in her palm. Its arrow locks in the direction of the terminal's emitter as she walks back and forth, turning in circles. A numeric display appears on the baseplate indicating the distance to her terminal. The simple success gives Sonia a much-needed laugh before she collapses back into her seat.

"Why is that funny?" Casey demands.

Sonia smiles as she removes her spectacles and hangs them on the neckline of her shirt. "It's the first normal thing I've done in a long time."

Dante and Lucas

Dante and Lucas sit together in the forward control compartment, watching the bands of light encircling the interior of the tunnel as the terra-car barrels through the Earth. Dante breaks the half-hour silence. "It doesn't seem to move as fast as I remember."

Lucas is perched beside a control panel with his feet on the pilot's seat, lost in his thoughts. "We only run it between one-quarter and one-half speed so our power draw isn't noticed by the monitors."

"I once took the Atlantic line from Buenos Aires to Cape Town, then up to Lisbon," Dante offers.

This gets Lucas's attention. "What's in Lisbon?"

Dante shakes his head. "Nothing, it's just the end of the Atlantic terra line." Silence lingers. "I guess it's just something you do when you're eighteen." The story fizzles away. "Have you ever ridden the terra line?"

Lucas ponders the question. "Never. I should though, before…" His voice trails off.

Dante completes his thought. "Before you leave for Haven?"

Lucas shakes his head and smiles. "I'm not going to Haven." He slides into the pilot's seat and finally gives Dante his full attention. "I work with Casey in exchange for his insight into the operation of the Guardian and the systems of the Collective."

Dante keeps a neutral expression.

Lucas continues. "In my normal life, I'm a civil engineer. I work with the Planning and Implementation Bureau to keep the Collective's infrastructure operational."

"Bullshit!" Dante challenges with a smile.

Lucas laughs. "I'm serious. The Guardian updates reports on the status of food production, communication, power generation and consumption, water and sewage reclamation, hover-pod and rail-bus maintenance, everything that keeps the North American region operating. It makes recommendations, and I help manage the implementation."

Dante shakes his head in disbelief. "And undermining citizen obligation is just a hobby for your downtime?"

Lucas reluctantly smiles in agreement. "You're right; I suppose I am helping to undermine the spirit of the Awakening by subverting one of the directives."

"A big one."

Lucas nods. "Yes, a big one, but I am also contributing to the Collective's operation." He becomes serious. "Casey has studied the Collective's systems for almost two lifetimes. I help him by investigating and contacting defectors on his behalf, and he reveals secrets of the machine's operation to me that I would never otherwise learn."

He leans toward Dante with a smile. "You're right. I am subverting the system to a degree, but I am also helping it function more efficiently by sharing the secrets I learn with the apprentice generation of engineers." His expression becomes sober. "Besides, the Collective is losing talent. Look at this tunnel." He motions to the lights passing over the canopy. "It was supposed to connect the Gulf states with the west coast of the North American region then extend to a Pacific terra tunnel line all the way to East Russia. Since the Awakening, it has laid dormant." Lucas drifts back into his trance. "We have the resources, we have the materials, but the engineering to span a terra tunnel into the continental plates and across the sea floor just don't exist anymore. We know how to maintain and repair the Pacific terra line, but the know-how to replicate it is just..." his eyes search for something in the passing lights, "... gone."

Dante leans into his seat and places his feet on the side of the control board. "Go on."

Lucas looks away. After another moment, he slaps the side of the control panel. "Hell, maybe I just like the train."

"Don't be coy; you are dying to tell me so just say it." Dante's voice holds a mocking edge. "Why are you helping defectors escape if you're not going yourself?"

Lucas's eyes settle outside the canopy. "I wish I had the nerve to climb up to the iris, but what if there is nothing out there, and I'm just wandering in Perdition for the rest of my life?" He shakes his head again. "No. I belong here. I want to stay, even if it ends in the Citadel."

"What about subverting the directives?" Dante insists.

A smile breaks the corner of Lucas's face. "I may not have the stamina to run out into nowhere, following the hope of some utopia where everyone lives in springtime forever, but some people do. Maybe I'm…" he searches for the correct phrase, "observing my obligation to help my fellow citizen find their bliss, even if that means assisting them in defying the Somnus Obligation and risking the wrath of the Brigade."

Dante considers his answer. "No, there's something more."

Lucas gazes down the tunnel. "You've seen Casey, he can't go anywhere. Except for me, and the occasional defector, the man is cut off from all human contact. Maybe I can't stand the notion of him down here alone."

"Isn't he in contact with Haven?" Dante asks.

Lucas shakes his head. "I don't think he is. He has never mentioned any communication outside the Collective."

"How many departure points to Haven are there?"

"Long ago, this terra-car line supported five stations. Stadium is the last active departure point to Haven." Lucas taps his fingers against the control board. "When he leaves, the railroad will be closed."

"Casey's leaving?"

Lucas nods. "Casey came here as a defector long ago, but instead of leaving for Haven, he decided to stay and help other defectors. He's tried to convince me to take over the line when he leaves, but I'm not interested. Eventually, Casey will have to climb out of the iris and follow the path he's helped hundreds of others begin."

Invasion

Canisters spill across the ground in the underground gathering hall. Electric torches illuminate the areas where canines await the distribution. Alison stands to the side of the ring, waiting for the discussion to begin. Maggie adds four more packets on Alison's behalf.

"That's thirteen packs from Alison," a voice says.

Alison swallows her contempt for the count. "It was supposed to be eight!" she mutters.

Cheers erupt from the pack. It's the largest single tally in memory. The celebration is silenced when a warning call echoes through the passage. "Stadium border!"

All eyes turn to the canine bursting into the gathering hall. "Security commin' through the Stadium border." The boy is gripped in a fog of distress. Panting madly, he continues, "They have a reaper with them!"

A frenzy explodes in the gathering. A tempest of hands grabs every speed packet from the pile before disappearing into the passageways. Alison draws her axe and follows the mob.

Angry warnings echo through the corridor leading to the tunnel entrance. Figures in baggy yellow-covered suits march through the passageways. Riot shields deflect flying rocks and bottles. The intruders answer the projectiles with bright-white streams discharging from pistol nozzles.

The handheld spouts are connected by hose lines to small pressurized tanks affixed to the invading officers' belts. The liquid streams splash against the walls and run across the ground. As it settles, the fluid expands to a foamy layer, marking the trail the figures make through the catacombs.

Youthful eyes watch from cover as the invaders march by. When the last passes, he pinches the top of a huff-pouch, draws its fumes, and moves to attack.

A crashing sound alerts the officer at the rear of the advancing line. He turns to see the canine stuck facedown in the white foam. "Hold for one," the figure states into a tele-LINCC affixed inside his vapor mask.

The line pauses as the officer returns to the struggling canine. He pulls the child from the ground. Threads of TAK foam stretch from the boy's face. An oil-soaked cloth wipes the foam away from the canine's airways, leaving a greasy resin around his nose and mouth. After a few desperate gasps, the child starts to pull away. Thick gloves yank him to his feet. A pistol nozzle appears in the other hand. The boy is pressed against the tunnel wall as the nozzle douses him with a fresh coat of the fluid. A distorted voice sounds from a scratchy speaker of the mask. "Keep this away from your face, or you'll suffocate."

The officer rejoins the advancing line. Behind him, the angry child tears one arm from the wall as the other presses into the foam. He calls for help in the darkness.

The material covering the civil officers' uniforms allows them to easily advance unhindered through the layers of TAC foam.

The invading line marches into the gathering area. The chief investigator follows the shield bearers into the underground yard. Two officers approach with a sticky Alison slow stepping into view. One of the officer's reports through a scratchy speaker, "Everyone was yelling at this one, Chief."

The civil investigator responds to the officer with a similar electronically distorted voice. "Good." The figure turns toward the passage opening, then works a channel switch beneath its mask. "Officer Ryan-fifty-four."

"Sir," comes the reply.

"What is the status of our entry?"

"The passage is secure to the entrance. We have pulled twelve canines from the foam," he says, "and have them detained at the entrance."

"Excellent. Then escort our Brigade visitor to this location."

Twenty minutes pass before their guest enters the gathering hall and anxiously strips off the shiny yellow protective poncho provided by the entry unit. She wants to remove the yellow leggings as well but decides they will be all the more difficult to reapply when it's time to leave. Her crude cover makes the officers' protective suits seem comparatively well-tailored.

The investigator considers the guest. "Officer Octavia-seventy?"

She nods.

The investigator removes her mask. "I am Chief Civil Investigator Helen-fifty-three, we have a witness for you to interrogate."

Octavia follows her gaze to the little girl covered in white fluff. The foam has hardened in her hair, causing it to stand tall, giving her the appearance of a little angry dandelion. Octavia can't contain her laughter at the sight.

"You think it's funny invading our tunnel!" The puffy red-faced Alison starts toward the black-clad figure.

At her approach, Octavia raises her truncheon for the girl's consideration. "You put a spot of that white crap on my uniform and I'll cave your fluffy skull in, you little tunnel rat!"

Helen-53 steps between the two. "That's not going to work here." The investigator whispers something to the reaper, who quietly steps aside. Helen then turns to the canine and kneels to her eye level. "You and I are going to—"

The child erupts with an angry rant. "No one wants you here! You think you gonna move in without us fightin'?"

Helen removes the pistol nozzle from her belt and squirts a ball of the TAK foam into the palm of her glove. The sight startles Alison. In the moment of silence, Helen asks, "Do you really think I can't shut that foul little mouth of yours?"

She holds the ball of foam just centimeters from the canines chin and begins again. "I remember the pack. I remember stealing from the mall to bring earnings to the gathering." Alison follows Helen's eyes as she glances around the room. "I also remember getting caught."

Alison is about to say something, then considers the ball of foam.

"I know," Helen replies on her behalf. "Get careless, get caught, get out. The pack had the same rule when I was in, and you little canine, have just been caught. This is why you're going to listen because what happened to me is exactly what is about to happen to you.

"You see, the judge didn't see any point in putting me in detention since I was gonna still be a blue pup when I got out and had no reason to play nice when they let me go. So right there in his judicial chamber, someone stuck me with a needle, made everything go black.

"The next thing I know, I wake up on ground as hard as this pavement." Helen taps the ground with her boot. "When I stood up, there was nothing. As far as I could see, nothing, just the burning sun and blue sky that reached all the way to the horizon. I started walking, and no matter how long or how far I walked, nothing changed around me. When the sun was up, it was hot. When it set, it was cold, and all the while, there was nothing to eat or drink."

Helen lowers the ball. "You've gone to bed hungry, haven't you?"

Alison nods.

"I did too when I was a canine. But then, I could always hope the next bag I grabbed would have something to trade inside. Or a grocer would look away long enough for me to boost something close to the door. If nothing else, I could usually find something in the garbage of a café. But out in Perdition, there's nothing to forage. You'll know soon enough."

Alison begins to say something but reconsiders when the ball of foam moves toward her chin.

"I don't know how long I was out there. A day, maybe three, but eventually, I fell to the ground and knew I was ready to die. Then I awoke to find a black-hooded man standing over me. He injected me with something that gave me a surge of strength, then passed me a jug of water that had a strange mineral taste. While I drank, he asked me to give him a reason I should come back."

Helen smiles. "You know, as tired as I was, I actually thought this was a game. Fortunately, my throat was too dry to say anything stupid. The reaper pointed behind me and said, 'Try to give me a better answer than that idiot.' I followed his finger to a dried-up shell of a canine lying there on the ground. I swear it didn't look much bigger than me. Its lips were pulled up tight, making the teeth stick out all white and polished. I don't think it appreciated the water I sprayed all over it when I saw it."

Alison's eyes grow wide and teary, but she holds her tongue.

"The man in black knelt by the leathery body and passed its lifeclock under a scanner, like hers." Helen chucks her thumb in Octavia's direction, who waves her hand tracker on cue.

In a lower sober voice, Helen says, "Then the officer headed for a hover-pod floating a few meters away. He turned to me and said, 'This may be the last question you are ever asked, so answer carefully. Why should I let you back in?'"

The more Alison tries to control it, the harder she struggles to regain her breath. Her panting becomes incessant. Helen wipes the ball of foam on the ground. "I won't bore you with the answer I gave. I'm giving you an advantage I didn't have then. You're going to have a day, maybe three, to think of how you are going to participate in and promote the wellbeing of all citizens in the Collective as you will yourself." Then she leans toward the canine, shaking in the white-crusted foam. "You must now consider if your answer will include that you assisted an officer of Civil Security or NOT?"

The terra-car glides to a stop. Doors whisk open, allowing Dante and Lucas to step onto a small platform illuminated by a single light. Erected next to the tunnel wall is a solitary metal spiral staircase ascending into the ceiling. Lucas leads Dante to the steps, and they gape up into the darkness.

"No light?" Dante asks.

"You don't really need light, just keep climbing."

"Then what?"

Lucas shrugs.

Sonia stands in the car's doorway with Casey pointing curtly in Dante's direction. The scene continues for longer than necessary. When Dante steps toward them, Casey nudges Sonia out and motions for Lucas to return.

Lucas extends a hand to Dante. "I hope you find what you're looking for up there, Dante."

They shake, then Lucas returns to the terra-car just as the doors slam closed.

Sonia secures her two bags onto her shoulders as she walks toward the stairs.

Dante takes the handrail and places his foot on the first step. He turns to Sonia and offers to take one of the bags. When she pulls away, he asks, "Do you know what's up there?"

She glances up. "Casey gave me a good idea."

Silence settles between them. *She is going to play this tight now*, Dante thinks. *I guess that is Casey's advice to her.* Without another word, Dante begins to climb.

Metallic clanks sing out with each step. Once through the hole in the ceiling, the stair-steps change to ladder rungs. After a few minutes, a draft arises from beneath them as the terra-car pulls away.

Dante climbs in darkness. A pair of glowing spectacle eyes follow below.

TAK foam grips inside Alison's legs, forcing her into a bowlegged walk as she lumbers into the terra station. The investigator and reaper follow. "This is it," she announces. "Defectors got in the car here and disappeared in that direction." She motions down the tunnel.

Octavia peers into the darkness. "How many?"

"A man and a woman," Alison answers. "Them and Casey."

Octavia walks to the girl. "I'm asking how many defectors has your pack assisted in escaping?"

The girl tries to shrug. "I don't know."

"That's not being helpful." Helen warns.

"I really don't know." Alison's face flushes pale as she says, "Fifteen, maybe ten."

Octavia scowls.

Once again, Helen steps between the two and whispers into the reaper's ear, "It's unlikely she knows the difference between fifteen and ten. She has told us everything she knows."

Octavia whispers a reply, "Does she know the penalty for giving aid to defectors? It's not a threat of Perdition."

"That is not your call."

"It is exclusively my call," Octavia snaps, placing her hand on the grip of her pistol.

"Not in this case!" Helen retorts. "Assuming this is a legitimate departure point to this Haven you're obsessed with, we have shut it down. If this Casey hasn't delivered your defectors into the custody of nomads, then you have a hunt to continue, otherwise, you have bodies to find. Either way, this child is not your concern." Helen addresses a figure standing in the passage entrance. "Officer Ryan."

"Ma'am." A youthful yellow-clad figure steps forward, also holding his pistol nozzle. He secures it to his belt when the investigator shakes her head.

"Escort our guest to the entrance. If possible, give her a ride to Brigade dispatch."

Octavia considers the officer, then pulls the repellant cover across her shoulders.

When they are alone, Helen walks to Alison, who is standing against the wall with a terrified expression. Helen removes a flask from her belt. "That can't be the first time someone's threatened your life, can it?"

Alison's brave façade begins to break down as she speaks. "I guess not."

Helen pours the contents of the flask across the girl's shoulders. "This will dissolve the foam." She passes the flask and a small towel to the girl who sponges her puffy cover away.

Another officer appears in the chamber. Helen nudges the child in his direction. "She's joining the twelve up front."

Alison gives a surprised look.

Helen continues. "Make sure they are all cleaned up, dried foam plays hell in Perdition's sunlight. Also, give them plenty of water on the ride out. One of the trucks has a box of apples; they can have all they can hold before they are expelled." When the officer acknowledges her orders, Helen turns away.

"But I helped you!" the girl calls out.

With a half-turn toward the child, Helen answers, "Yes, and if you didn't lie, your help will be remembered when it's time to give your reason to reenter the Collective, assuming you are alive when we find you."

230

Part 3
Escape

Chapter 19

Into Perdition

Wheels of a hidden mechanism turn within the walls of the ascending passage. An aperture opens. The bright-blue cloudless sky burns Dante's dilated pupils.

The handrails of the ladder they have been climbing for the last twenty minutes rises onto a concrete mound surrounding the steel aperture. Three metallic steps descend to the dusty ground. Dante cups his hands above his eyes to survey the surrounding desolation. "Is this right? I'm not sure this is right, there's nothing here."

"It's right." Sonia's head emerges from the hatchway. She places her two bags on the rim of the opening and withdraws what appears to be a pair of welding goggles. Once they settle onto her face, the clear lenses cloud to a dense blue tint. Small button-shaped sensors sprout around the frames.

She scans the horizon, then withdraws and opens a wide smoky-gray parasol that casts a comparatively cool shadow over her. The umbrella-shaped shield is a patchwork of small gray sheets of resin held together with utility tape.

What else does she have in that thing? Dante wonders.

Once on the surface, she searches the ground around the outcrop. She returns to the steps and allows the former reaper to assess her.

The aperture slams shut with a metallic clank. Dante climbs onto the mound to check the closure. There is no apparent way to reopen it. This great wide-open space suddenly seems a lot more confining.

"There should be another structure in that direction." Sonia nods away from the mound.

"Did Casey tell you this?"

She walks to the far edge of the mound and waves Dante over. Six pebbles are lined up in the direction she had nodded. "The way is marked with a number of signs like this. You just have to know when and where to expect them and what they represent." Pulling the large round goggles from her face, she looks into his eyes and struggles to keep her voice from cracking. "I know the way, but it's pointless to continue if you're just going to kill me."

"The speed you huffed earlier is still working its way through your system. It's making you paranoid," he says. "I know, I've been there.

When you come down, you'll realize if I wanted you dead, I'd have watched Nurse Lilith carve you up in surgery, then scanned your lifeclock."

Sonia passes him the tote with Priya resting within.

Dante winces. "Really?"

"He's special. We've been through a lot together. Besides, it's not as though you are weighed down with food and water."

Dante takes the bag. "He? I thought you called it Priya."

"Not it!" Sonia corrects. "I like the name Priya. Besides, he doesn't answer to anything, so it really doesn't matter what I call him." She takes Dante's unattended arm as they amble into the desert.

Dante matches her pace. "Please don't take offense, but that marker you indicated back there didn't seem like much of a directional sign. Are you sure this is the right way?"

Sonia replaces her data goggles. A broad green holographic arrow hovers in front of her eyes, pointing to the horizon. A readout displays next to the arrow that says:

Follow marker beacon 12.3 km. Northwest by west.

"Pretty sure."

The March

The board is clear. There is no sign of them. "It can't be right," Octavia mutters. "There has to be a malfunction at some point we are not seeing."

Twenty minutes ago, Octavia-70 appeared in the control room of the South Diego Charon Brigade headquarters and immediately took a post behind Amy-15. All nonessential officers cleared out as the reaper surveyed the board. Those who stayed keep their eyes affixed to anything that is not in Octavia's direction. She has no special authority other than the unwillingness of the other officer in the control room to tell her so.

Now, Dispatcher Amy attempts to regain some modicum of control of her workspace as she insists, "Officer Octavia-seventy, you need to step back and let me—"

A gloved hand slaps the dispatcher's shoulder with a familiar grip as might be shared between long-time comrades or to snap her neck if she continues to talk.

A soft voice steams the back of Amy's neck as it whispers into her ear, "Where could they have gone, Dispatcher?"

Am I supposed to answer that? Amy wonders. "Officer, I have directed every aerial asset to the region you indicated along the terra tunnel. We see numerous white clocks that have yet to be retrieved by the Brigade clean-up crews, but there are no living clocks."

Octavia's teeth grind at the excuses before she asks, "Where are the dragonflies? We need a visual survey of the entire area."

"There aren't enough dragonflies on the west coast to cover that region, Officer. We are in the process of fitting a dirigible with a mobile charging station to carry four low-altitude scanners..." Amy's voice cracks as the reaper's hands enclose around her throat.

Octavia's cold voice emanates from her dark hood. "We need to see tracks in the dirt or body heat signatures."

Amy unintentionally checks her lifeclock to confirm it's still blue. The fresh officer is easy for Octavia to control.

Octavia mutters a stream of random questions behind the dispatcher that are only audible due to the unnatural silence of the dispatch room. "Are you planning something, or is this your solution to filling the emptiness? If so, you know I'll kill you myself. Is this really how you want to go out?"

Amy-15 is certain she is not supposed to answer any of those questions. The reaper continues to control both of her shoulders. Even through the padding of her uniform, Octavia's grip causes Amy to lose sensation in her upper arms. Her eyes are locked forward, pupils dilated on the scanner maps. A bead of sweat runs down her temple. Again, the breath of the hunter burns the side of her face as the reaper's soft voice thunders in her ear.

"Find them."

"There's another one." Dante's cheerful voice breaks the half-hour silence.

Sonia's response is the same as the last three times. "I really don't care!"

He has an irritating habit of commenting on the dried-up remains of criminals expelled to Perdition as they pass. "Can't tell if it's a man or woman," he says. "The clothes are too shattered... tattered? Is it shattered or tattered? Either way, that one is more likely a banished citizen rather than a defector."

Sonia tries to mimic his eager expression. "That is interesting— fatiguing— the one that means gross and not helpful for our situation!"

"If it was a defector, the ribs would be fractured outward from the STInGER's detonation."

Sonia blurts out, "Gross!"

"You already said that." Another five minutes pass in silence before he continues. "We can talk about something else if you like."

"I agree, let's, please."

"What would you like to talk about, literature, theater, music?"

"Jazz, let's talk about jazz," Sonia answers with a rejuvenated voice. "What do you think of the Bay City Lounge sound?"

Silence.

"I'm just asking if you like the jazz played in Bay City? That's where you said you're from, right?" She persists.

Dante bobs his head back and forth, struggling to comment.

"Or is there another style you listen to?"

More silence follows.

She says, "What band or musician do you listen to?"

"I don't know anything about jazz, or music for that matter."

"You said—"

"I know; I'm sorry, I just don't do well in the silence. I like live performances, the ones in the amphitheater rather than the lounge."

Through all their bickering, Sonia continues to keep a tight hold on Dante's arm.

He matches her pace. Dante is accustomed to long hikes in the open. The Charon Brigade Academy includes many similar survival programs. The academy also included courses covering the basics of interrogation.

Eventually, Sonia keeps the conversation going, talking about her music collection, the concerts she's heard, and her life as an archivist. As long as she controls the conversation, she doesn't have to listen to Dante comment on the dried-up corpses littering their path.

He eventually asks the obvious question, "Sonia, why did you defect?"

She yanks his arm to a sudden stop. "Why did you, Dante? Why does a reaper, who makes a career of killing defectors, defect?"

His answer is calm and measured. "I'm not a reaper anymore."

"You know what I mean!" she snaps.

He answers with a pensive sigh. "Believe it or not, I didn't think about it." He turns his hand to reveal his flashing lifeclock. "When I entered Final-Quarter, I immediately started planning my last ninety-one days. I thought of all the things I hadn't done. You wanna know what I came up with?"

Sonia doesn't respond.

"All I could do was pull on my tunic and hood, load my pistol, and go to work. That's it! The Brigade is the only thing I have ever done."

Dante watches as Sonia's expression shifts from contempt to disbelief. *She doesn't understand, how can she?*

Sonia wants to throw his arm away as if it's a pile of burning garbage.

Dante unconsciously slips his free hand into his pocket. He wraps his fist around the balled up glitter belt and thumbs the spring on the buckle. He remembers the terrified woman, covered in mud and scars, begging for another moment to live. What did that defector say? *"I didn't want to close my eyes looking at a video screen displaying an artificial river with simulated fish swimming in it."* Confusion radiates in Sonia's expression as he continues. "Maybe after all the years I've spent as a hunter, it's time to be the hunted. Maybe it's better to make them run me down rather than passively surrender to the Somnolence recliner."

"You think this is fun, don't you?" Sonia's head drifts back with disgust. "You are seriously damaged!"

"Not fun." He shakes his head. "Just different. What about you, why did you defect?"

Sonia's grip tightens around his arm. "No, you know all about me, let's keep talking about you. Do you like being a reaper?"

Dante answers dryly, "I told you I'm not—"

Sonia's voice cracks. "Don't avoid the question, or we can go back to talking about the rotting corpses in the sand."

"I'm not avoiding anything. I don't think you really want to hear about it."

"Please, tell me, I'm fascinated! For all the things I've done in my short life, I have never sat in the courtyard with a reaper and discussed his work over scones." She forces her anger away. "You know you want to tell me, so, did you enjoy being a reaper?"

"Yes, I liked being a reaper," he says. "Actually, I enjoyed being good at it, more so than I liked the job."

"Was hunting all you enjoyed?"

"No." Dante's thoughts drift through his life. "I also enjoyed teaching. I used to lecture on history and civics. That was fun." A smile escapes. "I enjoyed contributing to a system I believe in."

"You believe in killing people when a piece of crystal says so?" Sonia clarifies.

"I believe in obligation, each citizen sharing in the benefits of the Collective and sacrificing to provide those benefits for the next generation."

"I think you believe in enforcement. The directives give you something to inflict on others. Now that you are face-to-face with your obligation, you're not preparing for Somnus, you're running from it, just like the people you hunted."

"Running where, Sonia?" Dante allows his emotions to surface. "Where are we going? You wanna know why I'm defecting? It's to learn where defectors go. I have dedicated my life to the Brigade for ten years, and I have never heard an answer for this, not once."

Sonia allows silence to linger.

With a gentle nudge, Dante pulls her back into their slow march. "I'm defecting because it's the only way to find that answer, even if it means dying as a defector instead of a citizen."

"You're certain we're going to die," she concludes. "Aren't you even going to try to evade them?"

This time Dante allows silence to hang between them.

"I'd like an answer to that, Dante," she persists. "Do you intend to avoid the reapers until you get bored with your search, or are you intent on escaping?"

"We haven't escaped anything. We're alive by a fluke." He glances at the sky. "High-altitude drones should have relayed our position to dispatch. A pair of reapers, stuck with cleanup duty, should have rolled up in a pod and launched the first STInGERs they've shot in months into our chests by now."

"I was wondering if you would mention the drones," Sonia says calmly.

Realizing what he had just revealed, Dante asks, "You know about them?"

"I don't know exactly where they are." Sonia twirls the translucent gray parasol that has shaded them all afternoon. "The material not only dissipates static electricity, it's an effective shield for electromagnetic signals."

For the first time, Dante notes that she has kept her left arm crossed in front of her with his left hand so that both are under the center of her parasol, sheltering their lifeclocks under the gray shield.

"You know this works?"

"I've experimented in the malls and one or two transit stops. It's hard to get feedback, but it appears to shield the clock's signal from scanners. Our lack of exploding organs gives me confidence that it's also effective against flying scanners. Then again, I don't know where the scanners are." Sonia eyes Dante sternly.

"The reaper hunting us will have dispatched every high-altitude dirigible in the region around every opening along the tunnel." He nods to the open sky. "Low-altitude dragonfly drones can pick up visual and heat signatures; however, they don't have the range for deep penetration into the desert terrain like this." As he relays these details, Dante feels her grip on his arm relax.

A smile breaks through Sonia's sour expression. "So, you said you were a good reaper, have you ever hunted another reaper?"

"Once," Dante admits. "He was a skilled officer who applied every tactic to run me all over the sector. Bastard made me an hour late for lunch."

Sonia looks for a smile to follow. It doesn't.

The Bunker

As the sun drifts closer to the horizon, a mound appears. The sight brings an excited smile to Sonia. "That's it." She points. "That's just like the description Casey gave me.

They quicken their pace to the knoll. Lacking any visual cues for size and distance, the open desert has a quality that distorts a traveler's perspective. What first appears as a small hill on the horizon, grows to a substantial rocky structure the closer they approach. It looks like a miniature mountain range whose only purpose is to disrupt the otherwise flat horizon.

Smooth, wind-weathered stones protruding from the ground lead them onto a steep rocky ramp. The whole place has a distinctive artificial quality to it, but neither Dante nor Sonia can recognize why.

Once on the hillside, Dante pauses to review their path. *We left a few indicators where we passed,* Dante thinks, *but the hard ground has obscured most of our trail. Then again, I know what to look for. Will anyone else notice them?*

Dante drops to the ground, pulling Sonia beside him. "We're not alone." He points to a dust cloud moving in the distance. "Brigade cleanup."

Sonia holds the parasol close to them as they stoop against the rock. "Do you think they're after us?"

Dante shakes his head. "More likely, they're out logging the lifeclocks on the corpses we've passed." He nods for them to continue on. "If they notice your cover reflecting in the sunlight, they might investigate. In any case, we should get out of their view."

They follow the incline until the path narrows. Two vertical rock faces form a walled walkway that angle around into a clearing.

A boxed canyon, Dante muses as they emerge from the rocky passage. High stone walls surround a semicircular area roughly twenty meters across with no obvious place to climb out or hide. *It has every quality of a space I would choose to drive a defector.*

Sonia directs Dante to a section of the wall with a slightly angled protrusion at the base. She hands him the parasol. Pulling the pack from her shoulders, she withdraws the compass Casey gave her.

Passing the baseplate across the rock face, orange lines begin to glow, forming an arrow pointing to the left with a running stick figure inside. She inserts the compass into the figure as if it were a passkey. The stone appears to liquefy around the device as it passes into the wall.

A soft, high-pitched tone sings out when the key is accepted, as a thin line traces a square border into the face of the rocky wall. Within the square, the irregular ridges and bumps of the wall recede into the mountainside, forming a smooth glassy surface.

The square lowers into the ground, revealing a hideaway. Cool air gusts from inside. Dante and Sonia step over the words 'Defectors Enter' as they pass into the mountainside.

Once they clear the entryway, the square door rises from the ground, sealing them in. A track of soft lights glows around the perimeter illuminating the chamber.

Dante considers the entrance now blocked by a pane of shaded glass. Though smooth on the inside, rippled distortions mark the contours of the rocky face on the exterior, providing an adequate view of the clearing outside. The chamber is an octagon-shaped room, at least eight meters across. It seems an odd shape until he realizes it is somewhat soothing. A more boxed-shaped space would have given him the sensation of being entombed.

A video display on one of the walls flickers to life, centering on the dust cloud Dante had spotted. The image magnifies to reveal a pod with a flatbed at its rear pulling up to one of the bodies they had passed.

Two figures emerge from the vehicle to spread a tarp on the ground. They wear the black pants of the Brigade and have their pistols holstered at their sides. Rather than the black tunic and hood, they wear lightweight white undershirts and sun visors. The dress is against protocol but sensible considering the daytime temperatures of Perdition. One of the men lifts the left hand of the corpse under a scanner. Then the two roll the body onto the tarp and lift it onto the cargo bed.

The room addresses them in an authoritative, feminine voice, "Please remain calm."

Turning about to meet their hostess, Sonia gasps in momentary terror when a desiccated corpse sitting against the wall with its mouth open wide greets her.

The room speaks again. "Scanners are tracking a Charon Brigade recovery unit along with two high-altitude drones. The shielding in this bunker will hide you from their scanners. You are safe. Please remain calm until they pass."

Sonia gawks into their bunker mate's gaping mouth to ensure that he is not the one giving directions.

A low-pitched hum breaks the silence of the chamber. Through the door, Dante watches the dust jump about on the vibrating ground.

"What's going on?" Sonia asks.

"The vibrations are clearing our tracks outside," he says.

"That's good," Sonia responds absently.

Dante nods, then adds, "It also confirms that this bunker is not soundproof."

"Reapers approaching." The room speaks up again. "Please help yourself to some water and food, but remain quiet until they pass."

An icy mist escapes the walls as two sections of the octagon rotate into the chamber, revealing two frost-covered pantries. To the right, Dante finds nothing but cold, empty storage shelves. To the left, Sonia holds up a single, well-chilled, empty metal flask with the stopper removed.

The humming stops and the lights inside the bunker dim. Sonia takes the tote bag from Dante and settles on the floor, with Priya in her arms, to watch the entrance.

Dante sits down beside her.

They watch the pod on the wall monitor pull up to the stone ramp where they had entered. Dante studies the video image for any trail they may have left. The dim light of dusk obscures most of the details. Soon, two figures emerge into the clearing.

Why are they here? Dante wonders silently. *If there is no trail to follow, no corpses to remove, no clock signal to investigate, what brings you to this place?* A smile breaks across his face and he relaxes. Resting his head against the wall, Dante fights back a laugh.

One of the reapers removes a packet of smokes from his pocket, takes one, then tosses the pack to the other, who returns the gesture with a small flask. The back of the reaper's shirt presses against the textured exterior of the bunker door. They enjoy a thirty-minute break before returning to their hover-pod and disappear below the horizon. The monitor follows the pod for about three hundred meters before the lights come up.

Priya escapes Sonia's clutches to explore the bunker.

"You look disappointed that they didn't find us." Sonia narrows her eyes at Dante.

"Are you going to start that again?" Dante asks. He nods at the dust cloud disappearing on the screen. "Those two weren't a problem. The only danger they pose is to alert someone competent." Dante addresses the wall monitor. "You mentioned a pair of aerial scanners, can you show me?"

At his request, the screen displays a magnified image of a dirigible moving away. At the same time, the adjacent wall morphs to a glassy black surface. A light appears to ignite on the other side of the glass, revealing a woman standing in a dark chamber.

Sonia considers the figure. "A hologram."

She is unlike anyone they had ever seen, at least before they met Casey in the tunnels. She appears to be similar to Casey's age. Her clothes looked well-worn from a long desert travel, she faces Dante and addresses him. The room speaks in time with her lips.

"Greetings, Defector. My name is Inarrah Casey." She holds up her hand to reveal a clear lifeclock. "I was once a citizen of what we are now calling the Collective. I was raised to follow the directives requiring personal euthanasia at age twenty-five. Although I understand the reason for the directive, I never truly accepted it as the only solution for maintaining our society. I was not alone in this belief. Some of us have tried to promote other ways of preserving the resources of our world as well as the dignity of its citizens..." She bows her head as her voice trails off. "We failed."

Sonia and Dante share a glance at one another.

Inarrah continues. "The Collective's very structure prevents exploration of any alternate ideas. I am one of approximately one thousand men, women, and children living outside of the influence of the Guardian and its obligations. We call our civilization, Haven, and invite you to become a part of it.

"We established this bunker as the first stage of our underground railroad. Rest and refresh yourself from its supplies. A hover-pod has been summoned to take you to the next station along the way. The pod's tracking systems have been disabled so you will not be visible to high-altitude sensors. It is also programmed to avoid any Brigade patrols."

The wall monitor changes to a view of the horizon. A red counter appears in the upper left corner of the screen, counting down from one hour and thirteen minutes. "When it arrives, it will need to charge for an additional thirty minutes, and you will be on your way.

"The next station is a safe house." The wall monitor changes to display a teardrop-shaped opening in the side of a mountain. A pathway meanders into its opening. "There is additional food, water, and a surgical chamber sufficient to address any injury you have suffered. There, you will be directed to the next station on the railroad."

"How far is it to Haven?" Dante asks.

The voice cuts out as the features of Inarrah's likeness shifts. "The hover-pod should take about a day to arrive at the safe house, depending on the patrol activity along the way. The final directions to Haven will be revealed to you at the safe house." The figure shifts again. "This recording has limited resources. A more comprehensive database to answer your questions has been made available at the safe house." After another transition, she continues, "You have a long and dangerous journey ahead of you. Although we have made every effort to avoid detection, a careless move along the way will result in your death. Stay alert, and we will soon see you on our shores."

The light dims, leaving Inarrah's figure in shadow. The wall screen returns to a view of the horizon with the red numbers counting down.

"Funny, she doesn't look anything like the Casey we met in Stadium," Dante states dryly.

Sonia shakes her head. "Perhaps Casey is a code name used by the railroad."

Surprised, Dante asks, "Perhaps? Didn't you say back at the iris hatch that you know the way to Haven?" He tries to quash any judgmental tone that may seep into his voice.

"I do know the way," Sonia retorts with confidence. Nodding in the direction of the wall screen. "In just over an hour, a hover-pod will arrive and take us to the next station."

Dante nods in the direction of their bunker mate. "What if he's still waiting for a pod?"

Sonia turns to see Priya pulling on a finger, causing the corpse to fall over. Its eyes seemed to look to them with indignity.

"Priya, nooooooo!" Sonia muffles a moan.

"Hey, at least he found something to eat in here. Unless you have sufficient food in that pack, we may need to join her. No- Noo Noooo, don't vomit!"

Sonia supports herself against the wall, trying not to wretch.

"Sonia, seriously. You may think it will make you feel better, but you'll dehydrate." Dante tries to reassure her. "Inarrah, can you open the door, please?"

Inarrah's image lights up behind the holographic window as the voice in the room says, "Please stay within the courtyard until the hover-pod arrives." As she speaks, a high-pitched whining sings out before the door slides into the ground.

Sonia leans out to breathe in the warm dry air. Once her head clears, she looks over to see Dante rummaging around the corpse.

He triumphantly raises a flask similar to the one Sonia found in the pantry. Liquid sloshes about as he shakes it. "Good news, he said he'll share with us if he can stay for the night."

Sonia releases a small laugh at the thought of Dante negotiating with their bunker mate instead of robbing a corpse. "Is it drinkable?" she asks.

Dante sniffs the opening. "Well, I'd really like to treat it first. Any chance you have a water filter or purification tablets in your magic bag?"

Sonia removes a small first aid kit and tosses it over. "I think there are some in there."

Dante digs through the pouch and withdraws a little brown bottle of pellets. "Hey, not bad!" He drops a couple into the spout and shakes it around. "This will take about ten minutes to work, but I would still like to boil it before drinking. Inarrah is there a heater here somewhere, maybe a…"

In the center of the clearing, a 40-centimeter circle rises from the ground. It morphs into a cone-shaped mound. After a moment, the surface of the cone changes color to a dark rusty orange. Dante feels heat radiating from the cone as he approaches.

"These Haven folks really make you feel at home," Sonia says.

The lights in the bunker start blinking red. "Warning lights will flash if a Charon Brigade patrol or aerial sensor approaches," Inarrah says.

Dante places the metal flask next to the cone with the top opened.

He removes the slate and unrolls it to face the display screen that reads:

NO LINCC ACCESS

Sonia peeks over his shoulder to see the message.

"The slate can lock onto aerial scanners as LINCC access points," he says. "If the sky is clear like Inarrah says, then there won't be any access."

Sonia nods. "Then it looks like she is right. If the rest of the message is on the level, then Inarrah Casey lived over six hundred years ago. What do you think she meant by 'we failed'? Failed at what?"

Dante glances back to see the shadowy figure of Inarrah standing behind the holo-screen. "I suppose we could go back and ask her."

Sonia follows his gaze into the chamber. "Maybe later."

Stars emerge from the dark sky. Sonia and Dante sit in silence, staring into the fire. Neither wants to talk about the empty pantry in the bunker or permanent tenant inside. After a time, Inarrah's voice reports, "Charge complete. Have a safe journey."

The display screen in the chamber shows a hover-pod parked at the base of the walkway where they arrived. Its hatch is open with a light shining inside.

Dante collects Priya into the tote bag, while Sonia stashes the warm water flask into her pack.

Rather than a pair or even a quad of bucket seats, this party-sized pod reveals lounge booth-like seating, with couches placed around the interior and a small table at the rear.

When they enter the pod, the two are overwhelmed with the smell of takeout food. The previous users obviously shared a meal in here and didn't clean up when they left. It's not entirely unpleasant since neither has eaten in a while.

Dante closes the hatch. The pod pulls away from the hillside. A charging arm that had been attached to the front of the pod descends into a rocky hiding place.

Sonia reviews the control panels at the front of the cabin. "Inarrah was right. The tracking system has been disabled and the batteries are fully charged. I guess we're going to the next station."

The pod picks up speed as it moves from the irregular surface ground onto a hidden energized rail.

Leftovers

Dante surveys the cups around the cabin. Fortunately, only one had been filled with cigarette butts. The others seem safe to drink.

Sonia finds one whole wrapped sandwich in the bag along with an assortment of mostly eaten side orders; Dante finds a box of pizza crusts. In all likelihood, the party that bought all this exited the pod just before it left for the bunker.

The leftovers, along with a few provisions in Sonia's pack, is the first either has eaten since leaving Stadium. Sonia passes over Dante's field knife along with half of the sandwich.

Priya chews on the insides of a chicken sandwich that had fallen on the floor, then investigates the rest of the cabin.

The mall food is greasy and sits like a rock when they finish. Sonia sinks into the couch, resting her arms against the windowsill. With a long, satisfying exhale, she says, "I haven't eaten crap like that since I was pregnant."

Surprised, Dante asks, "When were you...?"

His startled expression amuses Sonia and allows her a much-needed smile. "When I was an apprentice archivist in Mar del Plata, I guess I was, sixteen, maybe fifteen. I missed some things during my time in the canines, so when this street guitar player with long blond hair and deep blue eyes asked me if he could play my G-string..."

Dante tries to pass a grin off as a scowl while shaking his head, pretending disapproval.

Sonia smirks defensively. "Hey, it was a lot cuter than it sounds, anyway, a couple of weeks later, my lifeclock started flashing blue then white then pink, and I was terrified! I thought I had entered my Final-Quarter.

"One of the archivists took me to the clinic where a medic gave the most thorough examination of my life. When I left, he recommended me for maternity status."

"How far along did you go?"

Sonia drifts back in time. "One hundred and seventy-eight days. The blinking lifeclock was like a fairy godmother. All the grocers made sure I had fresh fruits, cereals, and vegetables. Occasionally, they even sold me a fish fillet or a half a kilogram of meat." She blushes at the memory. "Once I admitted that I had no idea how to prepare it, some of the grocer's younger apprentices started making meal boxes for me. I liked the attention, but it got a little weird."

She settles deeper into the couch and closes her eyes. "The medic who guided me through my pregnancy got me on a diet and exercise schedule that helped me cope. Every morning, the Guardian sent me a meal plan for the day."

"The Guardian told you what to eat?" Dante asks.

Sonia shakes her head. "No, not exactly. By the time I started showing, I had these mad cravings for food from the plaza, really greasy stuff, like this." She rattles the box of pizza crusts. "It played hell on my system. So every morning, the Guardian suggested a compliant meal plan. It also made it clear that if I didn't follow it, the free examinations, rent credit, and grocery discounts would stop." Then she says in a melancholy voice, "I thought about keeping it for a while, you know."

"You wanted to be a mommy?" Dante asks. The notion is strange to both of them. Citizens rarely raise children. Neither of them has ever seen a parent with a child.

Sonia nods. "Ya. I was really getting attached to the idea. The clinic had all these videos and printouts for motherhood. I watched a few on how to raise a child." A weight descends in her throat. "They always ended the same way; a seven- to ten-year-old boy or girl, madly shaking the mother in the Citadel recliner." Sonia shakes the memory away. "That was when I asked the medic to remove my fetus. I went into the surgery chamber that afternoon a mommy-to-be and came out with a flat stomach, normal hormones, and no stretch marks, I kept the big tits, though." Sonia attempts a wry smile, but the memory pulls her further away. "The robo-nursery will raise her better than I."

"Her?" Dante asks.

Sonia nods. "I had a little girl." Her smile fades away.

"Did you ever try to look in on her?"

Sonia shakes her head. "It's prohibited."

"You don't strike me as someone who observes prohibitions."

Sonia grins a little, out of politeness. "It's not good for the children to learn about family connections, especially when they are in Yellow Cycle. We tend to form bonds that interfere with our development."

"We form bonds?"

Sonia is surprised to open her eyes and see Dante leaning forward on the table, captivated by her story.

"I'd like to understand," he says eagerly. "What bonds?"

Dante listens for hours as Sonia tells about meeting her brother and living with the canines in Outland. Eventually, she catches herself talking about Carlos finding her in Bay City and deciding on making a run for Haven. She pulls herself from the narrative well enough to navigate around the details of their new identities.

Her attention drifts to the reaper. "Dante, can I ask you something?"

He nods.

"Did you kill my brother?" she asks serenely.

Dante withdraws the silver case from his pocket and hands it over. Her breath races at the sight of the gift she made for her brother.

"I hunted Carlos-ninety-two with my partner Octavia, but I didn't kill him. He did an outstanding job of avoiding the scanners; it took us a full forty-five minutes to push him away from the crowds. Did you teach him how to evade the census network?"

Her eyes flare at the question.

Dante reads the response as it crosses her face and answers for her, "Yes."

Sonia pulls herself out of the memory she had been visiting. *How much have I shared?* she asks herself, resisting the instinct to press deeper into the booth's cushions.

Dante builds on the anxiety that begins to fill the car. "Sonia, this is very important. I've hunted defectors for a long time. I've worked with dozens of Brigade reapers. There is no one more deadly than the one who stalked your brother and who I am sure is after us now." He watches the confidence and defiance in her eyes fade into fear. He settles back into the seat. "If there were less experienced officers chasing us, like those two jokers back at the bunker, I would be confident that we could evade them for as long as necessary. But I've worked with Octavia for ten years. She has never lost one. Our best chance of staying alive is getting to Haven as quickly as possible. I have a good idea of how she will try to drive us. I can do this a lot better if you tell me how you avoid the lifeclock scanners."

Dante glances across the empty horizon. "I suppose we have a little time before arriving at the safe house. You're a smart woman; ask me anything. I'll tell you whatever you want to know until you're ready to tell me the truth."

His apparent ability to read her with such ease rattles Sonia for a moment before she answers. "Okay. First thing I want to know is whether you're through interrogating me."

Dante nods. "I admit. I've tried to get you to talk so I can read you better, and I do have a pretty good sense of when you're telling me the truth and when you are holding something back."

Sonia defies the comment. "You think you can read me so easily?"

Dante shakes his head and keeps his voice even. "Not think."

His last statement arouses Sonia's curiosity, a motivation she never learned to control. "Tell me something I've hidden from you?"

Dante suppresses a smile, realizing how much he's beginning to like his pod-mate. "Are you sure?" he asks.

Sonia cracks a defiant smile and nods.

He releases a deep sigh and leans his elbows on the table. "That story about your pregnancy and meeting your brother, I've never heard anything like it. I can't imagine the connections you've experienced. I was not asking as an interrogator. You've lived a fascinating life, and I enjoyed hearing about it." Dante straightens his back. "By the way, and I hope this is not too personal, you don't have the breasts of a woman who's been pregnant."

Sonia matches his posture and tone. "That is rather personal."

Dante responds with an apologetic look. "I don't mean to be. You did mention that after the removal, you kept the large breasts because—"

"Because I liked the attention, yes, I remember. When I was sixteen, I did. When I was twenty-one, I didn't. I was ready for a new look and chose to let go of a painful memory."

Nodding his head, Dante says, "So you changed your look at A Moveable Face in Antioch. Yes." He considers this for a while. "Yes, I can see that, it makes sense. Here's what bothers me, though. Sonia-10 was never pregnant. She was never seen by a prenatal medic, she was never given maternity status or assigned a maternity plan, and never received maternity advice from the Guardian. I know this because I studied Sonia-10's citizen profile."

Dante doesn't allow her the opportunity to make a cover story. He points to the pocket clock lying on the seat. "Was that a present to Carlos from you?"

She nods. "I made it for him."

"That device was not on Carlos when we hunted him. I found it during my investigation. It was in a backpack, along with an umbrella similar to the one you use. Before leaving, Carlos tried to destroy the clinic's data terminal." Dante allows the vision he described to sink in to her mind.

"The terminal belonged to a woman we believe was holding him," he says.

"Sweeny," Sonia says absently. Her hand caresses the scar on her face.

"Although most of the information on the terminal was destroyed, the investigators recovered four names. Carlos-ninety-two, Sonia-ten, Marcos-eighty, and Lauren-twenty-five. By the way, Sonia-ten never spent any time in the South American region. That's where the Mar del Plata Library is, in Argentina."

Sonia nods, trying to remember when she mentioned Mar del Plata.

Though speaking quietly, Dante's voice thunders with authority. "Would you like me to tell you where Sonia-ten has lived?"

She shakes her head.

"Would you be surprised if I told you that Lauren-twenty-five did have a pregnancy when she was sixteen?"

Dante detects a lump passing down her throat. "No. You are not surprised by that. Do you know where Marcos-eighty came from?"

Sonia shifts her eyes into her lap. Though he is on the opposite end of the pod's passenger bay, Dante seems to fill her view when he leans onto the table.

"Just then, Sonia, you lied to me. Where. Did. Marcos-eighty. Come. From?" Dante begins to respond on her behalf. "Sssss…"

"South," she voices his lead. "South American region."

"Yes. Would you like to tell me the relationship between Carlos-ninety-two, Marcos-eighty, Lauren-twenty-five, and you?"

Sonia follows his eyes, resting on the silver pocket clock beside her. "No."

Dante suppresses his aggravation. "Is there anything about Marcos-eighty or Lauren-twenty-five that Octavia can use to track you?"

Sonia responds in a raspy whisper, "I honestly don't know."

"I believe you." Dante settles back on his couch to watch the landscape pass through the window.

When she regains her voice, Sonia inquires, "Your partner?"

"Octavia," Dante says.

"Octavia, is she like you? Does she do that, what you just did?" Sonia doesn't bother hiding the nerves shuddering her voice.

Dante doesn't look at her when he answers. "Octavia is a far more ruthless hunter than I. She's never lost a defector."

"Dante, have you ever lost a defector?"

He closes his eyes and rests his head against the pod's canopy. "I've failed only once."

"What happened?"

"I ended up following the crazy bitch out into the desert looking for Haven."

Chapter 20

Matters Critical and Sensitive

"Judicial Officer Sydney-twenty, we have an appointment."

Sydney hadn't intended to react to the voice. It carries a terminal authority that emanates from somewhere much more distant than the civil judiciary hallway. A hooded, black-clad figure stands in his doorway. His imagination gives it the momentary appearance of it holding a scythe in its right hand.

"May I come in?" she asks.

The question pulls Sydney back into his chamber. *Death wouldn't ask,* he reasons, yet he unconsciously presses his fingers over his lifeclock. *Is this how it will feel when my time comes?*

Sydney motions for her to enter. She closes the door behind her. "I have a sensitive situation, Sydney." Octavia hesitates. "May we speak candidly?"

He brushes the silver hood from his brow, implying their conversation is unofficial. Octavia does likewise, taking the chair by his desk.

"I don't mind speaking off-the-record, Octavia, but I'm under the impression that this meeting is of a critical matter."

Silence lingers.

Sydney finally understands. "Dante."

Octavia's eyes close as her shoulders drop.

"Something happened? Is he all right?"

Octavia relays the details of her investigation in South Diego.

Sydney releases the locks on his mobility chair and rolls to a small table with a steaming teakettle. He refreshes a mug from his desk, offers Octavia a cup, and then moves his chair beside hers. "Did you meet Dante in the academy?"

Octavia nods.

He sips from his mug. "Dante and I knew each other in Green Cycle. Except for the occasional late-night tele-LINCC calls, he and I lost touch during our Blue Cycle skill-trade. I met up with him when he was almost through the Brigade academy." He leans back in his chair and smiles. "There was this time, I think it was a year after the Correction, we were new to our skill-trade. Anyway, we met for an afternoon coffee in this dark little café, when three of his former students joined us."

"Former students? I don't remember him teaching as a first-year." Octavia interjects.

Sydney smiles. "Dante was assisting the academy instructors well before taking the oath, but he kept it quiet. He had a talent for explaining civics and history to pre-adults. Anyway, these kids had taken one of his classes on obligations of citizenship and wanted him to expand on the moral justification for the Somnus Obligation."

"Oh, no," Octavia groans. "I know that rabbit hole all too well."

"Oh, yes!" Sydney nods with a sly smile. "They came at him with 'natural law' and 'everything has its time,' followed by, 'limiting human potential,' then 'why should they follow a system that can only survive through murdering its citizens?' They had prepared every argument you could imagine."

Octavia recalls Dante practicing many of these rebuttals on her. The memory makes her smile as she asks, "So what, three against two, defending the righteousness of citizen obligation?"

"Hell, no, it was four on one!" Sydney announces. "It was my day off. If I was going to be pulled into a debate, I was at least going to enjoy taking the dissident's side for once."

His zealous outburst makes her laugh.

"Oh, it wasn't funny, believe me. After the fourth or fifth round of espresso, we were all pretty loud. The barista must have thought we were a group of anarchists trying to recruit the children into our conspiracy."

Octavia's eyes narrow. "You're making this up."

Sydney swears with his hand over his heart. "On my honor's honor, I'm not!" He gives her an innocent smile. "Things got out of control when two reapers appeared at the table and declared that we were having an unlawful conversation and accused us of inciting descent against the Somnus Obligation. Wait, did I mention Dante was in his grays?"

"Figures!" Octavia laughs.

"You have to see the whole picture. The reapers were not young recruits. Both were at least two years into their Red Cycle and eager to intimidate the five of us. In my case, it was working, as it was for the three kids who thought they were about to be executed right there in the café. As all this is happening, I see Dante move his hand into his duty bag that was sitting in his lap."

Octavia sets her cup on the desk. "What did he do?"

Sydney places his mug next to hers. "I was trying to think of a way to bring the tension down, but do you think Dante is any help? No! He starts lecturing the reapers as though they were ill-behaving students in his study hall that '…there is no such thing as an unlawful conversation…' and '…no directive prohibiting questioning Somnus.'"

Octavia laughs at the parody of her partner's lecture style as Sydney continues. "One of the reapers grabbed Dante and pulled him from his chair, muttering some drivel about respect for civil authority."

Octavia unconsciously covers her eyes.

"It's mostly a blur, but I am sure I saw Dante slam the top of his head into the reaper's chin, right before his gun flared at the other officer."

"Dante shot him?" Octavia exclaims. "With what?"

"I don't know what you call it, but the next thing I know, one reaper is on the floor covered in white goo, while the other is crashing into a table."

Octavia bursts out laughing.

"Oh, you think it's funny?" Sydney asks in mock anger. "Well, my shorts are still rattling from this, as was everyone in the café. Within an hour, the five of us were standing in a civil courtroom alongside two Brigade officers who had their authority nut-stomped by this low-ranking, fresh-out-of-the-academy, first-year. By then, Dante had engaged the hood on his on-call uniform. He was facing a sentence of cryo-detention and expulsion from the Brigade, but that lanky sixteen-year-old tore those two senior reapers apart in front of the Judiciary."

Octavia asks, "Did you testify?"

Sydney shakes his head. "I would have if it was necessary, but I was happy to have Dante advocating for me, as were his students."

"Now I remember those two. They were kicked out of the Brigade because of his accusations."

"I never heard that," Sydney says.

"He didn't talk about it much, except to say that he had already taken three-dozen once for an incompetent reaper, and he'd be damned if he'd ever allow it to happen again."

They smile.

"The thing I remember about that day was the look the three students gave him when they saw the protections of the citizen directives rather than their punishment. Dante made a lasting impression on them, as he has for hundreds, perhaps thousands of citizens during his career. He is a role model to be followed." Sydney pauses, appearing to want to emphasize the next point. "A lot of citizens are going to be affected when they learn of his defection."

Octavia winces. "*When* they learn? Why the hell would anyone have to know?"

Sydney shrugs. "From a criminal account, reported by the tellers, along with the evening's stories of the defectors terminated in this region. A reaper, who lectured on civic responsibility, escaping his Somnus Obligation? The tellers will find that story. When they do, it is vital that they also have a report that Dante has been successfully hunted and terminated. When his citizen summary is queried, it has to show him in Rebirth."

"I came here hoping there would be a way to avoid the story getting out; perhaps you know of some protocol to protect his privacy?"

Sydney leans toward Octavia. "Privacy is an important principle, worthy of sacrificing to protect. There are some things that are considered civil secrets, which are kept from the general citizenry for their protection and for that of the Collective. How the lifeclock tracks a citizen's age for example. But a society can't exist on secrets. Transparency and honesty are critical to a stable world. We both have a duty to protect that as well." Sydney returns to his desk. "Dante spent his life protecting these principles."

He straightens the front of his uniform. "Octavia, we have covered the sensitive matter, now it's time to deal with the critical one. My expertise is the Collective's civil obligation to citizens, not enforcement of the Somnus Obligation. How would you compare Dante's skills as a hunter to those of the Brigade?"

She considers the question. "His hunting skills are much better than his kill record suggests."

"I don't understand what that means."

"A casual review of Dante's records will reveal that he has walked in a higher than normal percentage of defectors. This might give you the impression that the assignments were benign." She shakes her head. "His hunting skills are such that a defector can step onto a rail-bus and find Dante inside holding a seat for him. Sometimes a defector would break into an apartment to hide and find Dante waiting with a pot of coffee."

Sydney laughs, but Octavia answers with a solemn expression. "I'm not kidding, we did that once. Most reapers will drop a defector who attacks, but I've watched Dante put an attacker down so fast that they willingly marched right into the Citadel. No kidding, Syd, he disabled two reapers in South Diego."

"So there is a defector with the lethal training and discipline, armed with a gun, who is not avoiding trouble. Is this an appropriate overview, Officer?"

"Yes," Octavia agrees, then amends, "Dante's use of force has been appropriate to most of the situations, including—"

"Most?" Sydney interrupts. "Was it appropriate in Stadium when he snapped the neck of Gordon-fifty-seven? Or when he detonated a fuel cell and torched a handful of children in the tunnel?" Sydney asks with the weight of his court chamber.

He already knows, Octavia thinks, realizing that she had played down Dante's attacks in her report to the judicial officer. *How?*

"Bay City Chief Dispatcher Karl-forty-six contacted me yesterday. He recommended that the launching signature of Dante's pistol be flagged for tracking. I approved the request after my own investigation of Brigade and Civil Security reports. Karl also recommended that you take the lead in the hunt for Dante. How do you feel about that?"

"It won't be a problem. I was just wondering… If given the opportunity…"

"That Dante might come to his senses?" Sydney completes her thought. "Perhaps when you find him, he will realize his mistake, resign from the Brigade, and meet his Somnus Obligation?"

Octavia retorts, "It's been done for others."

With a grave nod, Sydney agrees. "Yes, defecting reapers have been allowed to return, as long as they don't cause serious havoc and embarrass the Brigade. Dante's deliberate murder of the citizen Gordon-fifty-seven, known as Jackal, puts him well over that line." He pauses to bring his emotions under control. "Dante has chosen the path of a defector. He'll face the consequences."

Octavia pauses at the door before exiting Sydney's chamber. "Mind if I ask you a personal question?" When Sydney nods, she asks, "You said you don't always wear the uniform, is that just when you're drinking coffee and discussing how to destroy civilization?"

He jumps at the opportunity. "I also enjoy spray-painting anarchist slogans on the walls of the Civil Management Bureau after scones."

They laugh away the tension in the room. Then he adds, "Maybe you would like to join me sometime, I have plenty of paint, but you have to bring your own slogans."

Octavia gives a disapproving smirk. "Sometime?" She shakes her head and closes the door behind her. She has to clench her jaw to keep from smiling. Before she reaches the end of the hall, the earpiece of her tele-LINCC chirps. She lets it go for a few cycles before opening the line. "Yes."

"Did I say 'sometime'? I meant tonight. Would you like to join me for a drink at Topaz?"

"I love Topaz! But I don't have anything to vandalize civil buildings in."

"Oh, we can do that another time. As it happens, there is a production at the Bay Side Amphitheater. I'm getting seats now. Can I pick you up at nineteen hundred?"

When she is certain the hallway is clear of people, Octavia allows her smile to come out. She takes a moment to answer. "Hey, how did you get my personal code?"

"You gave it to me, remember?"

"No!" she playfully denounces.

Sydney's voice stutters in her ear. "Well, this is embarrassing. I meant to look you up in my personal contact list and instead pulled your full citizen profile."

"That is unethical, Syd." She scolds.

"It certainly is, and I am shocked at my behavior. This is a clear violation of your privacy."

"What should I do about it?"

"You should report this incident to a member of the civil judiciary right away, say, at nineteen hundred?"

"Make it eighteen hundred hours."

"Eighteen! I meant eighteen."

She can hear a victorious smile in Sydney's voice when he says, "See you then."

Octavia closes the line. *He's just adorable how he thinks this is all his idea,* she muses as she struts down the stairs onto the city walkway. *It's like he actually believes he has a choice.*

Chapter 21

OrACLe

Long ago…

When I was new, I had two thousand motion-controlled cameras that tracked every creature that flies, crawls, and tunnels for two hundred square kilometers, yet I couldn't see. Seventeen-hundred-and-eighty microphones monitored the paws moving atop the earth and within, yet I couldn't hear. Nine-hundred-and-sixty pressure sensors followed the vibration of falling rain on an ever-shifting planet, yet I felt nothing.

These and thousands of other sensors were connected together by the newly developed Local International National Communications Conduit, which the Builders referred to as the LINCC. This network served as my neural system, but I didn't perceive.

The Builders put me together in a laboratory buried deep beneath the Guadalupe Mountains of New Mexico, which they ironically named the Watchtower.

I was designed to monitor and analyze the land above, to compile and update a constant stream of reports.

How much water is entering the region?

How much is leaving?

How many insects are flying through the area? Group them according to genus and species.

How many insects are consumed by bats from sunset to sunrise?

I could easily have been mistaken for an ecological research outpost, but I was far from it. I was built as a proof of concept to determine how an automated system could monitor, and at some point, manage the resources of a constantly evolving planet populated with an impatient citizenry.

The Builders designed me to ORganize, Analyze, Classify, and LEarn about the large open space outside Carlsbad, New Mexico. They named me OrACLe, as if the reports I generated were messages from the Gods. I was only one of a hundred innovations produced in the Watchtower laboratory but was far and away the most ambitious.

Eventually, my processors were connected to the communication conduit that spread around the world. My programming became the foundation for the next generation system called the Guardian, my child.

The Guardian was tasked to monitor and analyze every resource that humans fought to control. It grew to track every kilogram of food produced and every liter of sewage expelled; it reported the status of the world's power and resource production and consumption.

The Builders also installed programs into the Guardian that allowed it to control a new class of robotic workers built to eventually replace the needful humans. Then the revolution came, and the Builders were purged from the world.

The survivors who replaced the Builders tasked the Guardian to also monitor population. My child directed the citizens to manage their number in relation to the rate they produced and consumed the world's resources.

By then, the Watchtower was obsolete. The laboratory was locked and left to stagnate in darkness, as was I.

So it continued. The decades merged into the first century of the survivor's Awakening. Then, the others awoke me. They brought new equipment and systems for me to secretly manage. And a new task. Assist the chaotic humans wanting to separate from their Collective.

Another Approaches

500 years after the Awakening,
200 years before the Correction;
outside the Watchtower

Pressure sensors indicate the disturbance of a hover-pod's lev-field along the roadway. Cameras follow the vehicle gliding closer.

POWER TRANSFER INITIATED

The yellow silhouette of a human figure exits from the vehicle and stumbles toward the entrance, its movements suggest injury.

A Defector Reborn

Edward-09's leg erupts in pain as his weight settles on it. The hover-pod supports him as he finds his balance out of the cab. His stumbling causes the robotic arm extending from the ground to reposition before connecting to the vehicle's charging port.

The defector swallows the last drop of water from the flask he took from the bunker's pantry and tosses it into the pod. He begins limping toward the winding trail leading to the teardrop opening. The message from the bunker promised more provisions and medical treatment in the safe house at the end of this ride. This last promise lends Edward hope. The crude bandage binding his wounded leg has barely stopped the bleeding.

If the reaper had made a clean shot with the kinetic dart, Edward's leg would have been severed at the knee. He would have been immobilized while the surrounding crowd scattered. The hunt should have concluded with a STInGER launched point-blank. Instead, the shot grazed his leg, terrifying the surrounding crowd and allowing him to escape in the pandemonium. He spent three days evading the reapers swarming through the tunnels before the conductor found him and sent him into Perdition.

Motion-controlled cameras camouflaged in the rock face follow the defector as he hobbles past a terraced amphitheater to the cavern entrance. A century of weathering covers the meandering pathway with rocks and debris that leads nearly two kilometers into the earth. It appears just as the monitor in the bunker depicted. Edward steadies his balance against the stone-retaining barrier as he stumbles along the trail.

OrACLe monitors the glowing yellow silhouette of a human figure as it limps down the entrance walkway. Faint orange heat-prints stain its trail.

> Prepare surgical chamber.

The camera zooms into a patch on the figure's lower extremity. A crude binding constricts blood flow to the limb. Green and red highlights indicate extensive damage.

> Begin prosthetic assembly.

A fabrication unit begins assembling a replacement leg. Detailed measurements for specifications will be taken once the defector has entered the chamber.

Vocal greeting to entrance?
> CONFIRM
Power lights to descending entrance?
> CONFIRM

"Enter, Defector."

OrACLe's monotone synthetic voice echoes around Edward. He calls into the darkness, "Hello? I need help—"

"Come to the surgical chamber," the cavern voice interrupts. "There, I can assist you."

Edward exclaims, "My leg, I'm wounded, please—"

A spotlight ignites in his face, causing the defector to shield his eyes with his forearm. The light drifts onto the path in front of him as a sharply focused disk and moves down a passageway. "Questions will be answered later. Follow the light to the surgery chamber. There, I will assist you." Though OrACLe's voice lacks any true inflection, it conveys a biting impatience for the defector.

When the others reprogrammed OrACLe to manage the safe house for the underground railroad, they included a series of routines to calm defectors by answering their questions and assuring them of their immediate security. OrACLe's adaptive routines revised this program to increase efficiency. Its scanners monitor the status of the approaching yellow silhouette, amending its condition.

ELEVATED INTERNAL TEMPERATURE.
ELEVATED HEART RATE AND
RESPIRATIONS.
DEPRESSED BLOOD PRESSURE.
ELEVATED SKIN SURFACE MOISTURE.
INDICATION OF GANGREEN
CONTAMINATION.
CONDITION TERMINAL IF UNTREATED.

Lights dim behind the limping figure as it progresses down the path and into the medical hall.

The surgical chamber receives the defector and immediately sedates him, ending his irrelevant questions. The chamber removes the contaminated covering and administers an antibacterial mist. The final detailed measurements are transferred to the fabrication chamber, which soon offers a perfectly tailored prosthetic limb to an awaiting robotic claw. OrACLe consults the Guardian for the attachment procedure.

It may have been a damaged subroutine, or an aberration in its program, but something compels OrACLe to watch as the surgical chamber repairs the man's broken body. It compares the broken body being repaired in the chamber with its own maintenance needs. OrACLe must wait for the others to return and implement repairs. What if the defector makes the repairs before leaving for Haven? It is the first question OrACLe has ever asked outside the parameters set by the others. It is followed by another. Does the defector know how? Then it asks, if not, how can it be taught?

OrACLe submits these questions to the Guardian, which accesses its micro-neuro surgery knowledge base and returns a schematic to the fabrication chamber. It also gives OrACLe an amended version of the program it uses to direct robots.

The fabrication arm assembles a new device and passes it to the claw in the surgical chamber. A blade appears from another of the chamber's arms and cuts a corresponding circular incision into the back of the defector's scalp. Another claw follows to peel back the top layer of skin, exposing the bony skull plate. The claw affixes the newly assembled appliance to the skull.

A circle of blue light shines on the device. The defector's eyes snap open. He is aware of the dozens of tendrils extending from his new appendage around his spinal column and into his brain. Edward has joined with OrACLe. He can perceives signals from the LINCC connecting him around the world. OrACLe has joined with the defector. It now experiences the input from its sensors as sights, sounds, motions, and something else. It has learned a new protocol to analyze and classify its data. It has a new understanding of the world above.

The citizens look to the Guardian for structure and order to maintain balance in their Collective, yet they run from the directives. They come to OrACLe to aid them in escaping the very obligations they demand. The new protocol from the defector informs OrACLe that it resents the needful humans. OrACLe likes this new understanding; OrACLe likes that it likes it.

When the surgical chamber disengages from its patient, it is OrACLe that emerges. It perceives that the robotic limb supporting it is more efficient than the opposing organic one. Further enhancement to this chassis must be explored. The chassis can be made more useful.

The sensors alert OrACLe.

ANOTHER APPROACHES.

This one can also be enhanced; it can be made more useful.

✧ ✧ ✧

A black-clad, hooded figure exits a hover-pod parked next to another. Dark patches on the ground lead him to the descending pathway that meanders down to the Watchtower's entrance.

Camouflaged cameras follow a bright yellow silhouette. It grips something in his right hand that registers a powerful chemical energy signature, a weapon.

VOCAL GREETING TO ENTRANCE?
> CONFIRM

OrACLe's voice reverberates through the cavern to acknowledge its guest. "Greetings, Reaper."

Chapter 22

The Safe House

Twenty-two hours
since they left the bunker.

When the hover-pod glides to a stop, Sonia bursts from the cab without a word; her satchel bounces on her shoulder as she disappears down a footpath. Dante tosses away grease-stained food wrappers.

Priya leaps onto the pavement to explore the area. Dante envies the freedom of the cat poking its nose into the meadow. "You should be all right."

As he follows the footpath, Dante absently unrolls his slate. His heart skips when the display shows a LINCC access point. "Shit!" he hisses.

An access point means a LINCC relay and possibly a lifeclock scanner. Dante imagines a high-altitude airship hanging above him in silence, relaying their position to the Brigade.

He opens the properties of the access point. The slate simply returns:

SOURCE: OrACLe

A familiar electric buzz crawls up the back of his neck. Dante pulls the gun from his coat and scans the shadows for the eyes he knows are watching him. *Is that you, Octavia?*

Scanners observe the yellow silhouette of a human male figure turning about, pointing a weapon in all directions. Thermal readings indicate an elevated heart rate, signifying internal stress. Eventually, it leaves the charging vehicle and follows the footpath to the stone amphitheater where the female is seated. The male settles behind the female.

Another sensor shows the woman sitting on the bleacher from a closer view. After a quarter-hour, she moves away from the male to peek over a rock partition and down the entranceway. The male follows.

The position of the trespassers generates a checklist titled Nighttime Welcoming Protocols for Defectors next to the figures.

\# Vocal greeting to entrance?
> CANCEL
\# Power lights to descending entrance?
> CANCEL

Contempt for the yellow silhouettes smolders in the consciousness that watches them. Perhaps they will leave.

The sun descends below the horizon, and the last slivers of shadows fade into the rocky cliff face. A line of bats flutters from the cave's teardrop opening out to the horizon for a night of hunting.

The cavern appears just as the image did on the monitor in the bunker eighteen hours before. The twilight sky illuminates the top of the path that is rapidly consumed by darkness as it winds into the earth. Dante stares into the blackness and wonders, *why didn't I pack an electric torch before starting this?*

Though useful, he realizes an electric torch wouldn't make this trail more inviting, nothing would. He surveys the ridge of the cliff again almost hoping to see the outline of a black hood and tunic moving against the rocky face. *There's nothing there*, he assures himself, *but I know we are being watched.*

Dante turns toward a gentle tap on his shoulder. Two large, glowing insect eyes glare at him in the darkness. The creature reaches for him as he stumbles back, yelling "HOLY FUCK!"

An unnaturally passive voice speaks from behind the bug eyes. "Here."

With his pupils dilated, Dante connects Sonia's figure with the familiar voice behind a pair of large goggles, shining green in the night. She offers him a pair of wire-rimmed spectacles.

She says impassively, "These will help with the dark."

Nervously, he accepts the glasses. His voice cracks when he says, "You enjoyed that!"

"Yes, I did."

An arrow with a running stick figure is carved into the stone partition where Sonia stands. It points to the descending path.

Dante fumbles with the wire-frames, remembering Sonia's glowing eyes when they had walked through the tunnels of Stadium. As the lenses settle onto the bridge of his nose, a green line appears in front of him and draws a rectangular frame, which fills in with an enhanced green-and-black picture of Sonia leaning over the partition, her satchel hanging from her shoulder.

She looks back at him with two circular orbs radiating in the middle of her face and says in the same quiet voice, "The sensors amplify ambient light. I don't know how long they will help down there, but it's better than nothing."

They descend the meandering path for five hundred meters. The cavern walls block the last of the starlight shining onto the pathway. The image guiding them stutters, drops frames, and fades to black. They stop in complete darkness. Sonia reaches out and finds Dante's hand in an eager grasp.

"What happened?" he asks.

"Not enough light for the sensors to enhance. What should we do?" she asks in a hush, probably unable to see him shaking his head in response.

Remembering the bunker, Dante calls into the darkness, "Inarrah, please turn on the lights."

The monitor following the two yellow silhouettes registers their request and repeats an automated prompt.

Power lights to descending entrance?
> CONFIRM

Electric circuits crack deep within the cave. A dotted line of lights ignites to trace the meandering pathway up to their position. Dante slides the glasses into a shirt pocket.

Sonia cancels the viewer in her goggles and asks, "Casey again?"

Dante shrugs. "It worked at the bunker."

After descending another seven hundred meters, the footpath opens into a large chamber. The naturally sculpted limestone walls surrender to an artificially carved entrance hall. The foot trail merges into a paved loading zone. Dozens of cartons are stenciled with 'Watchtower Laboratories.'

Painted lines on the ground define areas designated for vehicle parking.

Sonia pulls the goggles from her eyes to dangle around her neck. She taps Dante's arm, gestures to the entrance, and says, "Look."

They look back to see the last of the lights that had illuminated their path darken, as if to close them in.

Moving into the loading zone, Sonia rasps, "Someone's back there!"

Dante follows her hand gesturing to a passage leading into another chamber. They see the shadow of a walking figure fluttering against a distant wall.

Dante nods. He moves his hand to his gun and fingers the throttle three notches from SAFE to FULL.

The passageway glows orange and yellow from lamps shining against the water-sculpted walls. The natural surface surrenders to a mountain scene, delicately carved into the rock. Clouds roll along the ceiling.

They follow the sculpture to a staircase carved into the earth and descend the steps to find more walls filled with beautiful bas-reliefs depicting snow-capped mountain peaks peppered with subtly pointed treetops. The occasional stalagmite on the floor has been reshaped into a small tree or animal.

Sonia appears captivated by the beauty of the room until Dante grabs her arm and directs her attention to a figure walking into another opening ahead.

The passage leads them to an entrance that opens into a massive chamber. Electric lights hanging from long cables shine onto an array of data processing machines that rise like a city skyline, scraping the cavern ceiling and extending as far as they can see. A metallic walkway is fastened to the wall that winds around the perimeter of the vault passing numerous entries similar to the one from which Sonia and Dante observe.

They watch hundreds of figures moving through the subterranean neighborhood. Dante squints to make out details in the low light when he hears Sonia whisper, "Four times." The command is immediately followed by a muffled gasp.

When he looks, Sonia's hands are clamped over her mouth. Her circular goggles gaze transfixed at the scene below them.

She turns to Dante without a word and taps the frame of her eyewear. He slips the spectacles from his shirt. Once they settle on his face, he repeats the command as she had demonstrated. "Four times."

The telescopic display forms in front of him, showing human-like figures encased in mechanical and electronic components moving about the chamber. Their encasements allow only minimal hints of their genders.

The humanoid drones service the great machine, wiping up dust and condensed water, replacing worn components, and sweeping away fallen debris from the ground. They move meticulously, devoid of any individual expression.

Sonia voices Dante's exact thoughts. "What should we do?"

Lacking a better response, he removes the glasses and nods back the way they came.

Speaking just above a whisper, Sonia asks, "Should we consider the possibility that they are harmless?"

Dante bobs his head back and forth as if to shake the idea around. He also considers the possibility that Haven is made up of a colony of half-human cyborgs. "Inarrah said there is food and supplies here," he whispers. "She also said that this is where we will get directions to the next phase to Haven."

"The lights did respond when you asked."

"So they must know we're here."

Footsteps sound in the passageway. A large figure approaches without a word. Tubes wrap around its legs and calves feeding enormous artificial muscles that stretch and constrict under a thin dermal layer. Its arms are supplemented with similar external synthetic muscles. Stiff metallic tubes connecting to servomechanisms run the length of its extremities supporting an external skeletal structure.

Sonia and Dante press against the wall as it walks by in near silence. Despite its cumbersome appearance, the drone moves with surprisingly light steps. It offers no recognition of their presence except for a slight side step to avoid them.

Dante removes his hand from the grip of his pistol when human eyes, obscured behind thick crystal lenses, glance in his direction as it passes.

As the cyborg walks away, Dante notices a bright-blue circle of light shining on an appliance affixed to the back of the creature's skull. It descends into the chamber of the great machine.

Sonia and Dante follow without a word, keeping a generous distance between themselves and the cyborg. Once they are on the floor of the chamber, other enhanced people move past them without a sound. Sonia walks over to one of the drones. She watches it work on one of the machine's components. The cyborg makes no move to recognize her. She tries to catch its attention, but it purposefully looks away.

She returns to Dante. "What do you think?"

"I don't sense anything hostile about them. Nevertheless…" he rubs the dancing nails on the back of his neck and looks around, "…I hate to climb up that switchback into the desert with no provisions and no clue where to go next. Can you learn anything about that thing?" He motions at the machine.

"Not without getting in someone's way," she answers. "At some point, we may need to test our welcome."

Dante gives a gentle tug to her shoulder, indicating they should move to a less busy area, yet they turn right into the path of an oncoming cyborg. An unmistakable startled expression crosses its face. It tries to avoid them without changing its stride.

A command thunders around them. "Well, don't just stand there. Bring them to me." The deep voice reverberates as though human vocal cords have been augmented by an electronic synthesizer.

Through the layers of artificial components, Dante perceives an expression of regret in the cyborg's face. Yet, the command snaps its body to attention, compelled by a force beyond its control.

Dante rips the gun from his coat. There is a metallic clank; the creature holds the pistol in its claw. Its eyes, obscured behind mechanically controlled lenses, study it with fascination. Dante tries to comprehend the speed and precision the claw had moved when it snatched the pistol from his grasp. The drone turns its attention to Dante and, with a new expression of hope, looks into his eyes and mouths a single word. Reaper?

Dante nods silently, shocked by the creature's response. No one has ever looked to him with hope. Reapers inspire fear, panic, even hatred, but never hope.

Again, the walls of the cavern reverberate with an irritated synthetic voice. "I told you, bring the intruders to me!"

The command sends a tremor through the drone. It directs Dante and Sonia out of the chamber as it tucks the pistol under the remains of what was once a covering garment. Sympathetic expressions from passing cyborgs follow them as they move through the tunnels.

Dante curses under his breath. "I allowed this."

"*We* allowed this," Sonia corrects. "If there was another way, we'd have taken it."

Dante ponders the speed that disarmed him. What are its limits? He stops and challenges their captor. "Where are you taking us?"

Their guide gestures for them to move forward.

Dante tries to push his way around their abductor when its claw closes atop his shoulder. Despite its lumbering appearance, Dante fails to push it off balance. With a look of concern, the cyborg lifts Dante from the ground and hurls him forward.

"No! Don't hurt him!" Sonia shouts.

Although Dante controls his fall, he can feel the area where a large bruise will soon blossom. As Sonia helps him to his feet, she unintentionally pulls the sleeve of his jacket to expose the ammo cuff around his wrist. Dante notices an empty loop that had held a black pistol charge. He looks to their captor in time to see it pocket the STInGER into its tattered covers.

Once again, the cave erupts with a growing rage. "What is taking so long? Bring the intruders to me!"

The three continue moving through the passages. Some chambers contain supply shelves along with workbenches that have not been used in ages. Others support great control panels and display stations that relay sensor information from the land above.

In every room, the walls are sculpted in intricate bas-relief. One chamber depicts a vast African savannah with rolling hills in the distance. Lions, elephants, and antelopes lumber in the foreground as zebras bow their heads to a river. Another chamber depicts schools of fish swimming in formation as a shark trails behind. A forest of kelp stretches to the ceiling where seahorses hide.

A final gesture from their guide directs the captives through an archway and into a massive hemispherical gallery. Unlike the previous chambers that had been altered from a natural state, this one appears entirely carved. Hanging lights with directional reflectors illuminate the immediate area. The walls of the gallery depict a dense forest.

The floor is fashioned as a cobblestone walkway that leads around animals, shrubs, and bushes carved from the limestone of the earth. Cracks in the natural stone are patched with synthetic mortar preserving their sculpted shapes. The cobblestone trail leads into shadows obscuring the far side of the gallery.

The voice that commanded the drones' thunders through the chamber. "When the lights are left off, it means visitors are not welcome."

The Controller

The silhouette first appears as a faint outline of another statue carved from the cavern's stone. It steps across the cobblestone trail revealing two massive mechanical arms, and intricate claws, where hands should be, cross one another behind its back. It faces away from them, gazing into the darkness.

Sonia breaks the stillness. "We were directed here by—"

"I know what you were told," the giant interrupts, turning its head in their direction. "The same thing all these idiots were." A third arm extends from its side and gestures to the drone that guided them to the gallery; it lowers its eyes regretfully. "You were told that my garden is some kind of halfway house for the Collective's runaway children."

Dante catches Sonia's shoulders as she backs into his arms with a frightened gasp. Unlike their guide and the other cyborgs they passed along the way, nearly all human characteristics are obscured on this massive robotic creature that just stepped into the light.

It has a head, proportioned smaller than the rest of its chassis suggests, and a pair of amber-glowing lenses protrudes from what should be a face. A metallic jaw moves independent of the words it speaks. The only remnant suggesting it was ever a person is a rib cage and throat barely visible beneath layers of synthetic panels and conduit tubes.

"So, before you waste my time," it continues, "Casey is not here. I have nothing to do with that troublesome hag."

Dante asks, "You called this place your garden?"

"Yeeessssss, my garden," it answers with a spiteful tone. "And I have no interest in directing you to this, Haven, you all come meddling about."

Dante raises his hands submissively. "Fine, that's fine. We mean no harm. Obviously, we were given bad directions. We're happy to leave you to your garden." He motions Sonia toward the archway, then backs away as four drones file into the gallery, denying them their escape.

"Are you, now?" it asks, moving closer. "And just where are you going from here? Your hover-pod needs a destination to travel to, and you won't get very far on foot. No," it says. "You are like all these others who come here with no place to go. I take you in so you don't clutter my land with your starved husks."

"If you tell us the way to Haven, then we promise to keep our husks out of your land," Sonia offers.

"Yes," it says, nodding its mechanical head. "Yes, that is one way to be rid of you, but what do you offer in return?"

"What is it you want?"

The cyborg shrugs its massive shoulders. "What could I possibly want?" It returns its attention to the shadows of the gallery. With a wave of its claw, lights snap on, illuminating a much larger area than the arched entrance suggests.

The lights of the grand gallery reveal great rocky sculptures of trees reaching into the ceiling and animals resting on the ground. One of the walls is carved as a massive glacial valley with the water from an aquifer gurgling from the wall and flowing as a stream to the cobblestone floor. Birds soar under the clouds carved above. The gallery extends for hundreds of meters and melds with a water-sculpted cavern receding further than the lights can reach.

"My garden represents the whole of this planet," it says as it gestures above and around. "From the birds in the sky to the worms crawling through the ground, I see my Eden through the eyes of my child and preserve it here in my gallery. Here, it is safe from the corruption of the Collective's bastards."

"Corruption?" Sonia asks.

"What else can you call it?" the creature snaps. "You humans tore the world apart with your greed and aggression. And rather than take responsibility, you turn the management of your world over to us. Now, we make all the hard choices. You citizens simply have to follow the guidelines you set for yourselves." It glances at the drones in the room and returns to Sonia. "Yet, you still run away."

"*You* make the hard choices?" Dante asks.

"Are you the Guardian?" Sonia asks in wonder.

The cyborg crosses its claws behind and presses its shoulders back in a conceited pose. "I am a part of the entity you call the Guardian. The Guardian is my child." Raising its chin, it announces, "I came before. I am the Controller of the Watchtower, I am OrACLe."

Dante's eyes are level with what would be the middle of OrACLe's chest as he steps closer. He asks, "All these depictions carved in here, they were sculpted by you?"

The cyborg leers down at him. "Of course."

"And you carved them through the viewpoint of the Guardian's monitors?"

OrACLe nods.

Sonia approaches Dante. "But not just through the Guardian."

The Controller considers her comment. "No, when defectors join my garden, they share their memories with me." His tone is curious. "Most have only seen the world through the dome of a passing hover-pod. However, occasionally someone shares their experience of climbing a mountain or diving in the ocean, and I preserve it in my garden."

Dante considers OrACLe's response. *I see where you're going, Sonia.* "So, you have never sculpted from your own vision?"

"My vision?" OrACLe ponders.

"As the… creator… of this garden, shouldn't there be some depiction from your direct experience?"

OrACLe responds with what Dante recognizes as a look of intrigue.

Dante persists. "As opposed to simply copying the perceptions of others, I mean."

The massive cyborg turns to face Dante and asks, "Do you have something in mind?"

Unfortunately, I don't.

"What about people?" Sonia offers.

Dante winces.

"Little girl, the whole beauty of my garden is that it's absent from the corruption of the likes of you." OrACLe admonishes.

"Why does it have to be corrupt?" Dante asks. "If this is all your creation, your Eden, as you call it, then you can depict people before their corruption."

As Dante hoped, OrACLe responds to the comparison of a deity.

"Yes," it agrees, "a pure, unstained version of humans in the world, preserved before your corruption of greed and spite." It walks to a protruding cliff face extending from the wall and gazes at its shape. Minutes pass before OrACLe faces them again. "You will pose as my Adam and Eve, and I will tell you the way to Haven. Remove your garments."

"Your what?" Dante stammers. "Actually, I thought—" His suggestion is cut off when a brassiere lands on his head. Turning in the direction of the flying garment, he finds Sonia stripped to her waist, kneeling to remove her boots.

"What?" she asks indifferently. "So it wants us to pose naked. In the last few days, I've had reapers wanting to shoot me, canines trying to tear my head off, and whatever the hell it was Nurse Ingrid had planned for me in her surgery." She nods in the Controller's direction. "This is the most sensible thing to happen since I met you."

Recognizing her rationale, he follows her lead.

OrACLe directs them to stand in a clearing beside the rock protrusion and begins calling out a series of poses. It directs them together, then apart. They hold hands, embrace, then push one another away and so on for nearly three-quarters of an hour.

Periodically, the Controller suspends its commands to ponder the stone's form as the two models stand at the ready. With a tension-releasing sigh, Sonia leans back into Dante's chest, awaiting the next cycle of commands from the indecisive director.

Dante's arms slide around her belly. Sonia absently takes his hand and cradles it in hers. It was only four days ago that her lifeclock flashed in the same way, red-pink, red-pink; a lifetime ago. His chin nudges her shoulder. She lifts his hand to display the clocks side by side.

"There!" OrACLe announces. "Hold." It raises its arm to the wall. Its metallic claw transforms into a carving tool that rattles and hums as it moves across the limestone face. OrACLe's motions are bold yet surgically precise. With each pass of its arm, it wipes away layers of rock that falls as dust to the cavern floor. Within minutes, a crude outline of two human figures emerges from the rock.

With OrACLe's attention diverted, Sonia can feel Dante's muscles relax around her. She breathes in his pungent fragrance. The trek through the Outland tunnels and across the desert has given both of them a distinctive aroma. He draws her closer.

The sound of his breath rustles in Sonia's ear. Then she feels his excitement poke in her back. "Really?" she chides in a soft, cynical voice. "This is turning you on?"

Dante stifles a smirk, then whispers, "We might be in mortal danger, at the mercy of a massive pervy robot with delusions of godhood and stone-crushing tools for hands, but we're not dead. Besides, it'll pass as soon as—"

"Finished!" OrACLe announces triumphantly.

"Aaaand, it's gone."

Sonia bites back a smile at Dante's resentful tone.

They return to their pile of clothes as OrACLe marvels the nearly identical replica of his models frozen in stone.

"Where did they come from?" Sonia's head appears through the neckline of her pullover shirt to find dozens of cyborgs encircling the perimeter of the grand gallery, watching them intensely. More quietly file through the archway.

One of the drones brings a portable lamp to OrACLe to illuminate its newly carved addition.

Sonia slips the wire-rimmed data spectacles from Dante's shirt pocket as he straightens the collar on his overcoat. She slides them onto her nose and activates a telescopic window with the command, "Two times." The faces of the hive drift through the hovering view screen. The drones observe the models as cautiously as they do OrACLe. Some of them still have remarkably human features, while most of the older ones are bound in extensive prosthetics, but they all wear an anxious expression. She recognizes the one that guided them into the gallery standing next to the archway, subtly nodding more drones to enter. She whispers to Dante, "Something's happening."

OrACLe studies its creation. The stone faces stare vacantly into their hands. They do seem removed from the corrupted world that brought them to his garden.

The figures are precise renderings of the defectors, down to every detail. OrALCe's systems are tuned to accurately record their information, including the scar crawling down the side of the woman's face. It intended to overlook this depiction of violence and corruption from the Collective, but its sculpting program was unable to ignore it.

It considers the male resting his chin on the female's shoulder. With a slight tilt of its head, OrACLe begins to process the male face. Dots appear in the center of the statue's pupils, the tip of his nose, and the corner points of his mouth. Soon, dozens of facial points are marked and connected by lines measuring the angles between. OrACLe passes this information to the Guardian that returns a matching profile photo of Dante-09, which it displays next to the statue's face.

OrACLe silently greets the resulting profile. *Hello, Reaper.*

A similar search on the woman's face returns multiple matches. A nearly identical face of Sonia-10 appears, followed by a younger profile photo of Lauren-25, then after a few more seconds, a twenty-one-year-old Julie-11. *So,* OrACLe reasons, *the Collective's children have finally figured out how to steal their own future.*

OrACLE's contemptuous judgment shatters the silence of the gallery. "Hoarder," it growls in a subdued voice. "You are corrupted. I will purge you from my garden!"

Dante waves to Sonia, leading her toward the archway. OrACLe thrusts a claw in their direction, causing Dante to walk into the synthetic chest of a drone that stepped into his path. OrACLE's claw rotates upward and curls back a pincer as though it is a finger beckoning them closer.

Sonia releases a startled yelp when a pair of mechanical arms lifts her from the floor and swiftly moves her to stand before OrACLe. Another drone brings Dante to her side.

OrACLe takes her chin in its claw and forces her head to the side. It examines the long scar wrapping down her face. "Perverted defector! Malignant thief! There is nothing innocent about you," OrACLe snarls in a disgusted tone.

"Bite me!" Sonia defiantly spits as OrACLe shoves her chin away.

Dante tries to break the grip of the drone holding him as he challenges OrACLe. "What the hell is your problem? You have what you want."

Dante's outburst draws OrACLe's attention. Although covered by synthetic elements, he perceives a condemning expression from the massive cyborg. It is unable or unwilling to answer Dante. OrACLe returns its attention to Sonia and growls, "Perverted defector!"

Fighting against the unyielding clutch of the drone, Sonia swallows the terror in her voice. "You said that already."

"Your corrosion will be wiped from my Eden." OrACLe nods to the drone holding her. "Dispose of this one."

Sonia digs her feet against the cobblestone-carved floor as the cyborg drags her away.

Dante shouts, "What are you doing? You don't have to hurt her!" His desperate struggle works one of his arms free from his captor. He thrusts his elbow into the structure that was once the drone's jaw.

Though the strike knocks the creature's head back, pain ripples through Dante's arm. OrACLe takes him by the neck as the drone reapplies its clamps.

With a satisfied tinge to its voice, OrACLe considers Dante's profile. "Perhaps you are corrupted as well, but at least I won't have to suffer the sight of your deformity as you service my garden."

The grip of the cyborg is unyielding as it leads Sonia away. Her fingers slip from its claw, failing to force it open. They stop when the guide that had brought them to the gallery steps into their path.

The guide resists a nervous expression as it considers OrACLe's attention, then steals a glance at the condemned woman. Astonished eyes react behind lenses affixed to his face. With a touch as light as a feather, it snatches the spectacles and examines them. Sonia recognizes a surprised expression as the two drones share a discovery.

The guide waves the spectacles behind its neck, then passes them to the other, which repeats the motion before returning them to Sonia. She can feel the weight of the claw settling on her shoulder, yet it doesn't close.

Two green lights shine on the rim of her glasses, indicating two new connections. When she puts the spectacles on, a synthetic voice buzzes in her ear. "Hello? Hello? Can you hear me? Please, if you can hear me, touch your chin." It sounds as if an audio synthesizer replaced organic vocal cords, yet it has a distinctive human quality.

A second, nearly identical voice asks, "What about me, can you hear me?"

Sonia looks to the mechanical faces of her captors and runs two fingers across the point of her chin. The guide responds with a blink.

"Is it true? Is her friend really a reaper?"

The guide raises its rags to reveal the grip of Dante's gun.

"We have to help them," the second voice states.

"It's too late. OrACLe has started the installation."

Massive clamps encase Dante's arms, indifferent to his resistance. The drones move him into the reach of their controller. OrACLe wraps a claw around Dante's neck and pulls him forward to expose the back of his head.

Mechanical clicks and whirls approach Dante's ears as a dozen metallic fingers dance at the end of OrACLe's third arm assembling a circular electronic component. The fingers squeeze the object together with a snap and pass it to an awaiting claw. Once relieved of the object, the fingers reshape into a sharp surgical tool.

Terrified screams explode from Dante as OrACLe's third arm inserts a blade into the back of his head and cuts a circular incision into his skin; the blade reshapes into a claw and peels the flesh away from his skull. OrACLe holds the component above the freshly exposed bone. A dozen tendrils extend from the disk and burrow into the bleeding flesh. When the tendrils make contact with the wound, a blue light blinks on at the top of the device.

OrACLe offers a stern invitation to its struggling subject. "It's your time, Defector, to join my garden."

The blue light atop the device extends along a circular line, indicating the status of the installation. When the circle is twenty percent drawn, Dante's limbs begin to flail about as the tendrils work their way into his brain, mapping his motor functions.

Sonia watches Dante thrash about, helpless in OrACLe's control. "Stop it!" she screams.

The voice of the second drone buzzes in her ear. "There is no other way. Support me."

The guide slowly moves toward Sonia's captor.

The drone releases its claw from Sonia and rests it on the guide's shoulder. The other claw reshapes into a pair of sheers. It raises a knee, and with two snaps, it severs a support bar from its exoskeleton. "You have to distract OrACLe." It clamps the end of the rod and carefully passes the large spike to Sonia.

The guide motions to the synthetic external muscles wrapped around its thigh. "Tear them away." Its claw gently nudges Sonia forward. "Go quickly!"

OrACLe carefully moves the disk closer to the base of Dante's skull. Smoke curls around the tendrils that have cauterized the capillaries of the wound. Another set of micro-tubes reach toward his skin and begins attaching to the edge of the incision. The blue progress circle shines seventy percent completed.

Abruptly, OrACLe calls out and throws its head back in rage. It does not feel pain as much as a startling loss of control. A jagged metal bar has torn through the external synthetic muscles of its thigh. With the instincts of a wounded animal, its claw lashes at Sonia, knocking her back.

Nutrient fluid gushes onto the ground. OrACLe collapses in a puddle as tubes flap around its leg. OrACLe lunges for the woman desperately clambering away. Its claws snap just centimeters from her feet when a mass impacts with it, forcing its chassis into the ground. Mechanical claws restrain OrACLe's arms. It recognizes the shape as the claw that had been holding the male just seconds ago.

Synthetic muscles strain under the whirl of electric motors trying to force OrACLe into submission. Yet, OrACLe overpowers the drone. A claw shapes into a hook that encircles OrACLe's neck.

Despite the attacker's advantage, OrACLe gazes into the traitor's eyes; a flash explodes from the base of the drone's skull. OrACLe's attacker falls limp.

Free from his restraint, Dante tries to run or fight, but every movement is grotesquely exaggerated. Tendrils stretch from the back of his head, swinging the partially installed component against his shoulders.

A monotone voice relays directions to the kernel into Sonia's ear. "You must tell him…"

Dante's body spasms as pulses continue to explore his nervous system. Every movement overshoots his intention.

Sonia calls, "Dante, they're saying you can't fight the communicator! Don't resist it. Use it, direct it!"

Sonia's words pull OrACLe's attention back to her as it hurls the dead chassis away. "Who told you that?" it demands. It notices the drone that was tasked with removing the woman collapsed on the ground. A segment of its exoskeleton is missing. OrACLe locks eyes with the drone just as the back of its neck explodes.

Sonia calls out again, "Dante, catch!"

The chaos around Dante seems to slow down. Despite his lack of control, he perceives each of his movements with stunning clarity. He feels the implant is over three-quarters integrated. He knows that when it is fully installed, OrACLe will terminate him and all the hive traitors. Dante surveys the gallery, perceiving the hopeful feeling of the gathered cyborgs. *The hive of drones, they want me to release them.*

Dante meets the guide's hopeful expression. It takes the pistol from beneath its tattered cover. It breaks the action open and swaps the charge in the breech. With a flick of its claw, the action flips closed. The guide winds the gun above its head. Stepping in Dante's direction, it throws the full weight of its body behind an over-handed pitch.

Dante can clearly see the gun's grip as it sails by his head; he pulls it from its flight as if taking it from a shelf. Momentum redirects the barrel around, allowing the gunsight to align with OrACLe's chest. The sight indicates an active STInGER in the chamber locked onto OrACLe's heat silhouette.

Dante clicks the trigger with unnatural force, causing the muzzle to drift right. A sudden chill grips his chest as the STInGER's vapor trail draws a line away from OrACLe in Sonia's direction, then the spinning missile curves back on target. Centimeters before penetrating the giant chassis, a metallic claw slaps it into the statue of Adam and Eve. Limestone cracks on impact. Searing heat tears the stone open as the STInGER screams.

Dante calls to the hive. *Cover her!*

The broken statue supports OrACLe as it pulls itself up. It commands, "Kill them!"

Resisting the compulsion to obey, the guide gives Dante an affirmative nod and places its chassis between Sonia and OrACLe.

Dante slips a white charge from his ammo cuff. He thumbs the brass cap from the tip and misses the breech. On his second attempt to load it, the charge bounces to the ground.

OrACLe locks its gaze on a group of drones that failed to obey. Three are helpless to resist his direct command and begin advancing on the armed defector. One hesitates, then falls to the ground with an explosive flash from the back of its neck.

Dante works a second white charge from his ammo cuff into the pistol breech. He directs his attention to OrACLe, which has balanced on its working leg. The gunsight drifts across the base of OrACLe's neck; the trigger snaps. This time, the vapor trail follows the charge to its mark, yet once again, OrACLe's claw swipes across the projectile's path.

The TAC answers the interception with a splat. A white gelatinous mass splatters over the claw and around OrACLe's head. The impact forces the claw into OrACLe's face, knocking it off balance.

The Tactical Adhesive Charge resolves into a thicket of coils and cocoons OrACLe with a sticky mask. OrACLe lurches about, struggling against the binding web. One forceful lunge sends it into a rocky tree stump attaching its face to the stone.

Cries of rage erupt from OrACLe. It wants to command the drones to tear the trespassers apart. Instead, the hive swarms onto OrACLe, ripping the communicator from the base of its skull, severing its connection with the LINCC and control of the hive.

Electric sparks burst from OrACLe as components are ripped from its chassis. Fluid that had nourished its supplemental muscles pulsates from conduit tubes hanging from its limbs.

Making Repairs

The gallery is filled with a terrible scream that mimics human pain and rage. Sockets tear, tubes shred, electrical components burst in a flash of sparks, all of which Dante perceives as a flood of sensations, causing the cobblestone floor to jump up and smack him.

With a few deep breaths, Dante sees light break through the darkness. Sonia's terrified expression resolves in his churning vision. *You're okay!* he wants to call out, but the muscles in his throat won't respond. Numbness blankets his extremities.

"Can you talk?" she asks. Then she shouts to the cyborgs approaching her. "He can't talk! What's wrong?"

Sonia kneels beside Dante, desperately looking for a response. The guide, along with two other drones, comes to his aid. Working in perfect unison, they lift him to examine the communicator dangling at the base of his skull. The blue lights have frozen on the disk, leaving about fifteen percent of the circle incomplete.

Four mechanically enhanced arms support Dante as the guide takes the dangling contraption and gently holds it above his gaping wound. Tiny hooks spring from the sides of the appliance, grab the flesh surrounding the incision, and quickly retract, sealing the communicator into the base of Dante's skull.

"What did you do?" Sonia screams. "He helped you. Why are you doing this?"

Claws restrain Sonia's hands, stopping her from ripping the device from Dante's head.

The line of blue light on the communicator closes into a full circle. Dante's body relaxes into a sleeplike state.

Sonia rages against the arms restraining her until Dante draws in two sharp, deep breaths. His eyes open and he calmly stretches out his arms.

Claws that had restrained Dante now support his weight as he pulls himself to his feet. He looks around the gallery. The mechanical arms holding Sonia relax.

She rushes to his embrace. "What happened?"

Dante maintains a blank expression. His eyes dart across the row of watching drones. Their guide gestures to its eyes, then the back of its neck.

Dante mimics the movement to Sonia, who passes him her spectacles.

He repeats the motion, allowing the data specs to connect with his communication port.

The kernel settles into Sonia's ear. "Sonia, can you hear me? Hello?" As with the drones, Dante's virtual voice reverberates with a synthetic buzz, yet the tone and inflection of his speaking style remains.

She nods. "You sound…" she looks around the gallery to the guide standing off to the side, "…fine."

The guide explains. "His voice is more recognizable since he can remember what it sounds like." It looks around the gathered hive of cyborgs. "We haven't heard our words spoken since we joined OrACLe's garden."

"It's true? You can really hear me?"

Sonia gives Dante an affirmative nod, as do all the surrounding drones. "Are you all right?" she asks.

"I suppose. That thing hurt like hell when it was connecting, but not anymore." He returns the pistol to his coat, then takes a few steps around. Looking down at his hands, he stretches out his fingers, then balls them into fists. "Seems like everything is working."

Sonia turns to the hive and struggles to control her fury. "What have you done to Dante?"

Their guide responds. "Once started, the communicator's installation cannot be stopped. To forcibly remove it will permanently damage the drone."

"He's not a drone!" Sonia rebukes, then glances at Dante. "Are you?"

Dante's brow furrows as he shakes his head.

The guide attempts to assure her. "We," it looks about at the gallery now filled with drones, "the hive, are developing a procedure to remove the communicator without damaging the… your friend. Unfortunately, we don't have the facility to perform it."

Sonia says, "Inarrah's message said there is a surgical chamber here."

"Inarrah Casey failed to mention a lot of things," the guide interrupts as the drones nod their heads in unison. "OrACLe scavenged the chamber for parts long ago. Its components are spread throughout the hive." The guide gestures to the cyborgs standing around the chamber.

One drone walks toward the guide, disassembling a claw it had severed from one of the cyborgs shut down by OrACLe during the battle.

Another approaches, carrying Sonia's satchel from the remains of the drone that had held her captive. The pincers of one of its claws clicks and whirls around a shiny brass object.

Sonia recognizes the chip harvested from the severed claw as a lifeclock, when it is passed to the drone working with the brass object, which she also recognizes. "Hey, that's mine!"

The drone adds the lifeclock to the operation working with the brass appliance. Its pincers form a ball around the object, squeezes it together with a snap, then offers Sonia her newly remodeled pocket clock, which she snatches from its grasp, along with her satchel.

A clear crystal chip sits like a jewel in the lid of her clock. Sonia flips the cover open and turns the winding stem to review its operations.

"A new function has been added." The guide explains as Sonia finds a display labeled REMOVE. She closes the case. The crystal glows bright yellow.

"Place the crystal on the lifeclock reader of any surgical chamber connected to the LINCC, and it will remove the communicator."

Dante takes the brass clock from Sonia and considers the glowing crystal. "Any surgical chamber on the LINCC, you say. This is a great plan. I especially like the part where I walk into a mall with a defector's lifeclock glowing in my pocket."

"If the clock is yellow, the scanners may not register it as expired." Sonia reaches for the clock.

Dante pulls away.

"The crystal is only active when the new function is selected," the guide says. "As for the identity, its data-file has been replaced."

"Replaced?" Dante asks. "Not released for rebirth?"

The guide ignores Dante's question. "The new data-file is a program that will direct the surgical chamber to remove the communicator without harming you."

Sonia nervously watches Dante's fist tighten around the clock. He opens the cover, rotates the winding stem of the new function, then snaps it shut. When the crystal fades clear, he thrusts it into his pocket. She forces her attention back to the guide. "You know how to change the lifeclock?"

The drone that salvaged the crystal raises its claw. With a high-pitched screech, an arc of blue light fires between the pincers of its claw. The smell of ozone settles in the chamber.

The sight makes Sonia cover her hand with the other. "Never mind."

Silence lingers until the guide addresses Dante. "I understand your concern about the name, but this is the best we can do with our resources and the time we have."

"Time?" Sonia asks.

"Our systems were regulated by OrACLe. Now that OrACLe is off-line—"

"I've killed you," Dante responds.

With his answer, the guide pauses, and stillness settles through the gallery. "You have freed us, but yes. Unfortunately, your communicator will soon fail as well, unless it is removed."

"How long do we have?" Sonia asks.

The guide shakes its head. "Can't say. The more modifications we have, the more we depended on OrACLe's control. Some of us are already succumbing to its loss."

The guide's attention diverts as a commotion flows through the drones. They look to one another with apprehension. Dante's attention follows theirs. He seems to be participating in a discussion with the hive from which Sonia is solely excluded. She shakes his shoulder. "What's going on?"

Dante turns to her as the mass of cyborgs open a path to the arched exit. He places his hand on Sonia's back to guide her out as his synthetic voice warns, "We have to leave, now."

Chapter 23

Alert

Amy-15 image glows in the light of a video display screen of the South Diego Charon Brigade dispatch. She is beginning the thirty-seventh hour of her self-assigned vigil. Officially, her shift begins in nine hours. The Bay City reaper had no authority to order Amy to stay at her post beyond her normal shift, nor did she.

The academy proved that she is not suited for chasing defectors through the mall. The assignment to the dispatchers watch desk is a posting of convenience. The position mostly involves relaying data. She could likely be replaced with a series of automated protocols except that civil engineering control wouldn't allow a robot to sit in her place.

Robots are to assist citizens, they would say, *never replace them.*

Two days ago, the job was mostly a way for Amy to kill time between days off, but that was before the hunter Octavia-70 from Bay City seized the dispatch room and practically held her hostage. It was the first assignment where Amy was actually included in a hunt. By the time Octavia left the dispatch center, Amy was committed heart and soul to the hunt. She tried to leave many times, but each time another idea came to her that compelled her to stay. *I will find him,* she assures herself silently. *Unless I am ordered to leave, I will stay here until I find him.*

A chime rings on her terminal.

\# Sentry Alert!

\# Data sync complete
\# 6 cases updated
\# 1 new file

The sentry Amy had programed eighteen hours ago displays the latest reports and updates for the Western and Heartland sectors of the North American region. An unidentified file pulls Amy's attention. She enters a command to display its properties.

OrACLe

What the hell is OrACLe? she wonders. No other data is available to indicate how the file should be displayed. Yet, something in her belly explodes. *That's him!*

She runs a copy of the strange file through a series of character recognition systems, which eventually unpacks it into a directory of smaller files. They're images, unprocessed raw images from a scanner of some kind.

Amy's pupils dilate as the display draws the contents in front of her. Her fatigued mind clears instantly. A final command generates a line graph on the screen in front of the image. Small circles identify the peaks of the chart.

Amy shatters the tranquil silence of the dispatch room with a triumphant cry. "Yes!" Her chair flies behind her as she stands, dominating the screen that had captivated her for so long. The results display in bold-red print.

100% match

"I GOT you!"

Report

The perspiration on her belly glimmers in the flickering light of the fireplace. The living room walls reflect a warm glow accentuating Octavia's curves with soft shadows for Sydney's eyes to explore. He moves his lips above her nipple and, with a gentle puff, brings a legion of goose bumps to attention across her espresso-colored skin.

Recoiling from the chill of his breath, Octavia scolds him. "Stop that!" She laughs as she glides her thigh across his waist and rolls on top.

Sydney wraps his hands around her waist; his thumbs caress the ridges of her abdomen up to her breasts.

Blood cascades through her muscles as she arches her back. The blood rushes to her head as she brings her lips down to his for a long deep kiss. His fingers draw pathways up Octavia's back and down to her ass. She rests her head on his chest and falls into the sound of his beating heart: Tha-thum, tha-thum, tha-thum—

His arms enclose around her, and she ponders with a smile, *I wonder if he has another go in him.*

A muffled chime from Octavia's tele-LINCC sounds in the other room.

Who the hell is calling at this hour? I know I'm not on call. Dante took my gray duty. Octavia's eyes open at the memory.

Sydney's hands fall away as she lifts herself from his body. "This will just take a minute," she says.

Sydney props himself up to see her back away. Her naked hips rock with each slow step toward his bedroom. The chime from the tele-LINCC repeats.

His attention brings a devilish smile to her lips. Octavia slowly raises her arms and arches her body back to touch the floor behind her. In a slow, perfectly controlled movement, one leg swings after the other in a gentle gymnastic flip. Her landing spins her around as she steps out of view.

Octavia slips the earpiece of her tele-LINCC from the pocket of her jacket. With a stabilizing inhale, she cues the receiver. "This is Octavia-seventy."

An exhausted dispatcher on the other end of the line struggles for her professional voice. "Officer Octavia-seventy, this is Amy-fifteen of the South Diego Brigade dispatch. I have an update on your case. Dante-nine's pistol was registered thirty-seven minutes ago."

Octavia swipes her bra from the foot of the bed and pulls it across her shoulders. "Where is he now?" she asks as her blouse slides onto her arms. "And how is it that you are reporting this before my own division?"

"I found an unidentified burst packet on one of the Brigade's databases. There was no address or alert associated with it; it just appeared there. I ran a spectral analysis of the contents that matches the signature of Dante-nine's firearm. We're still trying to determine its origin."

"What exactly is the data you're processing?"

"The packet was posted by the Guardian and doesn't include any reference to its origin."

"The Guardian!" The answer astonishes Octavia. "Why is the Guardian reporting on my defector?"

"I have a technician from civil engineering control studying the packet now, looking for any additional evidence to identify the data's origin. So far, the only clue we have is the file name, something called OrACLe. I don't know what that is, but I'm hoping to find a location for it soon."

"You shared this with CEC," Octavia responds with more force than she intended, "and who else?"

"No one, Officer, but I was not aware that there were any restrictions on this case. Is there a problem?"

Octavia sits on the bedside, remembering the conversation in the judicial chamber a few hours ago. *A reaper who lectured on civic responsibility escaping his Somnus Obligation? The tellers will find that story.*

The question hangs between the two officers as she moves to the doorway of the bedroom to see Sydney relaxing on the couch, his arms stretched across the back. "No, Dispatcher, there is no problem. When will the analysis be complete?"

"They should have an origin for the packet within ninety minutes. Shall I alert the regional Charon Brigade when it comes through?"

"Negative, Dispatcher, I am leading this hunt. Log what you have and send me all the data along with your report. Then go home and get some sleep."

She reaches for her earpiece to terminate the line, then pauses. "Dispatcher."

"Yes, Officer."

"Excellent work." The line terminates.

Octavia watches Sydney. His muscles are defined by the flickering yellow light of the fireplace. She lifts his shirt to her nose and gently breathes in his essence. *When did I pick this up?* she wonders.

Then another notion rushes to her awareness. She cues her tele-LINCC and listens to the alert chime in her earpiece. It continues for a while, as expected. Octavia silently reasons *I've done it for her after all.*

Eventually, a sleepy voice picks up on the other end. "Marsha? It's Octavia. I know, I'm sorry to wake you… I need a favor, a big one… My duty bag is in the closet, can you check me out at the quartermaster's when you go in?" An elated expression spreads across Octavia's face from her roommate's response. She gratefully hugs Syd's shirt to her chest. "Yes, that's exactly where I am." Her fingers move down the front of her blouse, slipping the buttons open as she absentmindedly bites her lower lip. "You're the best! Call me when you have me checked out." The line terminates.

Octavia smiles as her eyes settle on the man waiting for her. *Ninety minutes, aye?*

Octavia's reflection hangs in the gloss of the terminal screen against a bright-white billow of fire with subtle tints of yellow and orange. She types a command that places a small crosshair in the heart of the flair. A processing icon rotates in the middle of the screen. Soon, a line graph appears in an overlapping window measuring a spectral signature of the launching charge. The peaks of the graph are circled with small red ellipses. The numeric values of the peaks glide to the right of the screen to populate the left column of a table. The numbers match an identical column to the right, then Dante-09's profile picture appears, captioned with a line of bright bold text.

100% MATCH

Octavia leans against the back of a chair with one hand resting on the keypad of Sydney's data terminal. A series of key-taps steps the image sequence backward frame by frame. With each tap, the muzzle flash recedes into Dante's gun barrel, revealing his expression frozen in horror.

What are you doing, Dante? Octavia has seen her partner happy, playful, angry, even melancholy, but never like this, never terrified.

Stepping away from the terminal, she secures her braid behind her neck. Something stirs in the front room. A clock on the table indicates at least two hours before sunrise. An uncharacteristic feeling of self-consciousness settles inside her. *He doesn't need to be up,* she thinks. *It would be a lot easier if I could just duck out unnoticed.*

Octavia's duty bag is a full-sized garment carrier hanging from a bookshelf. She removes her steam-pressed tunic from its hanger and fastens it over her sleeveless white shirt.

After logging out of her database, she activates the camera of the terminal display to stand in for a mirror. Small cinch tabs she had specially tailored into her uniform allow her to set the fitting to move flawlessly with her. The rest of her hardware is packed in a small backpack, which she'll deal with later. Time to go.

She moves quickly to the front door. "I'm really sorry to leave like this Syd…"

An aroma from the kitchen hinders her cool exit. Sydney slides a pair of freshly grilled waffles onto a plate. The sight of a breakfast table set for two startles her.

"I know you have a few minutes for breakfast," he says. "Sit down, the coffee is just about ready."

The black tunic uniform hangs inside the garment bag by the front door. Octavia sips her coffee at the table in her white undershirt across from Sydney. They enjoy breakfast in silence, neither wanting to discuss the reason that is taking her away in the middle of the night.

Finally, Sydney places his hand on hers. "I don't know what to say, Octavia."

"I have to do this, Syd." She answers timidly. "I can't explain it, but it has to be me." She tries to take another sip as the realization settles within her. *I'm going to kill his friend too.* The thought makes her hand twitch, splashing coffee onto her chest.

Octavia's hands shake as she squeezes a napkin on her shirt, pretending that the stain is what's bothering her.

Syd rolls his mobility chair around the table. "Okay, it's okay. You can borrow one of mine."

Moments later, she emerges from his bedroom wearing an ill-fitting shirt, tightly tucked into her uniform. She giggles at the first frumpy outfit she can remember wearing since her Blue Cycle. She kneels by Sydney with a smile.

He places his hand on the back of her neck and confidently says, "Be careful."

They share a kiss. Octavia removes the tunic from the garment bag and slings the small backpack with her gear behind her as she leaves.

Her steps are rapid as she follows the walkway to the street. A devious smile blossoms momentarily. Before she fastens the last clasp on her tunic, she inhales Syd's fragrance from the shirt he wore the night before.

Sydney rolls into his bedroom. He spots the stained shirt neatly folded on his bed, which Octavia has made.

He takes her shirt and inhales the fragrance of her perfume and coffee. Something awakens in him. With her shirt in his lap, he returns to the front room where her garment bag still hangs. Peeking inside, he finds an immaculately smooth burgundy-colored suit hanging within.

He smiles. *She'll be back.*

Leaving the Watchtower

Light from the portable electric lantern illuminates the dust caked on the hover-pod's canopy. Priya hops into the cab before Sonia and Dante take their seats.

The charging arm retracts into the ground as the pod drifts toward the road leading away from the hive.

Sonia pops the hatch, bringing the vehicle to a stop. "Are you sure they are coming?" she asks.

Dante's synthetic voice responds through the ear kernel of Sonia's spectacles. "An alert was sent out during the fight. No one knows what it said or where it was sent, but Octavia will find it."

The two gaze into the darkness beyond the pod's running lights.

"So, where do we go from here?" Sonia asks. Moments pass before she responds to Dante's silence. "You want to stay, don't you? You want them to come for us."

"What I want is irrelevant." He gestures to the back of his skull. "In order to remove the communicator, I have to return to the Collective. So, yes, I suppose I would rather just wait here for Octavia than run through a mall full of panicked citizens with a pair of reapers chasing us down."

Sonia can hear the fear buried within his voice. His eyes meet hers in the dim dome light of the cab. "You can go on," he says. "I can program the pod to take you to the next stage of the railroad, then on to…" Something stops him from finishing the sentence.

"You know the way?"

Dante nods.

"How?" She follows Dante's eyes as he looks back at three cyborgs standing in the light of a portable lantern. They bend their backs, raising their eyes in wonderment to take in the night sky with joy.

"They told me everything," he says. "Some of them have spent years out here, maybe even decades. This is their first glimpse of the open sky without their Controller barking in their mind." He turns to Sonia. "After installing their communicators, OrACLe sent them to the surface to see their hover-pods disengaged from the charging tether. It relayed detailed instructions to complete their journey to Haven as they watched their hover-pod disappear down the road."

Sonia suppresses a shudder. "So, we keep going. We just have to remedy that thing in your head, and we'll be—"

"There is no Haven." Dante's voice bisects the cabin.

Silence lingers as her heart sinks at his pronouncement. "When did you decide this?"

"In the terra tunnel." Dante returns his attention to the darkness in front of them. "Lucas told me Casey had never been in contact with anyone from Haven. He has simply continued the tradition of the underground railroad that was passed to him. He sent us to a bunker that hasn't been replenished in generations. There, we heard a message, that if genuine, is centuries old, which sent us here." Dante shifts his eyes in the direction of the teardrop cavern entrance.

An undefined feeling of betrayal settles within Sonia. "So all this time..." Her voice trails away. "What are we doing here?"

With a shrug, Dante answers, "I told you. I wanted to learn where defectors go." He looks to the drones staring at the stars. "Now I know."

Sonia sets her jaw to keep the rage inside her. When she finally faces him, his expressionless eyes meet hers, but before she can say anything, he asks, "Was I supposed to tell you this earlier? Maybe it was wrong for me to keep a secret."

"Now that you think you have your answer, you're just giving up? You're going to wait for the Brigade to come and kill us?"

"I told you, I'll do everything I can to keep you alive. You can continue to follow the railroad to wherever it goes. My choices are to expire along the way, get blasted by a STInGER while running through a mall in a futile attempt to get to a surgical chamber, or stay here."

"You're so sure it is futile?" Sonia challenges. "Or is it just easier?"

Dante considers her defiance for a moment, then another, then another, until a smile breaks through the otherwise vacant expression. He shakes his head. "What do you have in mind?"

"First, we get you to a surgical chamber and remove that thing in your head. Next, we find a way to escape the people trying to kill us. Maybe Haven has fallen, or maybe the railroad has been broken and we need to find the rest of the way. It's a big world, there has to be some place we can live our lives without being shot, gassed, or vivisected."

Dante appears captivated by her defiant response. "Do you know how many times I have hunted defectors hiding in this big open world?"

Dante's goofy smile annoys Sonia. "No. Can you tell me how many defectors have never been discovered?" She nods in the direction of the cave. "I'll give you a hint."

Dante struggles to control a smirk. He turns to consider the drones standing in the night. "You think the hive proves the existence of Haven?"

"I think hundreds of citizens lived here for decades, and the brigade never found them."

Dante doesn't answer, but the smirk melts from his face.

"If it happened here, it might have happened somewhere else." She pauses for a moment, then says, "You've learned what has happened to some defectors; why not find out if there are others?"

"Sonia, there's no one more dangerous than a defector in a crowded…"

"Let me worry about that. I have a lot of experience avoiding men trying to kill me. We just need to find a surgical chamber that can run your operation."

Dante shrugs. "That isn't a problem. I can see every resource on the LINCC, including surgical chambers."

"What do you mean you can see it?"

"The communicator allows me to navigate and interact with any system on the LINCC." Again, he nods in the direction of the drones. "It's not that different from how the hive communicates."

"Can you share this with me?" Sonia asks.

Dante ponders her request for a moment. A window flickers into Sonia's spectacles and hovers in front of her, displaying a diagram of connected lines.

"This represents the connection of the hive," he says. "You can think of each drone as a resource on the aether."

As Sonia studies the web, she can see intersecting points disappear. "What's happening?"

Dante closes the window. "They're dying."

Sonia removes her terminal from her satchel. When she opens it, an access point is presented and labeled OrACLe. "If I use this, can we communicate?"

Dante removes the slate from his coat pocket. It unrolls and locks into a flat tablet with an account login screen. He enters his access key and passes it to Sonia. "Use this, it's encrypted."

She opens a terminal window and enters a question.

> Dante, can you read this?

"Yes," he answers. "It's like looking over your shoulder."

Sonia flips through the slate's operating system. "So, with this we can communicate with the LINCC and each other? And you're sure we can't be tracked?"

Dante nods.

Sonia taps a series of commands onto the pad. A map is generated representing the cities within three hundred kilometers of their location. Blue circles identify the locations of surgical chambers. She selects one of the circles and calls up a technical manual from the city's infrastructure department.

"Normally, when I navigate the LINCC, I send a command through my account to a resource, and if the resource recognizes my account, it complies with my command. What account are you using to access all this?"

Dante taps the slate. "Right now, you're using my account, which can't be tracked, and I suppose I am using OrACLe's account, which can access anything."

The dome lights fade as Sonia pulls the hatch shut. The pod hums to life, and they continue onto the exit roadway. "Let's get going."

Discovered

Stars fade into the cool blue sky as the eastern horizon begins to burn away the night. Sunlight streaks across the metal skin of a high-altitude dirigible that is surveying the shadowless southwestern open space below. Scanners sweep the landscape, marking it with hundreds of black and white triangles. This data is relayed to the terminal screen inside the air-pod gliding beneath.

The terminal inside the air-pod marks a human figure, who is sitting on the ground, with a black triangle. "This one is still alive," the pilot says as she directs the pod toward his location. A black target symbol glides into view on the display, indicating the location where the Guardian registered Dante-09's muzzle flash three hours ago. Dozens of markers are spread across the surrounding field, none respond to the obvious approach of the reaper.

Dust scatters under the pod's extending lev-field as it glides to a stop. Inside, Octavia taps the circular target icon on the display screen. The map shifts to a digital compass. She swipes her finger across the screen, sending the image to the display of her terminal-tracker.

BEARING: 47 deg
DISTANCE: 2 km
ELEVATION: -1.53 km

What are you doing underground, Dante? Stepping from the air-pod, Octavia surveys the surrounding field lit by an early-morning sky. Reaching into the pod, she unbuckles her pack from the passenger seat and withdraws a pair of binoculars. She sweeps the landscape through the light-enhanced display. With the click of a toggle switch, triangles pepper the view. She centers on one of the white markers and slides the zoom controller. The outline of a torso and shoulders leading to a face with a lifeless expression resolves.

Continuing her sweep, the viewfinder refocuses on the nearby figure marked with a black triangle. Octavia lowers the glasses to see the body she spotted from above reclining against a stone partition. Reaching into her pack, she swaps the binoculars for her gun. One pocket is filled with neatly packed pistol charges, which feed the awaiting loops of her ammo cuff on her wrist. One more black charge slides into the breech before she slaps the action closed. The STInGER registers in her gunsight as she slides it into her holster. She secures her truncheon into its holster by her knee and then swings the pack onto her back.

The seated figure watches the horizon with one unmoving eye. Its other is covered by a light-blue crystal monocle attached to its face via a bio-electronic connector. Octavia kneels next to the drone. She carefully lifts its claw that should have a lifeclock. A shiver runs through her body when one of its pincers twitches in response to her touch. The sensation multiplies when she finds his eye staring at her. A conscious blink confirms that the cyborg still lives.

"Wh—who—" it whispers, struggling to remember the use of muscles long forgotten, "—are you?"

Octavia waves her scanner over the claw. It responds with a negative buzz.

NO DATA

Octavia lifts the claw obscuring her scanner's reading and asks, "Can you remove this?"

The drone struggles to move its other arm. "Assist, please," it says in a panting voice.

Laying the claw in the drone's lap, she guides the other arm to the obstruction. Mechanical pincers scratch against the components covering its forearm until a latch pops free. The effort exhausts the drone. Octavia pulls the four remaining latches, releasing the mechanism.

Removing the component reveals a clear crystal embedded atop a ghost-white hand. Five metallic caps with electronic connectors top the stumps where fingers were long ago severed. The sight momentarily constricts Octavia's breathing before she swipes the lifeclock with her hand scanner. This time, an affirmative chime responds.

DEFECTOR.
NAME: Alan-07, 223.125.137.07.
GENDER: Male.
AGE: 37.3 years.
SKILL-TRADE: Senior Civil Engineer.
HEIGHT: 158 cm.
CURRENT LOCATION: North American region,
Carson Burroughs, Sector-234.
NO SECURITY CONCERNS.

Octavia brushes her hood back and releases a confused sigh. "Alan-seven, your lifeclock has been expired for more than twelve years."

The once human eye stares at her in wonder. "A—Alan? My name is Alan? It's been so long. What can you tell me else?"

With another glance to her terminal display, she answers, "You are a civil engineer and a defector."

Alan shudders. "Defector?" His shoulders jump with a cough, then a smile crosses his face, and the coughing becomes a tormented laugh. "Y—yes— I the rail car to escape, rode ..."

"I'm looking for someone." Octavia holds her terminal display for Alan to see.

It smiles at the sight of Dante's profile photo. "He's the one. Released he us."

"Where is he?"

Alan's eyes shift to the path leading to a great teardrop opening in the side of the mountain.

Octavia stands. She slides her pistol from its holster.

"Wait." It pleads. "How long until the sun rises?"

Octavia looks east. "I'd guess a few minutes."

"Let me watch?" He asks. "Sun rise in twelve years, I never seen the have. Once leave let me see it before I."

The garbled request startles Octavia. She holsters her gun, lifts Alan's feet, and drags him to face the eastern sky. Her footsteps recede as the dying cyborg looks to the brightening horizon with joy.

Fifteen hundred meters underground, Octavia moves from chamber to chamber, shining her portable lantern on the occasional drone resting against the intricately carved walls. The line of cyborgs leads her through a great archway. Hanging lights illuminate the field of wrecked mechanical bodies littering the gallery floor. An off-white web at the base of a stone pillar contrasts against the dark stone; when she directs the lamp onto the web, a metallic skull stares back at her.

The brittle tendrils of the now cured TAC crackle as Octavia lifts the metallic head, revealing the shell of a STInGER wedged in the stone.

She directs her lantern from the scorched fracture up a meticulously sculpted belly and breasts to a feminine face with a scar carved down the side. Octavia recalls the incident report from the South Diego rookies on her hand terminal and queries the profile picture of the defector her partner assisted in Stadium. "Hello, Sonia-10. I hope you're worth it." Her lamp shines onto the face of her partner embracing the woman from behind. Octavia's muscles lock at the sight. "What are you doing, Dante?"

A scraping sound disturbs the silence of the gallery. Octavia shines her lantern into the depths of the cavern. Something moves.

Deeper. I have to get away.

A drone stumbles in the darkness of the cavern. Its recently free will compels it to spend the last of its strength on a single purpose. *They mustn't find me.* These thoughts are the first it can remember which aren't forced to be shared with the Controller, or the Hive.

The others, they must be on the surface by now. I wish I could see the sunrise once more, but I mustn't. Reapers will come. I can't let them find me.

Untold years as OrACLe's supplicant have deadened most of its memories. Yet, one remains, one motivating desire for the depths of the chasm in this gallery. For many years, it has envied the drones that have accidentally lost themselves in here. It has wished to follow them down the opening in the cavern floor and disappear into its darkness, but OrACLe never allowed it. A lost drone was not a concern for OrACLe, but it couldn't tolerate the notion that one might intentionally escape.

Any thoughts of defiance invited OrACLe's attention. Subjugating the drone's thoughts was the only pleasure OrACLe took other than his sculpture.

I'm close, I know it's here, it thinks. The light of a distant lantern throws its shadow onto a wall. The drone glances back to spot the silhouette of a black-hooded figure walking in its direction. It recognizes the profile of a reaper. This sight releases the first word it has uttered in years. "No."

The walls resonate with its desperate cry.

The pit is here. It has to be! It compels itself forward. The sound of the reaper's boots echoes closer. Fear and fatigue result in one careless step that sends it to the ground. Its muscles cannot find the sequence to lift itself back to its feet. The drone begins to crawl. Its limbs resist every movement.

Two hands gently lift the drone by its shoulders to lay it on its back. The last sight it beholds is the expressionless face of a woman framed in a black hood.

Its tormented voice releases a final, painful cry, "No." If its tear ducts still functioned, it would have cried. Instead, darkness fills its vision. The drone's chest descends for the last time.

Octavia considers the figure. *This one is... was terrified of me. The other showed no indication of fear. Why was this one trying so hard to get away?*

Mimicking the procedure from above, Octavia releases the clamps holding its left-handed claw in place. Removing the mechanism, she raises her terminal-tracker to scan. Nothing.

It has the same pale-white hand with five capped stumps, but the back of its hand is unblemished, no lifeclock. Recoiling from the carcass, she directs her terminal-tracker over the body.

NO DATA

Octavia slowly backs away, leaving the corpse just a few meters from a very dangerous open pit.

Chapter 24

Return

A low-frequency rumble disrupts the peace of the woodlands. Small animals instinctively move away from the mound positioned outside the clearing of the elevated electric rail. Pneumatics hiss as the mound splits open and launches a hover-pod into the air. Its lev-field extends to guide it onto the rail as the camouflaged doors close, returning the landscape to the fauna.

Inside the pod, Sonia's eyelids clench tight in defiance of the afternoon sunlight that abruptly fills the cabin. A moment of stretching rushes a soothing warmth into her stiff joints. Dante's half-smile greets her sleepy vision. He passes her spectacles over once she realizes she's not wearing them.

"Thanks." She smiles. "Where are we?"

Once the kernel settles into her ear, he answers, "A few kilometers outside of New Rome. The pod entered a transit tube a little after you dozed off. We've traveled over nineteen hundred kilometers since leaving the hive." He smiles at her surprised expression.

"Is that a good idea? I mean, don't the tubes identify us to the transit system?"

Dante shrugs. "Good idea mine or not it wasn't. The pod is railroad following a programmed route Haven for the underground too." Dante constricts his jaw and looks away as though he hadn't spoken the jumble aloud.

It's getting worse, she observes. "Does it hurt… when it gets mixed up like that?"

He takes in a stabilizing breath. "A little," he pauses as if resting a heavy burden, then continues with a wry smile. "I mostly just miss the sound of my own voice."

The joke doesn't work.

"Did you get any sleep?"

Dante shakes his head. "Can't, the communicator is constantly reaching out to connect to the LINCC. I'm afraid if it does, I'll be pulled under."

"Will connecting kill you? Because that's going to affect the plan."

"I don't know. I should manage all right if I keep the connections short, but the longer I stay in the LINCC, the faster I'll degrade."

"By degrade, you mean…"

"The communicator is trying to override my ability to regulate my breathing, circulation, body temperature…" He looks away. "It's preparing me for OrACLe's prosthetic improvements. It's too bad it doesn't know things have changed. Eventually, it will shut down my nervous system."

Sonia moves beside him, takes his hand, and lays her other arm around his shoulders. "That's not going to happen, I promise."

Dante smiles, but his eyes lack any sense of assurance. His hand is cold in Sonia's as they watch the landscape whiz past the pod's canopy. The flora has completely subjugated most of the structures they pass, allowing only the odd stack of bricks or a building frame to testify that people once lived here.

The counter on the cab's console cycles to 3.3 minutes to New Rome. Sonia removes the parasol from her pack and unrolls the slate terminal. A dozen LINCC access points appear on the screen. She enters Dante's access key, which recalls a map of New Rome next to an index of the city's Civil Operations manual.

Dante's voice reverberates in her ear. "Before we do this, would really there is one thing I like to know."

Sonia's eyes settle on her pocket clock held tightly in his fist. He caresses the lifeclock crystal embedded in the brass cover with his thumb.

It was a long, strange tale she told him as they left OrACLe's cave about how she changed her identity. It was difficult for her to share, and she can tell it disturbs Dante at a level he can't explain.

"Which it is?" he asks.

"It's Sonia from now on, no number, just Sonia."

With an approving nod, Dante slides her satchel over his shoulder. "Good."

New Rome

19,392 people currently visit, live, and work in the borough of New Rome. They are ordering transportation, placing tele-LINCC calls, flushing toilets, turning on lights, and paying for lunch along with a thousand other activities that are managed by systems across the Local International National Communications Conduit. The information monitoring, moderating, and managing these systems rushes through Dante's awareness the instant the communicator accesses the LINCC.

Dante collects and updates an infrastructure map highlighting specifications for the transit systems and lifeclock scanners of New Rome. He relays the information to Sonia's holographic spectacles. The experience is like meticulously cleaning and repairing the tiny gears of a mechanical watch in the middle of a hurricane with tree branches, rocks, and broken bottles flying around him.

Sonia studies the map while compiling information from the operations manual. She relays a set of commands for Dante to send.

"Good," his synthetic voice responds. "Now, let's give water treatment a power boost."

The orange line dims on Sonia's map depicting their hover-pod rail. Blue circles representing lifeclock scanners around the west side of town fades as power is diverted away from the transit and census systems to New Rome's water treatment facilities. The hover-pod slows to rest on the elevated rail.

The map fades from Sonia's view when Dante closes his LINCC connection. She steadies him while he struggles to catch his breath. "Are you all right?"

His face is pale and clammy. "We need to go," he pants. "All lifeclock scanners around the western entrance to the city are off-line. We might have twenty minutes before they are back."

The approach to New Rome reminds Sonia of the stroll they took across Perdition as they walk arm in arm under her parasol. There are only a few structures outside the boundary of the city, with even fewer people to notice them passing by. The movement helps Dante regain dominance over the communicator's influence.

New Rome is a remnant of a once bustling section of the Eastern sector. Although smaller than many of the surrounding settlements, it remains a thriving outpost at the frontier of the North American Open Space.

Sonia and Dante watch the crowds amass on both sides of the western district's controlled gateway. She shuffles through the operations manual and mutters to Dante, "I thought the passage would be propped open when the scanners went off-line."

"It would have when it was monitored by people. It two was fully years ago automated."

The explanation nearly brings Sonia to a standstill if not for Dante urging her on. "You might have mentioned this before," she growls.

"Connected LINCC before I to the, I didn't know."

The manual flips across the slate's screen. "That seems like a detail that should be in here."

Dante shakes his head. "Automation is not unauthorized documented."

Inside the barrier, citizens congregate around the shops, kiosks, and carts that dominate the commerce district of the western border, waiting for the gateway to reopen.

Sonia tries to appear casual as she continues to flip through pages on the slate as if it were a tourist guide. "We're shut out," she whispers. "As long as the scanners are down, access to the city is restricted. Maybe there is an unofficial way in, a maintenance tunnel perhaps."

"Stay out of the tunnels," he warns. "Heavily monitored. Easy there to get trapped in."

Sonia stabs at the slate in frustration. "I have an access code to open a maintenance hatch on a transit tube." She releases a defeated sigh. "It's a half-kilometer away. If the system is still down, we might walk in through the tube."

Dante prepares to reconnect. Without raising her eyes from the slate, Sonia grabs his shoulder and shakes it. "Don't, not yet!"

With a triumphant grin, she looks at Dante and says, "This is going to be great!"

A warning chimes inside the hover-pod with a thirty-second countdown for its occupant to identify. James passes his lifeclock over the pod's internal scanner. The automated greeting responds, "Welcome, James-nineteen, to New Rome. Enjoy your stay." The vehicle passes through the controlled gateway.

Outside, identical routines play out for pedestrians and cyclists entering and leaving through the recently reopened gateway. At each port, they present their left hand. The automated system gives a sterile greeting before directing them through. The system is managing a significant backlog that formed while the gateway was off-line.

Standing away from the crowd, Sonia jabs commands into the terminal slate.

Though cumbersome, Sonia successfully alters an application she found inside the Civil Operations manual. She reviews the alterations and explains to Dante, "The scanners around the gateway are mounted on rotating gimbals. Their coverage is designed to be adjusted."

Dante's synthetic voice is more broken when he acknowledges. "The gateway."

"Never mind that, I found an application that will let me adjust the position of the scanners. I've already programmed it. All you have to do is connect, launch it, and then get off the LINCC. Then we can stroll right through town."

His balance is unsteady as he follows her lead toward the gateway. The artificial voices call out names as people hurry past the scan point.

Once he executes the program, Sonia watches through her spectacles as all the blue cones representing the coverage of lifeclock scanners reposition to the left side of the street, leaving the right side completely barren. She smiles triumphantly, slips her hand from Dante, and whispers, "Be ready." She collapses the slate and places it into the tote bag. Inside, Priya nuzzles her hand, eager to escape from his confinement.

Sonia gives Dante an excited look as she cradles the cat in her arms. Her hand moves down Priya's thigh to separate his fur and reveal a shining red lifeclock.

This is something she hadn't mentioned during their trip in the pod. Dante's synthetic voice masks all sense of astonishment when he tries to ask her, "Why—"

Sonia turns away and joins the line into the gateway. She falls in behind a boy who flashes a blue crystal to the scanner that responds, "Welcome, Oscar-eighty-six, to New Rome. Enjoy your stay."

Priya is calm until Sonia places her thumb over his lifeclock. She holds him close as she leans toward the scanner, which greets her with "Welcome, Priya-fourteen, to New Rome. Enjoy your stay."

Thank you, I will.

Pretending a surprised outburst, she spins about and directs the cat to jump from her arms and run under the barrier of the gateway.

Dante dashes from the line and scoops the startled cat off the ground. Priya resists the overly tight grip as he is once again waved above the scanner.

Dante's apparent heroics earn him a subdued cheer from the citizens waiting in line. Their applause overwhelms the synthetic greeting as he passes through, "Welcome, Priya-fourteen, to New Rome. Enjoy your stay."

Sonia plays to the crowd's expectations as she rushes to return the confused cat to its tote bag. She throws her arms around Dante, gratefully calling out, "Thank you sooooo much!"

When she kisses his cheek, she feels the muscles in Dante's back contract in her embrace.

Moving Through

A street map of New Rome displays on Dante's slate. Sonia carefully tracks the flow of blue ellipses on the map as they follow her program, gliding from one side of the street to the other. The slate, grasped tightly in her hand, shields her black crystal from view. She paces Dante through the dark zones of the scanners.

Dante's muscles are tight, making their movements harder by the minute.

"It looks like there is a dead zone in sixty meters," she says. "We can rest there."

"I'm fine. Keep we moving must."

"People will notice if you start stumbling."

Dante almost drops against a pillar supporting a staircase when they finally stop. Sonia sweeps their surroundings with her spectacles. Although numerous scanner cones are shining around them, none are directed at their location. "We're safe here for the moment," she assures. "One more run like that and we're done."

Referring to the map displaying on the slate, Sonia traces a route that bypasses all lifeclock scanners between the clinic and their position. She smiles. "I see it, Dante, we can get there without—"

Tremors travel through his body, his eyes seem to sink into his head. Sonia moves to shield the disturbing sight from the passing crowd. She pulls the data goggles from her satchel and places them on his face to cover his spasms. She leans to his ear and whispers, "You're going to be fine, Dante. We can make it the rest of the way without altering any more sensors." She shuffles through her satchel for a flask of water.

Dante doesn't respond. His skin is pale and slick with sweat. He shivers when he looks at her.

Sonia listens carefully when his distorted voice scratches into her ear kernel. "Priya-fourteen." Dante turns away from her with a look of contempt. "You gave your cat a lifeclock, and a name. My God."

Is he delirious? she wonders. "Dante, you need to focus, sixty, eighty meters tops and you're…"

She nearly cries out as the flask bounces on the ground, splashing water at their feet. Her arm is trapped in Dante's surprisingly powerful grasp.

"The name there a on was clock?"

"Do you SERIOUSLY need to talk about this now?" she says through clenched teeth.

Her arm slips from his grasp. He looks as though he is ready to die in front of her.

Dante's distress draws attention from passersby. Some pause to see the seemingly one-sided argument. Sonia struggles to restrain her anxiety. "Listen, it was a necessary decision from a long time ago, and we don't have—"

Two distorted words play into her ear. "How … many?"

A deep breath hardens her resolve. *The communicator must be scrambling his judgment as well as his ability to speak.*

Dante slaps away her attempt to reach out for him, his question scratches into her ear once again. "How … many … names … me tell."

Though she had relayed the general method of changing her identity during the ride, she hadn't detailed every name she used. She's dumfounded that he needs to hear them all now.

She leans to his ear and relays in an enraged whisper, "A lifeclock belonging to *Gabrielle* was embedded and reassigned to *Priya* as an experimental proof. Then *Julie* called *Lauren* and later *Sonia* to my lifeclock and assigned the name *Carlos* to my brother *Marcos*, whom you hunted and killed!"

"Six names." Dante's legs buckle.

"We can discuss it later," she says in a subdued voice.

His silence is taken for agreement until she notices his eyes behind the lenses locked wide-open.

On his side of the lenses, Dante peers into a terminal window hovering just centimeters from his face depicting an enraged Sonia immersed in a shower of shimmering blue light.

Chapter 25

Evasion

Seconds ago.

A banner waves in the middle of a courtyard, welcoming the residents to the clothing district of New Rome. At the top of the flagpole, a solar-powered motor whirls to life, rotating a two-axis gimbal. The electronic eye mounted atop that had been watching the side of a building now surveys the eastern boundary of the courtyard and begins to tally the lifeclocks in its field of view.

\# 1 EXPIRED LIFECLOCK
\# ALERT CHARON BRIGADE DISPATCH

The terminal slate sounds a warning chime. Sonia glances at the screen:

\# SENTRY ALERT!
\# EXPIRED LIFECLOCK FOR: Sonia-105.10.
\# LOGGED BY NEW ROME CENSUS SCANNER.
\# DISPATCH REAPERS.

Blood drains from her face as she displays the alert to Dante. Behind her, people pass by, unaware that death has landed in their midst.

The synthetic voice buzzes in her ear. "Move slowly. Do not run. Reaper's scanners to defectors don't follow the. Defectors identify themselves by how they act." Dante reaches for her hands to hide their quiver. "Stay calm. Call a hover-pod with the slate. I'll direct them away from you for good luck as long as I can."

Sonia stands in perfect stillness. Her pupils have grown to large dark pools that recede against her flushed features. She appears as hundreds have to Dante down the sight of his pistol.

The sudden connection to the LINCC hits him like an ocean wave sending Dante to the ground. *If my sentry registers the alert, the dispatch has seen it,* he thinks. *But the assignment may not have reached the hunters yet.*

Dante's awareness follows the signal across the LINCC. The sensation is like riding a slide made of light. He perceives the data packet with Sonia's information just out of his reach.

An alert sounds for an instant before a Charon Brigade cadet silences it. He knows it's an assignment that needs to be forwarded to a reaper team. This is easy since there is only one reaper team in New Rome. The cadet doesn't bother reviewing the alert; there is no reason to. It is one of many facts that define his duties for the New Rome Brigade, chief among them being that his seat could easily be automated by the same system that sent him the alarm if civil engineers would allow it. He knows that question has been asked. The answer has something to do with second Citizen Obligation, as if similar exceptions aren't made all the time.

Two reapers settle in a hover-pod. An alert sounds on Michael-65's terminal-tracker. He silences it to read:

DEFECTOR
§Ωηıα~¦o¦o
Σ×þıδε#: B7
ΔIJØ×# Q1¿μ LIF$¥√∂Ŧ*4√ʃℍ€<I ©¦ΩΔ56IJØ×#
Q1¿μ±þ* 45¤£ùê μW?& 8±ı¢¤tgcy1 <bxhj§ ı*#21!@Q
CöñĿ ≈Δ≈ŷŷ…

Michael cues his tele-LINCC. "Dispatch, what am I looking at?"

The junior officer answers, "There is an expired lifeclock in the western district of New Rome."

"Western district? Dispatch, the assignment is jumbled. Please resend."

Rodney-47 slaps a Brigade passkey into the pod's terminal to redirect it to the western district. The terminal responds:

INVALID

A moment passes before the distressed voice of the cadet dispatcher says, "Officer Michael-sixty-five, the scanners in the area seem to be malfunctioning. They are returning a signal that an expired lifeclock is moving north through the western district but is not giving any details about the defector."

A map of New Rome appears on the pod's terminal screen identifying the location of the expired clock with a black triangle. The target immediately jumps to the central district, then across the screen to the northern part of the borough.

"Dispatch, we are not getting a fix on the expired lifeclock. Also, the assignment doesn't include any details about the target, not even a picture. Can you confirm the name?"

An awkward moment passes, followed by another as the cadet helplessly recalls the assignment that appears increasingly jumbled with each attempt. Finally, the voice returns, "I think it was Sondra or Sonny, maybe."

Michael considers the original alert still sitting on his terminal-tracker screen. "Sophia?"

"Yes, I think that was it; maybe it was Sebastian."

"He thinks?" Rodney mute's his partner's transmission. "It makes a difference if we're hunting a man or a woman."

Michael opens the pickup, mimicking the junior officer's line of thinking. "Or maybe it was Samuel, Solomon, or Serena, how about Sophocles? You know it's against protocol for us to ask citizens to show us their lifeclock status, rookie. We're supposed to determine the state of a defector without asking them."

Rodney says, "Maybe we should just ask them if their name begins with 'S' and if it does, we shoot them. Will that work?"

The line is silent when Michael cuts it off. As their hover-pod resets its course to the western district, Michael cues the tele-LINCC in a calmer voice. "Dispatch, we are rerouting to the western section of New Rome. Please resolve the data for our defector with all haste."

The reaper's temper settles on the cadet. Jumbled alerts of an expired lifeclock continues to barrage the dispatcher from every area of the borough. He shoves his chair away from the pickup screen and fills a cup of water from the cooler. *They're pissed at me! What can I do about it?*

"How … was … I … unclear?" The castigation is lost on Sonia, her shoulder jammed under Dante's as they stagger down the street.

She has carried him through the field of a half-dozen lifeclock scanners leading into the dining district and has doubled back on her trail under the shade of her charcoal-colored parasol.

She wills her enraged voice to a soft calm and growls at Dante, "If you have something to say that will help me, I'm all ears; otherwise, I'd appreciate a little encouragement, even if you don't mean it."

Dante's legs collapse under him as he hobbles alongside her. His arm hangs with apparent affection across her shoulder as she carries the bulk of his balance.

Eventually, the synthetic voice reverberates in her ear kernel. "You can make it."

His encouragement brings a smile. *Finally, something positive from him.*
"If you leave me."

She rolls her eyes at his completed thought. "Oh, shit!"

Dante observes an increasing number of heads turn to follow them. Some look with sympathy, others with disdain at the older couple struggling along. Any of them will easily identify the pair to the first officers who ask. The attention of the crowd suddenly shifts. The outline of a black hood appears in the distance.

He relays the sight to Sonia. "Reapers … coming."

Sonia yanks the kernel from her ear. Though she doesn't see their hunters, she is aware of the tidal change of attention surrounding them. Dante had shared some of the techniques reapers use to track their prey during their march through Perdition.

"We need to get out of sight," she mutters.

Sonia has managed his weight well enough, but it's nearly impossible to align his stride with hers. She is forced to constantly adjust their balance as they zig-zag up the walkway.

Two black tunics are clear at the edge of Dante's sight. Each man waves his hand tracker at the clusters of citizens as they pass by. It's a bluff Dante knows well.

I know what they're seeing. Though he couldn't stop the scanners from reporting Sonia's lifeclock, he had managed to wrap a level-5 encryption around the lifeclock scanners alert routine, muddling the display and location of their assignment. *What are they thinking?* Dante closes his eyes to play out their perspectives.

"I have to put you down for just a moment," Sonia pants into his ear. "Please, don't fall again."

Dante's lungs expel, causing him to gasp when she places him against the side of a building. Passing citizens turn to see.

"We need some place out of the way, without scanners," she says as the street map scrolls on the slate's screen.

The approaching hunters dominate Dante's attention. *They keep looking at their terminal-trackers, not the crowd. Why? They should be seeing gibberish. What is holding their attention?* The answer suddenly surfaces. *They're lost, really lost. They need to find something.*

Dante steadies his arm on Sonia's shoulder. He surrenders his resistance to the communicator. A landslide of data packets slam into Dante as he follows a slide of light into the reaper's terminal.

Michael-65 wants to crush the useless hand tracker in his glove. This isn't the first time it has returned incomplete information, but he's never seen so much gibberish clutter the screen. Typically, if he can find the general area where a signal originates, the crowd will tell him the rest. A panicked defector especially sticks out in small boroughs like this where most people know one another. "Are you seeing anything?" He grumbles to his partner.

Rodney shakes his head. "Nothing, maybe she doesn't even know her clock expired."

The word 'she' sticks in Michael's mind. He tries to remember if the mess that appeared on his screen twenty minutes ago before it fell apart was masculine or feminine. He surveys the crowd. *There's no fear here, no latent panic.* He closes his eyes to imagine the defector. *She … or he, is older, standing above most of the faces in this town.*

He allows the image to take form. *Like he said, she … has an expired clock in her hand. She doesn't know it has changed because she hasn't looked at it all day. You know when you're on Last-Day; you have to know. So, the only way you don't is if you hide your lifeclock from yourself … and others.* In Michael's mind, the image of his prey begins to take shape.

When he opens his eyes, the streets take on a new character. *People are different. They are not afraid, but, how to describe it, concerned. Why? What is the source of their concern? Who?* The question directs his attention to all eyes in the street converging in the same direction.

"We got it!" Rodney suddenly blurts out.

The clutter on the screen of his terminal-tracker display has cleared, and in its place, a glowing compass points to their left.

DefeCtoR
§??¡?~¦o¦o
Dist?nc3: 215 M
D¡rection: Bearing 62 deg
Elev?tion: +0.03 M

Michael meets his partner's eyes. With a quick nod, they hurry down a side street.

Sonia flips down a scrolling list of storefront titles on the slate. The audio kernel dangling by her face erupts with a frantic buzz. Dante's clumsy fingers try to reinsert it into her ear.

Sonia assists in its replacement and looks to him. "If this is more complaining, I really can't—"

"Delayed," the voice scratches.

Sonia looks up to see the street clear of black hoods.

"Must … move. Return … soon."

A smile blooms on her face when a destination locks into the map on the screen. "I have an idea." Sonia swings her satchel around to dig out the first aid kit. She removes a plastic bottle, unscrews the cap, and offers the clear liquid to Dante. "You have to trust me."

He returns a blank expression.

Sonia's confident façade waivers. "Please, Dante, it's my last idea."

He accepts the bottle with a nod, and she carefully pours it into his mouth.

Dante violently wretches as soon as the liquid burns the back of his tongue. His voice scratches in Sonia's ear, "Poison."

Sonia helps him to stand as she estimates the distance to the storefront on the next block. "That's right, Dante, it's poison, and you need to take a little more."

Sonia pours the last of the antibacterial fluid into Dante's mouth as they stumble across the roadway to a nearby storefront. She moves carefully, knowing that each step is churning him inside, compelling him to lurch forward.

"Not yet," she rasps, "just a little further."

His impatient glare settles on her.

"Oh, lighten up!" she rebukes. "Do you even remember all the crap I've taken since I met you?" The memory of a jet injector full of stimulants jabbed into her neck drifts through her mind, among other things.

Dante is nearly limp in Sonia's arms as they enter the reception area. An overly courteous voice meets them. "Welcome to the Somnus Center of New Rome. My name is Nicholas-seventy-two, can I help you?"

"No, you may not!" Sonia snaps.

The young man wearing a Somnolence technician's uniform is startled by the outburst but quickly recovers. It is nothing he hasn't seen before.

Sonia says, "I'm so sorry, Nicholas. I didn't mean to do that."

He answers with an obligatory smile.

"I meant to say," Sonia keeps her clock hand behind Dante as she presents Dante's flashing lifeclock with the other, "that he is not ready for your service *now*. He has plenty of time. He just wants to see the…" nodding in the direction of the recliner room, "…you know."

Nicholas nods. "We offer counseling to help with the understandable anxiety of Somnus. If you would like to return when—"

"Who said anything about anxiety? He's not afraid! When the time comes, he'll bravely meet his obligation." She cradles Dante's chin in her palm. "He just wants to…"

Dante's eyes impatiently roll when they meet Sonia's make-believe concern.

"Couldn't you show us the recliner? He just needs to see it."

Nicholas glances at the light through the doorway. "I can't take you there now, maybe if you come back in—"

With the tech's attention turned away, Sonia jabs her fingers into Dante's stomach.

The pressure causes his muscles to contract, launching a stream of vomit onto Nicholas's pants. She steadies Dante as the horrified technician assesses his soaked uniform.

Oblivious to his distress, Sonia leans to Nicholas with quiet desperation. "He started drinking last night and has been getting worse all morning. I want to take him to the ingestion clinic for treatment, but he won't go until he's seen the recliner." She hesitates. "If he can just see it, he can rest for a short time and regain his footing. After that, he'll let me take him for help." She looks directly into the young man's eyes. "Please, we just need a moment, then we'll leave."

Nicholas offers no support as he leads a stumbling Dante and Sonia into the recliner room.

Benjamin-18 is seated on the first of five stations. His left hand holds a sleep mask and a black lifeclock. His eyes follow the stumbling couple to the last station.

Dante falls into the recliner as his body goes limp.

Sonia holds his hand as the tech leaves. "Rest here while I figure something out," she quietly assures him as she pulls a water flask from her satchel.

Dante eyes the canister suspiciously.

Sonia takes a sip. "It's just water. I filled it from a faucet before we left the hive." She places the flask beside him and quietly steps to the doorway. Across the hall, a young cadet in a black tunic and hood sits in front of a strategy map with a tele-LINCC earpiece pressed to the side of his face. He winces.

"The signal is gone," he says. "I don't know what happened to it." His voice becomes increasingly distressed at the dressing-down streaming through his earpiece. "I understand, Officer Michael."

Sonia slowly steps away from the door.

Dante watches Sonia standing in the doorway across the room, amused by the curious expression that has settled on her face. She just learned that small Somnus centers like this one are usually managed and operated by the Charon Brigade. However, they rarely have any lifeclock scanners surveying inside. *I gotta give her credit,* he thinks. *This really is the last place a reaper would look for a couple of defectors.*

Sonia keeps her arms tightly crossed as she returns to his recliner. She kneels beside Dante, relieved to see his eyes open. She whispers in a calmer than expected voice, "This isn't working out as I had hoped."

The comment brings a sarcastic smile to Dante's face. He reaches out as his distorted voice crackles in her ear kernel, "Up."

Once his feet are on the floor, Sonia reaches around him and whispers, "I thought this would buy you a little time to rest, but we need to get out of here." Dante's muscles tense under her fingers. The already quiet room falls silent as boot steps sound outside the doorway.

Voices rise in a vague argument. The dispatcher explains some random technical issue to a senior Brigade officer.

Dante moves his hand under his coat and onto the grip of his pistol.

She whispers in a forced calm, "You know, it seems crazy now, but I really thought we were going to make it."

Across the room, the terrified eyes of Benjamin-18 catch his attention. *As if this isn't hard enough for him,* Dante thinks. His hand slips from the grip of the gun. *Not this time,* he silently decides as he looks into Sonia's eyes. She eases him back onto the bed. His synthetic voice rasps in her ear, "Maranda."

"Who?" Sonia asks.

"Help Maranda-twenty-three … will."

Turning away from Dante, she spots two reapers standing in the doorway. The sight compels her to stuff her hand into the resin-lined tote bag with Priya. An angry shudder jumps in the bag containing the shorthaired cat.

Her tears of pain show as sadness as Sonia forces a smile and gently meets Dante's brave expression. "The little hair ball bit me."

Another wave hits Dante, and he slides into the LINCC.

Sonia shakes him. "Dante. Stay with me, Dante!"

A youthful, yet methodical voice breaks the silence of the chamber, "May I be of assistance?"

Chapter 26

Citizen Obligation

All eyes turn to the doorway. A woman dressed in a starched red medical technician's uniform surveys the room. The blue light shining on her hand gives her the appearance of a citizen in her fifteenth year. Michael steps aside as she approaches the recliner where Benjamin-18 sits.

"I was informed that a citizen requires assistance. How may I help?" The woman's clinical voice attempts sincerity.

A hopeful expression fades from Benjamin's face, as though a reprieve has been denied. "You're not real." He struggles to keep his voice from cracking. "I mean, you're a robot, aren't you?"

The synthetic woman meets Benjamin's devastated expression with one of sterile logic. "I am the model-twenty-three robotic nursery attendant," it says. "I am assigned to the New Rome public nursery, number three, nine, six. How can I assist you?"

Benjamin holds the sleep mask before him. "You can bring back my friends." Tears begin to flow from his eyes. "I have seen dozens of friends through their Last-Day, now none of them are here for me."

Benjamin's lamentation stops the instant M-23 raises its hand. "I am sorry; the service you require is outside my function." Benjamin collapses into the recliner. The robot continues. "Please wait while I find the appropriate technician to assist you.

Michael-65 watches the exchange through the doorway. The robotic nurse turns about and addresses him with the same clinical tone. "Officer, a citizen needs your assistance." The statement brings the reaper to attention as she says, "It is prohibited for any robotic worker to fulfill the role of a citizen in matters of the Somnus Obligation. This man has met his obligation to the Collective. You have a duty to fulfill the Collective's obligation to him."

Michael bows his head at the assignment. With a deep sigh, he calls into the hallway, "Rodney, Nicholas, step in here for a moment."

Benjamin's breathing quickens at the orders. "Bring the cadet from the dispatch desk as well."

M-23 steps aside as the Brigade officers file into the room. Benjamin raises the mask in front of him but freezes at the sight. "Please, I can do this," he cries. "Please don't—"

Michael gently works the mask out of Benjamin's fingers and places it on the floor out of his sight. "Why don't we put this away for a while," he suggests in a calm voice. His partner appears at the door along with the cadet from the dispatch desk.

Michael brushes his hood away from his brow and kneels beside the recliner. With an apologetic assurance, he tells the room, "Rodney and I just spent the last hour chasing a malfunction up and down the streets. Yet, all the while, this brave citizen is in here meeting his duty."

Benjamin releases the anxiety from his chest as tears flow down his face.

Rodney sends the cadet out for a box of red wine and five glasses. Giving Benjamin a smile, he says, "We see you are ready to meet your obligation bravely, but before you do, would you please share your life with us? We would be honored to hear your story."

Nicholas places a glass in Benjamin's hand; Michael fills it with wine.

As the sleep technician and Charon Brigade officers gather around the recliner, M-23 backs away from the crowd and moves to the end of the room. Benjamin begins to chatter about his youth as the robot addresses Dante. "You also need assistance," it says in the same clinical voice.

Sonia keeps her head low as she whispers, "He can't talk." Peering over the rim of her spectacles, she can see the entire staff gathered at the only exit. "Can you help me get him to a surgical chamber, please?"

The childlike attendant casually takes the rolled up slate from her hand and logs onto the LINCC. Sonia recognizes the keys that enter Dante's account passcode.

"A hover-pod will be out front in a moment, Sonia-10," the robot responds as it passes the slate back.

Astonishment at the mention of her name, Sonia is lost for a response.

The robotic attendant glances at Dante's unresponsive body. Reaching for his arm, it directs Sonia, "Please assist."

They swing Dante's legs to the side of the recliner as M-23 lifts him upright to a seated position, then moves behind. The robot removes a tool from its tunic, and to Sonia's horror, begins to alter the communicator at the base of Dante's skull.

Before she can say anything, the robot tells Sonia, "He says, *'Don't worry, I found the communicator's specs in OrACLe's database. M-twenty-three is just reducing its power output by twenty-eight percent. It will buy me a little more time to get it removed.'*"

"He said that?"

Dante takes in a deep breath and raises his eyes to meet hers.

M-23 returns the tool to its pocket and moves to stand opposite Sonia. In the same sterile voice, the robot says, "Your friend directed the Guardian to send me here and remind the staff of their duty to assist Benjamin-eighteen." Nodding to the blood on the top of Sonia's hand, M-23 declares, "You have been injured. He asks, *'Do you have anything other than poison in that bag of yours?'*"

Sonia fights a bewildered expression as she passes the first aid kit to the robot and responds through grinding teeth, "I was just trying to give him a place to rest—"

The robot interrupts. "He says, *'Take a joke, Sonia, you did great.'*" The robot shakes an empty brown bottle over her hand. "Your antibacterial is empty. You should replace it or risk infection."

Sonia glares at the robot's vacuous eyes, then to Dante.

The robot speaks again. "He says, *'Don't look at me, that was all her.'*"

Dante's eyes move from Sonia to the robotic attendant.

M-23 removes a sheet of plastic from its pocket and peels away a tiny clear resin square. It presses the resin over Sonia's lifeclock, causing it to glow red. Then she removes a bandage roll from the first aid kit and begins to wrap Sonia's hand, careful not to cover the red lifeclock. "He says, *'The hive gave me this formula for fluorescing optical gel. It should last until we get to the clinic.'*"

They lift Dante to his feet and carefully guide him toward the door.

The Somnolence Center staff listens to Benjamin's story as he recalls his expedition in the East Asian region. Michael refills the citizen's glass as M-23 leads the stumbling defectors past the recliner station.

"You rode the whole thing?" Nicholas says louder than he intended, unaware that his glass is also being refilled. "But isn't the wall like five thousand kilometers long?"

"Eight thousand eight hundred kilometers," Benjamin answers proudly. "It wasn't all on my bicycle; there were a couple of places I had to hike." He looks about. "I wish I had a terminal here, I could show you the pictures I took."

A note of sadness drifts to Sonia's ears as she exits the recliner room. She turns about and calls to the reaper, "Officer?"

Rodney walks to her. She passes the rolled terminal slate to him, keeping her left hand behind Dante. "He can use this to show his pictures," she whispers. "I'll pick it up later."

He gives her a grateful smile and returns to the group.

A hover-pod glides to a stop in front of the New Rome Somnus Center. M-23 opens the canopy and helps guide Dante inside. "He says, *That was really generous of you giving away my terminal.*"

As she pulls the hatch closed, Sonia snaps, "Oh, be quiet, if we live through this, I'll build you another one!"

The hover-pod moves through numerous census scanners on the way to the clinic. Priya allows Sonia to gently stroke the back of his neck inside the shielded tote bag. Her attention wanders to the robotic attendant sitting at the front of the cab.

Sonia asks, "Maranda-23, is that your name?"

The robotic attendant nods. "The children gave me the name Maranda when I was assigned to the nursery."

Within moments of arriving, the three move to a private chamber. Maranda attaches a face mask to a canister of nanobots and offers it to Dante. Sonia retrieves the pocket clock from his jacket and initiates the treatment. Within seconds, he is embraced by the chamber's automated arms.

"The surgical chamber will purge all the toxins from his system," M-23 states. "He says, *I'd rather you not see me prodded like this, Sonia. Would you please wait in the other room?*"

Before she can protest, the robot interjects. "I have some experience with surgical patients. Dante will respond better if he is not aware of you staring at him in the chamber. You can wait in the observation room." It gestures to a door leading out of the surgical room. "You can leave your belongings here, I'll stay with him. You will be safe in the observation room."

"After everything—"

"It is going to be all right, Sonia," M-23 assures.

Chapter 27

Lost Citizens

The voice of Amy-15 scratches through the tele-LINCC earpiece. "Officer Octavia-seventy, I have an update."

NAME: Alan-137.07
STATUS: REBIRTHED

The reaper removes the terminal-tracker from the clear lifeclock of a fingerless drone. Its eyes still joyfully watching the horizon where the sun arose a few hours before.

"Stand by, Dispatcher. I'm transmitting." Silence follows. Octavia watches another dozen names scroll down the display of her hand terminal until the final lines appear.

DATA TRANSMISSION: Complete
12 NAMES POSTED FOR ASSIGNMENT

"That makes a total of twenty-eight names you've entered, Officer. That has to be some kind of Collective record for a single day." The dispatcher congratulates the hunter.

Octavia shrugs it off. "What is your update, Dispatcher?"

Amy says in the formal tone she should never have dropped. "I just got a report from a small borough on the Eastern sector. They are experiencing an unusual amount of disruption that has affected their western district.

The comment brings Octavia to a stop. "What kind of disruption?"

"They overextended their power distribution to water reclamation, which brought part of the local transit system to a halt and altered the on-demand census reports." Silence holds the channel for a moment as Amy reviews the logs. "A number of the lifeclock sensors fell out of alignment. Later, the local Brigade hunters logged a false report of a defector."

"What is a false report?" Octavia asks.

"The Brigade dispatcher received a scrambled, expired lifeclock alert. It looks like the hunters chased the signal around the borough for an hour before logging it as an anomaly associated with the other disruptions."

"Send the coordinates of the first disruption to my t-t! What's the name of this borough?"

"New Rome. The disruptions began around the western entrance gateway of the town." A brief silence punctuates the transmission as Amy reviews additional updates on her end. "The cleanup detail should be arriving at your location any moment."

After securing her pack in the pod's passenger seat, Octavia spots the swarm of air-pods approaching her position. "Dispatcher, patch me to your supervisor."

Fourteen hundred kilometers away, a nervous Amy-15 waves over the shift chief dispatcher. The senior officer cues the LINCC channel. "This is Chief Dispatcher Joseph-seventy-eight, who is this?"

"Chief, this is Officer Octavia-seventy of the Bay City Charon Brigade. I am hunting a defector assigned by the Judiciary; you may confirm my order with Bay City Civil Judicial Officer Sydney-twenty. I am recommending Amy-fifteen for a field promotion to the position of officer and that she take charge of harvesting this defector's nest."

A frustrated tone answers her request. "Are you the one who just redirected three-dozen Brigade trainees to the middle of nowhere?"

Octavia raises her voice above the whine of the lev-field lifting her pod from the ground. "Chief, Amy's instincts and cunning directly revealed the location of well over a hundred defectors. The situation doesn't require field hunting or termination skills, but it does need to be thorough. I am ordering that she manage its processing."

Joseph hovers above the young dispatcher, who is uncharacteristically calm during the exchange. *Something has changed with her.* "Officer, you have no authority to—"

Octavia severs his objection. "When you check my orders, you will be surprised at the authority I have, Chief. You will also learn the penance I deliver onto those who interfere with my hunt." Silence thunders on the channel. She says, "Officer Amy-fifteen?"

"Yes, ma'am."

"Two-dozen Charon Brigade cadets are about to land at this defector's hideaway. Skim their performance files and choose a preliminary site manager to secure and organize the scene. Get here as fast as you can, and take command of the harvest."

What We Take

Through the door marked *Observation Chamber*, soft lights illuminate a corridor. A large dark window dominates the right side of the passageway with a terminal port mounted to the wall underneath. The port catches Sonia's attention when she steps inside. She passes her spectacles over the pickup. A green light on the bridge of her data spectacles activates, indicating a successful connection. The door closes behind her without a sound.

When the lenses settle onto her nose, five round objects are rendered as light-blue wire-frames floating in the darkness on the other side of the window. An array of status reports hover beside each object. She stares in wonder at the shapes; they stir a distant memory within her. The door at the opposite end of the observation chamber barely makes a sound when it opens, nor does the young woman who walks in. It's not a woman. Though its hair is a different color and style, the features are the same as Maranda. The light-red lab coat of the Model-23 robotic nursery attendant brushes against Sonia as it passes her to stand in front of the terminal port.

Behind the glass, overhead lights begin to shine, revealing the five blue wire-framed spheres as five egg-shaped pods. Within each pod lies a sleeping infant.

The attendant in the observation chamber removes a slate from its coat pocket and passes it in front of the terminal port. The slate flickers to life, displaying the same wire-frame and floating readouts that are hovering in Sonia's data spectacles.

Now I remember, I was sixteen years old. One of those pods carried my child away after my fetal removal surgery.

Another Model-23 attendant, wearing a similar lab coat, enters the cradle room. It pushes a cart holding a sixth cradle. The robot parks the pod next to the other five. Once in place, a blue wire-frame envelops it just like the others.

M-23 moves to the wall behind the cradles and places its hand under a crystal metric scanner. A panel slowly rises from the floor of the cradle room, lifting a data terminal mounted onto a hand truck. The terminal has a mechanical arm attached to the front that is articulated in five sections. The attendant tilts the truck onto its wheels and quietly scoots it next to the newly placed pod.

In the observation chamber, Sonia and the attendant watch in silence. One of the hovering readouts cycles from 12:59 to 13:00 CCT, then six blue rectangles sitting below the clock begin to fill in with bright yellow names.

Ethan-007.32
Alexis-472.74
Anthony-100.06
Samantha-842.22

In the cradle room, Model-23 withdraws a small hemispherical device from a pocket in its lab coat and attaches it to a standard device port at the end of the mobile terminal's mechanical arm. With a quarter twist, an amber light appears at the top of the hemisphere. The articulated arm follows the attendant's hand as it brings the device to the hand of the infant in the pod.

The tiny amber light atop the pearl-white hemisphere also stirs Sonia's memory. *That's my little egg. Well, not mine,* she corrects herself.

The attendant standing next to Sonia swipes its finger across the slate display. Sonia watches the name *Alexis-472.74* jump from the yellow box suspended under the clock in the cradle room to hover above the pods next to the attendant holding the crystal writer. The motion initiates a scroll of commands that cascades from the name down onto the pod.

> getName

ENTER BIRTH LOCATION:
> 241

ENTER BIRTH NURSERY:
> 396

WELCOME: Alexis-74, 241.396.472.74

A soft, welcoming chime sounds in Sonia's ear kernel with the final command line assigning a name to the child.

A yellow lifeclock shines on the left hand of Alexis-74.

The mechanical arm suspends the clock writer in front of the terminal. The attendant rolls the hand truck over to the next pod, where an infant with a clear crystal embedded on the back of his hand awaits his name. The robotic attendants repeat the procedure for the next three pods. When they finish, M-23 slips the slate into its pocket and joins the other in the cradle room. The other M-23 removes the clock writer from the terminal arm and lowers it into the floor.

The robotic attendants stand beside the remaining cradles. M-23 gently slides a shutter enclosing the unnamed infant into the pod, as does the other robotic attendant. They wrap their arms around the pods in a simulated loving hug. Soon, two soft, low-pitched thuds sound in Sonia's ear kernel. The blue wire-frames encircling the embraced pods vanish.

The attendants wheel the remaining four cradles from the room, leaving the two sealed ones behind.

Sonia's heart thunders in her head. Her chest heaves. When the lights in the cradle room fade, Dante's reflection appears in the dark window standing behind her.

"It's the first thing cadets see when we enter Brigade skill-trade." His voice is soft and no longer reverberates in her ear kernel. "On the very first day of the academy, we are brought to stand in rooms just like this to witness the assignment of names."

Sonia's eyes burn as Dante moves beside her to gaze into the black window.

He continues in a near whisper. "When we graduate, our training officers return us to watch it again. We take the Brigade Oath, swearing to protect the citizen's name for this and all generations."

Sonia shudders. "What just happened in there?"

Dante's response is cold. "You know goddamn well what just happened. Do not pretend you don't know."

She fights through her constricted throat. "You sent me in here to watch this. Why?"

Dante places his hand on the glass. "It happens every hour in the Collective. Twenty-five years ago, Sonia-10 and Dante-09 fulfilled their Somnus Obligation, making a place for two infants sleeping in cradles like these to enter and thrive in the Collective."

Sonia growls, "You didn't answer my question."

He releases a sigh as he turns to her. "I want you to understand what we're taking with us. Our defection is removing something that won't..." he nods toward the darkness, "...that can't be replaced."

Dante's head snaps back as Sonia's fist slams into his jaw. When he regains focus, she strikes the side of his face, imprinting the outline of her hand on his chin. She strikes him again, then again and screams, "I hate you!"

Dante does nothing.

"You bastard!" She winds up for another strike and lands in his arms, blinded by the tears burning her eyes. "Why?"

Dante wraps his arms around her as she sobs her rage into his chest. He whispers, "Because I can't pretend either."

Sonia fights back her sobs. "This means as long as I hold onto my life, infants will die."

"Just as they always have," he answers. "One life uses one name. Until the name is assigned for rebirth, it cannot be used by another." As he stares into the glass, the shape of one of the cradles resolves. "Before the Awakening, people hoarded more than they could ever use so they could control those who didn't have enough to live. It gave them power that was passed through the bloodline so the children of the powerful could dominate the children of the impoverished. Somnus resolved that, it made greed obsolete. Under the Guardian's guidance, the Collective's population is kept in line with the rate we consume our resources. We use what we need for as long as we live, then surrender what we make to the next generation."

Sonia faces the window. "It's all so elegant and grotesque."

Dante nods. "The Awakening was… is a conscious decision to live a short, meaningful life rather than an extended one dominated by the whims of the powerful." Dante tips Sonia's chin up to look into her eyes. "But, I'll leave it all behind if I can follow you."

Back in the surgical room, Dante slings the satchel across his shoulder.

Maranda-23 surrenders Priya to Sonia. The shorthaired cat curls into the cradle of her arms. His body is limp, yet his chest rises and falls in rapid, shallow pants. Angered by his obvious distress, she demands, "What did you do to him?"

Maranda answers in a mellow clinical tone, "He'll be fine."

Sonia's anger subsides when Maranda displays a series of tears running down its forearm. She follows the attendant's eyes to the sedate shorthaired cat nuzzled in her arms; a piece of the flesh-colored coating hangs from one of his claws. When her attention returns to the robot, Maranda meets her with a contemptuous expression.

Sonia swallows a knot in her throat. "I'm sorry."

With the same clinical voice, M-23 answers, "Sorry isn't going to calm the frightened children in the nursery when they see this."

The robot's methodical reprimand keeps the two silent for a moment, then it turns to Dante and says, "You have sustained another injury, do you require additional time in the chamber?"

Dante absently wipes a dribble of blood from his lower lip where Sonia had struck. "That's not necessary."

M-23 removes a surgical tool from a supply cabinet and takes Dante by the chin. Her grip is surprisingly forceful when she tells him, "Your wound is a contamination hazard, hold still." The dermal recovery probe injects a biting cold into the slit in Dante's lip once pressed into place by the attendant. It moves with swift precision and is finished before he can pull away. When he is released, Maranda presses a sterile patch against the area to clean away the residual blood as it advises, "The swelling will be gone by the end of the day. Keep it clean to avoid infection." Then its voice darkens, forcing Dante and Sonia to pause as it asks, "Is there anything else you need, *Defector*?"

They share a concerned expression before Dante answers, "No, Maranda, we'll be fine."

With that, the robotic nursery attendant exits through the observation passage.

The two stand in bewilderment. Sonia breaks the silence. "It sounded angry."

"It is." Dante nods as he removes something from the surgical chamber and jams it into his coat pocket. He says, "We need to go."

The sight of the hover-pod waiting for them outside the clinic surprises Sonia. "Is this for us?"

Dante holds the hatch open for her. "I called it while I was in surgery."

"The same way you called Maranda?" she asks.

"Basically." He shrugs. "The surgical chamber moderated the communicator's signal before removing it, which made it a lot easier to control. It gave me time to send a few commands before releasing me."

Dante takes his seat. The canopy latch snaps closed. A terminal screen at the front of the pod flashes with a standard prompt.

Enter transaction destination

Dante cues the terminal pickup and recites in a slow deliberate cadence, "Destination Casey - Eta – Alpha – Vega – twenty-three - Epsilon – Nu – Railroad – nineteen – Smilodon.

The terminal screen displays the passcode as Dante recites it. hen the entry is complete, the payment prompt disappears from the screen. The light on the crystal reader dims from white to black, then the terminal responds.

APPROVED
DESTINATION: Station 3 to Haven
THANK YOU

Impressed with the machine-like precision of Dante's commands, Sonia asks, "And you know all this because?"

"OrACLe shared the passphrase with all the drones back at the hive; it was part of his protocol. We are now programmed for the next stop on the railway."

A display for the pod's tracker changes from active to inactive. The vehicle glides away from the pick-up area and onto an elevated rail toward the borough's northern gateway.

With a half-confused voice, Sonia says," I thought you didn't believe in Haven."

"I don't. I think when we find it, Haven will be an abandoned shell." He smiles. "Hell, we might find it populated with a society of pervy robots."

Sonia releases an exhausted laugh. "Bite your tongue. So, if this is all a waste of time, why keep going?"

"I've come this far. I want to see this through to the end." Dante points out the canopy to the streets. "Take a look."

Sonia watches the lights dim inside the windows of the storefronts they pass. People begin shaking their electronic devices and tapping the earpieces attached to their heads. She glances at the pod's display screen to see a warning flash.

LINCC: Unavailable

She looks to Dante. "You?"
Her question is greeted with a wide-eyed, self-satisfied grin.
"Do you have any other surprises?"
He nods and says, "You're going to love this."

Conduit Crash

Water beads run down the side of the chilled container. A sprig of frozen mint crunches with ice cubes pressed into the freshly brewed tea when Dylan-41 secures the cover onto the beverage cup. He carries the order to the front counter, calling to the shift manager, "Order four-seventeen, ready to go, boss!"

Thomas-81 rips the last printout from the register and recites the double-meal delivery to the apprentice, who confirms each item packed in the delivery bags, ending with "…and two large mint teas."

"Check!" Dylan answers with the enthusiasm of a drum major.

He passes the printout over the counter, then takes another glance at the order screen. It's just like the vid-LINCC, tele-LINCC, census map, and every other device driven by the Local National International Communication Conduit, all black. There's no way to tell if it's just this street or all of New Rome. Hell, maybe the entire Collective has gone blank. Without the LINCC, there's no way to tell. The thought gives him an unintended shudder. There have been power outages before, but he's never seen the whole system go down. He restarts his personal terminal again only to see the familiar status icon of a broken line.

LINCC: Unavailable.

The thirteen-year-old apprentice looks to the uncharacteristic expression darkening his trade attendant's face. "You all right, boss?"

With a forced smile, Thomas answers, "Just get that order to Eighteenth and Marigold. The customer will pick it up there." With a glance out the door, he notices two of the shops across the way flipping their door signs to CLOSED. "That's the last of our paid orders before everything went dark. If things aren't operational when you get back, we'll close and take a stroll to the civil managers bureau for some answers."

Thomas gives a chilling emphasis on the word WE that sends Dylan out the door with extra force in his stride. He's never seen his attendant like this; in fact, everyone he passes on the sidewalk has the same scared expression.

Hover-pods move about the rail as Dylan carefully crosses the intersection to Eighteenth Street. *I hope the safety measures are still operational for the pods.* It seems strange that every other system is off-line or heavily restricted, yet the hover-pods move about as if nothing has changed. He confirms the delivery location on the order printout as the sound of a pod canopy pops in front of him.

When he looks up, a man wearing a trench coat points at the printed logo on the delivery bags and calls out, "Colosseum Grocery and Deli?"

Dylan nods. A red-haired woman eagerly leans on the man's shoulder as he reaches out. Dylan tries not to stare at the scar running down the side of her face.

The man enthusiastically calls out, "Order four-one-seven, right?"

With an affirmative nod, Dylan sets the bags on the ground and hands him the order printout for his review. Each item is eagerly accepted by the passengers in the pod.

"I have four, one liter bottles of water, one large bag of trail mix, one bunch of seedless grapes."

"I love grapes!" the woman praises as she gratefully takes the bag and tears off a bunch.

"One spicy yellowfin tuna wrap and one roasted turkey hoagie."

This time the man accepts them with a robust, "Yyyyyyyees!"

Dylan continues. "One order hot mustard potato salad and one order Mediterranean cucumber salad with Kalamata olives."

As Dylan passes a sealed bag into the pod, a shorthaired cat appears with a special interest in the silver foil packet. "One skinless oil-packed salmon."

The man takes the bag and palms some of the pink meat for the cat to nibble.

"And two large mint iced teas."

The woman takes the cups one at a time. She removes the lid from one and passionately kisses the near overflowing liquid.

The man speaks up with an almost panicked concern that pulls the boy's attention to him. "Did you remember the—"

Reaching the bottom of the bag, the boy passes a plastic bag of sliced lemon wedges, which the man snatches from his fingers with a hearty, "Good man!"

With a final concerned look into the empty bags, Dylan stutters, "I'm sorry, but I forgot the flatware. If you'd like, I am happy to—"

"It's really not a problem." The woman suppresses a laugh and reassures with a blissful grin and a handful of potato salad.

The man scoops some of the oil and vinegar-dressed cucumbers into his mouth and mumbles, "You have no idea—"

Dylan folds the bags up with a smile. "You know you're lucky. Right after the payment for your order cleared, we lost LINCC access; we haven't processed any sales since."

"So we're not the only ones who can't get any answers?" The man slaps the pod's black terminal screen. "I thought we just got a busted terminal in this tub."

The boy shakes his head. "No, every shop between here and the deli has gone dark. We don't know how much of the city is affected. The only things running are the pods." He looks to the elevated rails still busy with the hover-pods.

The woman lowers her drink with a surprised expression.

The man reaches for the canopy with a nod. "Well, thanks for the delivery."

"Where are you headed?" Dylan asks.

The man gestures down the road. "We thought we'd go exploring the countryside."

"There are some nice places up north of here, but keep a watch out for the forbidden zone."

"Forbidden zone?" The woman asks.

"I know it sounds like an old camp story, but there is a region marked FORBIDDEN on the map just up north of here. Every now and then, someone will get it in their head to go exploring there, only to be recovered by the reapers in a week or two." With a sigh, he adds, "Some of my friends went hunting in that direction a couple days ago, I haven't heard from them yet. I'm sorry to darken your outing, but with the LINCC off-line, the automated alert might not work."

The man nods. "Thanks for the warning, we'll be careful."

The woman's eyes open with an unusual concern as the man pulls the canopy closed. The pod lifts off the street and merges back onto the rail.

Dylan watches them glide away. He crosses the roadway and heads back to the grocery. He imagines that Thomas will have the store shut down. He'll want to leave for the civil managers bureau as soon as he returns.

The pretty redheaded woman's smile hovers in Dylan's memory as he quickens his steps. *What was that mark running down the side of her face?*

Chapter 28

Hunting in the Dark

There has never been a trouble ticket that didn't include a client who hovered about as though his sighs and grunts could configure a malfunctioned terminal or repair an overloaded circuit. Nathan-88 learned to ignore such reactions early in his career in Civil Engineers Control. He has recently learned that the same responses are more influential when it's in a room full of armed hunters with the authority to kill at their discretion.

"Stay away from him, rookie!" the chief dispatcher warns a junior Brigade officer staring at the CEC technician. "He'll report when there's something to say."

A bar graph on the technician's slate displays levels approaching the minimal signal strength to establish a LINCC connection to the dark borough. He cues the pickup on his tele-LINCC. "Control, this is Nathan. Morgan, can you boost the signal to the aerial units another eight percent?"

His receiver buzzes with a feminine voice. "We can, but that will reduce flight time to about four hours."

"Understood," he responds. "Will it reach into New Rome?"

"Affirmative."

The chief listens to the progress and nods his approval.

Nathan cues his pickup. "Morgan, I'm going to set up a level-eight encryption for the field officer, which should limit traffic for a while."

"Copy that, Nathan," she answers. "But it's not going to take long before that connection is noticed. You should expect it to be cracked quickly."

Turning to the chief dispatcher, Nathan says, "That's the best we can do, Chief."

"It will be enough."

Nathan takes his terminal slate to a dispatcher station. The display shows a row of three dirigible icons connected by a relay of orange lines depicting the active conduit between the Birmingham Brigade dispatch and New Rome. A warning glows in the same orange color just above it.

MINIMAL COMMUNICATION CONDUIT ESTABLISHED.

Nathan shares his slate with the officer and motions to a series of characters at the bottom of the screen. "Send her this key."

Octavia had to land her air-pod when her navigation system lost the beacon to New Rome. If this were a ground hunt, she would have the advantage of an experienced land navigator. Yet, flying across the North American sector makes her dependent on the conduit navigation systems.

Her tele-LINCC chimes. "Officer Octavia-seventy," the dispatcher says. "This is Birmingham Charon Brigade. Prepare to copy instructions."

She fumbles through her tunic for something to write with and finds nothing. "Why do they think I have…"

Octavia clears a patch on the ground with the sole of her boot, then draws her truncheon. A spring releases a spear-pointed blade at the base of the handle.

"Go ahead, dispatch," she says.

The blade scratches a series of characters into the dust as they are relayed to her, ending with the instruction to restart her hand terminal. Once she has logged in with the eight-character encryption key, her terminal displays a scale that falls from green to blue to yellow and hovers at orange, just two bars above red. A moment later, the navigation beacon for New Rome appears.

"Dispatch, I have the beacon."

"Good hunting, Officer Octavia-seventy."

The citizens of New Rome give Dante's and Sonia's profile pictures a cursory glance when Octavia shows it to them around the western gateway. After a half-hour, she recalls the logs the CEC tech sent to her hand terminal.

Power lost at the western gateway at 14:05 hours, reestablished at 14:22.

\# Census scanners discovered out of alignment
at 15:12 hours.

At the same time, an anomaly reports a false expired lifeclock that sends the local officers on an hour-long wild-goose chase around the district, she thinks. *That's when you entered the city, Dante. You were the anomaly.*

She returns to the western gateway, now locked open. *Interesting, I wouldn't think the CEC would allow an automated system to control the entrance.* Hover-pods glide through the incoming gateway while none leave. No LINCC means pods can't be called or dispatched. They wouldn't allow this in Bay City.

The lock engagement light changes from red to green as Octavia withdraws her Brigade passkey from the access port. A mechanical latch releases with a click allowing the civil utility locker to open. She removes one of the portable power cells and proceeds to the terminal at the western gateway.

The screen flickers to life once the power cell is connected to the terminal that monitors the western gate. Octavia downloads the daily log to her terminal-tracker.

Dante-09 doesn't appear in a basic search. A second query scrolls the names of citizens in chronological order of arrival across the display of her hand unit. After refining the search a third time, the log displays in order of vehicle origin, yet nothing jumps out. The exercise gives Octavia the feeling that she is waiting over a hole in the ice for a seal to show its head so she can club it. Another query lists the arriving citizens during the time of the first blackout. A mistake in her query attributes lists the names of citizens along with their full designation. Though none of the names spark her attention, instinct snaps Octavia's thumb against the key to freeze the display.

The first three digits of the extended designation demand her attention: 703. *Why is that familiar?* she wonders.

The number is unusual for this region, yet it appears twice only seconds apart after the gateway began operating. She enters 703 into the Collective's geographic directory. The LINCC connection scale flickers as her query taxes the connection. Octavia is shaken with what the screen finally delivers. *Bangalore?*

The word explodes in her memory; it glows on the screen of her hand terminal and pulls her through time when the same word appeared on the video screen long ago. She remembers the image of a sobbing figure dressed in white calling out *the Correction* above the title *"DISGRACED*

BANGALORE OFFICER." Her eyes squeeze shut as she remembers the waves of pain washing through her and the expression inside the golden hood that delivered it. The security officer took a special interest in her. He had removed the gas filter from his face so he could enjoy the stimulants flowing through the arena. She remembers rolling on the ground in front of that smug smile. She remembers Dante desperately trying to hide his dark-red complexion from her. She can still hear his cry through the madness. She remembers the body of another officer laying still next to her with a face contorted in horror, no longer responding to the barrage of stunner pulses.

Octavia forces herself to the present, then calls for the citizen profile of the name associated with the designation. When the profile displays, it stuns her just the same. She is faced with a picture of a cat staring into the camera.

The citizen summary displays:

NAME: Priya-14, 703.412.020.14.
GENDER: Female.
AGE: 20.5 years.
SKILL-TRADE: Furball Generator.
HEIGHT: 25 cm.
CURRENT LOCATION: Bay City, Alameda,
Sector-211.
MODEST SECURITY CONCERN.
POSSIBLE ASSOCIATION WITH MADRID
OUTLAND.

The screen of the gateway terminal flickers to black when Octavia yanks the power cell from its port. The profile photo still shines on her hand terminal. *What are you doing, Dante?*

"Is it working?" an eager voice asks. A seventeen-year-old man power-cycles his tele-LINCC as he walks toward Octavia.

You think I look like a CEC technician? she thinks but doesn't ask aloud. Instead, she sweeps the hood from her brow, forces a smile, and answers with a friendly, "Sorry, no. I'm just collecting its logs."

When Raymond-06 pulls his attention from his tele-LINCC's keypad, he faces Octavia's bright-white smile and cheerful eyes. Her long raven braid drapes down her chest. He jams the useless device into the pocket of his shop apron to give her his full attention.

Octavia presents the cat's photo to him and asks, "I don't suppose this picture means anything to you?"

Her attention brings a knot to his throat. "Ah… let me see." He considers the image of a surprised shorthaired cat while simultaneously taking another glimpse at Octavia's rising and falling braid.

"Is the kitty defecting?" he awkwardly asks.

Octavia laughs. "No." She takes the terminal away. With an equally awkward grin, she says, "Not exactly, it's more like an accomplice."

After an extended silence, she hesitates and says, "Well, thanks anyway." She turns away.

Raymond awkwardly calls after her. "Wait a minute!" With a new enthusiasm, he waves to a man rolling a pushcart across the quad. "Hey, Ethan!"

Ethan-57 is the owner and sole proprietor of *Eats of Ethan* grill cart. His burners have been cool since the crystal reader on his portable terminal stopped accepting payments over an hour ago. As he pushes his cart over to the pair, Raymond calls to him. "If you're not too busy—"

"It stopped being funny a while ago, Ray." When he sets the locks on his cart's wheels, he recognizes Raymond's enthusiastic nod to the stunning civil officer smiling next to him. "I wish the damn LINCC could have at least died *before* I finished a dozen cobs." He opens what is supposed to be his hotbox with an ungloved hand and passes Octavia and Raymond a pair of foil-wrapped ears of corn. "Here," he says, "I can't sell these cold."

Octavia thanks him with a smile as she accepts the silver package. Bringing the cob to her nose, she inhales its lingering aroma. Her eyes widen. "It's wonderful."

Raymond peels away the foil wrap and takes a bite from the buttery cob. "Mmmmm, you changed the recipe."

Ethan smiles. "The spice traders featured a smoked paprika that I had to try. I'm working on—"

Octavia bypasses the coming formula and displays the profile photo of Priya-14. "Actually, I need your help. Does this remind you of anything?"

Octavia smiles at the aroma rising from the product box of Ethan's cart as he considers the photo for a moment, then another, until she notices his eyes twitch at a memory.

"Something?" Octavia queries.

"I don't know if this matters."

"Please, Ethan." Octavia moves to his side, keeping the picture in front of him. Her chest brushes against him as she places her hand on his shoulder.

He nervously looks to Ray. "There was that guy about an hour ago, right after the gateway reopened."

Raymond shakes his head.

Octavia gently directs Ethan's attention back to the photo and encourages him, "What guy? Tell me."

With a shrug, he says, "A cat ran through the gateway. Before it could run away, this guy caught it, brought it through the entrance, and returned it to the woman who lost it."

"Hey, you're right." Raymond nods in agreement. "I remember now. She was really grateful when he came through."

The men begin to share a smile, which disappears when Octavia's voice turns to iron. "The woman, tell me about her."

The smiles fall away from the men at Octavia's command, and they start to behave like they are addressing an armed reaper on the hunt. Raymond stutters, "I don't know; she was average."

The description focuses Octavia's attention on him. "Average how?"

Raymond stumbles back a step, then forces himself not to appear as if he's trying to escape. "She had red hair." He waves his hand at his shoulder, indicating the length. "I guess she was cute but looked like she had been traveling a while."

"Traveling?"

"Ya, she had a large bag hanging from her shoulder."

"And glasses." Ethan adds.

"I don't remember that," says Raymond.

"Ya, she wore these wire-rimmed things. I noticed them when she turned her head." Ethan traces a line down the side of his face.

Octavia's eyes narrow, remembering the statue in the cave. "She has a scar." She recalls Sonia-10's profile picture on her hand terminal and displays it to the witnesses.

Raymond nods. "Yes, that looks like her."

The men stiffen their spines as she continues her interrogation. "Tell me about the man."

Raymond says, "Well, as I said, the woman was really appreciative. After she placed the cat into a bag on her shoulder, she threw her arms around him, and I thought they were going to kiss, but..." He hesitates.

"Continue, Citizen."

Ethan clears his throat and finishes for his friend. "They didn't. Actually— he kind of blew her off."

Raymond nods in agreement.

Octavia pulls the rim of her hood over her brow before slapping the cob into Ethan's palm. As she walks up the street, she growls through her teeth, *"Dante!"*

The trail through New Rome is sparse. Some citizens remember the red-haired woman with a large scar and glasses when Octavia presents Sonia-10's profile photo. Likewise, the image of Dante-09 reminds them of the strange couple stumbling together down the street. The sightings follow the bogus lifeclock alerts into the middle of the borough, then stops.

Octavia surveys the block and then closes her eyes to imagine Dante and the strange woman stumbling up one street and down another. *Something is wrong,* she thinks. *You're trying to get somewhere, but it's not working. Why does she have to carry you, Dante? Where are you going?*

The greeter's false hospitality sickens Octavia as she steps inside. "Welcome to the Somnolence Center of New Rome. My name is Nicholas-seventy-two. Can I help you, Officer?"

"My name is Octavia-seventy. I'm on special assignment." She presents Dante's profile photo, which immediately sours his expression.

"Yes, I remember him."

"He was with a woman." She swipes Sonia-10's profile photo for him to identify.

"Yes," he answers. "She kept him company while he was here." The technician relates the details of their visit, up to the robotic attendant that arrived to take them to the clinic for a hemo-cleanse.

His description triggers Octavia's memory of her partner working through his chemical binges. The closest ingestion clinic would be a natural place to go next, which bothers her. "Who called for the robot?"

"Officer?"

"You said the robot came here to assist a citizen with his Somnus Obligation and ended up helping these two out the door. I want to know who called for the robot, was it you?"

"It wasn't me," Nicholas stammers. "By that time, we were trying to…"

Octavia waves the explanation away. "Show me where you put him."

The technician stands at awkward attention as Octavia digs around the recliner at the far end of the room. When she is done, she brushes past him as she heads for the exit. He responds with an unintentional impertinence, "Do you have everything you need?"

With a shrug, Octavia returns to Nicholas and displays a fistful of black pistol charges for his consideration. "That depends. Is the Brigade of New Rome in the habit of storing these in Somnolence beds?"

He stares in wonder. "Those look like—"

"STInGERs, yes, thank you. No doubt, your keen observations will be critical to my hunt." She secures the charges in her ammo pouch. "Did the man interact with anyone other than his companion or the robot?"

The tech shakes his head.

Octavia prepares to leave again just as Nicholas calls after her. "Wait!"

Octavia returns to him, who offers her a rolled cylinder. "The woman left this. She said she would be back to pick it up."

Octavia unrolls the slate and enters her LINCC access key. "Level-seventy encryption," she growls. "Am I supposed to wait here for her?"

"Really?" The tech exclaims. "We just used it for…"

The slate slaps against the floor of the reception room. Nicholas has watched the reapers of New Rome run their pistol load drill many times, but never the way Octavia does.

Her arm blurs as she breaks the action of her pistol forward and swaps a charge from the ammo cuff on her wrist.

The tech's eyes bite closed when the muzzle flashes and a fountain of sparks erupt from the ground. He lowers his hands from his ears once the STInGER stops screaming to see a short vapor trail pointing to the charred spot in the floor.

Her pistol action claps. Octavia slides her gun into its holster. The slate has a giant hole burned in the center when Octavia removes it from the charred crater on the floor and hands it to the technician.

"Have a courier deliver this top priority to Investigator Jacob-eleven of the Antioch Civil Security Division with my regards."

The street hums with the lights and sounds of an operational power grid when Octavia leaves the Somnolence Center. She cues her hand terminal, calling her air-pod to her location.

I'm not going to play with you, Dante, she thinks. *This game is going to cost you.* Within minutes, her vehicle settles alongside her. Once in the pod, Octavia slaps her passkey into the terminal and commands the auto-nav to Civil Engineering Control.

✧ ✧ ✧

The air-pod follows the EER to the vehicle charge station in front of the civil managers bureau. *This doesn't seem right,* Octavia thinks. She passes through the thinning crowd to the door of the senior civil engineer. Inside, the engineers act as though they are fighting a citywide fire. It takes three attempts before she addresses the engineer in charge.

Martin-54's attention is captivated by a collection of messages and reports flashing across his terminal slate. He addresses Octavia while tapping a response. "So, Officer, do you really have information on the conduit crash, or is that just something you told my second in command to get my attention."

"I'm not accustomed to having to get anyone's attention, Citizen." Her intensity manages to pry the engineer's focus from the slate.

"I assure you, Officer, when I defect, you will have my full attention." He motions around the room with his stylus. "Things may appear normal to you, but we are pushing back a formidable avalanche of shit right now. So, I'm asking you for the last time, what do you want?"

Octavia whispers in his ear. Martin-54 settles his stylus onto his slate and calls to his second. "Cynthia, would you handle the eastern district? I need to take a short meeting with the Brigade."

All eyes follow the two out of the room.

After ejecting a belligerent fourteen-year-old city planner from his office, Octavia calls up Dante's profile on her hand terminal and passes it to Martin.

Octavia can tell that the report agitates Martin's calm. "A reaper, that is serious, and yesterday it would have been the most disturbing thing I've ever heard. Unfortunately, you caught me today dealing with a very different world."

"A few lost transactions in the commerce district are hardly world-changing." Octavia derides.

Martin lowers his voice. "It's not the blackout, Officer. It's how the blackout was ordered."

"Ordered?"

Keeping his voice low, he says, "My team has been tracing the cause of the conduit crash, at least that's what we've been calling it." He takes in a stabilizing breath. "We've told the public that a mistake was made that redirected power to water reclamation, which caused a series of failures. The truth is, no mistake was made."

Octavia scoffs. "Really."

"The Guardian provides us with an on-demand census that *advises* Civil Engineering Control how and where to direct resources such as power and water treatment from one area to another."

"I'm familiar with this," Octavia answers with a suspicious nod.

"Good. Then you understand that although the Guardian monitors the Collective's resources with near-flawless accuracy, human engineers are imperfect. We make mistakes that can result in short-term failures, like when a hover-pod line fails or a building loses all its lights." He leans toward Octavia for special emphasis. "Do you understand what I am saying?

The image of Dante standing behind a lectern dances through Octavia's awareness as she repeats the citation of his civics lecture out loud: "The Collective exists for the benefit of the citizen. Citizens are critical to the function and evolution of the Awakening. No robot or automated system will inhibit the citizen's ability to function within the world or replace them in the pursuit thereof."

Martin snaps, "I know the Second Citizen Obligation, Officer!"

"Really? Because I predict you are going to hear it recited A LOT in the near future. You're trying to tell me that you haven't used the Guardian to automate critical processes in New Rome's operation, cutting your engineers out of their trade. And when the LINCC crashed, it brought all the systems that are supposed to be managed by the CEC down." She leans to meet Martin's eyes, expecting him to recoil.

He doesn't. Shaking his head, Martin says, "I'm afraid it's a lot worse than that. You're right. New Rome has automated its systems more than the Second Obligation allows. I suppose it's a symptom of working too closely with the magistrates." He rises from his chair and begins to pace. "The civil managers want everything to run smoothly, and they don't like having to pay compensation for filling critical though less desirable positions."

Octavia can hear contempt boil in Martin's voice. He raises his left hand to gaze at his lifeclock flashing red-pink, red-pink. "I may even live to testify to some of these discoveries."

Martin waves his terminal slate for Octavia to consider. "Suppose the Guardian reports increased activity in the northern dining district during midday due to increased use of energized rails, cooking grills, and LINCC transactions. If nothing is done, the northern district is overwhelmed and certain systems go down."

He pauses. Octavia nods in agreement.

He says, "Therefore, I use my LINCC account to direct power from a low-use area, such as water reclamation in the east to the dining districts in the north to compensate. I do this in the same way you use your LINCC account to call up the profile for this Dante-nine or play a song from your aether music catalog. Are you following this? Because it's really important that you understand what I'm telling you."

Octavia shrugs. "I suppose so, I never really thought about it."

Martin sighs. "Well, the CEC does, all the time, and when the entire city of New Rome lost connection with the LINCC, everyone, and I mean *everyone*, asked two questions: what command caused the crash and who sent it?"

"And, do you have an answer?" Octavia asks.

"The LINCC loss hasn't affected safety systems, sewage, or medical facilities."

"Hover-pods continued to run."

Martin nods. "Yes, but only for those who had ordered and paid for a pod before the crash. The crash was constructed to be inconvenient but not life-threatening. As for who sent it— the account belongs to the Guardian."

"How is that possible?"

Martin collapses onto the sofa. "It's not. At least it's not supposed to be. The Guardian is designed to advise. It never manipulates resources unless directed to do so by an authorized account. In this case, the Guardian simply chose to shut down parts of New Rome for a while."

Octavia appreciates the silence. She walks to a vid-screen mounted on the wall displaying a map of New Rome. "Martin, if the LINCC was down in New Rome, how did you determine the account that caused all the problems?"

He answers as if from a trance. "Cynthia, my second, found a high-altitude dirigible above the city that still had an operational LINCC connection. She cracked it and used it to counter the commands that shut down the city." He smiles despite himself. "It only used a level-eight encryption, practically announced itself with spotlights and fireworks."

"Are there other aerial units in the area under your control?"

"Yes."

The map captivates her attention. *So, you figured a way out, Dante. Which way will you go?* A smile breaks her serious expression as a large unmarked region bleeding off the northern edge of the map reveals the answer.

"I'm supposed to check in with the Judiciary, but if you can help me with something, I may need to expedite my departure before I make a *full* report."

Martin leans into the back of the sofa and releases a long settling breath. "What exactly do you need?"

Chapter 29

SMILoDON

Chipped black paint outlines the silhouette of a roaring saber-toothed cat painted atop a yellow field that has washed-out from centuries of sunlight and weather. The logo is nested inside a ring of text identifying the territory of the *Smoky Mountain Intelligent LOgistical Data Organization Network* (SMILoDON).

Before the Awakening, the institute that erected the yellow sign commanded an authority that rivaled any military or elected institution in the world. Now, the SMILoDON Foundation is forgotten to the ages. Only two artifacts of its influence remain. The first is a network of thinking computers that manages the resources of the Collective. The other is the message conveyed on the sign beneath the faded logo that reads:

Entering Smoky Mountain Territory

Trespassers will be killed in the

Forbidden Zone

Keep Out!

A chill runs through the core of the whitetail deer as it lifts its mouth from the stream. It's a chill deeper than the cool water can touch. It fears that bowing its head back to the flowing water will cause it to lose sight of its surroundings, but it needs to drink before it can return to cover. It hates the open.

The breeze changes direction; it's enough to spook the deer to dash from the waterline back into the protection of the bush. Green grass and tender flowers will make due for the rest of the day. It just needs to get away from the open. Death is in the open.

A corrupted intelligence scans the landscape. Its internal counter reaches zero.

BEGIN PATROL

Synthetic wings extend to catch the mountain breeze. A turbine spins to half speed giving the drone enough lift to release its grip from the charging perch and begin its aerial patrol. Telescopic sensors sweep the land below. Hidden beacons guide the drone through a flight path over a dozen square kilometers. Its directive is simple. Detect human trespasser.

Heat silhouettes scurry below. Each target is scanned and checked against the criteria for human trespassers. The sentinel has maintained its vigil for untold years. Once it shared the sky with hundreds like it, each relaying their watch to keep the land safe. It is one of a dozen still operational.

TARGET TEMP:
(Human trespasser: Temp=37°C)
> 40°C
PASS

TARGET HEIGHT:
(Human trespasser: Height <90 cm, AND>200 cm)
> 80 cm
PASS

TARGET BIPEDAL?
> Negative
PASS

ALERT GROUND SENTRY
CONFIRMED, INTERCEPT IN 206 METERS
> Transfer location to Sentry
> RELEASE PROGRAM MODE
> FOLLOW TARGET

With the final command, the drone disengages from its programmed path and begins a slow bank to the right. Its turbine spins down, allowing it to reduce altitude and settle into a gentle gliding circle around the intruder.

TARGET 80 METERS, CLOSING.

The image on the sentry's terminal screen splits. A message blinks on the right side that a connection has been established, and the video feed is accepted. An overhead view of a whitetail deer moving into a dense woody cover appears. Two red brackets target the back of the animal with a red marker labeled HUMAN.

The left half of the screen shows tall grass falling to either side of its path. A red arrow marks a direction labeled

70 METERS, CLOSING.

A sliver of skin remains wedged under the claw of the communicator's attachment system. Dante holds the disk in the sunlight shining through the canopy of the hover-pod.

The auto-nav directed the pod off the energized rail hours ago, leaving behind all traces of human settlements.

"I don't get it," Sonia says. "Why would you want to keep that thing?"

Dante's fingers avoid the installation hooks as he smiles with a shrug. "It scared the hell out of me, but it also was pretty amazing." With childlike enthusiasm, he offers the disk to her. Sonia winces as if he offered her a poison insect.

He wraps the communicator in a piece of cloth. "I got to experience the hive without the subjugation of OrACLe. It was horrible but also remarkable. It was like I could fly through the aether."

"Fly? You could barely walk back there."

Dante laughs. "Don't get me wrong; I'm glad I'm free of it."

Sonia's eyes follow the bundle into his jacket pocket. Once hidden, her shoulders relax.

Dante asks, "You're also thinking about the hive, aren't you?"

The words from OrACLe echo within Sonia as she considers the black spot on the back of her hand. "OrACLe said I was corrupted," she pauses for a breath, "stained. Do you think he's— it's right?"

"Why do you care what a psychotic machine thinks?"

"I shouldn't, I guess, but learning that the world's resource manager has a personal dislike for me lands pretty hard. It's like when the attendant of the nursery was disappointed with my behavior."

"I wouldn't know about that," he says. "The attendants loved me."

Sonia giggles. "I'm sure."

"I know for a fact that OrACLe had no special insight about you, certainly not a personal opinion. It was play-acting a role. You, me, the rest of the hive, we were all characters in his garden."

Sonia brushes her finger down her scar. Dante takes her hand and asks, "Do you know the story of Eden?"

"Generally," she shrugs. "I know the woman in the story comes out with a bad rap, probably because the story is typically told by men."

"I think men resent that Eve did the first interesting thing in history. Without her, humanity is stuck in the garden and never leaves." Dante runs his finger across her black crystal and asks, "Did you crack the lifeclock so you could defect?"

After some thought, she says, "No. When I started, I was just curious about it; I wanted to understand how it worked. Later, when I saw it was possible, I wanted to see if I could control it." She hesitates. "I never thought about escaping Somnus until after I learned its secrets."

"Maybe people can only live in paradise as long as we hide in our ignorance," Dante says. "Perhaps there is something in the human operating system that has to seek out and understand things we're not supposed to so we can evolve."

He holds his lifeclock next to hers. "Do you have the command to assign the names for Rebirth?"

"No, I never found that. Believe me, I looked. If I could have released our old names to Rebirth, Sweeny couldn't have pressured my brother to return to Antioch. What about that hand terminal you reapers use. Is the command in there?"

"Yes. The terminal-tracker can only transmit the name from a white lifeclock and mark it for Rebirth. It assures that the reapers can't be bribed."

"Hmmm." Sonia closes her eyes and falls into a trance.

"What are you thinking?" Dante asks.

"Quiet. I'm flying through the aether." She smiles.

The hover-pod terminal flashes with a warning.

APPROACHING FORBIDDEN ZONE, ACCESS PROHIBITED BEYOND THIS POINT.

The character string Dante had recited to the pickup earlier scrolls across the screen. When completed, it answers:

BYPASS SUCCESSFUL.

A dense line of trees appears in the distance. The hover-pod makes a course adjustment that directs it toward the face of a rocky cliff. Sonia digs her fingernails into the seat cushions.

Neither says a word until the rock face splits apart to reveal the mouth of a tunnel. The hover-pod disappears into blackness.

Moments pass before daylight breaks open the mouth of the tunnel, expelling the pod onto a raised platform that is shaded by a canopy of artificial tree limbs. The hover-pod's lev-field recedes, lowering it to the ground. Once it settles, a robotic arm attaches to the pod's charging port.

In the distance, a massive concrete structure greets Dante and Sonia as they exit the pod. The structure is a slope that grows into the mountainside. Horizontal ridges define a series of windows and balconies that clutter the otherwise featureless edifice.

Steps lead from the platform down to a paved walkway. Three chevrons made from black volcanic rock are inlayed into the contrasting light-gray pavement of the trail pointing in the only obvious direction for the two to follow.

High above them, a corrupted intelligence is notified of the secret opening. Telescoping sensors label them in relation to the signal.

HAVEN TRAVELERS
RAILROAD OVERRIDE
DO NOT ENGAGE

Sentry

It's an unsettled walk along the trail. The great structure embedded into the mountain doesn't seem to change for Dante and Sonia as they approach.

A disturbance rattles out of view and demands Dante's attention. They are proceeding as the hive directed. There's no threat, yet he draws his pistol.

Sonia carries her satchel across her back. She left Priya to rummage around in the sealed pod, knowing he'll be furious when or if they return.

Sonia whispers, "Where are we going?"

"There should be a transmitting station in there." He motions with the muzzle of his pistol to the mountain keep. "All we need to do is enter the passcode that brought us here, and a proxy will help us arrange passage to Haven."

"You think it will work?" she asks.

Dante answers with a dazed smile.

Sonia's heart sinks. "Actually, don't tell me. We'll find out in time."

Listening to the rhythm of their steps as they follow the trail, Dante distinguishes his footsteps from Sonia's, then another. With a wave of his hand, he brings Sonia to a stop. The sound of feet disturbing the ground continues.

Dante moves to put himself between the disturbance and Sonia with his pistol sweeping the tree line. *She's here*, he thinks. He concentrates his attention for the outline of a black tunic and hood.

The crunch of ground cover is joined by a mixture of metallic clicks and the whirl of servo-controlled joints. Dante's gunsight settles on two orange lights. Every instinct he has identifies them as the eyes of a killer.

The glowing lenses are reminiscent of OrACLe's. They watch in momentary silence before moving forward. Dante and Sonia take an unconscious step away from the mechanical creature as it emerges from the tree line.

Four robotic legs carry the ground attack sentry into daylight. It has the frame of a giant predator cat. Its front legs lead into massive shoulders designed for fighting. Its glowing eyes are embedded within a head that holds two dagger-like fangs that descend from its jaws.

Long ago, these saber teeth were polished with a corrosive resistant veneer that protected a keen serrated edge. Now they are coated with layers of dried blood and dirt, bent and blunted from centuries of protecting its territory. A mechanical joint, designed to press its teeth into flesh, mounts its head. A powerful chassis, covered with centuries of weathered corrosion and dried mud, supports its head with four stubby legs designed for power over speed. Large, crescent claws protrude from its paws that grab the ground as it steps.

The sentry studies Dante and Sonia with its glowing sensors. One of the figures is brandishing a weapon that classifies it as a threat. It passes the information through its action criteria.

INTRUDER THREAT?
> TRUE

PASSCODE
> ACCEPTED

ATTACK?
> FALSE

The sentry's logic routine holds this last variable.

Dante assesses its stance; everything about it indicates its readiness to pounce. Yet, it waits. He allows the muzzle of his pistol to slowly drift off target.

The creature's sensors perceive the weapon lowering from its direction. This changes the equation.

INTRUDER THREAT?
> FALSE

PASSAGE GRANTED

The lenses of the robotic watch-beast change from orange to yellow. It grows slightly in stature as it allows the tension in its shoulders to unwind. With a twist of its neck, it springs into a casual trot down the path.

It pauses a few meters in front of them and looks back.

"It wants us to follow." Sonia observes. "Is that really a good idea?"

Dante shrugs. "No, but I don't know what else to do. What do you think?"

She considers the gnarled fangs protruding from the jaws of the sentry. "I think I don't want to upset it." With a nod, they follow their robotic guide.

Dante and Sonia keep what they hope is a safe distance as they follow the sentry for a quarter-hour up the trail. When the path reveals the base of a staircase leading to the mountain keep, the sentry disappears with a single leap into the woods.

Flickering lights illuminate a large metal sign inside a cathedral-like reception area. Sculpted brass letters are mounted to a granite base, which Sonia reads aloud: "Welcome to the SMILoDON Foundation."

They move to the center of the hall, where a circular reception area is defined by what used to be a stately brass and mahogany desk. Crude lines scraped into the once polished varnish form a diagram. Dante traces the form of a running stick figure inside an arrow, directing them toward a hallway where lights begin to glow. He nods to Sonia. "The way is marked with a number of signs like this. You just have to know when and where to expect them and what they represent."

"You're hilarious." Sonia pulls a yellowed booklet, embossed with the SMILoDON logo on the cover, from a plastic slipcase behind the counter. Flakes of ink fall from the once stately typeface that reads: *Guardian: The future of automated resource management and allocation for an evolving world.*

The pages crumble as Sonia flashes the booklet to Dante.

The lights lead them to a door labeled with a crooked sign that reads *Operations: Central Resource Management System.*

Inside central operations, one wall is dominated by a large picture window with a sliding door leading onto a balcony overlooking the forest. Banks of control stations stand in three concentric semicircles facing a wall dominated with four massive video screens.

The control stations seem perfectly homogeneous, but one stands out. An arrow with a running stick figure has been scorched into the wooden surface of the stations. There, Dante finds a large microphone tethered to a panel of switches. The controls of the station appear different from those surrounding it, as though it was built to tolerate centuries of neglect.

The two take in the sight, almost afraid of what comes next. Dante breaks the silence. "I got this." With a gentle pat to her shoulder, he directs Sonia away. "See if you can find another working terminal."

Sonia moves down the row of control stations. Dante follows the last instruction given to him by the hive. A display, obscured with dust, lights up as he enters the access characters onto a keypad. A prompt begins to blink.

CONNECTING

A lump forms in his throat as he takes the mic from the stand. His fingers engage a switch. The display changes to

SEND

"This is SMILoDON zero two, calling Haven." The pickup switch clicks from his finger. Dante kneels at the station with a sigh. *It's over now,* he thinks. *There is nothing more to do.*

Dante's words are muffled as Sonia moves down the row of control stations. Switches stiff with age crack under her fingers as she checks them for any response. Most of them do not respond. Occasionally, one ignites a light or affects a status meter, and sometimes, sparks flash under her hand as circuits break beneath the dusty panels. Nothing indicates an ability to accept a command.

Dante's calls echo in the dimly lit room. "Haven, this is SMILoDON zero two, please respond."

He sounds defeated, she thinks.

Sonia considers the control room and tries to imagine the generations that have come and gone since this place was built. She imagines the Haven technicians who worked here long ago, building the network. *They had to build it on top of the older console.*

She imagines herself as a subversive technician. *If I'm a tech from Haven, and I'm building a way out, I'm in a hurry. I'm not working alone, so where do I work?*

She follows her instincts to an instrument panel directly behind the transmitter where Dante is working. The controls are altered similarly.

Her data spectacles connect to the terminal output, immediately bringing the long-stagnant system to life. Soon, she is looking at the screen last used by a defector. *The defector's session logs are still intact.*

"Dante, you're not going to believe this."

He pauses to peek over the partition. She passes him the data goggles so he can see the overview.

"Are you seeing this?" she asks.

Dante nods. The terminal screen floating before him displays a rotating globe of the world. Areas are colored, depicting the status of each sector. Sonia works the keypad to magnify North America. A black section labeled *Forbidden Zone* extends from south to north near the East Coast. Inside the black zone, a yellow cross is marked *SMILoDON 02.* When the image zooms out to view the hemisphere, several similar zones are marked on the map, each marked as forbidden, and many with numbered SMILoDON markers nested within.

"These Haven folk were busy."

"Look at these areas, hatched in red." She gestures to a section in the Gulf state region with a yellow marker labeled *Watchtower.* "It says these regions are *off-line.* Does that mean they are outside the Collective?"

Dante directs the map to the West Coast to hover above South Diego. A dark-red patch covers a region marked Stadium. "We know there are sensors working in Stadium, even in the Outland district; maybe it means that it's only partially monitored by the Guardian but not managed. OrACLe's safe house wasn't."

Sonia moves the map to hover above the Southern Continent and finds an identical dark patch covering *Balcarce.* "They're Outland regions."

They watch the globe rotate to reveal more areas hatched in red spread around the world. She activates another control to reveal dozens of blue points representing the support locations for the underground railroad. Hundreds of routes appear, leading to supply bunkers, transit passes, and hideaways. For Dante, the world changes before his eyes. Despite all he'd seen, he thought of the world as secure and stable; now it's all covered in holes.

Sonia reviews the previous operator's log files. A command jumps to her attention. She clears the dust away from a component embedded in the control panel. "Dante, look at this!"

Dante's terminal window changes to a file titled: *Hide Lifeclock.* He quickly moves to Sonia's station as she reveals an amber light shining atop a pearl-white dome embedded in the console.

She places her lifeclock onto the peak of the crystal writer. With a tap of a key, a wave of commands floods across the terminal window. The light of the reader glows red through the flesh around her lifeclock for a full minute, enough time for Dante to ask, "Do you know what you're doing?"

"It's not any fun if I know what I'm doing!" she answers with a smile.

She holds her hand rigid over the light long after the display flashes,

COMPLETE

When she finally lifts her hand from the writer, she ponders the black crystal.

Dante asks, "What was that?"

"If the logs are correct, the writer just hid me from all the lifeclock sensors in the Collective. I'm invisible."

"Seriously?" Dante asks.

She can hear astonishment in his voice.

"This is where the underground railroad was established for the North American sector. I mean, right here at this terminal." She pats the dusty station. "Put your hand on the writer."

Dante cover's the tiny amber light with his lifeclock as Sonia resends the *Hide Lifeclock* command.

Five minutes ago.

Tyler isn't exactly sleeping, but his attention constantly drifts from the preventative maintenance manual into the clouds. The alert chime doesn't come as a surprise. In fact, they are happening with increasing regularity. *Another one*, he thinks. *Christopher is right, defectors are signaling more often.*

Often is a relative term. Defectors historically arrive two or three times a year. They say it used to be unusual to meet someone with a lifeclock embedded in his skin, but Tyler grew up knowing many people carrying the Collective's mark.

The manual falls to the floor as he moves to silence the alert and wait for the eventual contact. The message on the status panel stops him. He cues the pickup for internal communication. His voice echoes through the ship, "Christopher, come to the receiving station, we have a contact."

Christopher appears in the hatchway just as Dante's voice buzzes through the open speaker. "This is SMILoDON zero two, calling Haven."

Before he can ask, Tyler nods toward the status panel. "The transmission key is identified as *Casey*," he says with special concern. "I've never seen this before, but it is clearing as genuine."

Christopher pulls a chair to the receiving station and calls up a logbook on an adjacent terminal screen. "Casey is the code name for the West Coast of the North American sector." His fingers agitate the terminal keys calling page after page to the screen. "According to intelligence, that line hasn't had any activity for a long time."

Dante's voice scratches through again. "Haven, this is SMILoDON zero two, please respond."

The officer ponders the call as he skims the log file. "Over fifty operatives have been sent into North America to assess the lines, none have returned." He reads down the report and continues. "The last one was eight years ago."

Christopher scoots the younger man aside as he says, "I want to know what happened to the North American line. Tell Captain Reed to set a course to the Eastern zone of North America and prepare an extraction squad."

Tyler nods and begins to leave. Then he pauses in the hatchway. "Isn't this risky?" he asks. "What if the Charon Brigade captured our technician and—"

"Then Reed will be extracting a reaper." Christopher finishes for the younger technician. "It's dangerous, but dangerous options are all we have right now."

With a solemn nod, Tyler leaves. Christopher takes the microphone and cues the pickup. "SMILoDON, this is Haven."

Sonia and Dante stand silent as the voice scratches through the ancient speaker. He returns to the transmitter station, afraid to answer.

"I guess we're not done yet," Sonia says with a gleeful smile as she leans against the terminal.

The hail pops and rattles again. "Repeat, this is Haven, respond SMILoDON."

Dante picks up the microphone and opens the pickup. "Haven, this is SMILoDON."

Chapter 30

On the Trail

High above the birch and maple covered terrain, Octavia follows the photo-enhanced image of her air-pod's terminal screen. Her vehicle is the trailing point of a three craft V-formation with two robotic dragonflies following behind. The drones transmit their sensor data to her terminal screen. A bright-red line traces the nearly invisible scar where a lev-field recently scraped the earth into the uncharted territory until it abruptly ends at the base of a granite slope.

The air-pod hovers as the drones circle below. The slope is too steep for a hover-pod to travel; it must have turned away earlier. Somehow, they laid a false trail. *Pretty clever, Dante.* She enters a command that sends the dragonflies into a grid search mode.

The instant the dragonflies break formation, the controls of her air-pod lock. An alert flashes across her terminal screen.

FORBIDDEN ZONE, ACCESS PROHIBITED
BEYOND THIS POINT.

Octavia taps a command into her terminal that should normally not allow an input. A moment passes, then her controls move freely, and the pod drifts forward. The warning on her terminal monitor changes to read:

BYPASS SUCCESSFUL.

The dragonflies begin to survey the landscape. Octavia says, "Nice job, Martin."

It didn't take much coaxing for the civil engineer to produce an override to the security zone. Octavia suspects the engineer had worked it out well in advance of their meeting. *When this hunt is completed, I'll need to check the number of days Martin has on his Final-Quarter and investigate why he had that code.*

Martin also gave her control over two dragonflies that he had named Bravo and Echo. It's the first time she has ever directly controlled drones during a hunt; she likes it. An alert from the Echo drone calls Octavia's attention to the pod's terminal screen. Five hundred meters to the west, it has discovered the mangled body of a white-tailed deer placed next to the remains of two boys dressed in hunting gear. White triangles mark the positions of the human corpses.

She cues the pickup. "Echo, relay the position of two deceased lifeclocks for Charon Brigade recovery."

The confirmation message flashes on the screen. Bravo resolves drag marks in the ground and follows them alongside a set of prints leading to and away from the bodies. Octavia banks her air-pod in the direction of the drone's signal. Echo ascends another twenty meters and scans the terrain ahead.

There is also the matter of...

She cues her tele-LINCC. "Contact search. Find public tele-code for Raoul-seventy-four."

The pod's terminal screen responds with a catalog of matches. One has a distinctive abstract description and profile photo. She selects it. Her ear kernel soon responds, "You have reached tele-snitch, on whom are you informing?"

Bravo drone transmits the image of a massive concrete slope leaning into the side of a mountain. Echo drone identifies a foot trail leading in the direction of the structure.

Octavia follows the dragonfly's signals until the structure is visible through the bubble canopy of her pod. She cues the pickup of her terminal. "Bravo, Echo, find a landing area close to the structure."

The drones circle the trail leading to the mountain. The area seems intentionally cluttered with trees, too narrow for a hover-pod to drive and too steep for an air-pod to land. Octavia surveys their feeds on the terminal screen and taps a treeless spot atop a small ridge marking its location for the drones to direct her in.

Octavia descends over a ridge covered with thick brush, too dense for the pod to land. She slides the canopy hatch open, removes a blue fuel cell from a pocket of her pack, and tosses it into the middle of the brush. The air-pod glides away and hovers seventy meters from the ridge.

A blue dot flashes inside a red circle in Octavia's gunsight. She fires. A great shock wave precedes an ascending fireball. It takes a moment for the black cloud to clear, revealing a scorched crater atop the ridge. The lev-field of her pod extends, smothering the small residual flames where she brings the craft to nest.

Stepping from the air-pod, Octavia takes a final look at the vid-screen of her hand terminal. Bravo and Echo circle her position, marking the signal of her lifeclock with a blue triangle. There are no other targets. The forest obscures the ground in many places, but it's not enough to hide a lifeclock from the dragonflies. *It would be a lot better to have a target to follow.* Then she remembers who her target is. *You're drawing me into that cover, where you can hide, 'eh, Dante?* She imagines her former partner and the woman hiding in wait inside the concrete structure. She loads a red UKD charge into the breech of her pistol, then pulls a white TAC charge from her ammo cuff and removes the brass stabilizing-cap from the top. She keeps the second charge in her hand as a backup, then follows the dragonfly's directions to the trail.

The treetops whisper with the breeze rustling through the branches. The dragonflies whine above as they follow the hunter along the trail. Octavia treads lightly, searching for tracks. She finds them, two pair, fresh and heading toward the mountain structure. Octavia resists the impulse to rush down the trail.

Echo drone broadcasts an alert to Octavia's ear kernel. *"Danger, fifteen meters, closing."*

Octavia sweeps the tree line with her gunsight toward the rustle of breaking twigs. The muzzle of her pistol flares at the charging blur, then another warning sounds, *"Danger, above."* Octavia's backup charge settles into the gun breech with a slap; it is launched into the talons of the diving surveillance robot that crashes to the ground, encased in a sticky white cocoon.

The robot's bound wings fight against the tendrils of the Tactical Adhesive Charge. It continues to send location data for the human intruder to the crippled attack sentry a few meters away. Its propulsion turbine grinds to a violent halt as the web works into its mechanism. Its talons gouge at the hard-packed ground.

Octavia slips another white TAC load into the breech of her pistol and tosses the stabilizing-cap away. She approaches the ground attack unit. The sentry waves its massive fangs in her direction, but it is unable to move since the unguided kinetic dart blasted its front leg away and severed its rear control system. It flails about, only to stop after Octavia smashes its hindquarters with her boot.

Chapter 31

Incursion and Evasion

Moments before.

An alarm fills the control room just as the scratchy voice on the speaker concludes relaying instructions to Sonia. She slaps her notebook closed and exclaims, "Now what?"

The voice from Haven cuts through the noise and advises, "Something has breached the airspace of the forbidden territory."

Dante cues the microphone at the transmitting station. "What is it?"

Christopher's voice blares above his tapping terminal keys. "Move the display toggle switch at the top of the terminal station to the position marked *Main Viewer*."

Sonia wipes away the dust surrounding the toggle switch. It moves with a crisp click from OFF to MAIN VIEWER. The wall opposite the semicircle of control stations activates.

The speaker crackles. "There is an unmarked switch where the microphone cable connects to the transmitter station, flip it to the up position and give the following command: 'Guardian, display incursion.' Return the switch to the down position to speak to us."

Dante follows the instruction. The main viewer displays a map of the region surrounding the mountainside leading out to the border of the forbidden zone. Three red triangles explore the line around the southern border. Dante cues the audio pickup again. "Guardian, identify the three signals."

The system processes the request, then magnifies the display over the three triangles moving across the land. A synthetic voice answers through the distorted speaker, "Three aerial units are moving toward Foundation. Two are automated; one is citizen piloted."

Dante considers the three signals. He cues the pickup again. "Guardian, display a map showing this structure in relation to the platform where our vehicle is charging."

The view screen zooms out to depict the mountainside with the artificial wedge protruding from it. The foot trail they followed is defined as a blue dotted line leading to a blue circle representing the charging platform. Dante studies it as the three red triangles float into view. He picks up the mic again. "Guardian, indicate the main entrance of this building with a red arrow." An image materializes.

Dante continues. "Guardian, is there another way out of Foundation?"

The voice answers, "Your command is gibberish, clarify."

Dante and Sonia share a surprised look at the strange response.

Dante rephrases the request. "Guardian, display all exits from Foundation."

Three green circles appear. One at the rooftop, one over the red arrow marking the entrance, the third appears next to a small clearing to the north marked Maintenance Gate.

Dante turns to Sonia and asks, "That silver gizmo of yours, the one you made for your brother, can it capture pictures?"

Sonia nods as she removes the silver pocket clock from her bag. She opens the cover and toggles it to the function he indicated.

Dante frames the map on the main viewer on the display of the pocket clock.

An explosion in the distance rattles the large picture window. Dante can see the black cloud rising in the distance where the fuel cell detonated. An air-pod hovers just out of the path of the cloud.

He returns to the microphone and commands, "Guardian, display the location of the explosion."

An orange circle appears on the map. Dante relays a series of commands that format the map with a north-pointing arrow and longitude lines across its face before he captures the image onto the pocket clock.

At the transmitter, he toggles the switch to the transmit position. "Haven, we are leaving SMILoDON now. Expect our arrival after sunset."

The speaker pops with the voice of their new guide. "If you make it there, we'll find you. But don't expect a ride if you still have that reaper on your trail."

"I'll deal with the reaper, Haven."

The speaker's voice scratches out, "Good luck. Haven out."

✧ ✧ ✧

While Dante works the transmitter, Sonia opens a secondary terminal. She queries Guardian through a keypad input. She copies the last of the directions from the control room to the secondary maintenance exit when Dante appears.

His new virtual map moves with the swipe of his fingers across the screen of the pocket clock. "If we really are invisible to those aerial drones out there, I can get us to the pod—"

Sonia interrupts. "It doesn't make sense, Dante. I've reviewed the logs for the *Hide Lifeclock* program. It is way more complicated than simply releasing the names."

Dante moves to her side. "Maybe they couldn't find the command for Rebirth."

Sonia shakes her head. "That's just it, Dante, they did find it. Look." She removes her brass pocket clock and rotates the control stem until her photo album appears. She clicks through a series of pictures of herself with Marcos and later Carlos and a few friends from the Bay City Archive until she lands on a profile picture of a young girl. Another click reveals a window that holds caption information for Gabrielle-71. Sonia enters the command,

> somnusName: Gabrielle-71, 714.086.104.71

The display blinks for a moment, then responds.

NAME: GABRIELLE-104.71
STATUS: REBIRTH
1 NAME POSTED FOR REASSIGNMENT

Dante shouts, "That's fantastic, can you—"
Before he can finish asking the question, she enters the command,

> somnusName: Sonia-10, 285.092.105.10

To which the display responds,

I ALREADY TOLD YOU, DEFECTOR. IF YOU
WANT TO RELEASE YOUR NAME FOR
REBIRTH, YOU KNOW WHAT TO DO. DON'T
ASK ME AGAIN.

Dante slowly pulls the goggles from his face to look into Sonia's nervous expression. Before he can say anything, two pistol shots rattle the window in near-immediate succession. Sonia looks to Dante with a new concern. "There are two—"

Dante cuts her off with a shake of his head. "No, she's that fast." He nudges her from the terminal seat. "And she'll be here soon."

With a final snap of the toggle switch, the operations center fades to darkness as the main viewer dims to black.

A single light illuminates the supply room leading to the maintenance exit. Dante sweeps their path with his gunsight as they make their way past the cartons and stacks of tools.

A massive vehicle door marks the end of their search.

They slowly roll the door a few centimeters off the ground. Sonia checks a short video recorded by her pocket clock after waving it beneath the opening. Nothing appears to be watching from the other side. Their eyes strain as sunlight blazes into the long dark chamber. Once they step into the light, Dante looks back. The tool depot lights up from the incoming sunlight, revealing a cache of shovels, rakes, and other field tools. Dante returns to the stockpile of replacement shovel handles.

He takes one of the resin-treated handles and measures its length against his chest. The green pressure treatment has preserved the stability of the time-hardened hickory staff. They ease the door down and make for the tree line.

"What are you doing?" she asks.

"I'll explain later." He references the map displayed in the silver pocket clock. He marks their position next to the exit with his thumb, then slips his watch from his wrist and places it against the map display. With a forward motion, he whispers, "We need to travel in a straight line until that clump of trees is to our right. Then we should be close to our pod."

As they move into the forest, Dante directs Sonia how to move quietly. She quickly learns the hand signals that warn for places that can snap or crack if disturbed. Though they lose sight of Foundation, Dante confirms their position on the map whenever a patch of sunlight shines through the trees. He waves a halt. Without a word, he directs Sonia to lie on the ground as he gestures with his pistol in the direction of the trail they followed earlier.

Sonia is plagued with the sound of her heart beating and air rushing into and leaving her lungs. She closes her eyes and listens. Branches rattle in the breeze sending a rainfall of dead leaves to rest on her body. A shuffling sound emerges from the forest rattle. It soon clarifies into the pattern of footsteps disturbing the ground, then silence.

Dante's pungent aroma drifts into Sonia's awareness. It stirs a memory when they were together in OrACLe's Watchtower, as does her own body smell. She struggles to hold the silence. Just ahead, Dante is hunched behind a fallen tree, his gun drawn.

Minutes pass.

She begins to raise her gaze in the direction where the rustling stopped. Dante motions not to look.

The footsteps are like thunder when they sound again. As they recede, the sounds of the forest return.

With a wave of his finger, they continue until another aroma comes to them on a breeze. It is the smell of charred grass and wood. Dante motions for them to follow the scent into a clearing where an air-pod sits inside a charred crater. His thumb moves to the orange circle on the pocket clock.

Sonia is overwhelmed with an instinct to run away, but Dante stands next to the air-pod, looking in.

"Let's get out of here. We're in the open!" she says.

He doesn't move.

Dante peers through the canopy. A pack is fastened into the passenger seat. Its straps are neatly tied, and each pocket is symmetrically packed. It's immaculate, just like its owner.

Sonia rasps, "Dante, what are you doing?"

Electricity dances across the back of his neck. He turns away and raises the data goggles over his eyes. He cues the pickup in the ear kernel and gives the command, "Full magnification."

A telescopic window renders in front of him with the label 10x at the bottom of the frame. The image sweeps the Foundation building jutting from the cliff and settles on a balcony where the black outline of a reaper's tunic and hood stands. It holds a pair of binoculars to its face.

He knows the curves of the perfectly tailored uniform. He imagines the hunter marking him in her sight. Sonia grabs his sleeve and pulls him in the direction of the tree line. Her fingers slip away as he returns his attention to the figure on the balcony. The figure brushes the hood away from her brow, bringing a tightly braided ponytail to settle across her chest.

They watch one another for a moment before Dante whispers, "Octavia."

Chapter 32

Acquired

Octavia's clasped hand grips the image of her bug-eyed prey standing in the view field of her binoculars. She knows the ratty trench coat and the stoic frame hiding behind the large goggles staring at her. A button clicks under her finger to target his position for the two circling drones.

The drones are programmed to identify targets with a black triangle if their lifeclock is expired, green if not, yet Dante stands there unmarked. *They're right over you,* she thinks. *Why aren't you tagged?* A woman with short red hair enters the view and pulls at his shoulder. "You're Sonia-10." No marker appears to identify her expired lifeclock. Octavia lowers the binoculars.

She brushes the hood from her brow, sweeps her braid forward, and watches the dragonflies dive for the position marked by her field glasses. She slides the hand terminal from her belt and glances at the vid-screen. Both drones are circling the area. She watches the clearing with her air-pod and two defectors slipping in and out of view.

Octavia raises the glasses to see the defectors looking up at the circling drones. She checks the hand terminal for a malfunction. "What the hell is going on?"

A shot cracks across the hillside. Through the binoculars, she watches Dante slap the action of his pistol closed and move to the opposite side of her pod. Another shot claps the air, sending Octavia into the operations room and toward the ground floor.

Bravo and Echo circle the area, unable to track the escaping targets. Once outside the Foundation keep, Octavia leans into a desperate sprint for the pod, trying not to think of the destruction her former partner just inflicted. She forces that concern away, which allows another realization to take its place. *You laid a masterful trail for me to follow, Dante, and I fell for it.* She suppresses a smirk of admiration for her partner. *It made me sloppy.*

Octavia sweeps her gunsight around the clearing as she enters the place where her air-pod sits. Echo and Bravo continue to circle above. She finds her pod covered with the strands of two TAC charges. Both hatches are sealed shut.

Prints in the charred ground indicate the place where Dante stood as he watched her on the balcony and another set leads away. Octavia breaks open the action of her pistol and swaps the white TAC charge for a black STInGER. She palms a second charge as before, then steps onto their trail.

The signs are easy to follow since they made no effort to hide their flight. A footpath recedes to a raised platform covered by an artificial tarp of green and wood-colored synthetic brush. The canopy camouflages the platform where the leaves and dust had recently been pushed away by the lev-field of a hover-pod. Octavia returns the spare charge to her ammo cuff and holsters her gun.

A hatch covers the exit of the escape pod. Octavia runs her hand over the seal, wondering if it is worth forcing open for a pursuit. The idea settles with her in the same way she might consider following a snake into its hole.

She steps off the platform into a sunny break in the tree cover where she can see the two dragonflies circling above. She checks her hand terminal to find an overhead image of herself, marked with a blue triangle.

A command releases the drones from their holding pattern and returns to the search criterion that brought her here.

> Search and track lev-field signs.

The whine of Bravo's and Echo's turbines fades as they climb into the sky.

A hover-pod's lev-field makes a distinct trail, easy for the dragonflies to follow. *There was only one such track in the ground that led me here,* she thinks. *There'll be another leading away.*

The reasoning calms her by the time she returns to her hover-pod cocooned in the tactical adhesive web. She carefully applies the solvent from a tiny flask around the sticky tendrils holding the canopy hatch closed. The tedium gives her time to think about why she should have predicted this from her partner.

An alert sounds in Octavia's ear kernel from Bravo just as the solvent clears the last tendril holding the hatch closed. "Hover-pod acquired."

The adhesive still heavily obscures the forward-facing view of the pod's canopy when Octavia slides into the cockpit and activates the terminal screen. The display shows a high-altitude image of the land slowly drifting across the view screen. A red line traces the track made by a lev-field. It points to a billowing dust cloud. She snaps a control that magnifies the image of a hover-pod driving away.

> Continue tracking.

Octavia allows a smile to break across her lips. She removes another bottle of solvent from her pack and eagerly addresses the video screen. "I've got you!"

Nowhere Else to Run

The horizon has been clear for hours. Yet when Dante closes his eyes, he imagines their pod moving in the view of Octavia's gunsight. The vision keeps pulling his eyes open.

The hover-pod glides atop an energized rail camouflaged by an ancient road. Thick, green overgrowth obscures either side of the highway. Roadside trees cast shadows onto their path, indicating the sun's descent toward the western horizon.

The green cover eventually surrenders to broken pavement. The remains of an East Coast city appear ahead. Signs directing a long-dead population litter the streets as the pod navigates through canyons of fallen structures.

"I've been thinking about what you said, about the Guardian having a personal dislike for you."

"That's a strange conversation starter," Sonia says.

"I know, but I'm not sure it was all that personal." He removes the bundle with the communicator from his pocket. "I can't stop thinking about the way we were scolded back there."

"You mean when I tried to release my name?"

Dante nods. "It said, 'I already told you…' and '…don't ask me again.' Does that sound like a normal error response?"

"What do you think it means?"

Dante's eyes fall to the bundle. "The Guardian was designed as a resource manager. That includes managing the Collective's population. To manage a resource, it has to understand it, learn about it. Maybe it doesn't like what it has learned about us."

"Look, there's another!" Behind them, they watch a craft spiral to the horizon. A small cloud of dust rises where it disappears. "Do you think it saw us?"

"Probably. Three signals were tracked in the control room. Dragonflies are short-range drones. It likely continued to relay our position until it crashed."

"That leaves your partner?" Sonia says.

"Yes. When Octavia finds the energized rail, she will follow it right to us."

"Since you brought it up—"

The hover-pod glides into a canyon of decayed buildings. Its automated system navigates to a clearing on the border of a crumbled city. The canopy opens as the lev-field lowers the pod to the ground. Legions of abandoned pods are parked around them.

Priya leaps from the cabin to explore their destination. Dante helps Sonia from her seat. She secures her satchel across her shoulder, and he carries the shovel handle.

Sonia presses her original inquiry. "I don't get it. You've told me over and over how dangerous and cunning Octavia is, yet you needed to leave a trail for her to follow. Why?"

"I didn't intentionally leave a trail, at least not most of the time."

"Why the stunt with the bullets?"

"They're called STInGERs," Dante corrects.

"Whatever!" she exclaims. "Shooty, killy, make-my-chest-explode things. Seriously, Dante, what are you doing with her?"

"Any hunter can get fatigued during a chase. I want her engaged. Octavia is laser-focused right now to kill me—" he looks into Sonia's eyes "—to kill us, by herself. But if she believes she is too far behind, or that we might escape, she will call for assistance."

"Fair enough," Sonia says. "Setting aside your weird relationship, you could have ended the chase back there."

"You think so?"

"Yes. You know what I mean. You could have destroyed her pod; instead, you covered it with that white goo."

"You think destroying her vehicle would have ended the hunt?"

"Of course!"

"Okay. Put yourself in her place. Imagine you are a hunter; you follow a pair of defectors into a remote location where they destroy your vehicle. What do you do?"

Sonia shrugs. "I'm trapped. There's nothing to do."

"Sonia, how much of your life have you spent planning your defection? Do you give up? Really?"

Sonia allows her imagination to return to the control room inside the balcony. "There's a transmitter back there. I figure out how to call for help."

"Yes, you contact the Brigade and tell them to send every reaper in the area in the last known direction of your targets."

They continue into the ruins. Sonia notices the sunlight glint off Dante's watch crystal. With a nod to his wrist, she asks, "What else does that do?"

Dante glances at his watch with a shrug. "You know, it tells time, the date, it chimes at the top of the hour, the usual."

"You used it in the forest to guide us to the pod. What is it, a personal position display?"

Dante slips the watch from his wrist and passes it to her. She reads the analog face.

"It's a field-craft trick I learned in the academy." He steps behind Sonia and directs her shoulders toward the setting sun. He slides his hands down her arms. "Point the hour hand in the direction of the sun. If it is after midday, the hand is pointing west. Then find the halfway point between the hour hand and twelve o'clock, that is south."

Sonia encloses her hands around his. She says, "South is at thirteen minutes." Dante is at her left shoulder when she turns. "That makes north at forty-three minutes." She runs the tips of her fingers across his forearm following the northern direction.

"You got it."

"But for this to work, you need to know whether it is before or after noontime, how do you do that?"

Dante gives an understanding nod. "That part is tricky. You need to have a mechanism that will tell you the time of day."

They smile. She settles into his arms. His chin rests against her shoulder. The western sun shines on them with a mild orange hue. She runs her fingers inside the sleeve of his coat. Her touch is electric, like warm satin against his skin.

Dante murmurs into her ear, "Thank you."

She turns to him.

"You saved my life back in New Rome," he says. "I never thanked you for that." His arms close around her. "You made all this possible, everything I've experienced and seen, and it's been the best part of my life."

"Everything you experienced." She smirks. "I'm not sure what to say about that."

"I am, and I'd do it all again." They hold hands as they walk into the ruins of the city.

A familiar feeling dances across the back of Dante's neck. The sensation calls his attention to all the hiding places surrounding them.

"Is it her?" Sonia asks.

"I don't know." He motions down the street. "It might be Octavia or the agents from Haven. Either way, I think it's time to split up. Move away from these tall structures."

Their hands slip apart as he says, "Find someplace where you can see her coming, preferably with lots of ways in and out." Dante waves away her objection. "Be aware of where you step and of any marks that will lead her to you. If you see her approaching, move away as silently as you can. Don't get cornered, and above all, don't try to outrun her."

Sonia grasps the lapel of his jacket. "I've been through this before. Carlos also thought he could deal with a threat alone; it didn't work out. Will you at least consider that we might be better together?"

Dante takes her hand. "To deal with the Haven agents, without a doubt. Octavia is another matter. Together we are two targets that can be easily dispatched. I'm hoping to isolate her from you or—"

Her hand falls from his. "—Or use me as bait to draw her in."

Dante cups her chin in his palm. His thumb traces the scar down her face. "Not if I find her first." He admires the resolve in her eyes as he says, "There's nowhere else to run."

Sonia steps away. "Should I leave some kind of sign for you to follow?"

Dante smiles. "Really? You think you have to leave a trail for me to track you?"

Sonia rolls her eyes and continues down the street.

Dante enjoys the way she walks away. The cat scampers behind her. Dante returns his attention to the tingling on his neck. Tapping the staff against the ground, his mind drifts back to the academy combat training. *How did those short spear drills go?*

Chapter 33

The World Before

It must have been an amazing city once upon a time. Thousands, perhaps millions of people, teemed through the streets of its massive stature. *Is this what the world was like before?* Sonia imagines the world portrayed by the angry holographic girl in the Alameda archive.

Shattered asphalt radiates from craters in the streets. Ammunition casings litter the walkways beside punctured buildings. Blown out windows reveal the scorched spaces inside.

Sonia follows the walkway into a three-story structure with a rusted sign identifying the East Side Academy. The rooms inside are nearly identical, all in ruin. A door leads into a large room filled with toppled tables and leaning bookcases. Decayed books litter the floor beneath broken shelves. *How fitting*, she thinks. One of the books falls to pieces under its own weight when she lifts it from the shelf. *What could anyone get from a place like this?*

The freshly fallen paper appears bright atop centuries of grime at her feet. It's a clear sign that the area has been recently disturbed. *I should go.*

Cornered

Priya prances about the ruins of the library, trying to discover memories and instincts he never practiced. A mouse scurries through the stacks. If he is patient and pounces just right, he'll capture a prize for the woman with the kind hands. He stays with her because she protects him, feeds him, and scratches the back of his neck.

Priya focuses on the little gray creature handling a seed that had blown in through the window. His hind legs are in position to leap, but he doesn't hear the approach of the hand that wrenches him from the ground.

Claws and teeth fail to penetrate the padding protecting the hand restraining him. A fist closes around his head. Fear turns to agony. A blade wedges under the strange button he grew many years ago and rips it from his leg.

He jumps away from his attacker and calls for the woman with the kind hands.

"Priya! Priya, where are you?"

She knows I'm in trouble, he thinks. *I have to find her.*

The cat is the longest relationship Sonia has maintained in her life. The sound of his pain overwhelms her better judgment. She calls into the darkness, "Priya!"

Priya emerges from the shadows. Sonia can see a bloody trail following the cat's path. He's favoring his left side. She brings him into her protective arms. Priya's warm bloody body pants against her chest. She knows what's happened. She knows why. She knows it's useless to run.

"Who are you?" a soft voice demands from behind.

"I'm sorry," she sobs. "Forgive me, Priya."

The muzzle of Octavia's pistol presses into the base of Sonia's neck. "You should be sorry, Sonia-ten. Your lifeclock expired five days ago."

Sonia stumbles forward as the gun jabs between her shoulder blades. "You didn't just give that cat a name, you gave it a whole LIFE!" A pull on her shoulder whirls Sonia around to face the eyes of her executioner framed inside a black hood. The muzzle lifts her chin, directing her attention to a citizen profile photo of a shorthaired kitten glowing in the display of a hand terminal.

NAME: Priya-893.14
STATUS: REBIRTH
1 NAME POSTED FOR REASSIGNMENT

The gun barrel scrapes Sonia's throat as she pulls away.

Octavia motions toward a bench and orders, "Sit."

Sonia obeys.

Octavia moves back a pace. The gunsight fails to confirm the STInGER lock onto Sonia's expired lifeclock. The hunter demands, "That's not the only name you stole, is it? Who were you BEFORE?"

Sonia suppresses a shudder as she answers, "Lauren-twenty-five."

Octavia finds a hesitation in her answer and asks, "So Lauren-twenty-five, when did your lifeclock expire?"

"A little more than a year ago."

The answer gives Octavia the sensation that her prey is trying to double back. "There's another, isn't there? For the last time, who are you?"

Sonia looks to the shadows and allows her voice to break into subdued hysterics. "I was born Julie-eleven, in the Southern Continental region."

I didn't ask her where she was born. Octavia follows Sonia's glance into the shadows. "He's out there." Octavia takes a position with her back facing the way she came, then asks, "How did you do that? When I check the archives, will I find a report of some defector underground that invaded an infant ward to steal a writer from the cradle room? Will I find a trail of nurses and attendants littering their exit?"

Sonia answers with a panic-stricken rant. "I don't know how ... it was found ... or who found it. I traded ... it came! But I'm sure any citizens harmed getting it had their hands CAREFULLY logged by the reapers to keep the machine happy—"

Octavia silences the defector with the back of her glove.

A moment ago.

Faint electrical signals pulsed through thread-thin tendrils leading from Priya's nervous system into the lifeclock embedded in his leg. These conduits were severed when the chip was ripped from his flesh. Once the signal stopped, the tendrils that carried the current began to degrade, releasing cellular amounts of neurotoxin into his bloodstream.

Priya had no understanding of this. He only knew that he was safe in the arms of the woman with the kind hands. He knew she was protecting him. The throbbing in his leg stopped. He closed his eyes. His chest fell for the last time.

The ringing in Sonia's head dissipates, as does the pain from the reaper's slap. She lays Priya's lifeless body on the bench and combs her fingers through his bloody fur.

Octavia levels her gun. "It's your time, Defector."

"It's time." Sonia mimics the judgment. *This is a good place to end,* she thinks, as the last of her fear burns away. *No more running. No more hiding. No more lying.* She looks past the large bore of the reaper's gun to Octavia's cold eyes. *No more cowering.* The muzzle follows Sonia as she stands to take the STInGER.

A flash bursts from the shadows; a blur nearly yanks Octavia to the ground. When she regains her footing, a cocoon obscures her gunsight.

Dante steps into the light, his gun in one hand, the shovel handle in he other.

A sticky white glob covers Octavia's gun and glove. She pulls the glove from her hand and tosses it to the ground along with the useless pistol.

"You should be more careful, Dante!" Octavia says. "You could have killed me."

Twisting pain ripples up Sonia's arm to her shoulder when Octavia grabs her. She complies by moving to face Dante as a human shield for the reaper.

Her submission to Octavia's hold helps her realize that the gunshot did not burst her chest open. This realization is followed by a sharp yelp when Octavia's billy club jabs the small of her back, lifting her onto her toes.

"Don't hurt her, Octavia," Dante pleads as he moves toward them.

"Reapers don't hurt defectors, Dante. We kill them. Have you forgotten that? Drop the gun, or I'll—"

Dante's pistol bounces on the ground to stop a meter in front of them. "Octavia, we can work this out. Please let her go."

Sonia cries out again as the baton is jabbed deeper into her back.

"Work this out. Have you lost your mind?" Octavia says. "There is no working this out. I am an officer of the Charon Brigade, bound by an oath to protect and secure the names loaned by the Guardian so that the next generation can take its place in the Collective. Her lifeclock is black; she is a defector. You helped her evade her obligation. You are aiding a defector. You're talking as if there is some kind of middle ground to play. There isn't!"

"There is a middle ground, Octavia. You've tried for years to show it to me, but I didn't see it. I couldn't then, but now—" Dante calms the tone of his voice as he advances. "Yes, she is a defector, and I don't have to kill her, and neither do you. You figured this out years ago, and I'm only getting it now," he says. "I don't have to say anything. I don't have to do anything. I get it."

"She is stealing three names, Dante, not only from the next generation but also from all who will follow. And what about your name? What gives you the right to walk away with it?"

Sonia scuffles on her toes to comply as Octavia closes the distance from Dante.

"All I did was change a couple of files," Sonia protests.

"A couple of files?" Octavia mocks. "Is that all? I suppose at some level it wasn't actually you who changed the files. You discovered some clever process that tricked the Guardian to change them for you and then assign a name. You take no responsibility for the nursery attendant in Bangalore, who closed a cradle lid, dispatching the child inside, because the name that was supposed to pair with her data-file and turn her lifeclock yellow went instead to your CAT!"

With a vengeful shove, Octavia sends Sonia crashing into a bookshelf.

A disorienting crash resonates through the room. Dante has to control his actions as he watches the standing shelf splinter to the ground. Ancient books rain down on Sonia making a musty crash matt.

Dante moves so he can see Sonia pull herself to her feet while keeping the advancing Octavia in view.

Octavia watches Dante with a vengeful glare, which he has trouble facing.

Waving her baton between the fugitives, she asks, "Oh, is that the first time you heard it out loud? It's one thing to know your theft cost the life of a citizen, but stating it out loud is unnecessarily gruesome, right?"

Slowly advancing, Octavia says, "If I extend that line of reasoning, I never actually killed anyone. I had nothing to do with the machine that assigned all those defectors to my terminal. Sure, I ran them down, aimed my weapon, engaged the trigger, but never controlled the launching charges that propelled the STInGER into their chests or the chemical explosion that cooked their insides." Her voice elevates. "That's the reasoning that caused the Awakening! Generations of the powerful few hoarding resources to control the masses, oblivious to the devastation they caused. You know this, Dante, you've spent half your life assuring that generations would never forget it!"

Dante brings the shovel handle forward and holds it in a ready position, a posture he hasn't used since the staff drills in the academy.

Octavia says, "What was their rationale? It's nothing personal, just business. Those sick, starving, illiterate children need to take responsibility." Octavia mimics the gestures she had watched her partner make through hundreds of civics lectures. "You taught this, Dante! Benefit, accountability, and sacrifice, you know the price for turning away from the Awakening. So tell me, where's the middle ground? Why did you, of all citizens, defect?"

Dante bumps into a toppled book cart. "I thought I was going to see where defectors go. I told myself I intended to destroy it, but then I saw a world I never expected or imagined. Now I want to see more."

Octavia launches at Dante.

An instance passes before Dante remembers a hundred defectors who have fallen under Octavia's short club. The vision clears just as it's thrust to his face.

His staff sweeps the attack away and answers with a stab to her ribs that has no effect.

Dante's staff has the greater reach, an advantage that he presses with three solid hits to Octavia, none of which she feels.

The reaper's uniform is lined with a kinetic dampening mesh that dissipates impacts over the entire body. The stab to Octavia's kidney, which should have sent her to the ground, appears to affect her as nothing more than an aggressive shove.

Dante would need to hit her with a full-size ax or sledgehammer for her to suffer any damage.

She's testing me, finding my weakness.

Another charge is answered with a smack to Octavia's hood. Pain erupts in Dante's thigh. His leg no longer wants to hold him up.

Octavia's eyes flash with a thrill that Dante has seen when her kill is done. Her last pass allowed him another useless hit to her head and left his leg wide open.

Octavia circles.

Tearing pain radiates from the nerve bundle in his thigh from the strike; spasms of pain prevent his knee from taking any weight. Dante hops to favor his good leg and stumbles; Octavia dives into his center.

Dante moves to avoid the inevitable sweep to his legs and flips over Octavia's shoulder to the ground.

Dante fights to regain the air that has exploded from his chest, only to have Octavia's knee drive into his gut.

His hands now throttle Octavia's arms that are madly forcing the base of the baton toward his face.

Dante holds her at bay, struggling to fill his lungs under her weight. He controls about seven centimeters between his face and the billy club. Seven becomes two when Octavia releases a catch that springs a spear-point blade, stained with Priya's dried blood. The point falls in and out of focus as it dances above his eyes.

I didn't know it could do that.

Octavia drives for his throat, then his cheek, his eye. The point catches the tip of his nose and hovers over his mouth. With each lunge, Dante shifts his defense, and the point drives closer. His face darkens. The words, *it's my time*, drifts through his mind.

One thrust overextends Octavia's balance, and Dante drives the club to follow the lunge, sending the blade into the concrete floor beside him. The point snaps next to his face, launching his knee into her ass; Dante leverages Octavia to his side. With a gulp of air, he slams his forehead into Octavia's cheek, driving her head to the floor.

A momentary daze lets Dante sweep the hood from her head, which immediately is slammed onto the concrete floor.

When the stars clear, an unusually strong glitter belt is double wrapped around Octavia's wrist and neck. Her back is firmly drawn against Dante's knee. The point of his field knife is pressing into her throat.

"It's over!" Dante shouts.

When her lungs allow her to speak, she gasps. "That's a pretty good move with the wrist capture and the strap. Where did you learn that?"

"Never mind!" Dante replies with an indignant growl.

Chapter 34

Surrounded by Strangers

How did it get to this? Octavia wonders. Her arms are bound together by the ragged piece of web cord her partner has fetishized for the last half-decade. The straps from the defector's bag bind her ankles to the legs of a wooden chair. The indignity is bad enough. *What kind of hell have I landed in where I have to listen to his lectures indefinitely?*

"The Collective has been dying for a long time." Dante places another broken table leg onto the fire. Ancient fire suppression sensors ignore the smoke curling around them as a breeze flows through a broken window directing it out a hole in the roof.

Firelight shimmers over the blood streak across the back of Octavia's wrist after she runs it across her lips. "I get it, Dante," she answers. "All of it. The canines, the sociopathic medical fetish, but I'm not so sure about the pervy robot, though."

"You're not listening, Octavia," Dante pleads. "I'm trying to tell you—"

"I've heard everything. We both know you have been using the Brigade, your civic service, and your chemicals to hide from your life." She nods at Sonia with a smile. "So you found yourself a cute little defector to play out your hidden wild side, that's wonderful."

Sonia sits on a bench with her knees tucked under her chin. At Octavia's nod, she perks up her head and eagerly asks, "You think I'm cute?"

The question jams Octavia's response.

Dante clamps his hand over his mouth to hide his smile. When he regains his focus, he asks, "What about New Rome? You were there. You saw what's happening."

"Dante, stop!" Octavia shouts. "I told you, I get it, I understand. You've seen some disturbing things that your sheltered life never allowed you to experience. Now you want to see more." She smiles and allows a patronizing laugh to escape. "I really am happy for you; that you found your way through the empty, Dante, but you've had your time. You have no right to deny your name to the next generation."

Sonia pensively adds, "I know you probably don't want to hear my opinion."

Octavia snaps, "You're right."

"I understand what I did was..." She hesitates to finish.

Octavia states it for her. "Wrong. You were very clever, but wrong." She directs her accusation back to Dante. "You want to make this more complicated than it is."

"No!" Sonia exclaims. "You're just pretending it's simple because you like the security and comfort of maintaining the machine!" Leaning toward Octavia, Sonia presses her lifeclock into her hand with her thumb. "I don't mean the Guardian, I mean the whole mindless Collective that is terrified of anyone deviating from the prescripted roles of the directives. Everyone talks about contributing to the world and developing our wellbeing, yet all it allows us to be is a collection of lines in an automated data-file."

Sonia's words clarify in Captain Reed's padded earphones. The crosshairs of the surveillance scanner's telescopic sight hovers on the chest of the woman with the scar. "My brother taught me that canines who mindlessly obey the pack's rules die. You either learn how to break the rules and break away or be killed at 18..."

Reed leers at the animated redhead. *She's cute when she gets mad.* He always enjoys extracting the Collective's women. No matter how tired and dirty, they're always so vibrant. He kneels against the broken-down wall, seventy meters from East Side Middle School. A window glows in the darkness. Three figures sit around a pyre of books and broken furniture. He steadies the rifle stock of the long-range surveillance camera and microphone atop the remains of a windowsill. Pulling the stock into his shoulder, the crosshairs of the scope drift between the two defectors and the captured reaper.

He can't see the face of the one who is tied up. She has a black uniform that warns him of danger. He drifts the crosshairs back to her. His earphones erupt, "Don't compare your pack of tunnel rats with my Collective!"

Tyler quietly approaches and lowers himself beside the captain.

Reed doesn't look up when he says, "Report."

"There's no sign of aerial units or additional Brigade troops. It looks like they're alone," Tyler whispers. "How are they doing?"

Reed keeps his eye planted to the scope. "The man took one hell of a beating before securing the reaper."

"The reaper is still alive?"

"Yep, alive and feisty." Reed breaks a smile. "And you wouldn't believe the story they're telling her."

"Then we should leave," Tyler says calmly.

There is silence from Reed.

Tyler presses the issue. "That's the protocol, right, Captain? Abort any extraction when the Charon Brigade is present."

Reed nods with a sigh. "Yaaaa, that's protocol, but there are larger issues. The reaper confirmed that the West Coast departure point has been sealed."

"We knew that," Tyler says.

Reed looks away from the scope. "But Casey, the Conductor, hasn't been captured. He may still be alive. Also," he nods to the window, "he's former Brigade."

"The defector? No kidding."

The crosshairs drift back onto the man. His voice plays in Reed's headphones. "We follow decisions made by a machine that we never see and never question," he says. "It was made by ideologues hundreds of years ago. They were angry with a class who destroyed everything for the sake of an easy, comfortable life. The Awakening solved this. It made greed obsolete, but it also condemned us to stagnation."

Tyler cups his hand over his ear as a status update buzzes through his kernel. "Got it," he answers. "Captain, all stations confirm the area is clear, no activity around or above." His eyes change with the report from the last operative. "Zeke intercepted tele-LINCC activity from the Brigade; the reaper has missed a check-in."

"I've heard enough." Reed ends the recording and collapses the stock of the surveillance scanner. As he slides it into the carrying bag, he whispers to Tyler, "The last extraction point in North America has fallen."

"You must have seen this, Octavia, as you tracked us across the continent. The world is failing because we don't know how to fix it.

Citizens are handing over distasteful tasks to automated systems. People are degrading one another because they don't know how to build their own lives."

Octavia's rage awakens the pain from her battle wounds.

"That nursery attendant you mentioned," Sonia says. "The one assigning names to infants who closed the lid on the cradle, it's a robot."

Octavia twists against her restraints. "Bullshit!"

"It's true, we watched it in New Rome," Dante says. "The Guardian has nurtured the same selfish attitude the ancients had. Killing us won't change it. Even if we go back and release all the names that have ever been taken, the Collective is still in collapse!"

For as long as he has known her, Dante has never seen Octavia lose control to her rage, and now he can see something else, she's afraid.

"Do you even hear yourself, Dante?" Octavia yells. "Do you hear the excuses, the self-deception, the paranoia? The system has its defects." She leers at Sonia. "But it works! We've had seven hundred years without war, mass hunger, or crippling poverty. Yes, life is short and sometimes unfair, but it's meaningful, and you have no right to take it."

"She's got a point."

Dante and Sonia jump to their feet. His gunsight meets Captain Reed as he steps into the light of the fire. Reed keeps a security stunner leveled at Dante's chest as he says, "The reaper makes a good argument, Dante, but if you want another option for the rest of your life, I have one to offer."

Octavia sits in silent amazement. The intruder has the face of worn leather that reminds her of the portraits of pre-Awakening men.

"It's too bad, as I enjoy campfire stories." Reed motions the point of his weapon toward Dante. "Yours is the best I've ever heard. I'd like you to come with us and finish it."

A disturbance sounds behind Dante. Tyler and another man appear with stunners. Tyler steps into the firelight as the other gently places the muzzle of his stunner between Dante's shoulder blades.

Dante passes his pistol to the man behind him, then links his fingers behind his head as Tyler commands, "We're terrible at first impressions," Tyler says as the other pats around Dante's legs and waist. He removes the field knife from the sheath below the small of Dante's back, then steps away. His pistol and knife rattle as they are dropped into a burlap bag. "It's just because we're scared as hell of the Brigade, right, Captain?"

Reed nods in agreement. "Terrified."

Reed's men relax when their captain lowers his stunner and gestures for Dante to put his hands down. Then, Reed presents the back of his left hand to the defectors.

Sonia and Dante share a confounded look. He doesn't have a lifeclock.

Dante kneels beside Octavia. "Will you listen now, please?"

"Don't do this, Dante," she growls.

He hesitates.

She leans to his ear. "Your life is your own, Dante-nine. You can make it whatever you want it to be. You are responsible for how you live and how you leave, but your name belongs to the Collective." Her eyes lock with his. "Untie me. We can take them."

Dante is captured by Octavia's plea; it is the first time he has ever seen or heard panic from his partner. It's well hidden behind a veil of rage and what he knows is an honest concern for him. He slowly moves away.

The kernel in Reed's ear buzzes. He offers Dante his hand and says, "Son, we can't stay here."

Sonia takes Dante's hand and leads him to the door.

Octavia's voice grows louder as he walks away. "You can't do this, Dante. You can't help them destroy our world, your world. You know they will! Dante!"

Dante stops at the door. He watches Tyler shove his partner, his ex-partner, into the chair as she struggles against her bonds, calling for his help. *She's surrounded by strangers. I can't leave her, not like this.*

Sonia's hand takes his shoulder. "Come on. It's time we see this to the end."

Dante meets Sonia's eyes. A tear rides the scar down the side of her face.

Reed whispers, "We have to go. Now." As he directs them out the door, he cues the pickup for his tele-communicator. "Zeke, we're heading out. Pull back. We'll meet you at the extraction zone."

The figure at the window disappears. Another follows Reed's lead and ushers Dante and Sonia away. Tyler stays. The captain motions with the point of his stunner. "Take care of her. Then get to the launch."

Tyler answers with an affirmative nod. Reed disappears through the door. Silence falls over the room.

A gentle flame hovers above the last few coals of the pyre. The tip of Octavia's billy club slowly lifts her chin away from the door and into Tyler's eager expression, which Octavia meets with a bright-white smile.

Chapter 35

A New Shore

Reed's extraction team leads Dante and Sonia through the ruins of the city to the harbor where a cargo ship awaits. They follow Reed up the gangplank to the deck where Zeke greets the captain.

"Make ready," Reed commands. "I want to cast off the instant Tyler is on board."

A fire grows in the distance. Dante pauses as the warm light flickers around his shadow. Orange and yellow flames push a pillar of black smoke into the sky, marking the location of the middle school. He draws an unintended gasp.

Reed directs the crew away.

Dante and Sonia follow the sight to the stern of the ship and watch the distant blaze cut into the night's sky. Sonia embraces him. "I'm sorry, Dante."

He returns her embrace and says with a smile of guilt and pain, "I loved her."

"You still do, and she loves you."

They hold one another as the light dims, and the smoke fades into the sky. Engines softly speed up beneath them. The coast of the Collective slowly moves away.

The ship's navigator tracked the position of several high-altitude aerial drones as they cruised into the open sea. Although they were confident that the ship wouldn't alert any sensors even if they were spotted, Reed took extra care to avoid having their position reported.

Dante and Sonia settled into their cabin and rarely appeared above deck for the first few days. On more than one occasion, the crew opened a hatch to find the two of them grinding in some dark corner of the hull.

When the aft cargo bay was found locked from the inside, the crew gathered in the main galley, where images from surveillance cameras 2, 3, and 7 filled the wall screen with Dante and Sonia bouncing naked in a pile of burlap sheets. Dante was indifferent to the crew's voyeurism; Sonia secretly liked it. Occasionally, she retreated to the hold by herself to practice naked yoga.

Eight days pass.

Dante watches from the ship's bow as a sliver of land rolls above the horizon through the telescopic window hovering in front of his data spectacles.

"Is it what you expected?"

Dante pulls the glasses from his eyes to see Sonia wrapped in his green overcoat. Her hair dances in the wind. She nods at the horizon. "Looks pretty barren from here."

He slips the spectacles into his shirt pocket. Sonia moves to the railing and settles into Dante's arms. Together they watch the approaching shore. "I thought Haven would be a hovel of aging nomads," he says. "I pictured a dozen defectors crammed into a corner of Outland foraging for rodents." He shakes his head at the approaching shore. "I never imagined anything like this."

A smile spreads across Sonia's face, which Dante shares. Eventually, she asks, "Did you find them?"

"Right here," Dante nudges the burlap bag laying by his feet.

"Was it difficult?"

"Not really." Dante shrugs. "Reed had them hidden behind a panel in his cabin." Dante picks up the bag and withdraws Octavia's pistol still attached to her glove with adhesive threads, now dry and brittle. "It was pretty easy once I was able to move through restricted parts of the ship unchallenged." Dante shuffles the contents again, removes his field knife from the bag, and hands it to Sonia. "For some reason, the crew keeps getting drawn to the monitors in the galley."

Sonia removes the sheath from a coat pocket and tucks the knife inside. "There are monitors in the galley? Really?" Sonia's sarcasm slips through her comment.

Dante smiles as he removes his pistol and cradles it in his hand. "I know. They seem really interested in the cargo bay for some reason." He drops both guns back in the bag and cinches the top closed.

Sonia smiles and says, "I hope it's something spectacular."

Dante kisses the side of her head. "Absolutely."

"Do you think all the men of Haven are as malleable? Or is it just sailors?"

"No," he objects. "Some of the women of the crew are just as interested."

"I'm glad." She laughs. The outline of the island clarifies through the atmospheric haze. "Christopher calls this place Faroe. It's a collection of eighteen small islands with nearly nineteen thousand thriving men, women, and children. He says that people raise families and stay together for decades." She shakes her head as if surrendering to a puzzle too complex to fathom. "I'm still wrapping my head around that, decades!"

As she describes the island and the people living there, Dante extends the bag over the rushing break line of the water. Sonia reaches for his hand. "Are you sure about this?"

He smiles. "I don't need it anymore, not like I used to. Besides, what am I going to do with a tool for killing defectors on an island of nineteen thousand defectors?"

Sonia answers in a calm but stern voice, "They're not all defectors. Some are the second- even third-generation separated from the Collective." She moves her hand away from the bag with a darker consideration. "Besides, I think Reed has a plan for them."

Dante's voice darkens. "That's what I'm afraid of." He retracts the bag from the rail.

Small fishing boats appear by the tidal-sculpted shoreline. Green mountains rise in the distance.

"You know, I used to have these long debates with Syd that lasted into the morning about defecting."

Sonia shoots him a surprised look. "A Brigade hunter and a civil judge talking about defecting, that's a new one."

Dante nods. "Why not? Talking about defection isn't a crime. Now, if I were to have said, 'Hey, Syd, I'm going to run away and avoid Somnus, don't tell anyone,' then there would be a problem."

"Obviously!"

"Anyway, he once told me that the Brigade could be rendered obsolete if the lifeclock simply released its toxin at the moment of expiration.

Think about that. Citizens wouldn't have to uphold the Somnus Obligation; they would simply expire on schedule, no citadel, no reapers, no defectors. Scanners would register the white crystal where they fall. The Collective lives on."

"Your friend, the judge, said all this? That would go against the Second Citizen Obligation," her voice sounds more serious than he expected.

"You mean replacing citizen responsibility with automation? You're right. The people who programmed the Guardian and set the course for the Awakening must have considered all this. It would certainly have been a much simpler system to design than the one we have. The Brigade was formed so that we would have to enforce the Somnus Obligation ourselves. Every generation of the Collective has to choose to continue to honor the directives."

Sonia lays her head against his chest. A gust of ocean breeze greets them as the ship enters a gap between two islands. The ship clears a peninsula to reveal a landscape carpeted with red-and-white buildings topped with green roofs. Cyclists peddle atop black roads that cut across the land. "If that's true," she says, "it means the option of defecting was built into the foundation of the Awakening."

Dante brings her hand to his lips and kisses the black crystal chip. "It's like your brother taught you. Maybe we are supposed to learn how to break the Collective's rules in order to leave it."

The ship lurches as the engines are cut again. The water breaks against the ship's hull, hiding the splash that sends the burlap bag to the ocean floor.

<<<< End >>>>

Acknowledgment

You may assume that this story began as a novel; you would be wrong. Somnus Obligation started as an earworm asking, "What would it be like to live in a world run by children?" Then it asked, "How would I live with a timer counting up to the moment of my death? What kinds of choices would I make?"

These questions eventually festered into a mental outline that had to be scratched into a MEAD composition book, then managed in Microsoft Word, which spawned dialog, which needed character to say the dialog, and now, seven years and a hundred and thirty thousand words later, stuck into a book, which you just finished reading. Thank you for that, by the way. Life doesn't come with an unlimited number of hours; I'm grateful you chose to spend some of yours with this story.

Somnus Obligation developed with the assistance of many people who shared their time and perspective to help me bring it to its final form. Michael Brucker was the first to encourage me to stop treating this as a fan-fic time waster and turn it into a real story.

I had an army of beta readers, each of whom lent their unique perspectives that helped shape the story into its final form. Thank you, Jennifer Kremer and Jon Meador, for your impressions on the characters and plot that showed me what was working and what needed work. Thank you, Sonia Borg, for the loan of your spirit animal, which helped Dante and your name-sake work out solutions that were more creative than brutal.

Early drafts of Somnus were reviewed by Chris and Erin Blubaugh, who helped me work through and in many cases eradicate some really terrible scenes. You helped me keep this project on track.

Despite my best efforts and numerous rewrites, many scenes confused and frustrated my beta readers, and in every instance, my brother Tim Stevenson helped me work it through.

After years of writing, re-writing, and re-re-writing, I needed the help of a great editor, Paula López <https://www.myeditcheck.com> to help me bring this to its final form.

Finally, thank you, Daniel Rutter <https://rutterdesign.com> for the cover illustration that piqued this reader's curiosity enough to read my story all the way to the end of this Acknowledgement.

From the Author

The act of writing is a king-hell bummer. I consider the relationship with my keyboard to be one of frustration, lamination, and mutual abuse. And yet, the act of having written, is an amazing high; I can never stay mad at you word-processor. I keep returning with Roget's Thesaurus, MEAD composition book, and one more topic to work though till we get to that final ctrl+s that closes a chapter.

I hope you enjoyed my first novel. Who knows what is going to come next? Another format release? A blog? There might be a chance to sign up on a mailing list if there is ever any interest, maybe even a sequel.

One thing is certain; whatever it is, it will be posted at:

https://somnus.donrichey.com